Three Strides Out

A Horse Show Novel
of Suspense

V. S. ANDERSON

THREE STRIDES OUT

By V. S. Anderson

Cover Design by 100Covers

Also by V. S. Anderson

KING OF THE ROSES
BLOOD LIES

Visit the author at https://www.virginiasanderson.com

For Bill, Tom, and Chris

I don't know what it is about the horses. I only know that from the first day they let me ride at that first job they got me back in high school, I learned that there was more than one world you could live in. No one had told me that. No one had told me I could shut the door on so much.

Son, you have to get over being so angry, they all told me, all those nice people. They couldn't tell me how. They couldn't know how a horse could take your mind and do things with it, sort of like wrapping you up in music. It wasn't like there was a tune, just something that ran through your veins.

The thing about horse people is that we live our horses. We live all horses. Even the ones that piss us off, break our hearts. I don't know where it comes from. The horses do it to you. They get inside you when you aren't looking. I once thought maybe it was because they were beautiful. But they aren't all beautiful. Because they're so kind? Well, some are. Maybe some people like their power. Or the power people can have over them. I never thought of my horses that way but I guess some do. So I really don't know what horses do, or how they do it. I know what they did to me, and I wouldn't be alive now without them. Whatever it is they do, they don't let go.

So when we heard a horse screaming, we all ran to stop it like it was our horse.

At least most of us did.

CHAPTER 1

LUCKY, LUCKY, LUCKY, THE TRAINERS and riders and owners and grooms all told me, *damn* lucky I never slept through the night. Damn lucky my night sweats had me prowling the horse show grounds like some lost zombie so I was there to see the stacked hay in that two-horse trailer start belching flames. I told them all I didn't do anything special. Anybody would have run up the hill to the trailer lot like I did, no breath for shouting, just get there. As for what I did when I got there? Brave, they told me. Some said crazy. They had no idea.

Because it wasn't the flames I ran toward. I ran because I had to make the horse inside that trailer stop screaming. His screams now on top of all the others inside my head every living minute. I had to make him stop.

You do what you have to in the face of that much desperation. You shut your lungs to the smoke boiling black out the side windows, out the back doors. The whole rig shaking with fifteen hundred pounds of horse slamming back and forth inside. I flung myself at the ramp to the front compartment where I could feel him struggling, found a padlock jammed through the locking bars. I ran to the far side and the narrow access door. When I yanked, it opened, the black horse rearing against the tie that held him, a beating heart of terror inside that smoky hell.

I did what I had to do to stop the screaming. I hauled myself inside.

Yeah, crazy, both of us in that suffocating cell together. He slung his head as he reared, then crashed, knocking me down hard. The flames wolfed through the stacked hay behind him, only seconds away. You can't wrench a horse that big and that wild to a standstill, can't get his weight off the tie that holds him to unclip the snap. You do what some sane pit in your mind tells you: while he lifts you off

1

your feet and slings you against the trailer siding by some miracle you get your hand on the throatlatch of his halter and undo that. You hang on the halter till he shakes both it and your dead weight off him and when he senses his freedom you huddle beneath him while he hurtles past you, scraping off hide on his way through that narrow door.

And for a moment with your breath knocked out from his weight on you and your lungs burning, you can't even see the door you came through. The heat beating on you, sizzling metal on your shoulders, the gasoline stench inside you, you're swallowed by a living dark. And you can still hear him, even though he's far down the hill now, toward the just-waking showgrounds, and you know you haven't stopped the screaming. You've never stopped the screaming. You can hide what it does to you but it just goes on and on . . .

Then I was flat on the grass outside the burning trailer, thrown there by some panic, rolling, too weak to walk, not really far enough away when it seared me, that sudden, final whoosh of flame. I got my legs under me, they worked, my body worked, my mind grappled and failed. Instinct turned me toward the showgrounds below, now full of lights, shouting. The thudding of Romp fleeing but not escaping, like me never escaping. I hadn't freed him, couldn't, any more than I'd ever managed to free myself.

Stumbling forward, I smacked into a groom running up the hill toward me whose dark face I'd seen around the barns. He stopped me from falling. "You okay?"

I broke his grip. "I have to catch him. Keep him off the highway."

"He ran to the show rings. They'll catch him." He put his shoulder under me. "Come on."

So we humped down from the trailer lot, past the car lot, past the rows of barns and campers, into the wild army trying to corner that horse. For me it was just a whirl of bodies, voiceless. The screams all I still heard. Even when Brett, my Highflying Farm partner, grabbed me and shook me, I didn't hear him say, "God, Robb, what happened?" Still it was only the screams. He dragged me out of the rush to a bleacher step at ringside. "That groom said Romp was in that trailer. Said you were." I found I could nod. He pulled me upright. "Come to the camper. Stop this shaking, wash this shit off."

2

I could walk, his hand on my arm. What I couldn't do was tell him why I was shaking. Not shock. Not pain. Not terror. Rage.

Then I was sitting on my bunk in our camper, showered, wrapped in towels, the shaking now in muscles inside me I couldn't tame. Drinking the coffee laced with bourbon Brett gave me. They caught Romp, he told me, but I knew that horse hadn't stopped running because he'd escaped what pursued him. I could tell him it would always pursue him. Nowhere to run.

"He's back in Malloy's barn," Brett told me. "Drugged up. They don't think he's hurt, just scared shitless." He flinched at the bruises I could feel blooming. "You need a doctor? Maybe some of those drugs?"

"No doctor." No drugs. I had a day's work ahead I had to make look normal. For the first of many times that day I said, "I'm fine."

"How the hell did Romp get in there? Did you see anyone?"

For the first of what I knew would be many times in the days before me, I shook my head, lying. "No, I didn't see anyone."

He went down to our stalls, to our horses, to our customers coming in from their motels in the nearby town on the edge of the North Carolina mountains, all of them thinking it was a normal horse-show day. Friday, second week of a four-week summer series. The show would go on as usual: too many entries to refund, this week's Grand Prix on Sunday, too many big international outfits on the grounds. Almost every year of the eight we'd been Highflying Farm Brett and I had brought our students and our own horses to this series, where our championships and high-points said louder than billboards that we ran a top-notch hunter/jumper barn. I dragged on breeches and a polo, a costume for a life I'd just been ripped out of. I had three students to coach and two horses to ride, and I wasn't sure I could.

Because I knew exactly how Romp got into that trailer. I'd seen Jeff Carr leading him up the hill in the last dark hour while the grounds still slept. I didn't know why Carr had done it. I didn't know who he had done it for. What I did know for certain: I wasn't going to tell the police what I'd seen.

I could guess what all the normal people around me would tell me. *Take this into your hands? That's nuts. Let the police do their job. They know how.*

Except they didn't know how to do what I wanted and wouldn't even if they did. All they knew how to do was stash the monsters who did this in some jail somewhere. Where I couldn't get at them. Where I couldn't make them feel what I'd seen in that horse's white-ringed eyes as he reared and slammed and crashed. Panic, pain, and terror. Where I couldn't make them pay for that horse's terror. Where I couldn't make *them* scream.

CHAPTER 2

THE CHIEF OF POLICE FROM THE NEARBY TOWN of Timberburg said, "How fast does hay burn?"

He'd come up to me at ringside, introducing himself as Kyle Wardle, a burly guy with short-cropped gray sideburns who could have played kindly uncle except for his big gun. We'd moved a few feet out of hearing distance from the show ring where the two girls I coached on their pony hunters would soon show in their over-fences class. Both girls were watching us, holding their ponies with anxious little creases on their foreheads. Someone killing horses was a lot for eleven-year-olds to deal with and I wanted their day to feel as normal as possible. Their eyes had gotten big under their helmets at the sight of the cop.

He started off friendly, with a comment about how cool I looked considering what he knew I'd been through. What everybody knew I'd been through, judging from the number of people who came up to tell me how brave I was. None of them knew how I'd stood in front of the mirror in Brett's and my camper, dosed up with ibuprofen, taking hold of myself muscle by throbbing muscle, dressing myself in the Robb Slaughter they all expected, nerve by nerve. So that was who answered his friendly questions, about our farm "up in Pennsylvania," about my "partner, I think I heard Brett Crider," with a hitch on "partner" that made it an ask. In the horse-show world, not an unreasonable speculation but I said matter-of-factly, "Business partner. We're not gay." He fished for a quick lecture on the difference between hunters and jumpers and even with my mind on how many trips were left in the Baby Green Hunters so I'd know when my kids had to start their warm-up, I explained how hunters had to be pretty but jumpers just had to get over, and yeah, the jumpers were the ones who jumped the big jumps.

"So this horse Romp was a jumper?"

5

"Yes" was the simple answer. But I remembered Romp winning the first series Grand Prix last Sunday. One of those special horses you rode with your heart and your breath even when you watched from the stands. He could jump any fence from any distance. "He could have gone to the Olympics," I said.

"Yeah, could have," he echoed, but if he felt loss like I did he didn't show it on his deadpan face.

All in all, the guy was perfectly pleasant, though it looked like you'd have to tweak the right knobs to call up a smile. On his phone he noted what I had told him: that I'd used my sleeplessness to hike up to the trailer lot for a new tub of supplements and that was when I saw the flames. I turned back to my girls to make sure they'd learned their courses, promising the cop I'd be around if he had more questions. Then he asked that question, "How fast does hay burn?"

It took me a moment to sense where he was going. I put on puzzled. "Sorry?"

"Well, you said when you got to the trailer the flames hadn't burned all the way through to where the horse was. So it hadn't been burning long. Somebody'd just set it. Odd you didn't see anyone."

I smoothed the edge off my voice in case those eleven-year-old ears were sharper than I imagined. "If I had, don't you think I would have said so?"

"No offense meant. Just trying to figure this out. Like that side door, the one you went through, not being locked like the ramp was. You wonder about that?"

Yeah, I thought, Jeff Carr saw me coming and beat feet out of there before he could get that door locked. No way to know for sure until I had him by the throat to ask him, but that was what I thought. I had anticipated the question and planned an answer. "Whoever did it must have figured the horse couldn't get out that way so it didn't matter. He was wrong."

"He?"

"She. Whatever." I looked back at my girls. Taylor's pony Whisper was snatching at the dusty grass under the ring fence while Cadence's pony Clown rubbed the tight braids down his neck on her coat. The loudspeaker said five more trips in the Baby Green class before ours, five more of the young, inexperienced horses to negotiate the seven fences, and please start getting your ponies down to the gate. My kids were forth and fifth in the pony order. And I needed to put some distance between me and this guy Wardle so I

6

could figure out what I should know and what I shouldn't. "Look," I said, "I'm working. Like I said, I'll be glad to talk later."

"Yeah, I'll eventually want a statement." He hung back to toss out one more question. "You think it's insurance?"

"Could be." I'd already considered insurance. That was where people's heads went when a valuable horse was involved. But people who killed horses for insurance made the death look accidental. Or tried.

He sighed, like a hill he had to climb had just gotten higher. "Be thinking about who around here might have done this."

I found a half-truth to tell him. "Nobody I know would have done it."

"Then I guess there's people around here you don't know, huh?"

Yeah, no kidding, I thought, turning. "Really. I gotta go."

I reached the girls as the jump crew rolled in to adjust the striding for the ponies. The girls wore their heavier show coats; the mountain mornings were chill, the ponies' breath clouding. "Is he going to arrest somebody?" said Cadence.

"Did somebody do it on purpose?" said Taylor.

"I don't think anybody knows yet." The creases still in their foreheads said I had to work harder on keeping their day normal. "Didn't I say something about learning the course?"

Shit, yeah, they'd learned it. Kids like these learned the basic hunter course patterns early, this one a standard variation. Reciting, they pointed at the jumps in the ring with their riding crops. Single back toward the gate, outside up the far fence line, diagonal line back, single diagonal up (a spread fence, an oxer, scary, looming all by itself after a long gallop), then back toward the gate, down the final outside line.

The numbers? "Sixes," said Cadence.

"I think the last line's a seven," said Taylor.

They had to know that, too, how to adjust their ponies' pace and stride length to make the two-jump lines smooth and flowing. "We'll watch some trips, see what it looks like. Let's get on."

In the schooling ring, my girls warming up at a trot, I knew I wasn't all the way back to normal, that would never happen, but I was getting away with my act, which included doing my job. Every normal moment gave me cover for the rage that kicked around inside. Every normal nod steered all the curious gazes, all the silent questions, all the riders, trainers, owners, away from me. True, I'd

7

V. S. ANDERSON

been told I was brave about fifty times so far and crazy at least twenty, but I'd shrugged and looked modest and backed everyone off with smiles. No one could know that behind the smiles I was thinking about how bad I wanted to beat the cop to the killers so he couldn't haul them off to some courtroom and a plea deal. Every moment I played normal was a moment wasted. When I crossed to set up a spread oxer for my girls to school over, for an imbecile moment I wanted to just walk away, leave the girls there in their pretty little canters, go start . . . start . . . what?

Storming around in a frenzy wouldn't get me where I wanted. I couldn't shut the screams off but I had to choke them down so I could do what really needed doing: think.

The struggle must have showed on my face because at the fence Mack Dever took the pole I'd picked up and set it in the jump cup for me. "You okay? You look a little peaked there, boy."

Dever was a rangy, sandy-haired guy, always in herky-jerky motion. He bounced around the shows like a kid, but he was well into his forties, at least ten years old than me. He ran a big farm in Nashville; he'd brought twenty horses to this series. I shook off the rush of madness. I wouldn't be storming off anywhere until I knew more. "Yeah, I'm fine."

"Hell of a thing you did," said Dever. He shoved his Skyhaven Farm ball cap above the sunburn line on his forehead. "You know, had to be one of the Mexicans did that. Some drug stuff. Or trafficking illegals. Had to be."

"Yeah, probably." I rolled out the ground pole that would help my kids find their takeoff.

"Cops'll be all over this place now," said Dever. "Yo," he called to his rider. "Left rein, kiddo. Steer that thing!"

The girl on the gray pony took up her left rein, straightening the pony's jump. I found my own kids holding the rail, eyes on me, waiting. Clown was full of his usual garbage, pinning his ears and sulling when Cadence legged him. I signaled her over. "Spurs."

"He hates spurs."

"He hates everything."

The tiny nubs would only impress Clown a little. We needed just a little for his natural canter to get him down the lines in the number of strides the judges expected. He was going to pin his ears and frown like a gargoyle no matter what we did. I grinned at her, full-stop the Robb she knew and trusted. "Remember, run!"

8

Tough kid, she gunned him along the schooling-ring rail, turned for the fence, goosed him when he raised his head to back off. He shot out in front of her, jumped like he meant it. "Good," I said. "Go with that."

We watched two other ponies' trips from the in-gate. "That last line rides tighter than it looks on paper," I told them. "Settle Whisper on the turn. If Clown's running like you want, coast. But don't trust him." The pony wouldn't add a stride, but he'd suck back so that even in a tight line the last fence would end up a flat reach.

Our turns came. These girls I coached weren't pros but you'd think they'd been riding for long lifetimes. Neither of them came from a horse family, but they came from enough money they could do this expensive and glorious and humbling sport for as long as they wanted. We had never talked about their privilege. That wasn't my job. My job was to make sure that if they ever wanted to ride Grand Prix, they'd have the foundation, and a sense of what it meant to lose most of the time.

Today my job was getting Cadence to rev her lazy pony from the moment he stepped on course. She got a gorgeous bold stride out of him, all the pieces in place for perfect fences, until the last line where she was a second too late feeling him shorten. There was the long last fence he'd been planning, just to show us. A tiny form break the judge could count off for. It was okay. Just not gold.

Whisper did his thing. His natural jump was a shade less brilliant than it needed to be to win every time. That day two superstars fucked up and his pretty knees tucked almost to his chin got him second. Clown was fourth.

"Good job," I said to them both.

"I blew it," said Cadence.

"We'll work on feeling the rhythm." I rubbed a dust ball out of Clown's eye. "It's sneaky."

She stretched forward, hugging the little bastard around his neck. "He was really good till then."

"He was really good. You all were," I said.

In the gap before our afternoon classes I went to see Romp.

Mel Malloy's operation occupied both sides of an aisle in one of a row of covered barns stretching from the show rings to the lots where the cars and horse trailers were parked. Horses filled some of the stalls, while other stalls held tack and feed. Some were set up for grooming with crossties and mats. That day the barn aisle was as muted and tense as a hospital ward. The regular show vet had commandeered a grooming cart for his vials and syringes. Five or six people stood around whispering. They stopped talking when I walked up.

Among them I recognized the Paxtons, Romp's owners. They'd be staying nearby so they could see Romp's Grand Prix on Sunday. The Grand Prix he would have gone in. They were older, maybe sixties, Mrs. Paxton little and pale, in a long quilted coat and soft brown boots up to her knees. She had that blond hair they all had, these women, the color of milk going sour, pulled back hard off her starved face. Richard—Rich, he'd once told me to call him—was a solid guy in jeans and a leather jacket, stockbroker type playing country. Malloy's show manager, a quiet young woman in gray riding tights, hung back about ten feet away.

Malloy was rubbing the graying hair on his temples. He was a hefty guy, maybe close to sixty, filled out but fit, with a wide, cheerful face. He'd always been easy to deal with and talk to, one of those trainers who always seemed to be headed somewhere important but who always stopped to see if you wanted to go there too. He'd brought fifteen horses to the series. "Jesus, Robb, if you hadn't been there—"

"Damn lucky," said Rich Paxton. "*Goddamn* lucky. We can't thank you enough."

"We're taking him home," said Mrs. Paxton. Dierdre. She wore those leather gloves that look like they've been greased. "As soon as he settles down."

I crossed to see over the bottom half-door of the stall. For a moment I thought Romp wasn't there. I listened hard, wanting to hear him breathing. Malloy stepped up behind me. "He's been on the—"

The darkness blew up, changing the words he'd meant to say to a shout. Fifteen hundred pounds of muscle slammed against the door. Romp's head came out the top like he was going to plow over the door or splinter it. But he bounced off, must have staggered, hit the back wall so hard the whole barn shook.

"Oh God," said Mrs. Paxton. Malloy jumped forward. "Whoa now. Whoa, son." No good. The horse flung himself at the door again, this time rearing, getting his forelegs over. The wood groaned.

Malloy stumbled backward. Mrs. Paxton's hands flew to her mouth, her husband pulling her away.

I freed the top of the door and pushed it toward where Romp hung half out, scrambling to heave himself over. I shoved the panel against his striking hooves. His steel shoes cut chunks from the top of the bottom door as he slid back into the dark. I got the door shut, held it, while Malloy, teeth on his lip, fastened the latch. From inside came popping snorts, raw kicks against the stall boards like cannons on automatic, bam, bam, bam. Mrs. Paxton made choking noises. "Oh, I thought he'd stopped that," she cried.

Then just the scrape of his hooves as he circled and circled. Malloy wiped his mouth with the back of his hand.

"We can't haul him like this." Paxton had lost color. "Can't you sedate him more?"

The vet shook his head. "Could make him worse. It'll take a while, that's all." He caught Malloy's gaze, rolling up his syringe kit. "Nothing to eat for twelve or so hours. Maybe in a bit check his water." He turned to the Paxtons. "Wish I could do more for him, folks."

"You're sure he's not hurt physically?" Mrs. Paxton had shoved the gloved hands into her coat pockets.

The vet shrugged. "Like I said, some scrapes, no other sign I could find. We'll be able to check him better once he's quieter. But it looks like mostly trauma. Leave him alone for a while."

More kicks. Mrs. Paxton flinched like the blows were landing inside her head. Her husband took her arm. "Come on. Nothing we can do here. You need to eat."

She dug her elbows into her ribs, blocking something that wanted loose. "At least he didn't hurt himself."

He pulled harder and steered her down the aisle. I thought, you should wish it was that kind of hurt. Instead of the hurt from the lifetime he spent in the path of those flames. Even if he broke a leg and it killed him. The vet packed up the rest of his equipment. Maybe he thought the Paxtons were out of earshot. "Too bad, all the talk about insurance fraud."

But Paxton spun back, boiling. "The hell it's insurance. He's not insured for half of what he's worth."

"To us," said Mrs. Paxton, her voice low.

The vet sighed. "Sorry, just trying to get my head around who would have done this."

"Had to be somebody crazy," said Paxton, his square jaw jutting.

"Makes sense," the vet said.

Paxton shifted his glare to Malloy. "I'll goddamn sue anybody who says we had anything to do with what some scum did to our horse."

Malloy nodded, arms crossing. "Nobody better say it where I can hear them."

"We'll be at the hotel. Anytime you need us. Or that cop."

He turned away again and she let him tug her. They disappeared around the end of the barn. I'd gone back to listening. From the closed stall Romp's breaths came short and cracked, like sobs. "The police talk to you yet?" Malloy asked.

"That guy Wardle."

"What'd you tell him?"

"Not much to tell. He said he'd get a statement later."

His sharp gray eyes narrowed. "Bad shit, Robb. Maybe you'll remember something that will help him."

"I'll try," I said.

The young woman came up with a question about bell boots on one of their jumpers, and they went off down the aisle. I stood there a minute longer. A horse shivered a fly off, another one rattled a feed bucket. Normal sounds in a day I had to try harder to keep normal. A fancy trick when I was the least normal part. After all, normal people wouldn't have lingered outside Romp's dark stall listening. To the screaming. That only I could hear.

CHAPTER 3

WHEN I WAS A KID I thought becoming Robb Slaughter would shut down the screaming. At seventeen I filled out the papers that finally claimed that name. They told me my mother's name was Smith at the home where they sent me, but Smith didn't mean enough to be about her. I wanted those papers to create a new future for me. I guess they did that, since Robb Slaughter was how the horses knew me. But that name didn't stop the screaming. Instead, it saddled me with a promise I shouldn't want to keep.

For one thing, I couldn't slaughter the thing I needed most to get rid of, the one sure, inescapable memory that was all my mother left. Science says I couldn't have a true memory of what really happened; you can't remember everything about every moment, minds don't work that way. You remember what you notice, and even then only what gets stored. Then you can't tell whether what's in storage is what happened or what you've made up. Minds are like hard drives, always getting written over. Science says.

So memory couldn't tell me how long she lived—ten seconds or ten minutes or an hour—while I hid under the bed and did nothing while the man who said he loved her killed her. Cowered afterwards hands over ears instead of running for help. But memory told me exactly how long she went on screaming because she never stopped.

A therapist once said to me, "Do you ever think about killing someone?"

"I shoulda thought about doing that when it mattered," I answered.

"So you'd have killed to save the person who mattered?"

"Yeah, I would have."

He didn't tell me the obvious, that I'd been just a kid, yeah, they all said that, helpless. He said, "And now?"

I knew what he was after. What they were always after. "I'd be killing myself, wouldn't I? The police would kill me. So I guess it would really have to matter." "So killing is killing yourself?" he asked me. "Who deserves your life now?"

Apparently not the guy who beat his kid for pulling up on a rogue horse in the show ring instead of letting the horse break the kid's neck. Or the grooms who'd harassed that slow kid at a winter show in Chicago, tripping him, locking him in stalls with horses they'd riled up, pouring icy water over him and leaving him to freeze. Sure, I reported the grooms and I told the kid's dad, big talk, that if I ever saw him treat that boy like that again, I'd kill him. But the kid killed himself, and the kid the grooms tortured died homeless. So I heard.

The closest I came to doing what needed doing was that year when I was seventeen and I saw a guy run over a dog. Veered to be sure to hit him. Then laughed. I saw the logo on the pickup and I took my adoptive father's gun and went to where he worked. My cousin Philomena put herself between me and what was going to happen. She had a lot to say about what mattered, about saving the rage for that. For a while that night I thought that if I could get the gun back I'd use it where it mattered. Only sure way to stop the screams.

It wasn't like the screams were sounds I could have played back on my phone. Sometimes they were flares off to the side of what I was doing. Sometimes they ripped through my chest. They played background to anything I was doing or thinking, telling me always how there were people in the world who did the right thing no matter what and I hadn't, and, yes, I had an excuse, I always had a reason for walking away. The night after the dead dog, looking for silence, I fled into a seizure, sweating like my veins had opened up. Phil iced the madness with wet towels until it surrendered. The very next day at that stable where I worked after school the lady said, "Your cousin bought you some riding lessons." "What for?" I asked the woman. "She thought you liked animals." The dog wasn't about liking animals, it was about his screaming, but I let the woman show me how to put my foot in the stirrup and clamber into the saddle. That very first day she let me scramble over a crossrail. "Butt out of the saddle, hands on the mane!" And I found out in an instant that there is no room to be angry three strides from a fence.

I quit seeing the therapists when they let me. If one had asked me after I started riding if I ever thought about killing people, I'd have answered, whenever I do I just get on a horse.

It wasn't vengeance I thought about when I sat there in that camper with Romp's screams still echoing. It was what I owed all the horses who gave me the only peace I knew. Someone had made a horse scream the way she had and no way now I could say I was only a child.

As I sat there, the rage chilled into a shape that had lived in Robb Slaughter almost from the day I made him. Once probably a nightmare but now always at the edge of my vision, a jump coming at me, not a crossrail, not three feet, not even a Grand Prix spread. No, more monstrous and daunting, a looming gray wall. I'd never made it over; the horse under me had always floundered, not wanting to take me there. We'd backed off, pulled up, found some excuse for failing. Now that damn wall hung there, closer and bigger and more solid than ever. I didn't know how I was going to make it over, didn't know what would be left of my life when I landed. Maybe I couldn't give what clearing the wall demanded. I just knew years of doing nothing had fixed nothing. Time to see what doing something fixed.

CHAPTER 4

ON PAPER IT WAS A GOOD DAY, that Friday I rescued Romp. Working a big show made acting normal almost easy; keeping up with my students' courses and questions and worries, making sure they had their heels down and eyes up and wrists flat, all filled a lot of space in my head. We racked up more good ribbons; Rianne, one of our Adult-Amateur riders, was second and third in her hunter-over-fences, in the running for a Reserve Champion if she could win the flat. Judges loved her flashy mare Baby Jane on the flat.

But through every school and every trip a chunk of my mind demanded, *what are you doing about Romp? What is the policeman doing? What would a detective do?* I had a couple of advantages I ought to be exploiting. I knew about horses and horse people and the policeman didn't. And of course he didn't know about Jeff Carr.

Carr was one of those guys who lurked around the shows but never seemed to be doing anything. He was connected to an Illinois outfit, I always thought something to do with wheeling and dealing, always on the edge of money changing hands. That was the little I knew of him, money that had tried to change hands from ours at Highflying Farm to his. We were selling a horse, with a price and commission worked out with the buyer's trainer, and Carr went behind the trainer's back to claim he could get the buyer to pay an extra ten grand, five of it his. We didn't out him but we made sure we knew who paid what and who the commission went to and didn't get tangled up with Carr again.

Now I had to learn a lot more about him. Who he hung out with, who he told his dirty secrets. All morning I didn't see him, though he should be easy to spot, with his broad shoulders like a still-fit wrestler's and his red hair curling out from under a long-brimmed ball cap. At last when I went down to the food trucks for a taco he was ahead of me in line. I put some people between us so I could watch from a distance. He had his back to me, his bright blue windbreaker emblazoned with his outfit's logo, talking to somebody else who was waiting to order. He shifted a step sideways so I could see past him. You'd think with all I'd been through that morning not much could faze me, but it jerked a knot in my stomach to see it was Jenny Silver he was talking to.

Jenny was a braider, our hunters just a few of the many she dolled up in the predawn dark every show day with tight little dominos down their necks and swirled plaits in their tails. She worked for the Frenchman Alain Ricoeur during the day, grooming his jumpers and walking his big dog and God knew what else. She and I had a history over her boyfriend Zack that made what she did or who she talked to none of my fucking business, as she'd often made sure to tell me. I got my stomach tamed: she and Carr could be talking about the weather, what she had for breakfast, how bad he wanted to fuck her, all kinds of shit. Maybe I could persuade myself she liked him. I heard women did, though one of them would have to explain that because I couldn't. He had a lot of white teeth he was always flashing, a mouthful. Some people took a lot of teeth for a smile.

But it didn't look like she was buying whatever his fake smile was selling. She shook her head as she listened, her chin ducked and her face slanted sideways, the way you do when you're dodging somebody's spit. After she broke away to get her order, she passed him with her head bent to her phone and a look like you'd give a turd pile somebody should have cleaned up. I stayed back so she wouldn't see me. Carr watched her so long the next guy nudged him to go get his food.

He saw me when he turned. Our gazes held for a second. No teeth for me; his ruddy brows came down like he was adding numbers and not liking how they came out. For now I wanted that sum to come out to zero so as I made my way to the window to order I ignored him. When I looked around again he was gone.

I'd made a decision early about Carr. He didn't come up with the idea of burning that horse alive on his own. He was a hanger-on, looking for a fast easy buck. On his own he wouldn't have risked slipping that well-known horse past an early rising braider or the Night Watch crew who were paid to keep an eye out for people exactly like him. The trick was to find out who paid him, because somebody must have. A lot.

But like an idiot, it was Jenny I searched for when I looked up the lane toward the barns. I wanted her and Carr to come out to less than zero. But it wasn't like I could go ask her and get told again she was none of my fucking business. And she wasn't. My business now was back in Malloy's barn screaming, and Jenny was a bitter heartache I wished I could kick out of my dreams.

Back at our barn everybody was ooohing and aaahing over Rianne's ribbons. Taylor and Cadence argued over who got to climb the stepladder to hang them on the Highflying banner over our tack stall. I flipped a coin and Taylor won.

"Take a load off," said Cadence's dad. Dads and husbands and boyfriends usually showed up for the weekends. "You could probably use it after this morning. Have a beer."

"Thanks, maybe later." I had to get my two jumpers ready for their afternoon classes. I looked around. "Where's Brett?"

"Flight's stall." Rianne came out from hanging her show clothes in the tack stall. "Helping Claryce with those boots." Claryce's jumper Flight could be ugly about having his back feet messed with so it could take extra hands to fasten the boots protecting his rear ankles. Rianne untwisted the elastic she'd used to hold her long dark hair under her helmet. "Have you heard anything from the police?"

"Talked to the police chief this morning. Sounded like he was on it."

Cadence was trying to tickle Brett's fat slab of a dog Dozer behind his ears. Hard because he had skin like a rhino. "They won't get Clown, will they?" she asked.

"Oh, honey," said her mom. "Robb and Brett won't let them."

Rianne shook her hair out. "I thought the Night Watch people were supposed to be on the lookout."

"Night Watch guy said he completely missed it," said Martha, our show manager, as she squeezed into the group and dug in the cooler for a soda. "Raul's sleeping out here tonight."

Raul was our younger groom; he and our older groom Jorge would have already curried and brushed my two jumpers. I took a bottle of cold tea down to check the horses out. Like Malloy, Brett and I had brought enough good-paying customers to this show for enough seasons we got great stalls, both sides of one of the wide sheltered barns close to the rings. Like most outfits we'd made the aisle between our stalls into Party Central for customers and parents

19

and the husbands and boyfriends, fancy folding chairs you could wallow in and tables and ice chests and piles of food. Brett came up beside me as I checked on my own horse, Zenith, who dozed in a corner. "I want you to watch Claryce school. Flight's not as sharp as he was last week and I've been looking at him so long I can't see it. Maybe something Claryce is doing. I don't know."

I nodded. "Sure." Claryce was his student, not mine, but all morning he'd been making a nuisance of himself, finding chores he suddenly needed help with or asking questions he already knew the answers to. Keeping me busy. He took off for the rings after Claryce and Flight, his jumpy energy as always like an overcharged battery sparking. He'd show Growly, our sales horse, in the higher meter-thirty class, one and three-tenths meters, later. Rianne came up with her phone so we could go over videos of her trips that her boyfriend had taken. So once again I did my job, playing normal, pretending I had nothing but the day ahead on my mind.

In fact, I was thinking how ordinary it all looked, our cluster of customers gathered in our aisle between classes, the girls' moms deciding the kids had outgrown pigtails and experimenting with ways to keep their hair under helmets, Martha shepherding everybody with her usual grumpy affection, Rianne and Claryce kidding me and Brett that some of their show friends kept calling us the "stud barn," Taylor wanting to know why and her mom trying to change the subject and Cadence bursting out with, "Because Brett and Robb're *hot*, dumdum." Martha saying "Handsome is as handsome does" as she cleared Brett's discarded vest and paddock boots off the trunk where he always dumped them. "Well, we do have the sexiest trainers on the showgrounds," Rianne said.

Brett and I turned that kind of remark into a joke pretty fast. Okay, we were young and fit and still had lots of dark hair; Brett's blue eyes got a lot of blushes, way more than my plain brown ones, out of all the young girls. But we had long ago set strict rules about boundaries with customers and we didn't need elaborate guidance from management about how to behave around kids. Eight years of hard work and fair play had won us the kind of happy barn family you invested yourself twenty-four/seven in protecting, since people who could afford showing didn't fall out of trees. They had entry fees and stall fees and office fees and grounds fees and dues to the United States Equestrian Federation and the United States Hunter/Jumper Association; they had to pay Brett and me to haul them to shows and back and coach them in their classes and Raul and Jorge and Martha to take special care of their horse in addition to the board they paid back home. One day the right customer would bring us a Grand Prix horse, maybe several, and yeah, we dreamed of that. But the people with us now were loyal long-time clients who trusted that the money they paid us and the time we all put in together would take them somewhere they wanted to go.

Besides, it wasn't Grand Prix dreams that kept me going. It was the pure joy of those moments when I lost myself on horses, when it didn't matter whether I was Robb Slaughter or Joe Blow as long as I rode. A joy that people like these paid for, not only with their money but also with their trust. For the first time since I'd stumbled down that hill that morning, I wished I could give them some warning, tell them what had grabbed hold of me and what I was about to do, not just to Romp's attackers but to them. Suddenly that little cluster looked painfully fragile. A whole past of shared memories and hopes I was about to turn upside down and shake hard.

Martha climbed the bleachers to sit beside me to wait for Flight's Adult-Amateur-Jumper round. Martha always had something to do with caring for horses hanging off her: a grooming glove shoved in a back pocket, a rag for wiping the dirt out of noses, a fly-spray bottle hooked in her waistband. Today she had Flight's cooler over her arm in case he came out sweating. She was mid-fifties, gawky, with short brown hair that looked like it had gone through a long drought. She'd babied Brett since before I knew him. She shifted the cooler to her lap. "I hope she doesn't blow that last corner to the triple," she said.

The horse on course now belonged to Tannenbaum, the trainer at Carr's outfit. They wanted to sell this one. A dark bay with one white leg, thick neck, square frame. He was strong off the ground but slow. Carr didn't ride. At least, I had never seen him on a horse.

The horse stalled at the triple, taking down the final oxer. "They won't get their price for that," Martha said.

The next horse came in, a rangy chestnut. It trotted in a circle, waiting for the forty-five-second buzzer. "Brett's worried about you," Martha said. "Hell of a thing for you to have to go through and he's worried how you're handling it. You really okay with all this?"

Any lies I tried with Martha would have to be pitch-perfect. I came up with a not-quite-lie I hoped I could slip past her. "I'm getting there."

Didn't work. "You went to see Romp, didn't you?" she said. The kind of thing she always knew though I could never figure out who could have told her. "Yeah."

"You did all you could, Robb. Nobody could have done more."

"I know that."

The chestnut had a good round going. He'd probably make the jump-off. She shook her head. "What I don't get, insurance doesn't make sense. Anybody trying to collect on their own horse would try to hide it some way. But then what was it? Who'd make money doing something like that?"

I hadn't come up with a way for the Paxtons to make money off a killing like that, either. I nodded but my own gaze had shifted. Where we sat overlooked not just the bigger of the two jumper rings but also the jumper schooling area beyond it where Jenny Silver was holding one of Alain Ricoeur's big studs. Romp had beat the horse in the Grand Prix last Sunday. Rumor had it the Paxtons were shipping in another horse, a Dutchbred, that could beat him again.

No sign of Ricoeur now. He'd show up when he was good and ready. The big horse swiveled around Jenny as she led him to the schooling-ring fence. Turned out Martha's eyes went there, too. "You think that girl could get any skinnier?"

"I hadn't noticed."

She bumped me with a bony knee. "Bullshit. Every move that woman makes dings your radar. Not one of your more intelligent obsessions."

Arguing with Martha was like swimming in glue. "You're just not a romantic."

"Not an idiot, you mean."

In fact I hated how Jenny had gone from alive and vibrant to worn and drained these past two years. My fault, probably, since she'd started fading like this right after I put her boyfriend Zack in jail. Her pale silk hair was wrenched back, dirt smeared on her cheekbones. Ricoeur must be working the shit out of her. At last he came stalking up.

He was over six feet, way over, had to ride big horses. He had a flat square face, hard as sheet-metal. "He's a fucking robot," I told Brett. "You just want his horses," Brett had said. I couldn't see that he even spoke to Jenny. He ripped the horse's cooler off, wadded it up, and shoved it at her, still not looking. The horse jigged sideways. He took the reins, led the horse down the ring to the mounting block, and snapped off at a trot. Jenny shrank into the fence even more.

At least he hadn't hit her like Zack had, not that I could see. He was an ass, but not that way. He was some of that trash that leaves a stink behind them. They don't leave blood.

Zack left blood. She wore her hair lower over her temple to hide the scar from where he'd slashed her with that hoof knife. She'd gotten the tooth he broke fixed. "Yeah, she's hot," Brett told me back when he'd first caught me tracking her after her braid jobs in the mornings. "But she's not some horse you can talk goo-goo to and cure her. Any woman who puts up with that shit is broken. When you fuck broken, you get cut."

Beside me Martha folded her storky body forward, elbows on knees, as Claryce and Flight came into the ring. "If she nails the triple he'll win it," she said.

Brett had decided Claryce was too heavy in her tack on her corners, driving Flight up in front of her where she needed him but making him hollow his back. This class he wanted her deeper in her heels, air under her, on the turns. Flight had a big canter. I'd ridden him; I knew how much power Claryce was feeling. His long stride let her ride slow and careful. I saw the fences ahead of me as he met them. Counted the strides the way we all did, it was as natural as breathing. He lofted through the triple with his big slow jump that still got him well under the time allowed.

Claryce would be tempted to rush the jump-off. Watching from the in-gate, Brett leaned forward, brows knitted, as if he was riding the course himself. Claryce took her best shot, quiet in the lines, shortening the turns, letting Flight's natural lift get him over. He stepped over the triple and she ran him to the timers.

"Damn," said Martha. His time was two one-hundredths off the leader. "Double damn."

"It was a good ride."

She stood to go meet Brett walking Claryce and Flight out of the gate but she turned on me like a tree toppling. "Anything happens to you, I'll have to take care of Brett by my lonesome. Don't make me do that." She prodded the toe of my boot with her toe. "Time will fix it. Let go."

"I guess. The vet said he'll get better."

She leaned even closer like she was going to rumple my hair, the way she knew I hated. "Wasn't the horse I was talking about."

23

She took off, no chance for me to answer. Beyond her Jenny still stood propped on the fence. She must have felt my eyes on her, like I thought she did sometimes, because she turned and gave me one of those looks I'd never learned to ignore. They weren't just full of disgust like the one I saw her give Carr, they dug in and twisted. Like she knew how it felt to want to kill someone you can't stop running into every day.

Time hadn't fixed shit for her. It hadn't fixed a lot of things. Hadn't fixed it for Martha, the kid she'd given up for adoption and still kept trying to find. Hadn't fixed it for our groom Jorge, who told Brett and Martha and me one night over beers about the wife he'd left behind in Guatemala and lost to cancer, tears running down his cheeks. Or for skinny little Raul, who still leaped six feet at every loud noise. And time sure wouldn't fix Romp, whatever Martha was preaching. Or me until I gave him at least some real justice. To buy that brand of justice, I needed a plan with more teeth than time.

CHAPTER 5

LONG BEFORE I WAS READY, I had to ride.

Alone in the tack stall, putting on my helmet, organizing the back numbers for the two jumpers I'd be showing, Oh Snap and my own horse, Zenith, I had to stop for a moment and face it: I was scared.

I'd never been scared before. Even with Zenith, who was a little bit crazy, I'd never doubted that whatever horse I rode the lines and turns and strides would sort themselves out once I had my rhythm and pace. I didn't always get to the fences perfect, but no one else did, either. I knew what my horses had to do and what I had to do to make them do it. It was a matter of listening to the horses and your own body. I'd never doubted it would all come through for me. Until now.

Stupid, I thought. Why should what happened to Romp interfere with my riding? Snap and Zenith were sound and fit and I'd dulled my own bruises enough I barely felt them. I shook myself, went out in the aisle to take Zenith from Raul where they waited. Headed for the schooling ring with a stumble in my step that spooked Zenith, made me have to drag him forward. What the fuck was this about?

As soon as I sank into the saddle, I knew.

Thank God it was on Zenith I was finding out and not Snap. We always put Zenith first in the order because he was an unpredictable challenge we liked to get out of the way. He was a gray Hanoverian, not that big, sixteen-three, quick and athletic, but the type who came out of his stall every day a different horse. Some days you could jump him four feet on a loose rein; others you wondered if you or the horse could survive one jump, let alone fifteen, tearing around at supersonic speed. At least if the trip went to shit the way I knew it would I didn't have to worry about disappointing anyone's expectations. Everyone watching would chalk the mess up to Robb's

freak show, which was what I'd heard people call Zenith. I wondered
who would look like the freak this time.

Brett seldom did more than watch me on him, almost never
coached. No point in it; he'd long ago put Zenith into the one
category of horses we disagreed on, the ones he thought I couldn't
save. Oh, I got it. The rogues, the Mach-10 maniacs, the ones who
spooked at their own footprints. "Money pits," he called them.
"Thirty K and you've got a horse nobody but you can ride."

Except that at least twice I'd talked him into second chances on
horses that ended up being winners, earning us six figures when we
sold them. "Brett doesn't get horses like that and you do," Martha
said once. "You ever wonder what he keeps you around for, that's
it." That day she'd been trimming stray hairs off Zenith's fetlocks.
"'Course, this one, you're giving him third and fourth chances."

"There's a spark in there somewhere," I answered.

"Let's hope it's not the kind that'll launch you over the ring
fence."

But today Brett didn't go his usual route of propping his elbows
on the top rail and lounging while I schooled. Instead he posted
himself in the center at the schooling vertical, arms crossed, watching
me like I was a ten-year-old kid getting ready for my first Short-
Stirrup class. He tracked me in sullen silence as I fucked up the first
warm-up vertical, riding too right, burying my horse in a near stall. "I
don't know why you're bothering to school," he said finally. "He's
just getting riled."

I was schooling in hopes of a miracle to fix this. But my warm-
up got worse and worse. Brett didn't even follow me to the in-gate.
Before me was the course, fifteen good-sized fences I had to
somehow get over without leaving a trail of shambles. Not a
goddamn chance.

It was the screams that were fucking with me.

Since that first ride on that first school horse after that first
sweating seizure, I'd counted on the horses to drown it all out. To
shield me from that incessant squall echoing in my head.
Remembering riding, thinking about riding, riding itself, had brought
me the only silence I could always count on.

Not now.

Now I sat hoping that rehearsing the course would wipe my
mind free of the new wails I kept hearing, but it didn't. It seemed like
every horse I ever rode was screaming at me now. How the hell

could I deliver? I would fail them. Moments like this, reins to pick up and a course to get over, would stop being a salvation. They'd be a reminder of what I'd failed to do.

The horse on course before me raced through the timers, circled, exited—and now somehow I had to go through that gate and ride. There was only one answer short of turning and running: what I told every frightened student. Get your horse moving and ride forward. Hope this wasn't the day my crazy little horse would pick for his own suicide. The forty-five second buzzer sounded; I picked up the canter for the long approach back down the ring to first fence I'd planned on, pure mechanics, *this is how you do it, stupid.* Looked for that first fence with no idea how I'd get to it, and by God, there was the wall.

Not an illusion. A certainty, looming beyond this fence, this moment, this horse. Daring me to come to it. Mocking me. *Go ahead, back off, pull up, crash.* Suddenly I wasn't riding for the plain vertical back toward the in-gate, Fence Number One of the fifteen I had to negotiate, I was riding past it to the challenge I really had to meet. The real, concrete fence became nothing to me and Zenith lofted over it, landed balanced, gave me a perfect lead change as we turned in a flowing arc to Fence Number Two. Then Three and Four and on and on, turns and combinations and always ahead, the wall.

We didn't win. Weren't even in the money. We had two rails, maybe because I was getting used to looking down that new line. When I rode out, Brett unfolded himself from the post he'd been leaning against to watch me. "What the fuck," he said.

"He was paying more attention," I said, my voice amazingly cool given the ruckus in my heart. No way I could confess to anyone what had happened: that I'd ridden toward true justice like I meant it. Like I really could, would, do it.

"Right, *he* was," said Brett, but he smiled.

After that, Snap was a lock.

Green as he was, he was the kind of horse who if you didn't fuck them up they delivered. He'd been the most exciting young prospect to come into our barn in the last couple of years. His owner was a wiry little woman with white whipped-up hair who had come down from Philly where she ran a headhunting agency for tech firms. She had given up riding when she broke her hip a second time at seventy-four. She didn't break it riding. She tripped on a rug. She'd just bought Snap when it happened, had been ground-driving him before sending him off to get started. From rehab she put me in charge of keeping tabs on his training and taking him on when he came back. An ache in her eyes every time she watched me ride him told me how bad she wanted to be the one riding, but she had decided those days were over. We didn't know what Snap had in him yet, but I'd be the one finding out.

Now she took Snap from Raul and checked the girth of my second saddle, the one Snap went best under. "So terrible, what happened to that wonderful horse of Rich and Dierdre's," she said. "You did something remarkable, I heard."

"I heard that, too," I said, and hoped I'd made it a joke.

What wasn't a joke was that not only did I know now I could ride my horses, I knew what to do when the sick doubt settled on me: ride for the wall. Gallop toward it, don't look back, don't flinch. For Snap's class now, I let myself drop deep into mechanics, mentally measuring strides, squaring corners, placing Snap head-on to the jumps. Mechanics got me the clean first round I needed, no time faults. In the jump-off the course designer was dangling a temptation: leave out a stride in the last line and shoot through the timers balls out. And of course, take the last fence down when you did.

We'd talked about it, Brett and Pat and I. Snap was young, still figuring out his footwork. We didn't have to scare the shit out of him. But winning would clinch the test I had just aced, scoring a good ribbon and a check for Pat. So I planned the tight turns they ask for in jump-offs, shaving inches off the corners. It worked. Even waiting for the added stride in the last line, we came out with the top time.

A big black horse Alain Ricoeur rode beat us by a full second. He did leave out the stride. "You rode really smart," Pat said.

Brett had a solid ride in the meter-thirty on Growly, third by the clock. Schooling, he had listened to me more than usual, getting the big Holsteiner straight so he met his fences square. Back at the barn everybody was all chatter as they took off to change for dinner, but I wasn't cocky. Sure, I'd handled myself today, but every ride from now on was going to test me. Every ride a reminder of what I owed the horses and what I ought to be doing to pay them back. And every day Brett watching me and asking me to prove who I was.

28

He went to the camper to grab the first shower ("You always use up all the hot water"), and after a last round of treats to their horses, everybody else headed out. I stayed behind to wipe tack, hoping the quiet routine would let me work through a rush of nagging guilt. Martha's words rattled the silence: *Brett's worried.* It wasn't like he didn't have reason to worry. I was about to rip his clean-cut world apart.

His world had never been one I naturally belonged in. Two guys so damn different should never have meshed like we did. For Brett, there was a straight line through every problem and if you couldn't walk it, you had rocks in your head. Par for a guy who grew up seeing every barrier open up for him; his dad had owned a big Virginia farm, white-columns and white-board fences, and his mom rode on the A circuit up north. So it was for "the experience" that he ended up working for the Canadian outfit where our paths crossed. Me, I'd been living in tack stalls and picking up losing rides for flat fees just to keep horses under me so the nightmares wouldn't kill me. I ended up at that outfit because they had a bunch of green and not very talented horses they needed to get rid of and they wanted daredevils who could make them look respectable around a jumper course.

Brett didn't want to mess with those cheap horses and he let that be known. One day one of the other riders said to him, "Not everybody has Daddy's money so he can pick and choose." A fight would have gotten even Brett fired but he carried that money like chips on both shoulders and suddenly he had to prove himself.

One of those cheap horses was a mare with some real talent but a brain like a Molotov cocktail in search of a match. I'd been nursing her along hoping I could keep her from ending up at the killers. Brett was technically my boss and he informed me she was the one he was going to ride.

I told him not to. "A horse like that reads you," I told him. "She'll feel all that shit in you."

"She wants a fight, she'll get one," he said.

Still, the day he picked for the fight I noticed he made sure it was just the two of us in the indoor, out of sight of everyone. I'd set up a gymnastic line I hoped would slow her enough to make her think about what her feet were doing. When he said, "Get off," part of me naturally wanted to say, "Fine, asshole, have at it." But another part of me understood things and didn't want to see him do that to himself.

29

Like I thought, she wasn't having any of it. He couldn't even get her to canter with her front feet on the ground. At last he got off, both of them lathered and blowing, handed me the reins. "They should shoot her," he said, and walked out.

I got back on her not because I wanted to show him up but because I had put so much work in her and I also knew I might get to keep my job if I could get this one sold. I didn't know he hung around the corner watching. I let her alone, the way I knew to, and before I was done she jumped through the grid without killing either one of us. When I bumped into Brett as I led her out, he said, "What the hell do you know that I don't?"

Totally unexpected reaction from a spoiled shit like that, admitting he didn't have all the answers. I saw into him then the way I sometimes saw into blustering horses, the true spark there. A couple of days later he wanted to buy me a beer and he said, "What are you thinking about doing after you leave here?"

Eight years now. We were well into those eight years before he knew anything about me, and then only what accidentally came out. My mother's death, my foster-care childhood, my adoption—for him that seemed to be enough. We had a lot to prove together: him, that it wasn't just Daddy's money, though he used some of it to get us going; me, that I had something to bring to the kind of world Daddy's money would have bought. I sometimes wondered if I was bringing as much to Brett as I took. I decided over time that the promise I made was what mattered: that when the time came for all the stuff our jobs demanded, from wiping kids' noses to picking up the reins on that Grand Prix jumper we dreamed of, I'd do what I always did and put whatever I carried over there somewhere and show up for the ride. Sometimes over the years I imagined telling him stuff about me he'd never asked, as if those truths could stitch a sturdier seam around what we had. But in the end I kept my secrets. Better he never knew how much I put into being what *he* needed, so the *us* we worked so hard to build would keep on being there.

I tried to shut out my guilt with the answer I should have given Martha: Brett would be fine. If I disappeared tomorrow, a thousand people would line up to take my place. Everybody knew how good Brett was. Not only was he a strong, precise rider, he had a great eye for talented horses and he was a hard-nosed pragmatic businessman. A rising star in a hard-assed universe.

So silence had always worked for us, and I'd thought until today I could keep it working. In all the shit in my head since climbing into that trailer, I kept finding a fantasy that if I just explained what was about to happen and why, he'd understand. Then maybe he'd get that I was doing what someone had to and he'd put whatever I did behind him and move on, if not to some other version of us, then to a new version with whoever replaced me. I tried to persuade myself that would happen. That he'd take a dive way deeper than he'd ever wanted to go.

CHAPTER 6

AS IT HAPPENED, I SHOULDN'T HAVE STAYED behind in the barn hoping for peace and quiet. Because I didn't get any. I got a strange woman with hot, quick eyes who cornered me in the barn aisle with her card.

I had to let go of the reins I was wiping to take it. Valerie Raymond, from the local paper I'd seen in convenience stores. She was tall, with narrow cutting hips and sharp shoulders and longish dark-brown hair she hadn't done much to fluff up. "Mr. Slaughter?" She said my name like she was throwing a net over me. "You can imagine this thing about the trailer fire is a pretty big story. It's already been picked up by the AP. I want to get the story from you."

I dropped the card on a nearby trunk and made a show of working cleaner through the leather. The last thing I wanted was to talk to a reporter. "I already told the police all I know. Get it from them or the horse's trainer or owners. Not me."

"Oh, I got the official story about what happened from Chief Wardle. That's not what I'm interested in." Her voice had a lot of her sharpness in it. "I want to know about *you*."

I pivoted to face her. It wasn't so much that the hero tale she was probably cooking up would be embarrassing, though it would be. But whatever she wrote would catch me in a spotlight, make everyone look at me when I needed to hide. I hung the reins on the tack hook, grabbed a nearby pitchfork. "So write that I was a hero." Like everybody was already saying. "Put that in your story if you want."

I went into Zenith's stall. As if I thought I could escape. When I closed the bottom door she gripped the top as if she meant to fight me for it. "You don't sleep real well, do you?" she said brightly. "People like you tend to have nightmares. A nightmare woke you up, so you heard something happening. You had to save the horse the way you couldn't save your mother. Do you think maybe that's why you ran into that fire?"

Not a spotlight. Klieg lights. She would broadcast all the broken pieces behind my hard-won front of normal Robb. "I ran into that fire because I was the one who was there, Ms. Raymond. What happened to my mother has nothing to do with it. That's not your story. Leave it out."

She crimped her mouth in what might have been a smile. Or maybe a grimace of pity. "Mr. Slaughter, I found out about you and there's a story here, and I'm going to write it. You can have some say in what I write, or you can't. Or more accurately you *won't*. It's as simple as that."

Zenith fluttered his nostrils, a warm weight at my back. "That sounds like a threat," I told her.

The smile sharpened. "Or an opportunity."

"Excuse me?"

"Why don't you let me tell you?" she said.

I didn't like taking her to our cramped little camper, still steaming from Brett's shower. He had planned on a trip down to the tack shops, so I had half an hour max. But this conversation had to be private and I couldn't think of anywhere else. I sat her at the table with her angular features catching the late-day sun.

She hadn't left me many real options. If I didn't get in front of whatever she was planning she struck me as the type who would do exactly what she'd threatened, and I sure didn't want somebody that nosy sniffing around on her own. If nothing else I could find out what Wardle had told her. I'd concentrated so hard on keeping things from him it hadn't occurred to me he might have secrets himself.

She shook her head at a glass of water from our filtered faucet. "I guess these RVs are pretty handy for you horse show people." Her wide shoulders looked sharp enough to jab holes in the flimsy siding. "You spend much time in this thing?"

I usually had to laugh when someone called our stuffy space an RV. Nothing "recreational" about it. It wasn't a huffing behemoth like some of the campers parked alongside us in the row of rental spaces behind the barns; it allowed for a main room with a stove and fridge and my fold-down bunk, the hall with the tiny bath off it, and Brett's bedroom at the far end. "Just a crash pad." I ran water for myself, propping my butt on the counter, as far from her as the narrow space let me. "So what'd you do? Google me?"

Her hungry gaze sparkled. "You ever Google yourself, Mr. Slaughter?"

"A while back."

"What'd you find?"

"A lot of Robert Slaughters."

She took out a pen and a little spiral notebook. "I have a Google alert on my name. Amazing how often I'm either the subject of a funeral or the survivor of someone else's funeral. Once in a while I get to be a museum curator or a university professor. How about you?"

"You should know. You saw the hits."

She crunched up her eyes. "You've been buried a lot, too."

"Did I survive anyone?"

"Your mother," she said.

So she had claws. Wrangling over what she could have raked up from old news archives and police records would only make her dig for more drama behind them. Might as well find out how much blood she planned on drawing. "So you want to write this story about how what happened with my mother thirty years ago made me run into that fire."

"What did make you run into that fire?"

"Adrenaline."

She scoffed. "You think everybody would have done what you did?"

I gestured with my glass at her little pad. "Write this down and make sure it gets into your story. Almost everybody I know would have done what I did."

She castled her fingers, elbows spread wide on the table. "So now, you can't help wondering which of them *wouldn't* have done what you did."

"When I see somebody like that, I'll know."

"And what will you look for?"

"Somebody who would hurt horses."

"What do they look like?"

"Two eyes, two ears, a nose and a mouth."

She laughed, a little humph. "A lot of those to sort through." She scratched the tangle of hair behind her ear. "Anyway, that whole thing about your mother—that is newsworthy."

35

"Why?"

"Oh, come on."

"I was seven."

"I know."

"I was too young to remember any of it. Sorry if it messes up your story but it doesn't have anything to do with anything."

She studied me, chin on her hands. "I see your problem. You don't want everyone pawing over your past, like they will if I write my story. I can see how that would be a bummer. You want to stop me but you don't know how."

"So can I stop you?"

She curled forward. "Actually, you can."

"How, by buying into this opportunity you're offering? Which is what?"

She spread her hands, her eyes glowing. "I've been around this town long enough to know the police aren't going to solve this. It's not like they've got a big city force to throw at it, and hell, it's only a horse." She smacked the pad on the table. "But I bet *you* want to solve it." Her voice took on an urgency. "And whatever the people who did this think they're doing, who's to say they'll stop trying? If you could catch them first, you'd do it." Her eyes found mine, unrelenting. "Wouldn't you?"

A question no normal person would say "no" to. "Catch them how?"

More hunger in her gaze. "I get the feeling, from this stuff I know about you, that you're not going to move on from this. You won't be able to let go of it, you're going to find out things. But I can find out things you can't."

"Using what? Magic?"

She laughed, but bore down on the exhale. "I'm a *reporter*. I have contacts."

"And?"

"You tell me what you learn and what you need to know. I tell you what I learn and what I need to know." She spread her hands at my silence. "A partnership, to find out who did it. Opportunity plus!"

"Actually, it looks more like blackmail."

She shrugged, grinning. "In that case, you don't want to be the story, that's my price."

I took a swallow of water to buy a second to answer. "So if we learn things, which one of us tells the police about them?"

"It's not like we'd hide a killer if we found one."

I didn't raise the question of what might happen to a killer if I found one. "Of course not."

"But you can't lie to me," she said as if I'd already surrendered. "You want to keep your mother out of the story, you have to tell me what really happened at that trailer. Everything."

I had to push past a tightening in my gut to get to *why not?* From the looks of it, she'd be underfoot no matter what I did, and I'd be better off knowing what she dug up. Maybe she did have contacts, ways of asking questions I didn't have time to learn. But she'd be a tricky accomplice. She jumped right on my lie when I repeated what I'd told Wardle. "Too bad you didn't see the guy. I mean, he must have been right there, setting the fire. That would go a long way toward solving it."

"Yeah," I said. I set my glass down on the table. Gently, so the water in it didn't ripple. I didn't say how much my idea of solving it differed from hers.

The story was spreading that Romp had gone crazy. At dinner Cadence's dad said, "To think you saved him for this."

Then he flushed, wiped his mouth with a knuckle. "That didn't come out right. This is better than that would have been."

That started the girls crying. Ice cream helped, but not much.

When we'd seen everyone off to their motels and blanketed the horses against the cool night air they had in these mountains, I told Brett, "I'm going to sleep in the tack stall tonight."

He looked at me crooked, like he'd caught me stoking Growly's biting habit by giving him treats. "Raul's doing that. He wants the extra money."

"I'll pay him."

"He's perfectly capable."

"I didn't say he isn't."

"Fine, but there's only one cot."

"I'll sleep in a chair." The damn chairs looked like they'd come off the flight deck of the Starship *Enterprise* and as much as they'd cost they might as well have.

"Not the blue one," Brett said. "That's the one I like and I don't want your farts all over it."

"Like you could tell the difference."

"Try me." He laughed. A sound I liked hearing. Like we were a couple of high school kids joshing. He did that sometimes, I think, when he got too close to one of those edges he saw in me and didn't want to fall over it. I had to keep looking normal, so I laughed back.

CHAPTER 7

I SETTLED FOR THE CHAIR Martha called pea green and Jorge called *guacamole podrido* (he thought nobody caught on that *podrido* meant "rotten," but I looked it up). I wound a horse blanket around me. The blanket smelled of the usual horse stuff you couldn't wash out, the smells you grew into if you were around them enough. Any horse person would tell you that horse shit and even piss smell cleaner than what you get from cows, pigs, cats, dogs. The dirt you brush off their hides smells like it's been mixed with air. People who don't know won't believe you, but it's a kind of dirt that's clean.

In the stall, Raul was tucked into a sleeping bag on an air mattress, sometimes breaking into a coughing snore. The tall sentry lights outside poured down a white glare, but the aisle was dark. I had chosen to back up Raul's vigil not because I thought the horse killers would try again so soon but because Brett would be staying in the camper instead of heading off with his current girlfriend, and I needed some privacy so I could finally sit and think.

I hadn't used those minutes with that police chief, Wardle, very well. He'd hinted he was looking at insurance; maybe I could have learned how he thought that kind of fraud would work. Except he'd need to know what I knew about horses and money. Hunters might be pretty but they seldom earned enough showing to pay an immigrant kid to groom one for a year. Jumpers—that was different. The Grand Prix classes, where the top international riders and horses competed, had started paying real cash. But a full campaign on the Grand Prix circuit took a lot of straw or shavings and a lot of hay, and alfalfa at that. A lot of vet bills. A lot of kids to do the grooming. You could get some of them cheap, but you needed a lot.

Those costs wouldn't be our worries until that special customer bearing that special Grand Prix horse came along. In the meantime, our income came from people like Snap's owner Pat, like Claryce, who I think wouldn't care if her horse could only pop over cross rails as long as she had one to ride. Part of the reason she rode with us and not one of the hotter outfits like Mack Dever's was that she knew we felt the same way. People who only wanted to be seen on their big expensive horses didn't get royal treatment from us. If we let someone like that in our barn, Martha would have sneaked into their hotel room at night and poked their eyes out with a hoof pick. Then she'd have come for us.

Sure, a lot of barns made selling ego their business, mounting their customers on the fanciest stock their money could buy. But horses wore out, and they weren't like cars, where you could go get a new engine. Sooner or later they didn't do what you paid all that money for.

Wardle had probably spent his whole day rounding up that kind of information, while I'd run my feet off being everybody's Robb. Two more weeks and the series would be over, all the outfits heading off in different directions, and behind me was a wasted day. I sure couldn't sit around and wait on this Valerie Raymond. For now my way forward had to be like Martha said, follow the money. Somebody somewhere planned to make money killing a Grand Prix champion and I had to get busy figuring out who and how. That came first, before I could drill down to what justice would look like and how I would get it done.

The air mattress groaned when Raul turned over. I got up, the blanket draped around me, looked in on him. Enough light to etch his drawn jaws and cheekbones, hard-cut from a life I couldn't imagine even though he was young. He and Jorge were the reason Brett and I ever got any sleep. Eight horses at a show wasn't much for the bigger barns, but that many to water and feed and muck and groom and coach and ride could stretch a couple of pairs of hands pretty thin. Without the guys and Martha we couldn't have made it all happen. I pulled the sleeping bag over his shoulders, wishing him a well-deserved sleep.

In the *sillón podrido* (*sillón* for "chair" was one of the few Spanish words Jorge had managed to teach me) I pulled the blanket up tighter; these mountain nights were staying cold. It had been cold in the trailer lot until I'd jumped into that fire. I made a cave out of the blanket and took out my phone. I didn't want to tie into the public WiFi the show provided. I killed the connection, let my phone do the search.

I could start by digging into a little history I knew but Wardle wouldn't. I typed "horse insurance killings." My screen filled with hits.

No surprise there. Everybody, even people a lot younger than I was, knew about that slew of killings—I counted back, forty years. Lore that got passed around, a big scandal that hung out on the edge of our worries about our horses, all the things that could happen to them. I'd never known the details. I hadn't heard any lore about fires. Electrocution was what I spent a couple of hours reading about. A wire run from ear to butthole, then plugged in. Vets had written the mysterious deaths off to the perennial killer of horses, colic. It had taken whistleblowers and wiretaps to clue them in.

Another thing I'd known but hadn't thought about was that some of the biggest names in horse showing had done it. That is, paid a guy to do it. There was some bizarre stuff. Like a really famous rider leaving his best horse out in a thunderstorm hoping it would get hit by lightning. At least I could read about that without my guts tying up.

I did find one story about horses in a burning trailer. They also got rescued. No word who the hero was that time.

After a while I finished with history. I opened a new tab, typed in "Jeff Carr."

Like I'd discussed with Valerie Raymond, when you Google someone you find out how many people share the same name. I didn't know if he was Jeffrey Carr or some initial, or Jeffery Carr, or even Geoffrey Carr. I got dozens of hits on each.

I started with the sites that would return basic info for free. No one on the first few pages of hits had any visible connection with horses. Maybe I should try Facebook or Tik Tok. More likely, I thought, a porn platform. Of course, users of sites like that would use nicknames. I was wondering where else I could search when my phone spat out a warning: "Battery Low."

Not a great start but at least I'd done something. Before the battery died I cleared my history. No point in leaving my searches for strangers to thumb through. Assuming it ever came to that.

I guess it was inevitable that sooner or later I'd shrug out of the blanket and slip up the row to Malloy's barn. In the shadows the show manager, Nia, was asleep in a chair. Her hooded sleeping bag made the one over Raul look like a feed sack. I stood for several minutes watching her, to see if she sensed me. She didn't stir.

That evening I'd seen grooms trying to handwalk Romp, flipping like toys on the lead ropes as he struggled, and behind me someone said, "They'll have to put that thing down." A chill went through my mind. Was that the best I could imagine for that marvelous creature? An end?

I edged closer. I wanted the horse to tell me what he needed, what I should do. What would fix something—not just for me, for him. All that reached me was his torment, through his closed door, his pacing, the rake of his hooves. Not for the first time that day, he cut his own space into me, where he circled and circled and screamed.

Back in my chair, I guess I slept a little. The police solving this case was the nightmare I woke up to. The monsters who'd done this wouldn't even get the punishment Jenny's boyfriend Zack had. They might skulk through a few tolerable years in a cushy jail somewhere but that would be the end of it. It was only a horse.

But the more I sat and fumed about that courtroom, the more I got clear in my head what had happened. Not just to Romp. To me. I knew why that afternoon I'd suddenly broken through the screams to ride clean to my fences. It wasn't only those distances I had started seeing. After years of pulling up, running out, sure I couldn't get over, when I looked through Zenith's ears beyond those ordinary fences, I'd finally seen a distance to that goddamn wall.

People who don't jump horses won't know what seeing a distance means. On paper it's all mechanics, so many feet calculated by the height of the fence and the pace that makes for the ideal spot for the horse to take off. Galloping toward the fence, it's all crazy fluid, all in your body and breath more than in your mind. You can't think yourself to that perfect spot, you have to keep your horse going like you set him and when you're right, there it is. You can get over without a good distance, but when the jumps are big, your odds are long. You only see a good distance when you're riding to a fence like you really mean it, and your horse knows you do. There's an old saying about really big fences: to jump a big fence, you can't think about crashing or landing or what comes after. You have to throw your heart over and follow. Your whole being has to dig down into your commitment. Once you do your horse will take you to your distance. All you have to do is hang on.

Why I'd always quit was clear now. I'd never thrown my heart over. I'd never given the horse under me anything to trust. I'd thought I could keep putting off what that wall meant, leave the screams unanswered. I'd known all along they wouldn't stop until I answered. But I hadn't, couldn't, because I hadn't given my whole heart to what waited on the other side.

Not to my surprise, I started to sweat. Not a few beads in my hairline. A full-blown dead-dog sweat. Dead-dog because they first started that night long ago when I grabbed that dog off the highway only to feel him die in my arms. Felt his screams knife into my heart as I held him and couldn't do a thing to help. Those sweats weren't ordinary little flushes. They gushed like every ounce of fluid in my body was spilling out. They came in sudden moments when I saw clear what the other side of the wall looked like. What throwing my heart over demanded. This time my head played a sick vision of the people, all of them, who had made that horse scream. In the vision they were faceless, even Carr. In the vision I obliterated those blank shapes by magic, blinked and they vanished. A stupid trick my mind was playing. It wouldn't happen like that at all.

I got up and stumbled into the feed room for a towel, ran the hose and soaked it, swabbing my face and throat. The sweat passed slowly. This time. Leaving me limp as if I'd had a bad fall. But I couldn't shake my anger at the person who could have stopped those screams but didn't. When you let things like that happen you're as vile as the people you let do them. And when they tortured the next horse because I let them? Because I didn't want to go to the other side?

Then without warning Romp was the horse under me, dragging me to that perfect distance. The wall more than a promise, now a place *he* had to get to. He'd thrown his heart over with me hanging on him, and he was three strides out now. Galloping. Locked in.

After a while I put away my chair and the blanket. Raul still slept, breathing softly. Our horses snored or shuffled in their bedding, quiet and safe.

Three a.m. Twenty-four hours ago I'd stepped out into the night and spotted Jeff Carr. Followed him into a world I'd run from all my life.

But my normal life was where I had to keep functioning, at least for a while. I had a full Saturday ahead and a couple of hours still before it started, a short window of peace when maybe I could rest or even sleep. Brett would be comatose in his back bedroom, Dozer snoring louder than any sound I'd make entering. If I couldn't sleep I could at least rehearse a feeble idea I had come up with to get me started tomorrow. The grounds hardly stirred as I slipped out the back way between the campers and barns.

Then ahead was Jenny's camper. Snuck up on me. It was dark; even the braiders stayed curled in their bunks. Sometimes, passing her camper, I would slow, as if I could send some kind of plea through the metal walls to her, but now I veered wide. I wanted to keep her as far as I possibly could from this world I'd stepped into. But halfway past, I stopped, blinking. It took me the strangest long second to make out a figure crouching before her closed door.

CHAPTER 8

I SHOUTED. THE FIGURE TURNED toward me. A man, too thin to be Carr, his face a pale oval under a dark, brimmed cap. He ducked toward the fence, between her camper and the huge RV beside it, and ran.

I plunged after him but skidded to a stop. A glow on the metal step at her camper door.

Flickering. Fire? I dove toward it. A paper bag like people line their streets with at Christmas, a candle inside.

I fingered the bag open, blew out the candle. Curled around the smoking wick was a photo, even in the shadows clearly a cutting from a magazine: a horse.

"Jenny!" I didn't climb the steps. Some trace, boot prints, fingerprints, might show who'd been here. "Jenny! Jenny, are you there?"

No sound from inside. Darkness behind the curtains. I stepped over, banged on the window. "Jenny! Are you in there?"

The big campers on both sides were shuttered, a faint hum of heaters running. No one would have seen or heard anything. But I'd damn well shout up the whole row if she didn't open the door.

I banged again. To my relief, the door opened. She looked down at me, hitching her sweats higher on her thin hips, the hollow camper shell dark behind her. She shook her loose hair back. "What the fuck?"

"Somebody . . ." I gestured. She looked down at the step where the bag sat. Her face was already blanched by the cool glow from the sentry lights, so I couldn't say it got paler. But her mouth opened and her throat moved. "Somebody," I said again, like the idiot she always turned me into. "I saw a guy run away. It's . . . a candle. It's a candle, in a bag—"

45

She shot down the top step and snatched up the bag. Raced back up the steps. I caught the flimsy door before she could shut it. "What the hell's going on?"

"It's none of your business." Her voice came out low and fast, like a puncture in her lungs was leaking. She hauled on the door. I held on. "Hell it isn't. It's about killing horses." I pointed to the bag in her fist. "Is that the one that's next?"

She poked her head out and looked toward the lane in front of the campers. She crumpled the bag with the candle and picture still in it, backing away. I stayed where I was. Someone threatening her? This the police would have to hear about, whatever my agenda. "You should call the cops."

She turned on a light. I'd been in her camper just that once, the time I pulled Zack off her, had seen how little she had. Even less now: a plate and cup in a dish drain, a single rag draped on the edge of the sink, a towel. Her phone by the sink charging. She dropped the crumpled bag on the counter behind her. "Forget it, Robb. Nobody's done anything."

"There's a photo of a horse in that bag. It would have caught fire."

She changed the weight on her feet like trying a boxing step. "Seriously, Robb. This is none of your business. You gotta stop stalking me."

"No. I wasn't. I was going back to our camper. I saw this guy—"

"No. You slowed down so you could see if I was in here. Don't lie, I know you do it. That's freaking stalking, Robb."

I'd made it up the last step without knowing. I reached past her and picked up the bag. Pried it open, rolled out the little candle with its darkened wick and set it on the table inside the door. I worked the picture of the horse loose and smoothed it. From its gloss I guessed it came from *Practical Horseman*. I offered it. "Who's threatening you?"

For a moment she hung there, hands on the counter behind her. Her frown went from fierce to uncertain. She wiped the back of her hand across her mouth, then put the hand out. "Let me see that."

I should keep it, I thought. There'd be prints. She snapped her fingers. After a moment I handed her the picture and the bag.

She spread the picture out. "Oh."

"Oh what?"

"I know who this is." She flicked the picture at me. Laughed. "For God's sake. It's all right."

I didn't trust the way her face had changed. Like she'd had to build the right face for that laugh.

"Threatening to kill a horse isn't all right," I said.

"He doesn't mean any shit like that. It's just a . . ." She waved the photo. "Stupid. Some guys have funny ideas about how to be tough."

"Funny."

"You know something? You're not funny." She sounded more tired than defiant. She folded the picture, creased the edges, folded it again into an even smaller square. Threw it in the sink behind her, then picked up her phone. "Really. I don't need your fucking insults, dragging innocent people into your garbage. Go to bed."

I pointed at the sink where she'd thrown the photo. "This isn't innocent."

She thumbed the phone, eyes on the keypad. "Didn't you hear me?"

"Jenny, whatever's going on, if you know something, please tell me. I can help you."

She held up the phone where I could see it, thumb hovering on the call icon. "You've helped enough already." She'd keyed in 911.

I slipped into my bunk in the camper without waking Brett or Dozer. I didn't sleep; forty minutes max and we'd all be up anyway. I leaned back in yesterday's clothes and cursed myself for stupid. Because now it wasn't Romp or Carr but Jenny who twisted around in my head.

I'd known what it could cost me when I decided I had to get her boyfriend Zack off her and I used his petty drug-dealing to bring in the cops. But I hadn't really added up what my choice would cost *her*. Where I left her wasn't where I wanted. Bad nights worrying about her I thought that if I had killed Zack like I should have she'd have had a chance to move past him. Not to me. After that I'd have been the one in prison. Prison might have been easier to take than seeing her wear away like this.

It took me a while to catch on about Zack. All I knew for a long time was that he was the reason we had to have other people around if she let me sit with her at the food stands or have a beer after classes, the reason she turned down the only present I ever tried to

47

give her, a CD of one of the singers I thought she sounded like when she messed with her guitar.

"You're sweet," she told me, "but I've already got a boyfriend."

"It's not . . . it's just a friendly little something. It doesn't mean anything."

"Oh, not trying to get in my pants a little?" In those days I was one of the people she had special smiles for.

"No, really—"

"Excuse me? You *are* a guy?"

"Not that kind of guy."

"No, you're not, are you?" She'd flipped the CD back and forth until I finally took it. "The sex is the one thing I could possibly give you, but it wouldn't do what you think it would."

So I became the best friend-non-boyfriend I could manage and she seemed glad. She let me go grocery shopping with her during the shows and let me fix her car all the times Zack mysteriously disappeared right when she needed him most. I never told her for fear of spooking her but the moments I stole from Zack—watching trips in the bleachers beside her on a spring afternoon, helping her finish off a pint of ice cream before it melted, letting her show me a new guitar chord she was practicing—brought a peace that so far only the horses had ever given me. Sure, I thought about what it would be like to sleep with her—who wouldn't?—but in those days before I did what I did she was more like a softness that settled over me and I thought could have remade me if I could have let it keep going. But then I found out all Zack was doing to her and to a lot of other people and that was the end of that.

I read someplace that people who take what she took from Zack think they somehow deserve it. Like they're being punished for something. I couldn't think what she could have done to deserve him. I couldn't believe she could love a guy who treated her like that.

I didn't try to have that conversation with her but I had the one about getting killed. I ran into her at a fast-food place right after she got the stitches from the hoof knife out. Halter buckle did that? Right. She'd started to notice how much more I was hanging around her, worrying about her, and she glared when I slid in across from her that day. My time with her was already fragile but I was getting to where I couldn't sit and watch any longer. She put down her burger, tucked the wrapper around it like it was something living. "Don't start, Robb."

"You can't fix him. Everybody knows guys like that don't change."

"It was an accident. Leave it."

"What am I going to do when he does kill you? What then?"

Her blue eyes went darker, maybe from the defiance in them. She got up, made a space between us wide enough that her breath settled. "You're the one in the fixing business. You think you can decide who needs fixing, and for what. I can decide that for myself, thank you very much."

"So you're deciding to die, is that it? Am I supposed to watch this?"

"Robb. Fuck off. Go find somebody else to fix."

She left, already ducking her head to drape her hair over the scar, the way she did from then on.

Yeah, I planned to fix something, all right, that day I heard her scream and burst in on them in her camper. I remember most of all the look on his scraggy, flushed face when he turned and saw me. I expected to have to fight him, drag him out of there bodily, but instead of coming at me he just stared at me, and the look was fear. Not of me. It was warping his mouth and brows when he pushed past me and left her there crying. I bent over her. She said, "Go away."

Go away. That was what I did for her that day, give her that broken record to play whenever I came near. "Go away" when I tried to bring a doctor. "Go away" when I told her she could live with me. "Go away." Then after I made my decision, told the cops at that upstate New York horse show what everybody knew about the drug stuff Zack was doing but looked the other way from, she quit saying anything.

CHAPTER 9

I'D SPENT A LOT OF MY LIFE hardly sleeping, so the brain-sloshing weariness I carried out into that Saturday daybreak was no big deal. Really, that day, like every day of showing, took all my concentration to keep running in place. Everything but teaching and riding faded to a blur that came back into focus at odd times with a snap. There'd been no follow-up from the policeman. If he was around I didn't spot him. No word from the reporter, either. From the looks of it, for now at least, tracking the horse killers was my problem. I had that idea to get started but I had to pick the right moment to act.

I watched for Jenny but Ricoeur's Grand Prix horse would rest today for the big money class tomorrow, so she didn't turn up at the rings. Twice I started for Ricoeur's barn to demand answers from her about the candle and picture but I stopped myself both times. A public scene for what? More denials? Maybe trouble for her when it was what she said, some jerk with a warped sense of humor, using what had happened to Romp to pressure her, probably into sex. All I knew for sure was that she wouldn't have been involved in killing horses. I did watch for the thin man I'd seen planting the candle. I saw him about six times. Same dark ball cap, same style of jacket, same narrow face. I couldn't charge up and question every could-be I spotted. Even if the candle was a joke, the guy who delivered it was probably some groom or grounds-tender who had taken ten bucks to plant it. If I found him, maybe eleven bucks would buy me some truth.

But I had to spend another day soldiering through normal. The kids had their equitation classes, where they could show off the perfect positions we worked so hard on, and Rianne on Baby Jane had her adult eq. As always, our high ribbons piled up. The only one who didn't pin was Taylor. Of all things, she posted on the wrong diagonal for ten strides right in front of the judge. "Mistake Number

212 not to make again," I told her. She pretended to think that was funny but she glummed around all the rest of the afternoon.

I also had classes on both Snap and Zenith. Zenith went first in the order, another not-so-great trip, but not the catastrophe it could have been. The wall floated in the distance of my concentration and I got by with only one rail down by not grabbing his head off on the turns. Snap took more discipline because I had to put so much away to let a good horse do his work. He was third by the clock. He shook his head when Pat stroked him afterwards but he let her reach on tiptoes for an ear rub. The pale tissue around her gray eyes crinkled in the sunlight. "You look tired, Robb."

"I'm fine." I gave her one of those lying shrugs I'd stored for this kind of conversation.

She shook her head, the crinkles tightening. "They built the courses a lot bigger this week."

So walking back we talked about our strategy for the rest of the series, two more shows. The ones I might not get to, but I steered my mind away from that worry and toward the questions I planned for her. She had been going to shows her whole life, from Wellington to Devon to Calgary. She knew people I didn't know existed. She'd once bought a horse from the Paxtons. She'd know a lot about the Paxtons. With luck she wouldn't notice me trying to draw her out.

In the wash rack outside our barn I rinsed Snap's deep red coat, then squeegeed, slinging the excess water off him. "Hard on the Paxtons," I said.

Snap shook her hand off his nose, the way they do. Ingrates. She transferred her attempt at affection to smoothing his forelock. "I can't imagine."

"I really hadn't met them much. Just to talk to."

"Nice enough people," she said. Snap pawed at the trickle of water running down his legs and she shook his halter to pretend to scold him. "We used to socialize at the shows, but they've been doing different circuits recently. I haven't seen them much."

Wardle or maybe the reporter ought to be asking the obvious questions, like whether anything, no matter how small, made it look like the Paxtons needed money. But Pat knew things they wouldn't. I asked, "The Paxtons don't ride, do they? They have any kids?"

"No kids. She rides. At least she used to." She tugged Snap's forelock when he lipped her jacket. "Yeah, carrots in that pocket," she said.

I nudged her back to the Paxtons. "Wonder what they're planning to do with Romp."

Her eyes darkened. "Take care of him, I guess."

I couldn't find any more coat to squeegee. I fingered Snap's short mane over. It never lay flat. "A big loss."

Her gaze softened. "For her it's even sadder. She used to do Arabians, you know. She lost a stallion. I don't remember all the details, only that it was tragic. I'm not big on Arabians but I heard he was pretty grand."

Nobody I'd likely run into would be big on Arabians. They couldn't jump with the warmbloods. Not many people around like Pat, who'd known the Paxtons long enough to remember the dead horse. She hobbled along beside me back to the barn, stabbing her cane in the grass. "It's Mel Malloy I feel bad for," she said as I draped Snap's cooler over him to keep the barn dust off while he dried. "You know he takes great care of his horses. To have someone get into his barn like that and just take one—" She looked around at our barn. The aisle open at both ends, the unlocked stalls. You couldn't lock horses in. A barn fire would kill them all before you could free them.

"We're sleeping here," I said.

"Oh, I know that." She touched Snap again, checking how much heat he still had in him. "I'm not worried."

How much could I push beyond casual before she started wondering? I risked a little more prying. "You think it was about the Paxtons in particular or you think someone picked Romp at random?"

Her eyes went thoughtful. "He was pretty special."

I waited. Willed her memory to work.

She shrugged, dismally. "I guess the police will try to find out."

I held her cane while she took the lead rope and guided her horse into his stall. It hadn't been an earth-shattering interrogation, but at least I'd learned that it wouldn't hurt to be curious about the Paxtons. The story of Dierdre's dead Arabian was one more thing I knew that the cop did not.

With classes over, everybody wanted to sit around the aisle and jaw about all our ribbons and all the championships and reserves we'd win Sunday. Then there'd be dinner, and I didn't know if the fairly torrid affair Brett was having with this chick Cindi would keep him out of the camper overnight. I had the beer I usually did so no one would notice if I didn't, then ducked into the camper for the half hour before we headed out for dinner. I had to find a way to insert more of these private moments into my crazy existence. Propped on my bunk in clean dinner clothes, I set my phone up as a hot spot and dug around the Internet again for Jeff Carr.

By damn, this time I found him. One of the hits several pages in gave an address in the same town as Tannenbaum's farm.

I clicked on "Full Report."

The site promised addresses, aliases, court records, criminal records—but to deliver them the screen wanted fifty-nine dollars, my email, and my credit card to set up an account. I would have paid the fifty-nine dollars, but I didn't like putting that much information about my interest in Carr in the cloud. Maybe once I knew more. I made a note on my phone of the hit, cleared the history, then typed in "Dierdre Paxton" instead.

The hits didn't tell me a lot about her horses, Arabians or jumpers. They told me about her money. All the things she did with it. Like children's charities and rescue centers for injured birds like owls and hawks. Art scholarships. This painting she paid five million for and lent to some museum in Chicago. I read about him, too. He was on the boards of corporations I didn't recognize, but I didn't have to. We'd had plenty of customers on company boards over the years. You get to the point that what the companies do is over there, somewhere, as long as they buy nice horses and pay their bills. During the show you get invited to parties where you get to drink a lot of the kind of whiskey you wouldn't buy for yourself.

The Paxtons had both served on the board of a Baltimore symphony orchestra. A bell rang and I looked up the orchestra board. Yes.

I didn't plan to sleep in the barn that night, Saturday. The Night Watch people came around to report they were doubling their staff, and Raul said he kind of liked sleeping with the horses. "So there," Brett said.

Normal would be trailing off for beer and pizza with our crew and Cindi to Timberburg, the nearby town where the show was officially located, so after I shut down my laptop, I did. We all clapped and cheered soccer on the big screen in the little sports bar on the square. Maybe on some normal night I would have hung around the sports bar a while, checked in with a couple of girls I'd hooked up with last summer. But this wasn't a normal night and I didn't see many more normal nights heading my way.

To my relief, Brett and Dozer went off with Cindi to her suite at La Quinta in the resort town a few miles up the road. He wouldn't bring her to the camper; we'd long ago agreed on a "no girlfriends" rule there. So I headed back to the show to steal a few hours of much-needed sleep. I had another set of questions to try in the morning. Not the greatest questions, like I guessed Valerie Raymond would have come up with, but decent for amateur work. Whatever I decided, each tactic I tried might make people wonder why I was interfering the cops' business, so with each move, I could count on only one chance.

CHAPTER 10

DYAN WESTERMAN USED TO BE a customer of ours. The kind of ex-customer who's really nice to you in the in-gate and the secretary's office and other people's parties, but who doesn't invite you to her parties anymore.

The barn she was with now, Mack Dever's outfit, rolled in to every show with the biggest semi, a fleet of golf carts, a TV half the size of an IMAX in their barn aisle, gold-trimmed coolers on their fancy stock. They won the series award every summer for their tack-room display. At the end of their barn facing the rings they laid out a fake tropical garden, with stuffed parrots in plastic trees and a fountain. Their Mexican grooms rigged a bed of black mulch with track lighting so the customers and the three trainers Mack employed could sit around at night and drink. The lights skewed upward to make the fountain look like it sprayed diamonds. Our kids and their parents pretended to turn up their noses at that kind of bullshit, but we knew they liked wandering past there on their way back to their cars after their classes. Nothing much you could do about it. If a fountain won in the end, that was that. So far, it hadn't, and maybe now that I was a hero, it wouldn't for a while.

Maybe it was the diamond fountain that sucked Dyan in. She drank a lot but I hadn't seen anything worse to pin on her. She had to go somewhere, and the fountain gave her something sparkly to sit behind. It hadn't done Brett any good to tell her it wasn't about her, he just didn't sleep with customers. She tried me, too, but that was to get back at Brett. Taking her horses was the one thing she could do to us, so she did. It cut a chunk out of our income for a while—she'd had five horses with us—but she hadn't trashed us, we'd have heard. The story we got was that she thought Mack's new young trainer would fit better with her riding style. The kid was gay, but gay riders had an edge that some women seemed to like.

57

In fact, Dyan was the only one of our customers Mack had picked up. The reason there weren't more wasn't lack of trying. Whenever we turned up at the same shows, he'd always managed to make it clear, with his diamond fountain and the way he'd clap me on the back after a gift of chitchat, that his outfit was a lot classier than ours. We beat him enough, though, that the summer before he made an awesome offer for Baby Jane. I knew Rianne considered taking that much money. I wished he'd make an offer for Growly. Brett might have said no, though. He told me, "They do shit over there I don't like."

"Their horses look good and they go good." Horses that weren't happy showed it.

"Just don't let our kids hang out over there."

Yeah, I knew. Rich kids, money flowing. Another time Brett said, "You didn't stop that garbage with Zack."

What I'd learned last night on my quick phone search was that Dyan had served on that orchestra board with Dierdre Paxton for six years.

She was in classes with Rianne that Sunday morning with her Hanoverian gelding Sputnik, so I hung around and watched her trip. She'd always liked riding hunters, and she was good at it, one of those riders who seem to be doing nothing but are really making sure every stride fits just right. When she rode out of the ring I gave her time to hand the horse off to a groom, then showed up at Mack's barn.

Mack passed me on his way somewhere. "Hiya, Robb, good man." He gave me that absent smack like I was in his club. He was good-looking, I guessed, in his nervous sort of way; more than once I'd wondered if Dyan was getting more from his coaching than how to ride her lines.

She came out into the sunlight, stripping off her helmet. She had long blond hair that our own history with her told me was dyed. They bought their looks, a lot of these women, but people who can buy that look usually buy good horses. When I paused, pretending I was just passing, she was pulling off the hairnet she wore under her helmet and shaking the blond flow loose.

She knew how to use a smile. "Well, hello, there, stranger." The smile turned off with a click. "I've been meaning to tell you what a brave thing you did."

"Didn't really have a choice." Every remark like that put me back in that trailer. I spent one of my normal-Robb smiles on her. "It's the Paxtons I really feel bad about."

"Oh, yes." She pushed her expression harder toward sympathy, a dip between her sculpted eyebrows. "Awful! Poor Dierdre. Her horses are really people to her. This has got to be tearing her up."

"Didn't she lose one of her Arabians one time?"

She squinted, tweaking up a bouncy ponytail. "Oh, that was a long time ago. Not like this. He colicked. This, though—anybody have any idea who'd have done such a thing?"

If Dierdre got tied to fake colics, I wanted to be the one doing it, so I steered Dyan in another direction. "I don't guess the Paxtons have any enemies who'd want to hurt them?"

"Well, if they do, I can't imagine. Of course—" her expression went thoughtful, "—when people have money, other people get jealous. You know, want some of it." She shrugged, shifting to move on. "People are shits."

I shrugged, too. "I guess maybe Rich and Dierdre have some idea who might have done it."

That trawl passed right over her. "Well, the cops'll ask 'em. Gotta go get some grub, I'm starving." She took a step away, turned back. "Really brave thing you did."

I gave her an easy wave, left her heading for the food trucks. So from this chat I'd learned I'd been really brave and that Dierdre Paxton's stallion had died of colic. I hadn't learned whether he'd died at the same time as the killings that were put down to colic, but really, it didn't matter. One Google search would tell you how to kill a horse like that.

The girls' eq would flat sometime after noon, all the divisions finishing up in time for that evening's big-money Grand Prix. Back at our barn, Cadence's mom sat in one of our chairs, scrolling on her phone. Taylor's mom had her head thrown back, sunglasses over her eyes even though she was in the shade. The dads were off in chairs by themselves, midday beers beside them. There was a lot of sports talk when the dads came around.

That familiar world had gone from looking fragile to looking like some kind of dreamland, where I used to live but wouldn't be able to anymore. I had to consciously snap back to reality to react like the

59

grownup I should be at Taylor swinging on the open bottom half of
Jane's stall door.

Raul, inside, was fluffing new shavings. I caught the door in mid-
swing. "Hey. It's hard enough to get these to latch right. Let's not
play on them, okay?"

She jumped down. "I only weigh eighty-five pounds."

I automatically turned scolding into kidding. "I would've thought
at least a hundred."

"I do not!"

Raul paid attention to what his fork was doing. When I looked
back from Snap's door, Taylor still stood watching him work. I
thought for a moment. Often my job meant paying attention to little
things that might turn into bigger things. Especially now, when I
didn't know who'd end up dealing with the bigger things. I drifted
back that way.

"*Caballo*," Taylor said.

"*Caballo*," came Raul's soft voice, correcting the Spanish "b" I'd
never managed.

She laughed. "*Zenith es un caballo gris.*" She looked up at me,
face shining. "Raul's teaching me Spanish. Good Spanish. Not like
my teacher. He speaks Spanish like a nerd."

"Unfortunately, so do I." It was a running joke with Jorge and
Raul that I couldn't remember half the Spanish they taught me. Jorge
had caught on that I sometimes fucked up to make them laugh. He'd
started telling me wrong words, and we had a game, me trying to
catch him at it. Raul tended to watch, not play. He had that luminous
smile but also a slow, secretive one that made me feel like I'd
accomplished something good when I could make him show it. Right
now he wasn't smiling. Little things.

Cadence came out of the tack stall with a package of Swizzlers.
"Brian will be sooo jealous."

Taylor skipped back from Jane's stall, blushing. "You are so
clueless. Brian is a dumbass."

"Taylor!" came her mom's voice from down the aisle.

"He's a dweeb," said Taylor.

Hmmm. A little thing more than big enough to be aware of.
Brian Hogarth was a kid who rode with Dever, lanky, in his teens,
with classic boy-idol deep-set dark eyes. Cadence gave a sneaky
glance in her own mom's direction. "You didn't think so yesterday,"
she said to Taylor. She whispered to me, "He let her taste his beer!"

"Did not!" Taylor wheeled to me and Raul. "I know all the Spanish colors. *Gris*. Gray."

"So do I," said Cadence. "*Rojo*. Red."

"What's Spanish for chestnut?" I asked.

Taylor's lips clamped. "That's not fair. That's a special horse color." She looked at Raul. He shrugged.

"Taylor!" Her mom sat up, pushing the sunglasses onto her own sleek blond hair. "Where's that navy coat? Robb said to make sure it fits if you're going to wear it in the flat."

Coats had to set off straight backs just right in an eq class, where posture was on the checklist when the rider and not the horse was being judged. Taylor was on the edge of growing out of her navy. But she had three coats, so her mom wasn't really worried about the navy. I did my job. All my jobs. "Both of you go get the coats you're wearing," I told them. "Let me see."

Cadence shrugged, cool. Taylor pursed up her mouth and gave Raul a commiserating look as she turned. He focused on a last swipe at the shavings and came out past me. "*Caballo zaino*," he whispered. I took his word for it that *zaino* meant "chestnut." He grinned, ducking his chin a little, and shook his head.

Of course Cadence also had to model all four of *her* coats. Even the dads were summoned to voice an opinion on which coats would win the class. I was probably the only one noticing Jorge, down the aisle, having a quiet talk with Raul. They kept their backs to us. No big drama: our parents learned fast that Raul and Jorge were family. Taylor's mom damn well knew it. Okay, she had to pay attention to what her kid got herself into. But I wondered if she and I'd been paying the right attention. There were a lot of cute guys on showgrounds of one stripe or another. That sip of beer might matter a lot more than a few Spanish words.

CHAPTER 11

AFTER OUR CLASSES, WE ALL went to the exhibitors' party in one of the tented pavilions, stuffed ourselves on shrimp and scallops on toothpicks and globs on crackers that fell apart before you could eat them, then trooped over to watch the Grand Prix.

Non-horse people might not understand why we'd hang around on a Sunday after showing all day to watch other people's horses jump. But a lot of us liked to see really good jumpers square off. This was the big arena, down at the tail end of the barn row, tall covered bleachers and blazing lights. From high up where I usually sat, these big-money classes, especially the ones at night like this one, glowed like an ESPN extravaganza: the shimmer on the ring dust, the wild-looking jumps, the horses' coats HDTV neon, and the voice over the speakers booming out of a cloud somewhere. I sometimes went because a horse I liked was competing. That night I went to watch the Dutchbred the Paxtons had shipped into Malloy's barn.

The crowd was good size; a lot of the people sitting below me were locals who maybe got a kick out of watching pretty horses on a summer night. Brett and Cindi sat with some of her customers in the first row, Martha a few rows down from me with a friend from another barn. Our kids sat with their parents, who'd bonded with another couple from a Florida barn. The other couple's daughter, a little girl in a thick down jacket, kept bouncing to her feet and craning to see into the shadows outside the ring where the jumpers schooled. Raul and Jorge were bunched with some grooms at the end of the top row, several yards away. I'd always itched to horn in on the bets I thought they had going, though they probably had more dope than I did about which horses were sore and which ones were schooling bad. The Paxtons sat together in one of the lowest rows. From my viewpoint above them, it looked like he had his hand on hers in her lap.

I remembered this Dutch horse of theirs from the spring, a long-strided high mover like Romp, one they hadn't gelded. Some of the big jumpers could pay for themselves with frozen semen. At least I wouldn't have to factor in how Romp's semen had tested, since he didn't produce any. A stud with bad semen might make it worth cashing in your insurance. I wasn't sure the Dutch horse was that good.

Maybe the Paxtons had a lot more like him. They had a farm somewhere; the details hadn't turned up when I searched. If they did have a lot more good horses, losing Romp might not have been the disaster I'd thought.

A guy named Greg Drakow was set to ride the Dutchbred. Drakow came in for the Grand Prix; he was German, I thought. He rode for a lot of big outfits across the country. Even if the Dutch horse wasn't that good, he was.

Some of the top horses like Ricoeur's were stabled on the grounds. Others hauled in for the big money. One of the guys in the secretary's office told me he'd fielded a lot of traffic about what had happened. "Nobody's scratched, but I'm getting a shitload of questions." I bet.

The formal welcome speech blasted at us, hollow and huge. I waited for some message to the Paxtons, some mention. Nothing. Maybe the attack on Romp wasn't the kind of thing you wanted exhibitors remembering next year when they decided whether to come back to your show. I was thinking the local press would pick up on that silence when Valerie Raymond climbed up the bleachers toward me, clutching a program. "Hi, can I sit with you?"

I wished I could say no. I wanted to watch horses. But it was past time to collect on that great partnership she had promised. Besides, even in our short talk she'd displayed some pretty sensitive radar that would launch sirens if I rejected her. I inched over, gave her room.

"Never made it to one of these before." She was dressed like I was, in a flannel pullover and thick vest, with a cap over her ears. "It's pretty damn cold."

"Thought you'd be used to cold nights here."

She dug her fists into her pockets. "Yeah, but I'm not an outdoor person. The sports staff usually cover these things."

"Are they here?"

She pointed with her chin. "Yeah, there's a guy down there who's pissed he's missing some sextuple-A high school baseball game."

"You should have offered to cover the ball game for him."

She hunched forward, concentrating. "No, I need to learn about this shit."

I leaned back on the rail at the top of the bleachers, stretching my legs to the empty bench in front of us. "Can't you ask your contacts?"

"My contacts know about money, not about horses. I need to figure out how those two connect."

"Well, there's a lot of money here." People like the Paxtons, times twenty, come to watch the horses they owned. The first horse cantered into the ring, a big gray, Ellie Muchin standing in her irons, asking him to collect as he waited for the buzzer. "Five hundred grand right there."

She humphed, not mean, just interested. "Five hundred grand? What the fuck for?"

"Rich people like to own nice things."

She looked at me. "You didn't strike me as cynical."

"I'm not. I think that particular horse is a nice thing."

The buzzer went off. She focused on the gray starting his gallop. "So what's that buzz for?"

"She has forty-five seconds to get through the timers."

"They're all timed?"

A lot to explain. But this was the simplest of FEI tables. "In this class, the horses have to be under the time allowed and clean to make the jump-off. Time in the jump-off decides between the ones who go clean."

She concentrated. "Those horses I saw yesterday, those jumps were a lot smaller."

Same thing I'd tried to explain in a few words to Chief Wardle. "Those were hunters."

"Um . . . hunters of what?"

"Used to be foxes."

Her mouth crimped, a twist that was already becoming familiar. "Like tally-ho foxes?"

"The idea was, you needed a horse that could take care of you over walls and hedges and ditches and banks and keep up with the field." I shrugged. "Some people still hunt but not that many. Show hunters have to look like you could drop the reins on their necks and they'd cart you around."

She frowned, maybe remembering yesterday's classes. "But they weren't knocking any of the jumps over. How do they win?"

I focused on the horse below cranking up for the first vertical. "They look . . ." I waved my hands like I could catch the words I needed. "Pretty. Smooth. Beautiful. Brilliant."

She snorted. "That sounds major subjective."

"Like gymnastics. Figure-skating."

"Oh, perfect tens, huh?"

"Yeah. Like that."

I didn't tell her showing hunters was an art, didn't tell her how much work it took for a rider to get that perfect ten even once, let alone most of the time. Harder even than clearing a full course of big fences where all you had to manage was not knocking one down. Below us, Ellie rode great and the gray lived up to his billing, a big horse out of Canada, shipped in. Valerie jumped every fence with him, tensing, then sinking. Because he'd gone first, he was in first place. "Cool," Valerie said. When the next horse pulled a rail on the last fence, she curled into herself like a kid who'd dropped her ice-cream cone.

The Paxtons' horse was fourth in the order, early. "Owned by Summergate LLC," the announcer said.

"This horse belongs to the same people who own Romp," I told her.

"Oh?"

"I guess they have an LLC."

Her lower lip jutted as she leaned forward. "A lot of these horses owned by LLCs?"

"Yeah, I guess so." Brett and I were an LLC. You did that so if anyone ever sued, the only assets they could get were the limited liability corporation's, not yours. It hadn't occurred to me that the Paxtons owned their horses through one, but why not?

"Maybe they have partners, then," Valerie said.

I said, as low key as I could, "Maybe." But I was thinking about insurance. If partners owned the horse, who took out the insurance? The LLC? Who got the payment? The LLC? If any of Brett's and my horses had been insured, maybe I'd know.

Below us the Dutch horse went clean. Had a blazing round in the jump-off. Led the class.

"These LLC people who own the horse that got attacked and this one," Valerie said. "They friends of yours?"

"Acquaintances."

"How do they make their money?"

"He's in some kind of stock stuff. I really don't know."

She had that sideways grilling eye on me. "Maybe you ought to be a little bit curious."

I shook my head. "It would be too obvious if it was the Paxtons."

"You like them."

"I don't know them that well."

She leaned back beside me on the hard bench, nodding and smiling. To herself. My mind started to dig. Whether the Paxtons had partners was the type of stuff my reporter partner ought to be looking up. Presumably she'd honor our pact, tell me what she learned. I was calculating how much I should trust her when, down below us, peering up and searching the bleachers, there was Jeff Carr.

I didn't know how long he'd been there, just that his gaze locked on the Paxtons. He hung there, hands in the pockets of the leather bomber jacket he probably thought made him look tough. The Paxtons huddled toward each other, talking. I waited, thinking that if they saw Carr, I'd learn something from their reactions. But when they pulled away from each other, their attention turned toward the ring, the next horse with a chance to beat theirs.

Carr saw me. To my surprise he burst into a snowy grin, almost instantaneous. Like I was some kind of present he hadn't expected anyone to give him. He raised a hand. Waved.

Valerie's gaze veered toward him. He climbed along the edge of the bleachers where he didn't have to step over so many people, then made his way past the row of grooms and sat next to Valerie, with her between us. He leaned across her. "Heard about your hero act, Robb. Had to come say 'Good job.'"

Like he would have crossed the street to say that if it was the only message he wanted to deliver. I didn't smile back, just dropped him a nod.

"Got a horse in this?" he asked.

He could read the program as well as the next person. "No."

Valerie shifted, like spooking from a ghost's touch on her shoulder. I needed to be more careful; I'd let my tone get pretty sharp. She shifted again, giving me a glance. Her hand went out to Carr. "Valerie Raymond."

His grin got even bigger, his blue eyes crinkling. He took the hand like it was candy. "Jeff Carr. Haven't seen you around."

"I'm with the *Clarion*. Covering the horse show."

"Hmmph." Carr sat back, his broad shoulders rocking the wooden seat back behind us. "I thought that regular guy did that. Thought I saw him down there." He pointed a thumb. "Yeah, down there. Don't remember his name."

The corner of Valerie's mouth went up, though I couldn't see whether her eyes smiled. "I'm doing human interest. How people are reacting to the fire."

Carr got all serious. "Yeah, that's a big story. I guess if I wanted to know all about it, I'd start with Robb here, too."

She turned toward me, not exactly a question in her eyes, more like another flash of alertness. "I definitely wanted his story." Her tone bubbled with innocence, to me a deliberate production, but I couldn't tell how Carr took it. "Really amazing what he did."

"Yeah," said Carr again. He leaned across Valerie toward me. "Too bad you weren't a few seconds quicker. You might have seen the guy."

Valerie's antenna, already jutting, had to pick up on the hitch in my shoulders. I hoped I didn't overplay casual. "Maybe so."

Valerie pivoted from one of us to the other, still looking silent questions. "You were around Friday morning?" she asked Carr.

He gave a short laugh. "Depends on what you mean by morning. Best I can tell, I was in my motel room stumbling out of bed when it happened. I think I got to the showgrounds about when they got the horse rounded up."

"Then you don't have a camper here?"

"Nah. I stay up the Asheville road at the Days Inn. Get a deal from them every year."

The message to her was that she should ignore him. Maybe the message for me was nobody could prove where he'd been when the flames went up.

"A shame," said Valerie. "One less person I could talk to."

She leaned back, leaving the space between me and Carr open where she could see any more tidbits that passed between us. I wanted nothing to pass between us, but already I saw she was sharp enough to spot how much effort I put into nothing. I leaned back myself, picture of indifference. "Yeah," said Carr to Valerie. "You really want Robb's story. Nobody saw what happened but him."

I folded my hands behind my head. Poster Boy for indifference. Valerie shrugged like he'd said something so obvious any asshole would have known it. "Robb's a good interview."

"Yeah, he's a good guy," said Carr, stretching. "Well. Got to go check on some horses. Make sure the Mexicans get the stall sheets on front side forward. You know that story." He stood before she could answer. "Nice meeting you."

Her distant nod looked like she was sliding him into a mental file. He gave me a snap of his chin. "Buy you a beer sometime, Robb. I'd like to hear about that bay you've been riding."

"Sure. Anytime."

Valerie watched him trot briskly back down the bleachers. "What the fuck was up with that?"

I still had a long way to go before fast answers became a habit. "I barely know the guy."

She chewed on whatever she was thinking. Two horses had come and gone while Carr had been there. From the scoreboard time-to-beat, the Paxtons' horse was still leading. "Talked to the police chief this morning," she said. "In my humble opinion, he's got zilch."

"That's not good."

"He's been asking around, though. I've got an informant who'll tell me if he scores." She scratched the back of her neck where her hair was bunched up. "You be around tomorrow?"

"Where would I go?"

"Yeah, well, it's not like this is Las Vegas." She stood, stretched. "Damn these benches are hard."

"Tell me."

The row below us let out a group sigh as the horse on course, a French-bred, pulled a rail at the triple. "Someone told me I should interview the people who braid the horses. Sounds like they get up really early."

Damn this someone. "Yeah."

"You know any in particular I could talk to?"

"There're several of them. Ask around."

"Who braids your horses?"

I caught myself rubbing my thumb over my fingertips. Stopped it. "Jenny Silver."

"You ask her if she saw anything?"

"Why would she?"

Her frown clamped on me a second too long for comfort. "I guess I'll ask some of them." She stood. "Speaking of getting up early, I have to cover a commission meeting at eight in the morning. If anything happens I should know about, text me."

"We're partners."

"Good."

She skipped down the bleachers after Carr. How long before someone told her about me and Zack and Jenny? Drama I definitely didn't want in her story. I was glad the police chief was getting nowhere with his questions, but hers were a different story. Sooner or later she was going to cost me some of my precious lies.

CHAPTER 12

AFTER A GRAND PRIX THE SHOWGROUNDS are lit up, a lot of people hanging around to talk about the horses or stopping by a tack room for a drink. Martha and Brett kept our tack stall open even though the girls' folks had whisked them off to bed. No showing on Monday; they'd head home, then be back for their divisions at the end of the week. Rianne and Claryce and their guys had gone to their favorite bar. When I came up, Martha was rattling the ice in a rum drink she mixed herself and kept in a V8 bottle in our tack-room fridge. Brett sprawled in that fancy blue chair with a can of beer. He was a wimp about the cold and had his vest zipped to his chin.

Cindi sat on an overturned manure bucket between them. She'd microwaved hot chocolate and she cradled the steaming cup in both hands. Cindi was tall, athletic, one of those people built from scratch to wrap her legs around a horse. Her hair was turning gray even though she was younger than Brett, but she disguised the gray with random colors. Tonight, bright blue and yellow. Dozer lay at her feet, a jumble of fat rolls and slick buff hide twitching in some sort of dream. The kids had decided Dozer wanted to go live with Cindi. Brett said nothing doing. He had dragged Dozer out of a ditch somewhere in Ohio, all flea blood and ticks. So he said Dozer owed him. Not that the dog was much of a prize. When we got food in him, he turned out to weigh about a thousand pounds, all of it low to the ground. Growly slammed a hoof against his stall door, louder than a gunshot, and Whisper did something unwise with his water bucket. Brett shouted at Growly, but that never did any good.

Martha swirled her cup, the ice clinking. "Great for the Paxtons to win it." She pushed out of her chair. "Sit here, Robb."

"No, that's okay." I looked in at Zenith. He stood drowsing, head down, hind foot propped. I pulled over a mounting block and sat.

"I thought you were sleeping out here," said Cindi.

"He came to his senses," Brett said. "Raul is plenty."

Martha settled back in her chair. "It had to be one guy. Somebody who knew horses. He could sneak in and out really quiet. Easy to miss."

Brett upended his beer, folded the empty can in his palms. "Why does it have to be a guy? Why not a woman?"

"No woman would do that," said Martha.

"Ohhh . . . I don't know," Cindi said.

Growly beat on the door again. Brett threw the empty can at his stall. Growly jumped back about two feet, snorting, then poked his head over the open half-door. "Definition of insanity," said Cindi. "When has that ever made him stop?"

He slid his feet off the bucket. "Whoever did it, they won't try anything else for a while." He stuck his hands in his vest pockets as Martha took a long, clinking swallow. "How the fuck can you drink something with ice in it? It's fucking cold."

"I have a warm heart." Martha gave him her rum-drink smile.

"Well, I want warm feet." He rubbed a toe on Dozer's neck, making him curl his bulldog lips.

Cindi stood, uprighting the manure bucket. "Come on, Doz. You can be a foot-warmer."

"'Bout what he's good for," said Brett.

The three of them walked together into the darkness. At least, Dozer sort of walked. Martha got up, folded chairs.

"Leave one out," I told her. Raul had gone with some friends to dinner. "I want to sit out here a little till Raul comes back."

"Really, Robb, they're not going to try anything. Not so soon."

"So when should I stop worrying? Two weeks from now? Maybe three?"

"The police'll catch him," she said. "They were here this morning asking questions."

"I don't want them to catch him." I grabbed the chair she'd set down, slung it open. "I want him to have a head-on collision with a semi on a deserted highway. Take hours to die. Or no. I want him to get drunk and smoke in bed."

"Yeah," she said, zipping her vest up around her neck. "I can see that."

Didn't ask her what she could see. The hell I'd live with until I settled this? "Been a long day," I said. "Leave the chair there."

I searched more, trying different tags that might show some connection between the Paxtons and a low-life like Carr. Tonight's little confab in the bleachers said Carr was worried I had seen him. Let him worry. He also wanted to know who I was talking to. If he started pumping Valerie to learn what I'd told her, her sharp nose might twitch.

Nothing turned up on my searches. I was probably too tired to look hard enough. Raul showed up at eleven, sleeping bag draped over his shoulders. "Glad you're doing this, " I told him.

"I like it," he said. "Peaceful. No Jorge snoring."

"God, I hope it stays peaceful," I said.

I had another chance for peace of my own, with the camper once again empty. The line of campers was quiet, the huge RVs' outdoor lights turned off, hums leaking through cracked windows from music or some movie someone was watching. Horse shows were like a gypsy camp, I'd decided. All of us blew in for the next stop on the circuit, hung around for however many shows there were in a series, then packed up our horse trailers and campers and moved on. The big outdoor shows even added tents with modular stalls for overflow in good years. A whole little mobile city. I ran into the Night Watch guy with his clipboard. He promised to make a couple of swings by our barn.

I had to pass Malloy's big camper. Hard not to stew over Romp. What would the Paxtons do with him, wait? Maybe time actually would work magic. But remembering that rampage on those lead ropes, I slid into crazy shit. He was useless to them like this; somehow I'd get past this in one piece and they'd let me have him. Visions rose in my head of taking him away, the wall I had to smack into fading into the distance, me taming the fear out of him, like he was one of those movie dragons. Winning over whatever lived in his skin now. Making him not what he once was, but what I needed. I'd be the one who waited and coaxed and did all the magic stuff.

I knew I was stupid, just this side of drunk. The Paxtons probably thought that out in the country all the birds singing would cure him. Like getting better just happened. Sometimes it never happened. Sometimes you had to forget what was wrong with you long enough to be somebody else for a while.

So I wasn't watching and didn't have time to think when a hand landed on my shoulder and yanked me around. Jeff Carr's face inches from mine, teeth flashing movie-star white in the sentry lights. I got the beer out of my head and a handle on my body fast. I'd assumed he'd limit himself to defenseless creatures, but maybe not. If he knew I'd seen him put Romp in the trailer he might figure I was a problem he had to act on. Part of me tensed for whatever he was bringing. Not good. I needed to pump him, not fight him. To my relief he let his hand drop as I stepped back. Something made him laugh. "Look who's wandering around in the dark again. Hero Robb."

I edged sideways. From the look of his stagger as he tracked me, I was way soberer than he was, sober enough I wouldn't need rescuing from any of the silent campers nearby. The last thing I wanted was somebody storming out to bitch about the ruckus. "What do you want?"

"You sneak around like this a lot, don't you?" He breathed on me, yeah, boozy. His red hair looked black in the sentry lights, dark lines scored in his face. "You ever sleep, Robb? You wander around every night?"

How drunk was he? What could I squeeze out of him? "So why are *you* wandering around?"

But his gaze bounced away, almost pulling him off his feet again. "Everybody's making such a goddamn big deal. You saved the damn horse, huh?" He gave my shoulder a shove, almost playful. "Big hero. Thanks to you, old Romp's goddamn fine."

Yeah, fine, flailing like a banshee on the ends of those lead ropes. "It was a big deal to some people."

"Yeah, like those rich shits. Like they don't have twenty like him." His eyes narrowed unevenly. "Here's what could be really funny. If you were the one who did it. How about that?"

Nothing on his face told me if he was serious. "What do you mean?"

"Nobody there to see you, right? Nobody there." A fist reaching to punch my arm, Carr catching himself when I swung clear of it. "Or did you see someone? You planning to blackmail someone?"

"Somebody I should blackmail? Anybody you know?"

But he waved an arm, stared past me as if I hadn't spoken. "I heard you told that guy Zack you'd kill him. He's not the only one, either. If you could kill people you sure could kill a horse."

"So you think I'm capable of killing?"

He sneered. "Oh, everybody knows you're a hero. Whoever you'd kill, they'd deserve it." His next punch found me, cracking on my bicep. "Me, if I killed anyone, they'd throw the book at me. You, they'd say, that's just hero Robb."

In the harsh light I looked closer. Goddamn tears. Drunken tears. He backed away, wiping his nose. Any minute he'd start puking. "God," he said. "What time is it? Almost fucking time to get up again."

I hadn't coaxed anything out of him except some spewed bourbon. "You need me to take you somewhere?"

He wove farther away, stumbled, righted. "She kicked me out."

"What?"

He turned back to me, raising his voice suddenly. "Damn cunt kicked me out!"

"Who did?"

A porch light came on from a camper behind me. I edged out of the sudden glare. Carr peered around as if he'd lost something. But he flapped a hand and stumbled into darkness. "Fucking cunt!"

I took that shit to the silent camper where I could think it out.

So that was it, Friday at the food truck. They weren't talking about the weather or what she had for breakfast. Or should I hope the showgrounds were full of cunts kicking Carr out of their campers? If I'd paid better attention over the years I might know who they were.

I tried again and failed again to put Jenny and Carr together. Did he have something she wanted, something she could buy? Safety? If she'd wanted safety, what was she doing with Zack?

I got up and poured a bourbon. Dumb wasting energy on what was over and already failed at. It was what Carr was up to now I should be worried about. Taking care of him would take care of any problem he caused Jenny. Whatever I did, I would make sure it stuck this time.

I sorted through the few times I'd spoken to Carr over the past couple of years. Not much there to give me a handle since we didn't do business with him. But a sneaky bitterness ran under some of what he'd said, maybe even jealousy—*if it was me, not you.* That idea had pulled up a snippet I'd overhead at an after-show party somewhere in Vermont, maybe, Carr in a group of men who might have been owners or horse dealers or even show dads, a lot of raised voices and laughing, Carr's voice loud. "Yeah, I rode some Grand Prix horses, won some stuff, but you know what? That's a tough way to make a living." A dank corner of the memory hinted at some reference to what gay riders got out of all that galloping, but I couldn't swear to that.

So maybe he did ride. He wasn't obviously built for it, but there'd been pretty good riders who carried their weight in their upper bodies like he did and supported it with short, strong legs. But what I remembered sounded like he'd given up riding. Maybe for the same reason a lot of people do—riding is hard. Works your body, and your mind. Makes you sweat on hot days and freeze on cold ones. And get well acquainted with the solid ground.

One possibility: if he thought I'd seen him, he might be laying the groundwork for an accusation of his own. Robb Slaughter acting crazy. Threatening people. How far would he get with that? Gossip about me and Zack had spread pretty far, but it had been two years now, and no one ever mentioned the whole mess anymore. All the more reason to keep the reporter from stirring up stories. At least she hadn't stumbled on Jenny. Next thing I knew, I'd circled back around to the questions I really wished I could answer. What the hell was that candle at Jenny's camper about?

Maybe it had something to do with Zack. But I couldn't connect him to harm to horses. He'd been a small-time player, selling a bag to some kid here and there. Even if he'd had a motive, he couldn't have engineered what happened to Romp, not from federal prison, unless he'd found a chunk of money to pay someone. No, I'd never seen him mistreating horses. Just the woman he said he loved.

I stretched out, some Neil Young playing, forcing my mind back to Carr. How much of our little conversation would he remember in the morning? I'd have to pass by Tannenbaum's, accidentally bump into him, see what he did. Nerves might make him break down and confess to the wrong person. Wardle, for instance. He might give Wardle a reason to shove him in jail where real justice couldn't find him. I lay awake worrying how to get ahead of that.

I woke In the dead hours from an Ativan-fueled sleep, hot and dripping. Another dead-dog sweat.

I sat up and breathed from my belly, in, out, in, repeat. One of those therapy regimens. Sometimes it worked. At last the light over the sink stopped hurtling toward me like a blazing asteroid and the sweat rivers on my jaws quit roaring. What didn't go away was the image from the nightmares, Jenny one of those faceless bodies in my vision. She held that burning candle. I blinked her out hard.

CHAPTER 13

WHEN WE DID A SERIES, Mondays were the days between shows. Some barns hit the road for other venues, but a lot stayed around. Head honchos like Brett and me could have slept in, but we never did. We didn't have to check on Jorge and Raul, but we both liked to start even a day off knowing our horses had cleaned up their grain and drunk enough water and turned to their hay with the blind concentration horses bring to eating. It made the day start better to walk through the barn and touch them all.

That morning I went from stall to stall, running my hands under their sheets for their warmth as they ate. Jorge and Raul were having a whistling competition as they scrubbed water buckets. Martha rooted around in the tack stall for her favorite brushes, and Brett turned up with wet hair from showering after he got back from Cindi's. Everything gloriously normal, except for the dead dog winding around my feet.

Routine helped. Like we often did on a Monday, all five of us went into town for a big, slow breakfast. The carbs and fat at that table would have floated a battleship. Jorge accounted for two full carafes of coffee and Raul for most of the little butter tubs. And this was the kid who actually did weigh about ninety pounds. Martha ate an omelet I could have wrapped her up in. Raul made me name all the food. I couldn't remember the word for pancakes, tried to get away with calling them "*tortilla gordo.*" "*Gorda,*" he said. I said, "Female pancakes?" "*Voluptuosa,*" said Jorge, making Raul blush.

Yeah, pretty lame, but it felt good, felt like an ordinary Monday on the road. Then it was back to the show for routine Monday chores.

We checked our week's entries online, but picking up new numbers for all our horses and riders meant a trip to the secretary's office. Raul held Jane and Growly while Jorge trimmed their ears and

Brett toured the mobile tack shops for the bit he wanted Claryce to try on Flight. He and Martha printed out the week's roster so the guys would know who needed bathing and tacking and lunging each day. In the camper I balanced our account online, paid the farrier's invoice and the feed store's, and transferred their pay to Raul's and Jorge's accounts. Jorge started taking the horses out one by one to hand-graze as the day warmed up.

Back at the barn, I distracted myself cleaning tack, Sarah Jarosz in my headphones. I had settled in a chair, switching out my worn-out spur straps, when Valerie Raymond made the whole day worse by showing up.

She actually bounded up, a lot of arms and legs and way too much sparkle, plonking another chair beside me almost before I could snatch my feet out of her way.

She thrust a folded newspaper at me. I fumbled it flat. The story with her byline showed up under bold type in the lower right-hand corner. "Timberburg Police Investigate Attack on Horse."

"Just the first one." Her perky voice warned I'd better like the gift I was about to open. "I'll shut up while you read."

The way she drummed her fingers on her chair arm said I should read fast. The story ran to an inside page, reporting, more or less, that the police had no idea what was going on. Much of the second page covered the horse-killings in the '80s and '90s. Paxton would like that. I handed the paper back. "I wish you hadn't named me."

"Come on, we talked about that. I promised not to make your history a big deal, but you *are* part of the story."

The talking I remembered hadn't made it clear how my part in the story was going to get told. "You need to let me see what you're writing first."

She gave me the insistent glower I'd probably have to get used to. "What are you afraid of? It's not like everybody involved in this doesn't know exactly who you are." She rattled her way through the flimsy newsprint to the end of the article and shoved the sheets at me. "Did you see this? I didn't say the horse was owned by the Paxtons. I said the owner was this Summergate LLC."

The article quoted the Paxtons expressing their deep sorrow for their horse and promising him a happy life ever after. "They confirmed it's their LLC?"

"Said it was a family business. I didn't push yet because I want to check some on my own."

"Like what for?"

She raced on. "Like finding out of there're any LLC partners. If there are, maybe they don't know what happened to their horse. Or that there's even a breath of a question about insurance fraud." She bounced in her chair. "I mean, maybe they won't like having their company named and I won't have to hunt for them, they'll pop up."

True, a lot of barns were building investor coalitions to campaign jumpers. Dever had tried to recruit some of our customers. I hadn't heard that kind of venture linked to the Paxtons. I was returning the paper when Jorge came and stood behind me. He had a way of making his waiting visible. I tilted my head to look up at him. "You want me to graze Zenith?" he asked.

"No, no. I will. In a few minutes."

He gave Valerie a look that said he'd remember her, then left. "These guys who work for you," Valerie said.

"What about them?"

"A lot of the people here, they have these kinds of guys—or girls—working for them."

"You mean immigrants?"

"Mexicans?" Her expression said her mind had shot off somewhere.

"All kinds."

"Because they're cheap?"

"Not the good ones." I shifted to sit up straighter, fill up the space she left leaning back. "You need to leave them out of this."

The frown came back. "I bet they know a lot about what happens around here."

"Even if they don't, you could get them in a lot of trouble."

Her voice jumped up a beat, a slap to it. "Robb, I hope you're up for what it'll take to get this done."

I stood, picked up my chair, and folded it. Managed to make myself lean it calmly under the string of ribbons over the tack-room door. She had no idea what I had to be up for. "We just don't want to get careless." I had to work harder keeping the reins on her steady. There was more than one way she could demolish any plan I came up with. "We don't know who these people are."

She gave a dry hmmph. "And exactly when have I been careless?"

"I said I don't want *us* to get careless."

She got up, rolling the paper into a messy tube.

"Sooner or later," she said, "we're going to find out something that's not public knowledge. Maybe about somebody you know."

I wrestled Zenith's door latch open. He came over to see what I had for him. She watched me push his halter over his ears. I said, "That's all the more reason to be careful."

Her face went stony. She put her chair back where she'd moved it from.

"I get it," she said, "about being careful. But there's such a thing as being timid. Our deal was that I wouldn't write a lot about your past. Your mother. All that. I'll stick to it. But either we're trying to stop this before they do it again or we're not."

Controlling this woman was going to be like trying to manhandle Zenith. You could never let him know you were making him do anything. I fed her Brett's line as a chill button. "They're not going to try anything for a while. We have time to be smart."

"Fine, be smart. Sounds like your kind of assignment. In the meantime, I'll go look for somebody I'm allowed to question." She whapped the folded paper against her leg, turning. "For Part 2."

I found Zenith a quiet place to graze beyond the wash racks. Horses would never stop grazing if you didn't make them. It must be nice to look around at your feet and find something as exciting as a blade of grass.

The two weeks till the end of the series stretched ahead of me like a marathon I hadn't trained for. Somehow I'd imagined I'd figure it all out overnight, some kind of eureka thing. But three days had passed and I'd learned next to nothing. From the looks of it, Valerie hadn't made much progress, either. I had the ugly consolation that Carr and I would meet up again after this series, probably at an August show. Valerie wouldn't be following when we took off; whatever she hoped to get out of me for her precious story, she'd better get it fast.

Around noon I yanked Zenith's head up and bullied him back into his stall. In our camper I set up my hotspot and logged on. For the lack of a better idea, I typed in Summergate, the LLC that supposedly owned Romp.

A whole page of hits. Summergate this, Summergate that. A lot of real estate stuff. Nothing looked right.

I tried "Summergate llc horses." My search asked, "Did you mean 'Sommergate'?"

I tried it. One listing for a horse boarding service in California, not an LLC. Then an article about one of Romp's Grand Prix wins.

So I typed "Sommergate LLC." Valerie had misspelled it in the article, because there it was.

Not that I learned what I needed. Sommergate LLC was a limited liability corporation registered in Delaware five years before. The only name attached, as something called "Registered Agent," sounded like another corporation, B&L Corporation Services, Inc., also with an address in Delaware. No mention of the Paxtons. I clicked on the link to B&L. Yes. A corporation of some sort. Connected to a long list of LLCs.

No reason the Paxtons couldn't have an LLC, possibly, like us, to shield personal assets. They probably weren't liable for the same risks we were. Even though laws in most states protected professionals like us from "the inherent risks of equine activities," someone could still get around the LLC if they could prove negligence. They could take Brett's house and his three dirt bikes. They could take my apartment and truck and Zenith.

I didn't know who Dozer belonged to. Maybe we ought to decide.

I looked up the Paxtons again. They did have personal assets we didn't, like five-million-dollar paintings. I found more tweaks on "financier Richard Paxton." His LinkedIn site swore he was somebody. His business site said I could trust him with my fortune. The company had donated a hundred grand to the United States Equestrian Team.

Maybe it was time to risk paying for Carr's full record, exposing my search to the cloud. I didn't think Carr himself was smart enough to track what I did from my hotspot. But maybe Valerie was.

By then it was nearly one o'clock in the afternoon. My head felt like a cabbage. I shut down my laptop and stretched on my bunk. I kept picking at my exchange with Valerie. Had she really hinted that I'd protect someone who would do that to a horse? I hadn't really considered that Romp's attacker might be somebody I liked, even cared about.

The next thing I knew I was dreaming again, something about Dozer running from me with some garbage in his mouth. Or maybe a little animal I had to take away. Then there he was on the bunk, spewing his wet breath right into my face. Brett stood in the open door, daylight streaming in. He crossed to the bunk beside me and swatted Dozer with a handful of envelopes and magazines, our forwarded mail. "God, dog, he doesn't want to smell your literally shit-eating breath."

"You let him eat shit," I said, waking up.

"All dogs eat shit." He thumbed through the envelopes, tossed some onto the table, held on to others. He opened one that looked like a tack-shop bill, frowned at it. "So what's up with this Valerie person, huh?"

I bunched a pillow at my back. In the mail on the table was the newspaper with Valerie's story. "She works for the *Clarion*."

"Yeah, I know that."

"She spelled my name right."

"She sat with you at the Grand Prix last night."

He didn't mention seeing Carr with us. Dozer was licking his prick, his butt squashed against me. I punched his neck to stop him. Futile. "So what are you worried about?"

He chewed on the words before he came out with them. "I don't want our barn getting messed up with all this. All sorts of shit could be going on. It doesn't have anything to do with us."

"People know that."

He thumped the envelopes onto the bunk beside me. "And Romp is not our horse."

Somehow he must know about my slow walks past Malloy's barn. "They'll be taking him to their place. Wherever that is."

"Can't be soon enough." He stood, looking tired himself. Maybe too much Cindi. "Dozer. Get the fuck off the bed, you trash hound."

Dozer panted in his direction.

"Whatever. Stay there then." He crossed to the door, the light behind him again so I couldn't see his expression. "Just tell that goddamn reporter no more stories."

"I can't stop her stories."

"Do something, sic Dozer on her."

"Yeah, that'll work."

He shut the door. "Don't worry," I told Dozer. "He was joking about you." But not about the rest.

Other Monday chores included doing my laundry in town and picking up deli stuff at the local grocery to welcome our customers Tuesday when they started coming in. Pat and Claryce set their own hours, but others had to plan around their businesses and jobs. This week the kids wouldn't show till Friday. At least I could hope for a weekend without tears.

Shopping for kids' snacks was tricky. Some kids had allergies, some couldn't have too much sugar, some had a thing for Cheetos and would rip the door off the tack-stall fridge for their fix. We'd have new mouths to feed; the Turners would haul in their large pony Steampunk for their son Scott to ride.

Scott was a shy kid, twelve, with all the moves that would make him a good rider if he kept it up. Boys didn't always stick with the slow-motion of hunters. Sometimes you had to move them into jumpers quick so they'd hang around. Scott liked the way with a hunter you could find a flow and let the flow be what it was all about. It seemed to me a lot of the gay riders had that kind of sense. I had no idea if Scott was gay or would be. One of those things the parents had to be thinking about but never talked about with you.

I was in the dairy aisle of the little grocery choosing dips when my phone rang. It was the police chief, Wardle. "I've come up with a few questions. I need you to come by my office. I'm here now."

He didn't make it an invitation. "I'm buying groceries right now. Maybe a half hour?"

"Sooner the better," he said.

CHAPTER 14

WARDLE'S OFFICE WAS A DOWNSTAIRS BACK ROOM in a two-story building on the town square. When I entered he was bent over a keyboard squinting at a computer, looking chunkier in a plain white dress shirt than he had in his uniform. Over the dark tie and white collar his close-cropped haircut made his ears stick out like pink handles. He took off a pair of dark-framed glasses when he saw me and nodded across the desk at a hard-backed chair. "Have a seat." Friendlier than "Sit down."

But he still hadn't spent any tax dollars on smiles. He pushed aside his keyboard. "You've got a pretty good reputation. You and your partner."

"That's good to hear."

"I'll still be looking for a statement at some point. But for now I need to ask you about something a little different. A woman who works a lot of the same horse shows you do." He leaned back. "A Ms. Silver," he said.

Her name landed like a weight he'd tossed me. It took me a moment to get my face fixed. "Excuse me?"

"A lot of people mentioned you and this Ms. Silver, so I thought I'd like to hear it from you."

"Hear what?"

"You were involved in an investigation into her live-in partner. Zack Cassidy, I think, was his name."

I kept a silent *bullshit* off my face with an effort. If there was some connection I had missed between Zack and Jenny and Romp, let Wardle tell me; no reason I should pave the path for him. "What happened with me and Zack is in the police records in Plattsburgh. It was more than two years ago. It's great you're being thorough, but if there's some way what happened then is mixed up with Romp, I don't know what it is."

He rubbed his chin. The big chair, plastic, squeaked as he shifted. There was a duct-tape patch behind his shoulder. "Word is you still carry a torch for her."

Bullshit times ten. By the time I got my ankles crossed I could answer. "Yeah, I care what happens to her. But I care about a lot of people and none of them have anything to with Romp."

He shrugged. "That guy Zack was mixed up in some pretty nasty business. Small-time, yeah, but still the kind of thing that might kill people, not just horses."

"If you know of some connection, she's the one to ask."

"We did ask. She said to ask you."

Damn her. At least she wasn't costing me one of the lies I'd been hoarding. "Like I told you, it's in the police records."

"Well, maybe not all of it."

"Maybe you ought to tell me what's missing."

He grimaced. "Well, for example, you ever had any issues with mental health?"

Double-damn Valerie. He was almost certainly one of her contacts. What had she told him? "Like what?"

"I don't know. Problems with women? Risk-taking behavior?"

I worked on not letting my jaw tighten. "Everybody who jumps a horse is involved in risk-taking behavior. So guilty, yeah."

He swiveled back and forth, an inch or so, in the beat-up chair. "Still trying to make sense of the risks you took Friday. Don't care what you say, not everybody would have done that. Almost like the fire didn't scare you."

Like he had any idea what scared me. "You don't know what everybody would have done. You don't know what *you* would have done."

Maybe the creases around his eyes were meant to look sympathetic. "I know, a murder investigation is no picnic. Have you had any conversations with Ms. Silver?"

Where *was* he going? "Like what about?"

"About what happened to the horse, obviously. What she might know about it."

More work on calm. "Why would I talk to her about that?"

He sucked his lip for a moment. "I'm just asking you to think. Help me out here. You sure you don't know anything that would warrant involving Cassidy?"

"Not a hint."

He leaned back again, lips pursed, and stared at me for a long moment. Finally he picked up a pen, twirled it, then tapped the point on his chair arm. "You're going to be here for another couple of weeks?"

"Yes, for the series."

He reached for his glasses. I grabbed at the cue, shifted to rise. But he stopped me with a sigh that had his belly behind it. "Mind if I give you a piece of advice, Mr. Slaughter?"

That line usually means that whether you mind or not doesn't count for jackshit. I shrugged.

"I just wanted an opportunity to tell you, if you hear something, don't be a hero. Ms. Silver says something, don't be a Romeo either."

I stood. "For the record, Ms. Silver doesn't talk to me. You should have heard that from your sources."

"Oh, I don't know. So far you've been pretty lucky. Maybe she'll think of something to tell you."

I made a break for the door with his unsmiling stare on me. "I hope you're not counting on my luck."

I did my laundry, then headed back to sort groceries between our camper fridge and the one in the tack stall. Brett and Cindi asked if I wanted to go with them for Chinese. We'd have to drive forty miles to Asheville for a decent place. I said I'd bought pasta sauce, I'd fix that.

"We could bring you back Moo Shu," said Cindi. She knew I liked it.

"No, really, I'm fine."

Which was a joke. I had sat watching my clothes dry and wondering what Wardle's questions about Jenny meant. Wardle didn't seem dirty enough to dangle bait just to see me bite. I'd sure bitten, and that had to stop.

Maybe he did know something about Jenny and Romp, something he wanted to learn if I knew. Could he possibly have heard about the picture and the candle? If so, how had he found out? Asking him directly would lead him where I didn't want him. At least so far he showed no sign that he'd stumbled on my lie about seeing Carr. If that ancient history with Zack was his best lead, he was struggling. Maybe for a little longer I could be the one counting on my luck.

When I went to check the barn later Raul and Jorge had gone for the day. We paid for a motel suite for them at the Days Inn, a kitchen and two bedrooms. Brett had decided Raul didn't have to sleep in the tack stall after all and I'd said okay. We paid for extra Night Watch stops.

Our tack stall was locked, like it should be, all the chairs and grooming and stall equipment inside. Our saddles we hauled up to our horse trailer at night to the extra protection of a special alarm. Malloy had recommended the app after an outbreak of major thefts a few years back. It signaled our phones if the tack compartment on the trailer was opened and activated a webcam like one we had in our barn at home so we could see who was messing with our stuff. We'd never had to do more than dry runs, but the system always worked, which was reassuring. I could buy a decent horse for what I'd paid for my CWD.

Maybe we should get a webcam for our show stalls. Tonight it would show the horses quiet, breathing softly, eyeball deep in good hay. I went back to the camper and put my earbuds in. A little Emily Barker, her voice dipping in and out of places I wished I could be. Music like that always took me to . . . Ms. Silver. And those songs, most of them her own, she used to play at night on her camper doorstep, a murmur that made me glad I'd walked by.

Sleep wouldn't come, all the shit I had to figure out a nagging whimper. After about forty-five minutes I swung out of the bunk, booted my laptop, and set up my hotspot. I typed "Sommergate LLC."

I sat and thought for a few moments about what the hits said. My last search had tickled a memory from when we'd registered our business. Someone telling us, at a party maybe, that we should have registered in Delaware. Taxes. By that time we were already doing business in Pennsylvania as Highflying Farm LLC, and if Brett paid more attention to this guy's advice than I did, he didn't say. But a line stuck with me, from the same guy, I think, some lawyer with some high-and-mighty job title, you run into those a lot at horse shows. "Everybody incorporates in Delaware."

The company that owned the Paxtons' horses incorporated in Delaware.

"LLC in Delaware" set the search engine on fire.

The very first hit told me that Delaware kept the names of the owners and members of LLCs private. The names had to be reported to the government but getting them would take a court order for a guy like me.

The pile of hits said a lot of people liked hiding their involvement in the entities they used to do business. Probably lots of reasons. I'd seen no sign that the Paxtons cared who knew they were "Sommergate," no sign they were hiding anything.

Wasn't this kind of information in Valerie's wheelhouse? When had she planned to tell me? When she made up her mind who I was willing to hurt?

About eleven I scrubbed the computer history. Maybe my caution was paranoia, but computers sometimes talked to people who knew how to ask. Like who? Brett? Brett would never snoop. Unless I gave him a reason. So far I was pretty sure I hadn't. But I was on a slope that felt steeper with every step I took down it, and who knew when he would decide I was starting to fall.

As always, the courses on Tuesday, the first day of the week's showing, were simpler, cleaner, than they'd be later. Good for Snap, who did well in the long, flowing lines and wide turns that put some horses and riders to sleep. Not so good for Zenith; tight turns and short approaches kept his mind on his job. As usual, Pat held Snap for me to get on and insisted on wiping my boots clean before I went in. As usual, riding woke me up. Blood where I needed it, in my brain.

Brett hadn't said much in the schooling area. He never did when things were going well. His gaze followed when I circled Snap around him on a loose rein outside the gate. "Looked all right. Did it feel all right?"

He was asking if *I* felt all right. Not snooping, just being my partner. It was the most direct he'd be ten feet from the ring. He put a hand on the toe of my boot before he left to go stand with Pat at the fence and watch the trip.

A little rain pattered in. If Snap cared, he didn't say. As always, once I set the pace and rhythm we needed, once I looked beyond all the clutter I had to keep my mind clear of, he took me to the spots. No jump-offs in this table, the Power and Speed. His time put him third, still in the money but with four to go. When I rode out, Pat sneaked him a treat. "Nice ride." Martha came up with Zenith. He was already looking for trouble, spooking when a horse cantered by too close.

"You look tired," Pat said. "We'll have a nice dinner later."

I nodded, sliding off. Martha held Zenith for me at the mounting block. "You look fine," she whispered as I shifted in the saddle to find my horse's center. I smiled, and so did she. Brett came over. "Now what do we do with this one? Make him trot the damn turns?"

I kept Zenith moving. "You tell me."

"Just stay on."

He couldn't have said anything more likely to make me go win it. So I did.

"Damn, I should have bet on that," Martha said.

CHAPTER 15

I HUNG UP ZENITH'S BLUE with our ribbons from last week. Raul offered to take care of him, but we all knew I would. So Raul started tacking Growly while I took Zenith to the wash rack.

It was raining again. I decided to rinse just Zenith's legs and chest and belly; without sunshine, the midday air felt chill. I turned from scraping his belly and found a woman I knew standing there.

Her five feet looked smaller than I remembered from the last time I saw her; she wore designer jeans that wouldn't last a day in a barn and a tight-cut jacket that slimmed her early-forties shape. Her natural-blond hair was cut short but still a soft mash of curls. "I watched you ride. Congratulations," she said.

Zenith pawed at the rubber matting. I'd sent him some kind of signal. Horses know. The woman sighed. "I guess I can't blame you for not being happy to see me."

"It's not . . . " I caught Zenith's halter. I wished I'd brought a cooler for him. Wished I could walk away and go get one. "You're the last person I expected to see."

"No, I never got much out of these horse events." She looked around, as if Pat grazing Snap a ways down or Jensen's grooms rinsing their horses constituted events. "A friend of mine who lives in Asheville said she saw a story in a local paper with your name in it. She sent me the link."

The tiredness the horses had taken away rushed back. One more fucking thing I had to figure out how to handle. God, I didn't want her near Martha. Or anywhere Valerie Raymond might suddenly turn up.

"Wait here," I said. "I'll go put him up and be back."

Too late. "Who's that?" Martha said.

"She's my cousin." My adoptive cousin.

93

"She live around here?"

More of the kind of thing that really was Martha's business. "I think she has a friend who does."

"Sell her a horse," Martha said.

Philomena wouldn't be buying horses, but she wouldn't have come down from Ohio for a casual visit, either. With a half hour till I had to spot Brett for Growly's class, I led her to a deserted pavilion behind the jumper ring where we could grab a couple of metal chairs from a stack. She wrinkled her nose. "At least this place doesn't smell like you used to when you came home from those stables." She directed a sniff toward me. "And you don't smell like that anymore."

"I earned a high school degree in stall cleaning."

"You've graduated from that."

"Yes."

We weren't completely invisible. Somebody in the jumper-ring in-gate was probably wondering whether I had a new customer, how much money she had, whether they could sell her their horse. She'd never been one to waste time. "Sorry to startle you like this, but when I saw that story I had a bad feeling. I got hold of the reporter. Valerie. She told me what happened. About the fire."

I caught my knee-jerk *shit* in the back of my throat before it escaped me.

"There's nobody left to worry about you but me," she said.

"I've gotten along fine without anyone worrying."

"So I thought the last few times I saw you." Those had been when my adoptive mother died and later when her own mother died, sisters. We'd helped each other with the arrangements. She shook her head, maybe at those memories. "So I stayed out of your life. I wasn't exactly a stabilizing influence."

"You aren't now."

Her face up to then held a familiar tease behind the smiles, a secretive tilt like she knew more jokes than the rest of us. She had always come at life as if she wanted to trick it. She'd mostly succeeded. She had married money, divorced it right, now she was a lawyer making her own money. But sitting there, watching me, she slipped into another mood I'd seen less often but remembered, grave and far-off like that day at the end of my seventeenth summer when she decided that being lovers wasn't the same as being in love.

94

"I hear you went into that burning trailer to save that horse," she said, lifting her chin in a challenge.

"I had to. He was tied."

"Most people would have opened the door Valerie told me about and tried to untie the horse from outside. Maybe would have shouted for help." She thumped her fingers on my chair as my mouth opened. "Don't tell me you're not 'most people.' That's exactly my point."

Yep, she was aiming for the same place as Wardle. Robb who did what normal people wouldn't. "I had to get in with him to get him loose."

A smile returned, one that spiked her mouth up. "I just can't forget the boy who ran into racing traffic to grab an injured dog."

Taking the dog's body from me: that was what she would be remembering. And later that night, taking the gun.

"The horse lived," I said, maybe too curt.

The smile flattened at the corners. "Valerie said no one has any idea who did this."

"They're working on it. They'll solve it."

"If I believed *you* believe that, I'd never have made this trip."

She would remember enough from that summer, her twenty-second, to figure out an awful lot from the little Valerie could have spilled. She reached toward my chair again but didn't touch it. "I don't know how much you've considered what this business of someone attacking this horse involves."

"I'm smart enough to know it's money. What else?"

She flipped a hand. "I've talked to some people, checked around. People are spending huge sums for horses like this Romp. They're not like racehorses, only a very few will earn back that money. They're like—" she waved the hand, "—like yachts. Ways to turn cash into tangibles. There may be more money involved than you know."

Yeah, horses were tangibles. I should know, I'd held onto them for dear life long enough. She stroked the slick denim of her jeans.

"My point is," she said, "that the police here aren't likely to find what these people are hiding and you won't find it either. Even if you do find what you're after, you may not be able to make it all come out the way you plan."

"So that's it. You're worried about what I'm planning?"

"Yes, Robb. I think you're planning the thing I once stopped you from doing." Her frank blue eyes pinned me. "Or some idiot thing along those lines."

I laid my hands flat on my thighs. Unclenching. "And you're hoping to stop me again."

Her gaze went where I couldn't follow. After a moment she said, "I should have told my dad. Your dad. What was I thinking, not telling anyone?"

Like a twenty-two-year-old, I thought, playing with something broken. Getting cut.

"So that's it," I said. "You feel guilty. You think if you'd told our dads then they'd have fixed me and you wouldn't have to worry about what I'm going to do now."

She smiled, this time sadly. "Nailed it," she said.

I remembered how baffled she'd been, not by what I had tried to do, but by what it did to me when I failed. When she made me fail.

"You thought I was going to die, didn't you?" I said. I'd been just coherent enough that night in that sweating seizure to persuade her not to call for help. That had been a hard time in both our lives. She was going off to grad school, not sure she wanted to, knowing she should want to; I was learning that my nice, supportive adoptive family could only help me so much. And all she could do was give me some sweet lessons in fucking and wipe the sweat off me and choose not to send me back where I came from, some sort of home for damaged kids. Helplessness was the memory she left for grad school with.

"I thought you were going to find a way to kill yourself," she said.

"If I'd wanted to, you couldn't have stopped me."

She ignored the first part of my sentence. "What did stop you?"

She had come a long way for truth and she might as well have it. "When you took the gun."

"Do you have a gun now?"

"Yes."

She left me again for those private spaces, but I was pretty sure of the part I played in what she saw.

And that part made my throat ache. I wished I could blink myself out then and there, become a blank spot in her future, whatever happened to me no burden of hers. Back then I'd wanted to give her some of my grief to carry, but I couldn't, and she couldn't take it, then or now. I swallowed the ache. "Listen," I said. "That night you made me make you a promise." Actually, she had bullied me into mouthing the words but I'd said them.

"I knew it was worthless when I made you do it."

"Do you want me to make that promise again?"

"Would you have kept your word?" Her voice went urgent. "Called me? Called someone?"

"I'll make it again, if that's what you came for."

"Make it," she said, her voice low. "Let me hear it. When you're there, and have to decide, you'll call someone. Me. *Someone*."

"Okay," I said. "I will."

She sat for a moment, lost in the stillness. She shook herself free of whatever caused it and drummed her fingers on her knee. "You're lying for my sake, aren't you? So I'll feel better." A quick hand stopped my protest. "One way to keep myself from leaving here feeling guilty would be to tell the police about your plans."

She knew better than that. She'd been in enough of her own courtrooms. "With what evidence? The cop here has access to all he needs to know about me." The records from my mother's murder. My history in the child-services system. "If he could arrest me for being nuts, he would have. He can't even take the gun, since technically it's Brett's."

She sighed. "Yeah, I know. Wishful thinking. I'm twenty years too late to absolve myself." A bend of her lip with no smile in it. "But I'm going to assume you *are* lying, you're going to do what you want and I can't stop you. So let me leave you with this." She leaned too close for me to escape her. "Forget me, forget the people who care about you. What about the horses who need you? I bet this Romp isn't the first horse you've saved from people who want to hurt it. What about that horse you rode today? What will happen to him when you're gone?"

"That's dirty."

A flash of her usual knowing humor. "If it works, like I think it will, who cares?" She sat back, rebuilding the space between us. "You'll get to that moment where you know you should call me, and you'll remember what I just told you. You'll know that someday a horse will need you, and you'll know you need to be there when it does."

"Probably," I said, as if I couldn't save horses now, not some hypothetical horses in the future.

She searched my face, frowning at what she saw; when she stood, she gathered herself as if picking up pieces. "You won't abandon the horses."

"Of course not."

"This is a good time to say goodbye, while I still believe that."

I stood, too. I put my hands in my pockets in case there was some tremor in them. "Can I walk you back to your car?"

She looked around, mapping wide spaces with no GPS to help her. "Don't you have some horse thing I'm keeping you from doing?"

"Horse things are a dime a dozen."

She gave a short laugh, a bite of surrender under it. When we reached her rental car, with a lot of empty conversation behind us, she got the door open, reached across it, pulled me to her, and kissed my cheek. "That's the goodbye kiss I couldn't give you twenty years ago. With all those people watching."

Not the kiss I wanted then. I nodded. Didn't return it.

As the car moved she lifted a hand to me, the way you'd wave at a stranger you passed on a deserted road.

CHAPTER 16

Martha texted from the schooling ring, "You coming?" and I answered, "On the way." Typing into the phone helped my focus. Phil had left me right where she wanted me, and I had to get my head straight fast.

The back side of the wall, what would happen there—that was what she wanted me to face. Too late. I'd dreamed it already, calling up those blank figures and blinking them out.

She couldn't scare me, or use her damn dirty trick about Zenith to block me. There would be no abject phone call. It would play out exactly as she predicted, and I didn't need her warning to know it would. Within only seconds a cop, or a security guard, or even a trainer I'd shared beers with, would take care of that. The after would come fast, and be over, and somewhere there'd be some horse who wouldn't suffer at these killers' hands.

So I hadn't needed her to make me face it. But to my dismay, as I made my way back to a major performance of normal, the blank figures whirled in my head and started the sweat.

I stopped in mid-stride. Fought to breathe. Played out all the hard work it would take to get to the base of the wall, let alone to the other side. I would have to put faces on the figures before I had to deal with any killing and so far I couldn't even see their eyes. The wall rose at the end of a long gallop and I was too far away to begin to see a distance. I breathed better. I tried a step. I could walk steady with effort. One foot after another, I walked on. After a couple of trembling minutes my breathing eased.

It helped that Brett and Martha's minds were not on me but on the horse and a problem that had to be solved.

The only glitch we'd found in Growly was that once in a while he'd come out of the stall with a hair up his ass. When that happened, it was like he didn't notice the jump until the last second.

That was a problem because he was one of those horses who really had to find his own spot. He was sensitive to aids and he'd start fixating on you instead of what he was doing. That day Brett kept trying to get him out of his messes and making things worse. I took up a post by the schooling oxer, where I could be part of the scenery until I got my heartbeat completely rated. I watched Brett survive a really bad distance and said, "Plan B."

He nodded. Hell, yes: our only hope this close to his round. It had worked the last time we'd had to try it. Brett snared another canter, his jaw working like he had a mouthful of wasps.

This time he didn't steady, adjust, encourage. Growly came to the fence with his mind on something God knew where. He took the square oxer with his chest. Brett picked himself up off the horse's neck and stomped on his stirrups to get his balance, didn't stop cantering, just turned. I scrambled to get the poles back in their cups. This time Growly's ears sat up like radar guns. He went OMG-there's-a-jump from eight strides back. When he landed ten feet out on the backside Brett took him straight to the in-gate. He had to wait out one trip, then galloped right in, kept Growly moving until the buzzer. Martha popped up at my shoulder, Claryce's dressage whip waving from a back pocket. "Excuse me if I don't breathe for the next ninety seconds."

"It'll be faster than that."

It was. He went all out, clean, chewed up ground in the jump-off. "I'm getting too old for this," said Martha. "Give me a nice quiet hunter class."

For once I wouldn't say no to nice and quiet, though I didn't confess that to Martha. Fortunately Claryce's ride was less stomach-churning. Flight didn't have Growly's stunning scope but he knew his job. After his trip, Growly led the class and Flight was third.

"Still that mare of Mack Dever's," said Martha.

"Ever the optimist."

"Realist."

The next horse was a chestnut gelding, not real big, okay motor, just not in Growly's or Flight's class. It pulled a rail on a fairly easy vertical. The announcer said he was owned by Sommergate LLC.

"Where did this come from?" I asked Martha.

"Guess it's another one of the Paxtons'. They must have shipped it in yesterday."

I studied the horse as it left the ring. Not what I'd expect the Paxtons to invest show fees in. "They haven't taken Romp yet."

"I heard he's not settling. They're still talking."

I nodded. Out in some fantasy world I was counting my pennies. Martha glared. "Don't even think it."

She stalked off, cutting her way with the long, whistling whip. No little shoulder bumps this time.

Rianne had two hunter classes I had to coach, then an adult eq class, where her petit, elegant line in the saddle won her a blue. All the horses that hadn't shown had to be lunged or walked, including the ponies, and the feed man came with our week's order. Then we had to set up standing bandages on the horses that showed.

The familiar chores gave my mind too much time to chew on worries. I still had no clue what to think about Jenny and that damn candle; gnawing at that made me watch for Carr. He hadn't surfaced Monday, but Tuesday as I hung out by the jumper ring watching horse after horse fail to beat Growly's time, I saw him. Across the labyrinth of ring fences he sprawled in one of Tannenbaum's golf carts talking to another of those thin men.

I circled the rings, hoping to get a good look. I had to thread through a throng of horses waiting for a flat class at the hunter-ring in-gate, and by the time I broke clear both the golf cart and the thin man were gone.

I got back to the jumper ring in time to see Dever's mare edge out Growly by two one-hundredths of a second. The kid riding her had paid a million for her. We only had fifty K in Growly. On his best days, Growly could take her every time.

By the time the five of us and Rianne and Claryce got back from dinner, I wasn't even sure where I was putting my feet. Cindi hadn't joined us. After we'd made final rounds, Brett said, "Cindi had to go to Asheville. She should be back by now."

Cindi went to Asheville to see her divorce lawyer. One day soon Brett might need somebody like Cindi. And probably his own lawyer. I hoped she could recommend some.

I went back to the camper, alone again. I put on my music and poured myself a bourbon. But the acceptance I'd reached after my talk with Phil didn't let me settle. It sank its fangs in my lungs.

And reminded me of what Phil had asked of me. *Call me.* And what I'd admitted: yes, inches from my elbow as I lay there was a gun.

It was a nine-millimeter subcompact handgun in its own leather holster in a locked case in a drawer. You could hook the holster against your belly in a belt or drop the whole thing in a windbreaker pocket. We kept a loaded magazine ready; if we ever needed the gun, there'd be no time for fumbling bullets into place. We both had concealed-carry permits that worked across most state lines. My copy of the keys I kept on a separate ring from my barn keys, inside a card case I carried on me. We'd never so much as pointed the gun at anything except a target. We'd both taken lessons handling the gun, all the safety and legal stuff.

I fished out my key and took the gun out. It was smaller than my imagination tended to paint it, small enough to remind me that on its own it was just a piece of metal. *You don't shoot to kill, you shoot to stop whatever's coming at you.* So the gun guy told us. Well, I'd be trying to stop something that had been getting closer and closer to me for a long damn time.

I put the thing away and waited for the rat-squeal of corraled anger to stop scuttling through my veins. Drifted in spite of myself into an image of Romp safe and whole and mine. Still so much hooey. They'd never sell him to me, even if I was there to take him. Because insurance. They couldn't collect—their company couldn't collect—unless he died. Was that the plan? To call him so damaged he'd have to be put down? I'd always thought of the Paxtons as ordinary rich owners, people who liked nice horses and liked to see their horses compete. Like our owners, like Pat. But our owners wouldn't kill a horse they could salvage, not for any amount of money. Had Dierdre sent her Arabian off for surgery that could have saved him, or had she just let the vet needle him? Brett and I had put two horses down since we'd been in business. When we'd had to. True, one of them, like Romp, I'd been sure I could save.

Still, Phil had been way off base, using Zenith against me. Whatever happened, I wouldn't be abandoning Zenith to any future worse than what I'd saved him from. Eaten up with fungus, shoes a month overdue and feet cracking to splinters, raw sores in his hide from where other horses in the field had beat up on him, an anatomy lesson in horses' bones. The woman promising he could "jump six feet." She'd thrown on a saddle with a broken tree and kicked him in a wild-eyed gallop at a pile of poles maybe four feet high. Goddamn if he didn't get over. So now he'd be Brett's, and half the horses in the world could wish for a fate like that.

But maybe the bourbon suddenly showed me a different picture of what would happen to Zenith if I wasn't there. Brett would keep him a while out of loyalty—his kind of guilt—but in the end he'd let somebody buy him cheap, wipe what happened to cheap, hard-to-ride horses from his mind.

I'd get a will. I'd leave my horses to Pat. Pat wouldn't justify killing horses because killing them was smart. Or kind.

But I had wished death for Romp, hadn't I? To end what he was suffering. People didn't shoot horses anymore to end their suffering unless they absolutely had to, in a moment of disaster when there was no vet and no time. To end a person's suffering, that was different. I'd read the statistics. Guns worked just fine.

CHAPTER 17

I WAS RIDING ROMP IN MY HEAD—Romp whole and airborne and glowing—when the booze and exhaustion finally got me.

Then listening to panicked shrieks from a dark stall where we'd shoved him . . .

Until a horse's sharp snort woke me up.

I thought it was a dream snort until I jerked upright at another harsh burst.

We never opened the small window between my bunk and the kitchen; nothing to see except some big camper, nothing to hear but their A.C. or heat.

And now a horse, thumping around in the space between campers, too loud for the closed window to block.

Ordinarily I'd have been more pissed than worried. Horses did get loose when people were careless. Here I'd been getting the sleep I needed and now I had to shove my feet into boots and shrug on my jacket and go see what the fuck.

But with Carr pissing at the edge of my world now, anything could be going on out there. My hand made a move to unlock the gun drawer. But if I shot the wrong person now, I'd forfeit any chance to shoot the right one later. Someone didn't latch a stall right. That was all.

My watch said one a.m. Chances were good the horse wouldn't be wearing a halter. No one left halters on horses; they could find ways to snag themselves in the safest stalls. I grabbed one of Dozer's leashes hanging by the door and went out. I circled the nose of our camper, listening. Silence, but you can feel a big animal around you, the way they turn the air.

Then I picked up low nostril flutters, the horse behind the camper now, apparently picking at the sparse grass. The campers backed up within a couple of yards of a long fence, and a horse

105

wandering along that fence could work back toward the barns, or it could turn to my left, toward the horse-trailer lot. From there, it might veer right on the road at the bottom of the lot, toward the dangerous main highway. If I startled the horse, no telling which way it would go.

"Hey, horse." The horse did lurch toward the fence when I stepped out from behind the camper; it stopped, though, ears up. If I'd had carrots, I'd have had him. A big horse, dark bay, with a wide blaze between his eyes. One of Ricoeur's German-bred studs, Emphatic something or other, one of those weird sport-horse names. Maybe he'd worried his door open by rubbing or scratching. Ricoeur would blame Jenny. She was supposed to be the one who double-checked everything.

Nope, no halter. "Hey, boy." He stepped away again, not worried, but with the sideways sashay that says a horse would just as soon not get caught. The big camper to my right looked locked up tight. For the best: a bunch of people pouring out with all their porch lights flaring wouldn't help at bit.

Neither would coming at the horse from behind. He'd think he was being chased, drift up the fence line away from me, toward the trailer lot and road. I turned to go back around our camper, get ahead of him, so I could nudge him toward the barns.

As I backtracked, I pulled out my phone to call Martha. Dozer's leash around the horse's neck would make him think he was caught until she could bring a halter. I was easing toward the fence again, about to tap the call button, when the black dog shot through the dark behind the campers, leaping at the horse and barking bloody hell.

Ricoeur's mastiff? Almost certainly. And almost certainly no collar. With no business being there.

I hurried forward. Where the horse and dog had been, nothing but a fog of thrown dirt spattering where the stud had taken off at a pounding run.

They make a lot of noise, running. By the time I plowed after him up the camper row, voices were ringing out, lights flashing on. I didn't wait. Not that I was in that big a hurry. On foot, none of us could keep up with the horse, or with the dog for that matter; he was still bellowing somewhere ahead. The two of them, horse and dog, would hopefully go to earth in the trailer lot, and I'd catch up there.

In the back of my mind I was thinking I could corner them both and haul them to Ricoeur's barn before anyone else realized what had happened. But that was stupid. Too many people spilling out behind me. Still, if I could get him back with minimum fuss, hand him over to Jenny—

I got Martha, talked between breaths while I jogged. "Loose horse in the trailer lot. One of Ricoeur's. Tell Jenny. Bring a halter." She wanted to sputter questions, but I hung up. Behind me, more voices, doors slamming, flashlight beams sweeping along the fence line.

First step, get my hands on that dog, so he'd leave the horse alone. He'd stopped barking. Maybe he'd bolted off on some other chase. Where had he come from anyway? He hadn't started barking until he was practically on top of the horse. For both the horse and the dog to be loose—that was more than careless. For the first time since I'd heard the horse snort, a worm of uneasiness inched up my spine.

For now, catch him. Once across the gravel road that led to the highway, I climbed the hill. At the top, the horse trailers and vans, more than a hundred of them, sat in their silent regiments under layers of cloud. A light on a pole at the distant tree line shone on the roofs and dropped dark shadows between them. The horse and dog could be wandering anywhere in those checkerboard rows.

I jogged along the bank parallel to the front line of trailers, searching through the gaps. No sign of motion. I didn't like the silence. The lot was big, but that was a big horse.

Below, voices, more of them now, lights playing along the fence line behind the campers, maybe movement below, already on the gravel road. I could use all that help to corral the horse once I found him. But I decided he wasn't on the hill among the trailers. I skidded back down. I had to hope he'd turned toward the rings.

But I'd barely reached the road when hooves rattled on gravel. From my left, toward the highway.

This time of night there shouldn't be much traffic, but even as I started up the road, a car passed on the highway, a swath of headlight beams. I'd made a few hundred yards when another went by. This time I thought I saw the horse's butt silhouetted against the passing lights. Still on the gravel road, nosing in the grass alongside it. For now.

Hurrying, I kicked gravel. I needed the horse to see and hear me coming so he wouldn't spook onto the highway. At last I got close enough to make him out against the sparse verge and the hedge lining the road. Another few feet and he'd be on the asphalt. The waving lights following me had stalled at the trailer lot. At this point, with the horse so close to the road, I had a better chance of catching him alone than with a big noisy group. So I didn't flash my phone; instead I eased toward him, hand out. "Hey, boy."

He raised his head with wary interest. His blaze shone eye to eye, a white wedge. He took a step toward me. "Come on, boy." His ears, prongs against a heavy gray sky with a moon behind it, rotated toward me, away, then back.

I took another step. A hot weight slammed against me, bounced off. Panting and wriggling. The goddamned dog.

Wanting me to fucking pet him. Then he saw the horse.

I dove for the dog as he lunged, grabbed for the back of his neck. Thank God, a collar. I wound my fingers around it, lifted him. He struggled, coughing out wild barks. He probably weighed a hundred-twenty pounds. The horse skittered sideways. Onto the pavement. With a metallic plock-plock of hooves, he trotted up the highway to my left.

I twisted the dog's collar to silence him. The horse clattered farther down the asphalt. I couldn't go after him and hold the dog, too.

I wheeled, dragging the dog around with me. With my free hand I fumbled my phone out, flashed it, shouted. Some of the lights were bouncing toward me. But from down the highway to the left, where the horse was, came the rush of an approaching car.

Goddamn the goddamn dog. I pulled the leash off my shoulder, doubled it through his collar so I could at least hang on. The car was coming fast but still a ways away.

I dragged the dog onto the pavement, yelling. The horse would bolt from me off the highway onto the far shoulder. Had to. All I could make out was his shadow against the approaching lights. A moving dark blur, hooves cutting sparks on the asphalt. Plunging straight at me ahead of the car.

I threw up my hand with the phone in it, waving frantically and screeching. The car's brakes wailed, the car—a small pickup—fishtailing. The horse exploded onto me, fireworks pinwheeling from his steel shoes. The blast of his body spun me as he swerved off the highway onto the show road inches from me. The dog ripped loose, raging down the gravel road after the horse.

The truck sat humming on the asphalt. I got to my feet, dusting off road grit. I couldn't see past the glare.

The truck door opened. The driver came out into the circle of headlights.

Jenny.

"Jesus Christ, Robb. What the holy fuck?"

I didn't answer. I'd dropped my phone; I bent, looking for it, found it and picked it up. A flashlight bobbed toward us, a voice calling, "Hey. What happened? Anybody hurt?"

She and I both looked toward the light, the headlights framing her frowning profile. She asked the guy behind the flashlight, "Holy shit, was that Emp?"

Mack Dever, lifting his light to show us his face. "I think so. Went by pretty fast. Bald-faced." He picked me out with the light. "Maybe you folks better get off the road."

Jenny climbed back in her truck, pulled onto the show road past us. By that time more people had come up. She braked and got out.

Malloy had caught up to Dever. On his heels was Jeff Carr. Not at the Days Inn tonight, it seemed. Malloy shone his light back and forth. "What the hell is going on?"

"Was it Emp?" Jenny asked.

"Looked like him. How'd he get out here?"

Martha emerged from the dark, a halter over her shoulder. And the dog. He was squirming on a lead rope she'd doubled in his collar. "Somebody want to take this thing?"

Jenny ignored her. She focused on Malloy, her jaw clenched. "Was he okay?"

"He was still running, that's for sure." Malloy's flashlight caught the dog. "Isn't that Ricoeur's dog?"

Jenny got back in the truck. "I gotta go see what the hell happened."

"Take this thing with you," Martha said.

Jenny got out again. Took hold of the dog's collar, let Martha spool the lead rope free. She dragged the dog over to the open truck door; tail snapping, the dog jumped inside. The truck's tires dug gravel as it shot off up the road.

A small cluster of people had caught up to us. A few I knew, not all. Carr, behind Malloy, swung his flashlight in sharp arcs. "Gee, Robb, you're good at finding horses out at night."

"He was outside my camper. The dog, too." If I'd been alone with Carr, I'd have pushed it. Instead I kicked at the asphalt. Somewhere on the gravel road was Dozer's leash. I flicked on my phone flashlight, searching. "Maybe the dog got loose and opened the horse's stall."

Malloy grunted. "Not very likely."

"Not fucking likely," Carr said.

I found Dozer's leash, picked it up. The glare from the circling flashlights caught Malloy's teeth working his lip. He raised his voice to the crowd. "Show's over out here."

He pushed through the group, leading. Carr looked back. "You coming, Robb? Or something else you looking for?"

I ignored him; I'd already started moving, Martha behind me. "Thanks for coming," I told her.

"Somebody coulda gotten killed." She drew even, her face shadowed now that all the lights were ahead of us. She snapped the shank she carried against her Wellies. "And not just the horse."

Some grooms had cornered the horse and delivered him to Ricoeur's barn. Jenny had him in a grooming stall, all the lights blasting, by the time Malloy and I and three or four of the others who'd followed us walked back. Carr hung off Malloy's shoulder, fidgeting in twitches that weren't just excitement. Making me itch.

The big horse pawed in the crossties, still riled. "Somebody call Ricoeur?" Malloy asked.

Ricoeur didn't stay on the grounds. Carr aimed his chin at Jenny. "He back at the motel?"

She cut him a look they both held for a moment. "I'll call him," she said shortly. She broke whatever passed between them, kneeling at the horse's legs, running her hands up and down them, cooing. Malloy caught the halter to steady him. He asked her, "He okay?"

She stood, her face numb and her eyes like bruises. "I think so. He needs to settle."

"I can get one of my guys to help you handwalk him."

"No, I'm gonna put him in the stall. He doesn't show till Sunday, so if he doesn't settle, I'll give him a little ace."

She led the horse into the aisle, ignoring Carr like he was a pitchfork someone had forgotten to put away. Malloy tucked his hands in his jacket pockets. "Well, let me know if you need any help." He gave a twitch of his chin at me.

I followed him to the front of the barn, stopping where I could watch Carr. He closed in on her as she latched the stall door, tying it shut with the lead rope. No telling what he was saying, but she turned to him and listened. "So what happened?" Malloy said.

I told him about hearing the horse outside, going to check on it, the dog appearing out of nowhere. I made it sound like one of those crazy things. He twisted his mouth. "You do have a knack with horses somebody wants to hurt."

I had my own thoughts about loose horses appearing out of nowhere but I wanted to see what Malloy was thinking. "You think somebody let him loose on purpose?"

He rubbed the back of his neck. "God, what do I know, people are crazy. We all gotta be glad you're such a light sleeper. Saving two horses in one week."

"Yeah, I gotta stop being so lucky."

"You *were* lucky! You coulda gotten hurt. Running into the road like that. You should be more careful. Maybe next time let somebody else handle it." He shook his head, looking from me into the barn where Carr and Jenny were still talking. "What was up with that between you and Carr back there at the road?"

I shrugged. "I hardly know him."

"He knows her."

"I guess so."

He looked for my gaze, things to tell me. "I don't know the guy that well either, just went out with people for a beer when he was there. All I know is that girl's had a hard run and you made it harder when you sent her guy to prison. No need to make it worse."

I brushed at my gritty sleeves. Someone else trying to drag what happened with me and Jenny into the mess with Romp. "Thanks. I'll write that down."

"No point in getting pissed, Robb. If you know of something between her and this guy Carr . . ." He seemed to listen, like if he waited long enough I'd tell him something. When I didn't, he took a breath, held it, like the air had gone bad, hard to get inside him. "I can't tell other people what to do, just what I'd do."

111

He didn't know about Carr and Romp, how could he? But he was guessing about things I didn't want him, or anyone, anywhere near.

"I've let go of all that," I said.

He finally got that breath swallowed. "For the best, in my opinion. Let people handle their own problems. If you hear anything the police ought to know, don't try to handle it yourself, tell that guy Wardle. That's the smart thing."

"Absolutely," I said.

He moved off heavily, pulling his jacket around him and zipping it. He didn't look back, but I had the feeling he didn't like leaving me standing there.

Jenny turned off the lights, Carr shadowing her. She swerved from me like I was so much road kill. On her heels, Carr stopped in the dark to face me. "Somebody trying to get you in trouble, huh, Robb?"

"I didn't get in trouble."

He looked toward Jenny as she crossed the lane to her truck, and I did, too. The dome light came on as she opened the door. The dog drooled onto the seat back, whining. Carr looked at me. "Lotta sick people around. You know?"

Jenny's engine started with a rough pop. I studied Carr in the glimmer from outside. No sign he'd been drinking. "Who're we talking about here, Jeff?"

He aimed a thumb as Jenny rattled off. "Scared the shit out of her, didn't it, nearly running down old Ricoeur's best horse. Funny if she turns out to be the only one smart enough to be scared."

"What do you think she's scared of?"

He laughed shortly, that way he had of making his teeth flash. "I'm just saying, lotta sick people. You keep making yourself an easy target. Next horse needs saving, maybe watch out."

First Malloy and now him. Everybody so worried about what I was getting myself into. "So when is the next one?"

"Like they put it on the Internet?" He laughed again, tapped my arm, turning. "Seriously, next time a horse gets in trouble, come get me. We'll be good guys who rescue horses together. Then we'll go have that beer and celebrate what good guys we are."

As he turned he reached around his right shoulder with his left hand and pointed a thumb-and-forefinger gun, fired it, and blew on the tip of his finger like it was giving off smoke. I stopped myself from taking an impulsive step after him. Something lurked under all this blather and I needed some trick to lure it out. That was how you handled a snake in the feed room; you didn't kill it until you saw what kind it was.

Then the aisle lights came back on. Carr was out in the lane already but I jumped, looking over my shoulder. A big guy in jeans and a sweatshirt stood glaring at me. Lots of muscle. "Show's over. Mr. Ricoeur don't like people in his barn."

"Sorry," I said to the muscle guy. "I'm going."

Carr was well out in front of me. He ducked between barns without looking back and I made the same turn. But when I reached the lane between the barns and campers, headlights came toward me, turning him into a silhouette. Jenny's truck. It stopped; he opened the passenger door, stood for a moment, then got in.

I thought she might pass me on the way to Ricoeur's. Instead she backed up, did a jerky turn, and drove back toward the road.

CHAPTER 18

I SETTLED AGAINST THE BACK WALL of the barn opposite her camper, in enough light to make sure she spotted me when she returned from parking her car. She was alone. Keys in her hand, she crossed. "Sheesh, what now, Robb?"

"Same as before. I want to know what's going on."

She jangled the keys for a moment, then went to her camper. I didn't move. She looked down at me from her step. "I really will call the goddamn cops."

"Go ahead."

She came back, the keys protruding between her fingers, the way they teach women to use keys as a weapon. In the sentry light, she was white and black, white hair and face, black jeans and jacket. Like somebody painting her had run out of colors. "You just want to know my business. I already told you it has nothing to do with you."

With the right colors I could've turned her into something different. Not hard blocks like this. "It's my business when somebody lets an expensive horse loose outside my trailer and then sets a dog on him. Was that Carr?"

I could smell her. Not weed or booze, not sex, but a burn that came off her, even though the air was cold. She raised the key tips at me, a handful of biting flowers. "The horse got out somehow. End of story. It happens."

"Who knew you were going to be driving back down that road tonight?"

"I wrote my senator. Jesus, what difference would it make?"

"You'd have hit him."

"*You* ran him up that road."

"So I guess I was trying to get you and that horse killed."

She spun. "I'm going to bed."

I called after her. "Did you tell Wardle about that candle and that picture of that horse?"

She stopped at the steps. "I told you, it was a joke."

"Maybe he won't think so. Especially when I tell him about tonight."

With a jerk she tromped up the steps to the door. She fumbled to unlock it, metal scratching on metal. I wanted to go over and help her. She'd never escape me unless I did.

Finally she got the door open. She reached in and switched on the inside light. So now all I could see was her silhouette turning toward me. "There's something wrong with you," she said, loud enough that the horse in the stall behind me snorted. "That's why you did that to Zack. That's why you want to drag me into some kind of shit you started. I have nothing to do with any of that. So. Leave. Me. Alone."

Her keys clattered onto the counter. The flimsy door rattled as it slammed.

She turned out her light right away, and I knew she thought I was watching, and she didn't want me to see whatever was in there with her when it grabbed her. Didn't want me to see her let it take her. Like she had with Zack.

Then before I even had time to fall back on my bunk and dream her, there she was, a shadow making a tinny rap-rap-rap on my camper door. I stumbled to my feet, clothes still on, and saw her on the steps through the tiny window. When I opened the door, she pushed in past me. By my watch it was three a.m.

Her hands were empty. No weapons. We'd come back from that edge.

She bit her lip, digging her nails in her palms. She looked at the door. I went over and turned the inside latch.

She sank on the bunk, the light over the counter laying a flush on her drained face. "You can tell this to the police but you can't tell them it was me." Her voice strengthened. "I'll deny I said it. I'll . . . I'll tell them you . . . whatever I have to." She worked her tongue against her cheek. "I don't know anything about Romp. But there's this stuff going on about insurance. Maybe it has something to do with Romp, maybe it doesn't. All I know is they wanted me to drug a horse I braid."

"Drug it? With what?"

"I don't know." More confidence in her tone. She'd drawn herself up, stiffer, taller.

"What was the drug supposed to do?"

"I don't know. Make it fall. Or colic. Or die. They didn't say."

"They."

"I don't know who it was. I got a text."

A text. "Did you keep it?"

"Of course not. Do you think I'm nuts?"

I propped myself against the back of the table bench, looking down at her, and worked through what she was saying. "Why are you telling me this?"

Her eyes weren't blue in this light. They were dark. She batted her hands at the question. "Because you keep trying to get me mixed up in what happened to Romp."

"When did this happen? The text?"

"I don't . . . last week. Thursday."

"You're sure?"

"It was before the thing with Romp."

"So did you do it?"

"Of course not."

I rubbed my hands across my face. She looked cold, crunched up there. I wasn't cold, sweat starting as beads but building to a heat on my skin. "Insurance companies test for stuff like that."

"Maybe it wasn't insurance. Or maybe it was some kind of new thing. I don't know." She flung her hands out. "I was scared because I didn't know if this thing I got asked to do had anything to do with Romp. I thought maybe if you knew something, saw something . . . if the thing with Romp wasn't insurance, what else could it be?"

She seemed to wait for an answer. I raised a brow. "Is that something I'm supposed to know?"

"You keep acting like you suspect me of something and I don't know any way to convince you except to tell you the truth."

Carr was right about one thing: she was scared. Something he'd said? Or my threat to turn her over to Wardle? Maybe whatever she was mixed up in was frightening enough in its own right. "That business with the candle, was that connected to this?"

"I don't know . . . you were right, it wasn't a joke." She shuddered as if a nerve had spasmed. "And . . . and this thing tonight. You're right, somebody let that horse out. And the dog. I thought maybe they're trying to make me do what they want. That

117

would be one way they'd do that. Hurt a horse I'm in charge of, make me look bad."

"Or maybe get you killed," I said.

She blinked, mouth opening as if I was sharing some big news. Then she dropped her face to her hands. "I could have killed him," she said.

Letting the horse out was the kind of gamble that would pay gold if it worked and if it didn't, no harm done. We would all decide to latch our stall doors better. I wrapped my arms around my chest and waited. It felt like a long time. Her shoulders didn't shake but I knew she was crying because of that time in her camper when I had seen her cry before. She sat up, not looking at me, wiping her cheeks and sucking in air.

I said, "Does any of this have anything to do with Carr?"

She hiccupped, the way you do when crying won't let go of you. She shook her head. "He's a guy I . . . he's nothing. He wants in my pants."

"What did he offer you tonight if you let him?"

"I didn't let him!"

"Or does somebody else want something you were giving out so late tonight?"

She wheeled. "For God's sakes, Robb. Why do you have to be such an asshole? All kinds of people hit on me. They don't all want horses killed."

I crossed to the counter, poured her a glass of water. She hesitated, but took it. "I'm sorry. I'm . . . I'm sorry about all the shit I've been saying about you. It's just . . . you shouldn't get mixed up in it. You don't need my shit." She coughed, wiping her mouth. "I just wish . . ."

Almost against my will, I crossed the narrow space to her and sat down. I waited for her to shrink from me. She drank the rest of the water, then sat, staring at nothing, with the glass on her knee. I took it from her, reached out and set it on the counter.

"I wish I hadn't made you hate me," she said.

"You know I don't hate you."

"You should. I know you were just . . ." He hands fluttered, trying to catch some word she couldn't say without their help. "You think I would . . . poison some horse for money? You think that?"

I wanted to put my hand on her. On her knee, her arm. Not for sex. To get hold of a moment when something I wanted seemed to be in reach. As if I could keep her there with me instead of letting her fade back into the grimness her face showed me. "I don't know what to think right now."

"Maybe you don't have to tell the police? I didn't do anything."

Still that need to touch her. I laced my fingers to fight it. Nothing I'd ever done had pulled her an inch out of that grimness, stopped her from sinking deeper. Maybe I'd even driven her deeper. "You're sure you don't have any idea who sent the text? Who's behind it?"

"No. I told you."

"The police could find out who sent it."

Another spasm and a fervent headshake. "I don't want any part of it. I don't know anything."

I sighed. "What if something else happens?"

"I won't let it." She used her thumbs on the tears. "If I have to sleep in the damn stalls with the horses, I won't let anything else happen. Then you don't have to tell them."

"I hope not."

"You do believe me? That I wouldn't hurt any horses?"

"I want to."

She pushed to her feet, huddling tight. "Please, one good night's sleep. Jesus."

I looked up at her. She was braced now. Taking it all out of my reach, what I had wanted to hope for. "Yeah, I'd like that, too," I said.

"Thank you."

"For what?"

"For not telling them."

I didn't ask when I'd promised. I rose and opened the door, stopped myself from putting out a hand to help her down the narrow steps. I closed the door thinking of that other time when she'd huddled against the wall of her camper and cried in front of me. Her hair flowed loose then, dripping into her blood and tears. Tonight it had been pulled back, so tight her bones cut through her cheeks. Trapped like that, it couldn't hide her. But nothing I saw in that strained face gave me what I needed. A way to bear every possible truth about her. A way to tell truth from lies.

CHAPTER 19

WEDNESDAY MORNING. I SHOWERED AND SHAVED at first light. Brett blew in while I was pulling on my boot socks, Dozer slavering after him. The dog wanted to climb onto the bunk beside me, but I'd had enough of dogs. "Look, he missed you," said Brett. "He likes you, God knows why."

He stomped back to the bedroom and made a racket pulling out and closing drawers. Dozer went to his bowl, which was empty. I got up in my stockinged feet and dumped dry food in it. I'd given up asking Brett why he didn't take a change of clothes when he spent the night with his girlfriend of the moment. He always answered, "I can never remember what the fuck I need."

I wanted coffee but left while he was showering. It looked like he hadn't heard about my night's adventures. I needed time to get ready for whatever he'd have to say. The food truck would be open in an hour. Outside, mist floated in the air from yesterday's rain. The fog in the still-burning sentry lights made Jenny's camper grayer than usual, sadder. She would have started working early, sleep or no sleep. She'd get to our hunters in plenty of time.

I beat everybody to the barn, floundering through a personal fog that for some reason kept me paying attention, like I had to be extra careful so I didn't walk off cliffs. I had all the stable sheets folded on their racks by the time Jorge came around the corner, our golf cart piled with hay bales he'd fetched from our trailer. Enough hay stored in that trailer to burn up several horses. I helped him feed, listening to the tubs rattle as the horses dug in.

Emptying water buckets so Raul could scrub them, I pawed over what Jenny had told me. If the plot she'd described involved insurance fraud, it was clumsy. You could always endanger a horse with an "accidental" colic, giving it bad feed or hay, or freaking it out, like letting it loose in the middle of the night. Any colic could turn

121

fatal. But that wasn't what Jenny had been talking about. Maybe they wanted the horse to jump bad, bring his price down. There was such a thing as a "loss of use" rider—an expensive add-on—for a horse that had been so damaged it could no longer do the task it had been purchased for. But even if I knew which horse was involved, how could I find out if it was insured with one of those? Could the substance be a new neurotoxin? Some way to give a horse some debilitating neuromuscular crap like EPM? The trick was finding somebody to ask about a drug like that without making them wonder why I wanted to know.

A good detective would have pressed Jenny about where she'd been so late at night, whether it was pure coincidence she'd come driving down that highway at exactly the right time. I decided again that her colliding with the horse wasn't anything my hypothetical perps could have counted on. Maybe they meant to endanger another valuable horse by setting him loose in the darkness, and if by chance she happened to hit him, that would have been a lucky score. But I should have bullied her about where she went with Carr after she picked him up. Did she knew any of his secrets? Did he know any of hers?

It was just uphill work thinking of her as a criminal. Those moments last night at her side proved I couldn't keep a cool head around her. With luck I'd learn that she wasn't a perp, she was a victim in whatever she'd gotten mixed up in. With even more luck, any crimes she'd committed would have nothing to do with Romp and I'd never even uncover them. Ignorance looked like the solution I should hold out for.

By then it was six. I swung down by the rings on the way to the food truck, but the jump crews hadn't finished setting up the day's courses. When I got back to the barn Brett and Raul had Whisper in the crossties, syringing his eyes with saline. He tended to react to the ring dust over the course of a show. As I passed, Brett stepped out behind me. "What the hell happened last night?"

I had wasted time worrying about Jenny when I should have been rehearsing answers. Now the simple truth would have to do me. "That bald-faced stud of Ricoeur's got loose."

"I heard *that*. How?"

"How the hell should I know?"

"It got loose where you were the one who had to catch it?"

"Well, it showed up outside our trailer."

He unsnapped Whisper from the crossties. "For God's sakes, Robb, next time let somebody else be the damn hero."

At least he agreed with everyone else about what I should do next time. "I swear." I put my hands up. "I'll try."

"You okay, then? You could've gotten hurt out on the road like that."

If my luck held he wouldn't hear about Jenny almost slamming her car into me. "I'm fine."

I didn't ride bad, all things considered. The sun shot through the fog and burnished everything. Maybe my being so tired helped Zenith. "I like you're not messing with him so much today," Brett said in the schooling ring. Snap was his usual businesslike self; all I really had to do was point him. A horse that can jump big with a comatose rider was priceless, which was why Pat had big plans for him. She hadn't been able to come that day, which was good, since I wasn't sure I'd managed to win it for her. When we went back to the barn, Zenith was out of the money on time, but Snap was leading, with twelve more to go.

"We should move him to meter-thirty next week," Brett said.

I nodded so I wouldn't have to answer. I was starting to realize this craziness wouldn't be over next week. Carr would still be alive, the people I hadn't found yet would still be alive, whatever they were going to do next still ahead of us, horses still to die, and me still watching and waiting and useless. I couldn't help stumbling into the after, where Phil had pushed me. I had a sudden pang of Snap jumping his course riderless, jumping high and wide, and me watching, sad like Pat, from the other side.

The hunter rings as usual were taking forever. It would be afternoon before our amateurs went. Rianne and Baby Jane were in a couple of divisions, and Bernie McCluskey, a sweet-faced redhead in her thirties, had arrived to show Gildy—the barn name the kids had picked for her mare, Good as Gold. In the lull with Snap's class still going I climbed the bleachers. I wanted to see if Jenny brought up the horse Ricoeur would ride in the meter-twenty. If the horse showed up with one of his grooms instead, that would tell me something, but whether I'd know how to read it was something else.

That horse of the Paxtons' I had seen the day before was in the meter-ten in the other jumper ring. A professional from a Florida barn showed it. She rode okay, but the horse took two rails, just careless. I wondered again why the Paxtons were campaigning a low-talent horse like that when I felt a shake in the bleachers, Valerie Raymond threading her way up.

I hadn't heard a peep out of her since she showed me the newspaper story on Monday. She plunked down beside me. "What's all this about you and another horse rescue last night?"

"I didn't rescue him. I didn't even catch him. There were a lot of other people around."

She dropped her voice as if the benches were listening. "This is aimed at you, Robb. Somebody's trying to make it look like you've involved in whatever's going on."

Aimed at me? Or at Jenny? "It was an accident. The door wasn't latched right."

"An accident somebody's trying to get you blamed for." Her voice picked up a jolt of excitement. "Somebody thinks you know something. That must be it."

"You're the one going around asking questions. I guess I better stop hanging out with you."

"At least I'm finding out things." She brushed back hair the breeze was ruffling into her eyes. "Get this. Dierdre Paxton had a valuable horse that died, about ten years ago. The insurance company wouldn't pay out." She undid one the barrettes in her hair and stuck it back in. "She sued them, claimed breach of contract and defamation. They settled." The glance she shot me glittered. "What about that?"

This had to be the Arabian Pat had told me about. "It means she wouldn't risk it again."

"But she got away with it! It's been ten years. Nobody I talked to even mentioned it."

Pat hadn't said anything about an insurance hassle, but she probably wouldn't even if she'd known. It wasn't a topic I could drop into a casual conversation. For now I had to mine what Valerie had brought me. "What did the insurance company accuse her of?"

"She'd given the horse some drug. Apparently something the vets didn't approve. I got my hands on the court documents. The company couldn't prove the drug would hurt the horse. They had their experts go back and forth." Her voice ran fast now. "She played it sort of like the way things happened with the fire. Nobody would think they'd do *that*. They're *horse lovers!*" She put a big exclamation point behind the words.

"So what drug?"

"A weird name. I had one of our interns go check on it. I'll text you what he finds out."

Jenny had said she'd been told to give some drug to a horse she braided. Maybe she'd been telling the truth. If the drug she was told to give acted like the one Dierdre had used, one that could possibly but not definitely cause colic, the owners might end up like Dierdre, getting their payoff even if the drug turned up in tests.

"Anyway," said Valerie, "that's what I've found out so far. What about you?"

My little bit of news about the Paxtons probably wouldn't impress her. "You know they registered their LLC for their horses in Delaware, where you can't trace who their partners are? It looks they might own a lot of horses through that."

"Hmm. That means their backers could be anybody." No exclamation points, but an uptick on "anybody." "Dirty money, maybe? That's why people register their businesses in places where who owns what can't be traced. I wonder if somebody around here knows who the partners are."

I couldn't connect my LLC news with insurance killings. My imagination toyed with the chestnut I'd seen earlier. People who showed horses like that were usually in the buying and selling business. All the signs so far said the Paxtons didn't need that kind of business. But insurance . . . maybe the low-talent chestnut was the kind of expendable horse you could insure for twice its value, then get rid of without anybody paying much attention. I didn't share that thought with Valerie. A vague suspicion anyway. Insurance companies usually wanted evidence of value. I couldn't imagine the Paxtons hard up enough to jump into a risky deal like that. Besides, an insurance game like Jenny had described—if it existed—had to be on hold now. No insurance-fraud ring, with or without players like the Paxtons, would try for a score with so many eyes on horses after the attack on Romp.

Except Ricoeur's valuable stud got loose, almost got killed on the highway. But maybe Jenny *had* been careless. Maybe it was easier to blame the escape on some mysterious bad guy than to admit she'd screwed up.

But Valerie's excitement reminded me of Phil's warning. Whether killing horses in burning trailers was or wasn't linked to some daffy insurance scheme didn't change the bottom line: somebody was trying to make money. People wanting money might not appreciate Valerie's reckless poking around. "Like I said before, you probably should be careful. Who you ask, and how you ask."

She grinned. "I'm not the one who almost got plowed over by a crazy woman last night."

"Nobody knows I'm interested in the Paxtons. Unless you ask the wrong people the wrong questions."

But her grin only widened. "So you think the Paxtons could be up to something?"

"I have no idea. There's no point in stirring shit up until you know who shit it."

"Just think," she said, to the air as much as me, "if it turns out they're mixed up with some Russian oligarch and we pin it on them, I'll end up with a byline in the *New York Times*."

"That's not worth getting anyone hurt over."

She jumped up, looked down at me. "You be careful. You're not a trained reporter." She looked way too happy as she tripped back down to the ground.

Jenny didn't bring Ricoeur's horse for the meter-twenty. A Mexican kid brought him, barely able to keep the big stud's feet on the ground. After a while Ricoeur came and got on. I leaned on the ring rail and watched him win Snap's class.

126

CHAPTER 20

R<small>ED-HEADED</small> B<small>ERNIE</small>, <small>OUR OTHER ADULT AMATEUR</small> who'd arrived late Tuesday, hadn't shown in this series before. The schooling area bustle, the fancy horses, the solid fences, all made the show a step up for her. We had to do a little psychology to keep her trusting smile going. Remind her that her major job was to get Gildy miles.

We'd bought Gildy the year before off one of Beth Hawley's owners who was getting out. A steal. When people quit, they want to be gone. Usually glad their horses landed in good hands.

Bernie put it together, ended up sixth out of twenty. Rianne pinned second. When Baby Jane was right to a fence, she had such classic form all Rianne had to do was not screw her up. The only psychology we had to do on Rianne was convince her she contributed to Jane's successes. We all knew that not screwing up your good horse was half the game.

We'd slipped the mares high in the order in their open-card classes, so we finished early. I set up Snap and Zenith and had a beer with Rianne and Bernie. Then I had an hour when maybe the smart thing to do was slip off to the camper and sleep. Instead I decided that next time, I wanted to be able to tell Valerie I'd found out things.

Malloy was one of those trainers who makes you wonder why they're in the business. The savvy and balls it takes to score big in hunters and jumpers could have earned him millions doing a zillion other things. Maybe he had made millions, had it stashed in an LLC in Delaware.

He was holding a mare for a groom to trim when I got there. The horse didn't like the clipper sound around her ears. Malloy had looped a chain over her upper gum and was wiggling it gently. That

127

trick does things to their brains that calm them. The kid perched on a stool, sculpting the rough growth off the edges of the horse's ears.

Malloy gave me a nod. "Got hot fast."

"Yeah, you forget it really does get to be summer around here."

The horse jerked when the kid folded the ear back to run the clippers inside. Malloy played on the chain. "Sorry I gave you a hard time last night."

"Didn't know you did."

His mouth thinned. "Strange stuff going on."

A trained reporter would have been slicker at guiding the conversation but at this point even a couple of clumsy questions were worth asking, especially if they involved the Paxtons. I dove in. "That chestnut of the Paxtons," I said, "the one today in the meter-twenty. I've got a rider I think he might do for if the price is okay and they're interested in selling."

The kid got down to change sides, carrying the stool around and climbing back on. Malloy massaged the mare's gum with his chain before he answered. "I think they've already got a sale."

"Oh. Well, nice horse." That feeler fell flat; you couldn't ask what the buyers were paying. "If you've got another one like that, let me know."

"Got a four-year-old on the farm that's a little like him. Priced a good bit lower. Owned by a girl up in Connecticut who never rides him. She needs something less juiced. All he needs is a couple of rides every week."

This whole idea was probably a waste, anyway. The Paxtons might own a lot of horses that weren't Olympic material. "Send me a video."

"Will do."

The kid cupped a hand around the second ear and began his art work. Malloy jiggled the chain. I had turned to go when he said, "This morning that police chief asked me about you and Jenny."

The sound of her name didn't hand me words that felt right. I nodded, sighing. "Yeah, he asked me, too."

"Like I told you, be careful around her. Keep out of her business. You don't want her dragged in."

"Of course not. I told him there was no connection."

He slipped the chain loose and rubbed the horse's lip as the kid stepped off the ladder. "He said he had read back over the records when you turned Zack in, followed up on some stuff that came out about you in the proceedings. Asked whether you had any . . ." He worked the word before he used it. "Issues."

"Like what issues?"

"He didn't say, I didn't dig into it."

"He's not paying attention to the right people."

"Yeah, that's what I told him. That horse last night just got loose. These things happen." He looked at me a long moment. "We better all be more careful."

"I plan to."

"I'm glad you're not worrying about Romp any longer. Nothing there you can help with."

I hadn't expected the comment. He watched me act out indifference. "That's something else I've let go of."

"Yeah, that's for the best," he said.

The jumper rings finished and the schooling area filled up with ponies. Most of the kids would turn up Thursday; for now, Wednesday, the barns were getting their ponies out with their pros and top juniors to loosen the kinks. We didn't have any of our own juniors at this show to school Clown and Whisper and we'd decided not to burden the customers with the cost of hiring another barn's rider. Martha could lunge Whisper, and the last thing Clown needed was settling down.

I'd flatlined with Malloy, got nothing helpful. If I wanted to shut Valerie up, I'd have to brainstorm new ideas for where to look. At least my regular chore of watching to see which ponies the other barns would be showing got me out in the open where I could see who was coming and going, like anonymous thin men. And I wanted my kids to win. Nothing I was doing changed that. In the melee in front of me I could see what they had to contend with. The later shows in the series paid more prize money, brought out the bigger guns.

Anyway, I was better off here watching one of our main pony rivals flatten over all his oxers than lurking around Ricoeur's barn trying to find out where Jenny stood. I couldn't help thinking that if he'd fired her I would have heard. She'd have finished braiding long ago so I wasn't likely to run into her by accident. It was better if I kept my distance, if I didn't lend credence to the idea that either of us had anything to do with the risk to Ricoeur's horse last night. No telling what people would put together if you gave them a reason to talk.

Like the ideas Malloy seemed to be trying to put together. He'd kept his mouth shut when I turned Zack in; I'd kind of wondered if he knew as much about Zack and his garbage as I did and maybe about the way Zack was treating Jenny, too. Maybe the way Malloy handled it, minding his own business, was the way people without something wrong with them acted. Even when—maybe especially when—bad shit was going on. Sometimes Malloy looked at me certain ways—like last night when he first asked me about Jenny— that made me think he knew I wasn't normal but was letting me deal with my own problems, like he'd said.

I hoped so. The fewer people who got mixed up in what I had to do, the better. Malloy seemed more worried about Jenny than I'd have expected. Maybe he felt like a father toward her. She could use someone like Malloy on her side.

A loud clatter jerked me back to the ponies whizzing by. In the center of the schooling area, Brian Hogarth, Taylor's alleged crush from Dever's, sat on his large pony in the wreck of the schooling fence. With a lurch the pony scrambled clear of the pile of downed poles. Brian's trainer and one of the Florida trainers set the jump back up while Brian gathered his reins.

I'd spotted Brian last night in a group of rowdy kids around Dever's diamond fountain. Maybe he'd crashed the schooling fence because he was tired from too much fun. He picked up a trot, but the trainer, one of Dever's assistants, crossed the stream of galloping ponies from the repaired jump to the rail and called to him, his voice clear: "Get out of the ring."

Outside the trainer talked low, Brian picking at the pony's short mane over its withers. Then he got off, shoved the reins at the trainer, and walked away.

Even at the distance, the look on his face struck me as kind of loopy. Unfocused. No, taking care of Zack hadn't taken care of that shit at all.

I made myself concentrate on ponies. On what I'd tell our kids when they came tomorrow to prep for their first classes. In showing you always think about what you did last time that got you second or nowhere instead of first. Usually the only reason is that you held your mouth wrong. But what makes riding and showing worth it is knowing that next time you can do better, and the amazing feeling from remembering that once you did it exactly right and might do it exactly right again.

So I was probably the most relaxed I had been for a week, in spite of myself actually imagining a future, when I felt a bump on my shoulder. I found Dyan Westerman propping her elbows on the rail beside me. In one hand she held a metal water bottle. Ice jingled in it, and I smelled the bourbon. "Cute little buggers," she said.

Ponies were cute if you didn't know them too well. "Yeah."

"You're showing those same two as last week?"

"Yeah, those two mediums. We've got a large coming in." Steampunk, Scott's pony, officially measured fourteen hands and one and four-fifths of an inch, right in the sweet spot under the fourteen-two-hand cut-off to qualify as a pony. That measurement could make a lot of difference in the ribbons he won and in his value; another half inch, and he would have had to struggle against the bigger horses, with their stronger motors and longer strides.

Dyan pivoted away from the ring, shoulders propped on the rail. "The one thing in the world I wanted when I was a kid was a pony." She sucked through the angled straw jutting out of the bottle tip. "Had to wait till I was an old lady and pretend my horses were ponies. You have a pony, Robb?"

It must be the hero stuff that pulled Dyan my way when she was drunk. She'd been drunk when she called me a few creative things because I wouldn't sleep with her to spite Brett. Afterwards she hadn't seemed to remember she'd even wanted me.

"I didn't start riding until I was older," I said.

She offered the bottle. "Want a sip?"

"I just had a beer."

"You're pretty sober."

At least we'd left the topic of my childhood. "Yeah, I guess so."

"You're too straight, Robb."

She'd accused me of that before, with one hand up the back of my shirt. Oh, well. My gut said shy away from serious topics. But then I remembered that I'd talked to her in the first place because she knew the Paxtons and at least some of their horses. Maybe with the bourbon in her she wouldn't notice a few more questions, maybe wouldn't even remember being asked. She gave me another bump, the pressure of her shoulder lingering. "Poor Romp."

"Yeah." I thought about what Malloy had said about the chestnut. "Glad they're getting good prices for their other horses."

She nodded. "Makes up for losing Romp."

I wanted to say, they won't lose him. He'll get better. It can happen, can't it? But I didn't like showing her what I cared about. Maybe I could steer her to the dead Arabian. "I didn't know they had so many horses."

She waved the bottle, sipped again. "Like that partner of yours has girl friends."

"That many, huh?"

"What about you? You know how all the little girls look at you."

I came up with a laugh I partly meant. "Beside Brett, I don't even make it to the jump-off." If I was steering her, she wasn't going. I tried again. "What's with that chestnut they showed today? He doesn't look like their kind of horse."

She frowned. "That thing? What's crazy is what they're getting for him. That horse is not worth a million five."

It took me a minute to get my face fixed. "Malloy said they had a good offer."

She tapped the bottle on my chest. "I could get you that kind of money for that gray thing of yours."

"A million five for Zenith?"

"If I had the right buyers." Her words were tangling up. "Buyers" came out "bryers." "The right buyers don't care how much they spend. They just want to get rid of money."

Like what Phil had said, more or less. I thought again about customers with restless money, the ones I'd had to talk down off bad buys. But Dyan's claim was almost crazy, not something I could take at face value. I let her wind our arms together. "Who told you that's what they're getting for that horse?"

"Her boyfriend," she said in a bubbly whisper.

"Dierdre's?"

"He saw the damn wire transfer."

I tried to imagine someone who'd be Dierdre Paxton's boyfriend in a place where he'd tell Dyan something like that. She snugged me against her, then let go, turned back to the ring, still sipping. I didn't want her getting sober. "Maybe he was trying to impress you."

"Impress me with what?"

"That's a lot of money."

She faced me again, eyes narrowed. "Maybe *I* ought to try to impress you. You never appreciated me enough."

"Apparently not."

Another bottle tap on my chest. "You can't play in those circles, Robb. We could." She took hold again, pulled me toward her. "You don't need that goddamn Brett."

"Who's buying the Paxtons' horses?"

She waved her free hand. "God knows. They've got some sucker on the line. They get big bucks for cheap horses all the time."

Martha bounced up in our seldom-used golf cart. I shifted around so Dyan would see her. It took her a moment to let go of my arm.

"The Turners are bringing SP tonight," said Martha. SP was what we called Scott's pony Steampunk. "Brett wants to know if you want to find somebody to get on him."

SP could be freaking his first day in a new place. His antics sometimes rattled Scott, and a more experienced rider would wear the edges off before Scott got on. "Let me talk to Causey. One of her juniors would work."

Martha was looking at Dyan squint-eyed. "Oh, and he wants you to see if there've been any new drops in tomorrow's classes."

Martha wouldn't leave until I did. "I gotta go," I said to Dyan. "I'll talk to you later."

She propped an elbow on the fence, cut her eyes at Martha. "Remember, ix-nay to that goddamn Brett."

Watching her take off, Martha said, "I hope you didn't just buy a horse."

"She wanted me to sell one."

"Who?"

"Zenith."

"God, get it in writing."

"You love Zenith."

"Honey, I love them all."

CHAPTER 21

SCOTT'S DAD SCOTTY SR. ARRIVED with Steampunk about six. The pony came off the trailer with the whites of his eyes flashing and sweat on his shoulders. We stripped his shipping boots and stuck him in his stall, let him traipse around snorting at the piled-up shavings. He finally grabbed hay, bringing mouthfuls to the door, chewing fast.

"You'd think he'd have figured all this out by now," Scotty said.

"He'll be okay in half an hour." Raul and I helped Scotty unload Scott's tack trunk and rinse out the deep layers of shit SP had deposited in the trailer.

"I'll go unhitch," Scotty said.

I told Brett, "Sherrin'll be here with Scott around seven. That girl from Causey's said she'd be glad to hack SP around."

He nodded. That flat work should settle the pony, make him okay for Scott. I did up Zenith in his standing bandages, thinking, somebody sold Dyan a bill of goods. Played on the way she liked being around the richest people. Look where she went when she left us. Probably she'd been Dierdre's friend for a reason.

But if there was any truth to it . . . if the Paxtons had sold that cheap horse for that much money. . . . Of course, if somebody wanted to pay a big price, you didn't blurt, "Oh, he's not worth that." But if it was one of your customers you had a duty. That such a big price for a middle-grade horse hadn't triggered whispers said that the Paxtons—and possibly Malloy—were ashamed of their scam and trying to hide it, like Brett and I would have if we'd done that deal on that horse.

I checked Zenith's water, double-checked his stall door latch, gave him a carrot from the stash in the fridge. People wanting to get rid of money? People with too much money looking for four-legged yachts to park it in?

By the time Scott's mom Sherrin drove in with Scott, we'd had Steampunk out half an hour, the girl cantering him around the schooling ring on a loose rein. Scott got out of the car in his half-chaps and paddock boots. I said, "Let's go see what SP's doing." Brett stayed to chat with Sherrin; one perk of having looks like his was that the moms always wanted to schmooze and that kept them from helicoptering their kids. At the ring, the girl from Causey's rode over, patting SP's neck. His head hung a lot lower than it had when we'd put her on him. "Doing great," she said.

Scott looked at me. He rubbed the pony's nose.

"He okay for Scott to hop on for a few canters?" I asked her.

"Seems fine to me."

She jumped off. We'd put her in one of our saddles because I'd known what would happen. I'd heard of people's eyes shining, but Scott's whole face lit up.

He swung on without a mounting block. "Nice ride," the girl said. I nodded. Brett and I worked hard to have nice rides.

At dinner Scott played a game on his phone while the rest of us talked about our favorite places in North Carolina. Cindi had gone back to Asheville, so I ended up with Brett and Dozer clomping around in the camper. He said, "I'd say let's stream a movie but you need to sleep."

"Yeah, I do."

"So sleep."

They disappeared down the hall to the bedroom where he had his own TV hookup and he closed the door. But I knew him. He'd come out for a drink after a bit and he'd want to find me sleeping. So I traded my dinner clothes for a T-shirt and shorts, kicked the A.C. up a notch, hooked up my headphones, and lay down.

I wished he could make me sleep. At dinner I'd had a hard time. That sick heartache again. I looked at those nice people and their nice son and thought, afterwards, they'll be here, just like this, talking about their lives and their horses, and there'll be a blank space where I sat. The wall and the blank space after. I still fought believing in the blankness. That it wouldn't keep receding. I hadn't found any answers, and until I did, I could push it back and back, the nothingness always before me. I was talking to someone on the other side of the wall when I fell asleep.

136

I woke up as always in the dim light over the kitchen sink. I took off the headphones and listened. No loose horses rustling around outside. Darkness and silence from the bedroom. Another wakeful three a.m.

I got my laptop, stretched out again, set up my hotspot. What Dyan had said nagged me. A strange piece of a puzzle with the Paxtons involved.

Ever since Pat had told me about the Arabian, I'd been walking my head around the Paxtons. Trying to find an angle that might show me what put their horse in that trailer. I hadn't quite found it in Valerie's news about the lawsuit over Dierdre's insurance claim. But Dyan's gossip had a little juice in it, not sure yet what kind.

She said they did it "all the time," sold cheap horses for more than they were worth. On its face, that practice was no big deal. More than once Brett and I'd gotten more for a horse than we'd have paid ourselves. But her "all the time" meant that for them, selling way high was standard practice, a piece of their role as rich owners they didn't advertise. It also meant that out there in the lists of horses showing were other horses like the chestnut, cheap horses they had owned and sold. Finding horses the Paxtons had owned and what had happened to them would shine light on at least part of Dyan's tale.

It wasn't like I was going to dig up a list of prices people had paid. No Zillow for that. But you could get a lot of info about horses roundabout, looking up class results and rankings at both the USEF, United States Equestrian Federation, and the Fédération Équestre Internationale, the FEI. You could get horses' names and riders' names, and with a click, you could get the show careers for both. Not for owners. Once in a while I'd researched owners on the USEF site when they came to our farm looking to buy or sell, but more often you scoped people out on their farm web sites or got to know them at shows. But now I searched "people" for the Paxtons, Dierdre and Richard. There they were. I set the date parameters well back and clicked "Rider Report." I hadn't expected much, since I was pretty sure they didn't ride. All I got from the .pdf file was that their "point state" was Connecticut.

I searched for Sommergate LLC, found it via a farm search, with the Paxtons registered as owners. They were amateurs, didn't take money for training or coaching. Any income for them would come from buying and selling—capital gains. The farm report didn't offer me info on any of the horses, cheap or otherwise, Sommergate had owned.

Thinking about it, I typed in Greg Drakow, the rider who'd been on their Dutch horse in the Grand Prix Sunday night. He rode for a lot of people. A rider report for the last ten years listed all the classes he'd ridden in and the horses' owners. It took a while to run through the entries. He'd ridden both for Sommergate over the last few years and for the Paxtons as individual owners before that.

Both Romp and the Dutch horse showed up among his many mounts, as well as a Sommergate mare I didn't remember seeing that ranked high on the Rolex and FEI listings; the mare mostly showed in Florida. I was more interested in six Sommergate horses Drakow had ridden only once, all at a meter-twenty, over the past seven or so years. In each case, the horse's results from Drakow's ride were DNP, Did Not Place.

A horse search on each told me they'd moved on from Sommergate after showing in fairly competitive company under Drakow. He wasn't riding the chestnut they were showing and apparently selling this series, but from what the horse reports told me, the six horses he'd ridden once were all middling jumpers who'd started in the Paxtons' barn, then ended up down the road.

No reason to link Drakow with the fates of any of the Paxtons' horses. He was a contractor, rode for a lot of people. He'd ride an occasional dud for the Paxtons because they were clearly good customers of his. They'd probably value his advice about whether to keep campaigning one he'd shown or move it on.

So. From the data, the Paxtons bought horses, found out whether they showed talent, then sold the ones that didn't. Perfectly normal. You couldn't always tell from a young horse's show record or how well it schooled what it was worth until you put it in front of big fences, a whole course full under a decent ride. Brett and I did that: bought, tried them, kept some for a while, sold the rest.

But Dyan had said this chestnut, a clone of the ones Drakow had ridden once before the Paxtons sold them, had brought more than a million dollars. I skimmed mentally through all the owners Brett and I had worked with over the years. Even among the few who had made bad buys, none had sprung for a price as far out of line as that.

I reread the horse reports for the six others. In each case, after Drakow rode them, they didn't turn up at shows again for about a year. When they did, they'd come way down in company. Rider reports on the new owners showed undistinguished placings, or none at all, at small regional shows. One horse had changed hands three times in three years.

From the meager records in the listings, the people who'd ended up with these horses didn't look like they'd had anywhere close to a million to spend. That made it likely the million-dollar buyers, if there were any, were middlemen of some sort. They'd paid a high price, then sold a lot lower. Successful dealers usually wanted their sales to work the other way around. These dealers, assuming they existed, hadn't campaigned the horses; if they had, they'd have shown up as owners or riders in the horse reports.

Of course, Dyan's "all the time" might be hooey. There might be nobody paying any millions. These undistinguished horses, including the chestnut I'd seen, might have been sold from Sommergate for five grand a pop.

I made a list on the computer: horses' names and USEF numbers, the chains of owners and their USEF numbers. The third on the list, Solomon XI, had most recently finished out of the money at .95 meters in a show in Georgia. Big comedown from Greg Drakow.

To check on Dyan's tale, I needed a handle on that first sale, the one from Sommergate. Again, I reminded myself, if the buyers never showed the horse, the change of hands wouldn't show in the USEF records. Marci Hagen, the woman who was most recently listed as the owner of Solomon XI—did she buy him from Sommergate, or from someone in the middle? How could I find out how much she paid?

I checked a corner of my mind where I'd stowed Jeff Carr. From the start I'd assumed he knew who'd hatched the attack on Romp, and I had let my mind dig at how to open him up. I'd seen him at a distance three or four times since our loose-horse escapades Tuesday night, once with Dever in Dever's golf cart, looking caught up in pretty intense talk. He hadn't approached me about that beer he wanted to buy me. He hadn't paid me much attention at all.

Had he played any role in getting big prices for cheap horses? Last night in Ricoeur's barn he seemed to be setting lures to see what I'd snap at. I had to start setting my own lures. Maybe I could figure out what kinds of lures would work and where to set them if my trained reporter and I found someone who was actually paying Sommergate prices in the millions for so-so jumpers. And why.

By then the light through our little window had grayed, day already here. I sat back and stretched, not really loosening any muscles. A clatter from the bedroom, Dozer knocking a lamp over, not for the first time. I turned off my phone, shuttled the laptop back to the table. Rolled onto my side, faked deep breathing. When Dozer bounded out, he jumped on my ribs and soused my ear with his wet slobber, not for the first time.

I pushed him off. Brett clomped out behind him. "You don't look any better."

"I feel better."

"Work on looking it. You want coffee?"

It was probably too early to text Valerie. "I'll get some."

He started the little machine to make his own. "Dozer."

From his place on my legs, Dozer leered.

"What do I pay you for?" Brett asked him. "Lick that shit face off him."

I shoved Dozer away and swung upright. "Lick more shit on is more like it. I gotta go meet the farrier for SP, thank God."

CHAPTER 22

SP NEEDED A FRONT RESET. Scott already had him in the grooming stall when I got to the barn. The farrier we used at these shows backed his truck with his forge up to the end of our aisle around six-thirty, the sun creeping up, well before classes started at eight. "Saw that gray of yours won his feed this week," the farrier shouted over the forge roar. "Good job." He pulled the left fore shoe and ditched it, shaping a new one over his fire.

SP had settled well, looked like he was still in dreamland. Scott picked hay strands out of his forelock. The farrier and I talked about SP's angles, whether he was moving his best. The right shoes could get you the free-swinging stride you needed to win on the flat. As always the front reset took about half an hour. The farrier told Scott, "Always buy a horse with good feet. Like this pony. Perfect feet."

Scott blushed. He loved it when anybody praised SP.

When the farrier drove away, I sent Scott down to the ring to see if the courses were posted. I went outside the barn aisle and called Valerie Raymond. "I have something for you to do."

"I have another commission meeting this morning. Can I call you later?"

"I'll text you. I need you to find someone."

The girls plowed in around noon and clambered all over their ponies. Clown and Whisper put up with the humiliation because it came with about sixty apples and a big bag of treats. "Two apples each," I said. Maybe you couldn't founder a horse on apples, but who wanted to try?

Having them there opened the day for me. That wall I was always galloping toward paled to a blur a long journey away. The distractions painted strokes in my mind I hoped I'd be around to remember: the girls giggling and digging their brushes out of their

141

grooming bags and their mothers pulling up chairs and opening five-dollar bottles of water and Zenith forgetting he was antisocial and popping his head over his stall door at the sound of treat bags crinkling and Brett zipping his boots for Growly's class and me thinking about the school the kids would do after lunch. Brett stood up, stomped to get his boots seated right and said, "Where's Scott?"

I looked around from snagging a treat for Zenith. SP was in his stall, deep in hay. "He was just here."

"He's out by the wash rack with Brian," said Taylor from Whisper's stall.

"Put detangler on his tail if you're going to brush it," I told her. "It's already thin and you don't want any hair breaking."

"I did."

Brett went to the end of the aisle. Hollering, a little urgent. "Scott!"

Scott appeared around the corner, cheeks oddly flushed. "You cleaned SP's feet?" Brett asked.

"The blacksmith just did him."

"Looked to me like your spurs need polishing."

"We weren't going to use spurs."

"Clean them anyway. You never know."

Scott looked at me. I coached Scott, not Brett. I said, "Make sure they're clean. I'll take them down with us, just in case."

Scott sighed, loud. He went into the tack stall and made a surly racket pawing in his trunk. Brett came to Zenith's door. "I don't want that Brian kid hanging around here." He looked over his shoulder. The moms were deep in conversation. "He's fucking high."

I nodded, said nothing. Scott came to me holding the spurs. I said, "They look fine." Scott made a noise and went back into the tack stall. I said to Brett under my breath, "Next time let me find something to tell him."

"Be here for it next time," Brett said.

He wheeled to the mothers, giving them his dimples. Scott's mom had joined them. I couldn't think of anything else to do with Zenith but I waited, pulling his forelock. One of the few things my horse didn't mind me doing. Apparently I was wrong thinking Brett hadn't started to worry. Stepping in with Scott was out of line and he knew it. He'd bury whatever was bugging him a while longer, that was his pattern. I hoped he'd hold it in until the series ended. If he called me on the lies I'd have to concoct to keep the charade going, there'd be no way to spare him. The longer I put off that explosion the better. So I let the heat settle out of my face before I turned and ordered, "Everybody get lunch now if you want it. Ready to ride at one."

My kids schooled in a warm-up ring that nobody used much, so they wouldn't get creamed by the older riders prepping for the junior class currently under way. I made them ride without stirrups for twenty minutes, which should cut back on the exuberance around our barn for a while. But they rode good, and I thought we had several chances to add to the row of ribbons on the banner above our stalls.

That afternoon that kid Brian had a fall. He fucked up a distance in the Low Jumpers and his fancy pony had to duck and twist, jumping him off. Like most kids, he bounced right up. But then he sank back again, sitting beside the fence while the jump crew checked the top pole. His trainer ran to him, and it looked to me like the kid was laughing. He got up again, took the pony from the groom who had caught it. His trainer walked him out of the ring, a hand on his elbow. Farther down the ring fence Mack Dever slouched in his gold-chromed golf cart, from the look of his smile to some woman beside him not much bothered that a kid from his barn had put on that kind of exhibition. Martha, holding Zenith beside me, said, "I hope somebody's paying attention to this shit."

After his trip Snap led in the meter-twenty with only a few horses left to challenge him, and our hunters with our amateur riders picked up two seconds, a third, and a fifth. Baby Jane had a shot at another Reserve Champion and Bernie was finding her stride. Back at our barn we were untacking and bathing horses, the classes still going and Snap still leading, when Valerie showed up.

I'd texted her to tell me when she was coming so I could steer her away from the barn, but surprise, she'd ignored my instructions. I couldn't put her off; my plan was too complicated to handle over texts. Brett gave her a nod he might have given to a feed salesman he didn't intend to do business with. Martha grabbed Zenith from me and followed Raul and Snap and Pat out to the wash racks. The whole aisle was filled with Taylor and Cadence and Scott and the echoes down the way from a bunch of shrieking teenaged girls outside Dever's aisle. I led Valerie to the food truck. I didn't want anything to eat but I had to get her out of there.

I ordered a cardboard shell of curly fries and got us one of the tables. She took in what I wanted from this Marci Hagen, the woman the USEF records listed as owning the Solomon XI horse now. Her face said she was speculating. "Okay, who she got the horse from. What she paid. You think she'll cough up what she paid?"

"You're the trained investigator."

She made a face. "You'll live to eat that snark. Why are you interested in this horse?"

"I was told—so far just gossip—the Paxtons are selling a horse they're showing here for a lot more than it's worth. I'm trying to find out if they actually do that. If they've done it before."

"There's no record?"

"Prices aren't public."

Her frown said she was still thinking. "So they sell horses for more than they're worth. But then if something happens to the horse they don't own it anymore so they can't collect. That doesn't work for insurance fraud."

"Let's see if there's any sign that it happens. That's first."

She eyed me. "You've got an idea about this, don't you?"

"Let's just find this out."

Her mouth pinched in suspicion. She pulled a strip of paper from her pocket. "This fit in with your idea?"

I read it, realized what it was. "What Dierdre gave her stallion and had to go to court over?"

"Yeah."

I flicked it back to her. "It's a homeopathic colic remedy."

"Yeah, like I said, we looked it up."

"It has a lot of belladonna in it. Vets don't like that kind of homemade shit."

"The court documents claim she gave the horse a purified form."

"Atropine?"

"Yeah, that's it."

I shrugged. "No, the insurance company wouldn't like that."

"So, is it something you'd give your horse if you wanted to kill it?"

Or something Jenny could drop in a morning feed? "It *could* bring on a colic. Any colic can turn deadly. I guess you'd have to give the horse a lot."

She pushed back against the little table. "You ought to be disappointed it's not a smoking gun."

"I am."

"Not enough." She considered me for a moment. "This idea of yours. It's not about insurance at all."

"I don't have any idea yet."

"How can I know what to ask this woman if you keep me completely in the dark?"

I considered what I was willing to tell. Sooner or later she'd figure it all out anyway. "Okay, as long as you realize I'm just thinking aloud." Explaining part of where I'd arrived helped me sort through it. "Marci Hagen didn't pay Sommergate any big price, you can see from her show record she's not that kind of player. But the records on Solomon are blank for eighteen months between her and Sommergate. That makes it likely that somebody, maybe several somebodies, owned him after Sommergate sold him and before she bought him. If they didn't show him, they wouldn't be in the records—"

"And you want to know if one of those somebodies actually paid Sommergate a lot for him."

"I want to know if that person exists and who it is."

"Maybe she did buy him from Sommergate herself, cheap, and held onto him."

"Then I want to know if she did."

"Why? What would knowing all this tell you about the attack on that Romp horse?"

I had a ways to go before I could lay out a complete theory. "Like I said, I don't know yet. It's a part of a puzzle about what they do with their horses. If they do this, it's just something strange."

Her eyes narrowed. "Fine. I'll make a couple of calls to this—" she thumbed to the address I'd texted her, "—fucking Roswell, Georgia. Provided I get to see the finished puzzle."

"Just phone calls. Check with me before you do anything different. And bail if things get sticky."

She scoffed. "It'll be real strange if 'just phone calls—'" she made air quotes, "—gets sticky."

I nodded. It damn well would.

A lot of us at dinner that night, reliving trips. Snap had won his class and Zenith paid his feed bill one more time. Pat glowed, but still with that sadness underneath, as if missing the days when she was the one reliving a wonderful trip.

Behind my smiles I toyed with what Valerie had told me about Dierdre and atropine. That news didn't fit in with Jenny's story. Atropine wasn't something you could casually drop in the feed. But in the grand scheme of it, Valerie was right. My idea—the one I'd told her I didn't have yet—had nothing to do with insurance at all.

CHAPTER 23

FRIDAY MORNING MEANT EARLY CLASSES. I'd actually slept. Five hours straight by my watch, with another hour right before the alarm went off.

Out of an impulse that had to be sheer meanness the series had put the kids' classes first this Friday, with the flats number one on the card, so you had to get your sleepy children on and into the ring while their ponies were still spooking at funny-looking dirt clods. Scott beat me to the barn again, SP already groomed. And long ago braided. All of our hunters were already braided. That meant Jenny had been working since probably four.

Martha brought me coffee. "Wonder if Brian slept it off."

Like I had time to care about Brian. The girls led their ponies down, Jorge superintending. Cadence parked Clown on my left at the rail. "Good morning," I said.

She yawned. One thing I'd learned about her, you had to get her pump going. "Run up your keepers," I said.

"This is my new bridle! They're too tight."

"Run them up every time and they'll stretch. Here, I'll do this one." I tucked the loose strap on the cheek piece into its keeper.

"There's only one on that side. There's three over here."

"Four, counting the martingale."

She let out a huge sigh but fumbled at the straps. I leaned over the pony's neck to inspect her work. "You pass."

Scott's warm-up was careful, an added stride in the first line, a push for the numbers in the rest. He came out beating himself up. "But you know what to do next time," I told him. "That's what warm-ups are for."

His first hunter trip went a lot better. I thought he might pin, fourth or fifth. He'd ride better and better as the day stretched on. I wished he could do a whole series because by the end he'd be in top

147

form, Champion. Ring nerves weren't his problem; he suffered from needing to be perfect every time. Repetition would quash that obsession. But a series was a stretch for Scotty and Sherrin financially. Maybe next year we could work out a job for Scott so he could show all summer . . .

It was so easy to forget that next summer was the other side of the wall.

I concentrated on now, on what he could work on in his second hunter trip. That went really well. I got going with the girls.

We'd finished warming up on the flat, the girls steering clear of the crush of other schooling ponies, when a groom shot across the ring inches in front of Taylor, making her pull up. The groom hurried up to Dever where he stood raising the back pole on the schooling oxer for one of his kids.

"Oh my God," said Taylor, riding by me. "Did you see that?"

I nodded. "Take a break." A face that had soaked up as much sun as Dever's could never really go white, but the crinkled tan had drained. He shouted to one of his assistants, a growl that sounded like "Take over here." Then he and the groom dodged back through the circling ponies. My girls were down the ring by that time, fortunately oblivious. I lowered the vertical beside me. "Hey, guys! Canter this!"

When we went up to the gate for our rotation, I deliberately didn't look for Martha. Whatever had happened, I hoped she'd save the news until we had trips behind us. Whisper was a little sharper than I liked; I hated to see them leave their best trips in the warm-ups. Clown was Clown, arguing every step of the way until the last line when he finally said what the hell. Fortunately Whisper had plenty of bounce left for a really crisp first trip, and Clown was a miracle of attention—for him. Then here came Martha, lips caught in her teeth. Rumors were sparking around me and maybe I already sensed what she had to tell me. She spoke close to my ear. "They found Brian in an empty stall. Dead."

"Do they know what happened?"

"Not yet. But I can guess."

"Don't tell Scott." But it was too late. He hurried toward me, his coat off, his collar open, his rusty hair tousled from his helmet. He wasn't crying yet but close to it. "I just talked to him yesterday!"

A mean part of me was glad there'd be no more "just talking."

"Is your mom at the barn?"

"Yes, her and Ms.—"

"Go back, get a soda, sit down for a while. I'll be there as soon as I can."

He stomped off, wiping his nose. The girls had been watching, picking up on murmurs. Cadence said, "What happened?"

"Brian had an accident."

"Is he okay?"

"I don't know yet. We'll find out in a bit."

"Probably fell off getting on," said Taylor. Cadence laughed.

I didn't scold them. Not long ago I'd heard Brian asking Cadence how long she planned to keep riding a big fat tick. She hadn't taken the comment as a joke. So far there'd been no announcement, no sign classes would hold up. I sent the girls in for their second trips on schedule. Cadence rode the shit out of Clown and he put in one of his best trips ever, but Whisper would probably still beat him. All the kids had a break before their eq classes later, so I couldn't avoid taking them back to the barn and into the rumorfest. At least I could hand them off to their moms.

I barely had time to count the minutes before an unmarked police car and a white van nosed along the lane in front of the barns to Dever's stalls. Claryce had arrived for her Friday afternoon class on Flight and Rianne and Bernie were tacking up when Wardle appeared on foot at the end of our aisle.

He jerked his chin at me. Brett was in Growly's stall and Martha in the tack stall. The moms and kids, Cadence in her mom's lap and Taylor and Scott piled together in one of the oversized chairs, all pivoted to watch as I drifted down to where Wardle stood.

"Come see me this afternoon," he said.

He wasn't any easier to read. He wore his uniform, tight and crisp.

"I don't know anything about any of this," I said.

He made hard knots of his words. "I want you to come and see me."

I looked at my watch. About one. "It'll be late."

"Text me when you have an ETA."

I walked back to where Jorge was straightening after fastening Flight's quarter boots. "Are you getting arrested?" Cadence asked.

"Honey!" Her mom bounced her.

Claryce pulled her helmet over her bunched dark hair. "Let's hope for no more tragedies."

"Bad things happen in threes," said Bernie from down the aisle.

When I told Brett I had to run to town before dinner, he cranked his brows down. "Yeah, I heard."

"Nothing I can tell him."

He was spraying detangler in Growly's tail. Didn't look at me. "I knew that shit with Zack would come back to bite you."

"You can check my ass for teeth marks later."

"*Our* ass," he said.

Wardle clicked his computer off when I entered, then swiveled to me. He put his hands behind his neck and stretched, sighing.

"So what happened with this Zack Cassidy?" he said.

"Like I told you before, there's a complete police report."

"I'm still waiting to hear it from you."

"Are you implying it has something to do with Brian?"

"This guy Zack was in the middle of drugs at horse shows. Kid ODs at a horse show."

I raised my brows. "So that's it? An OD?"

"Haven't got the coroner's report yet, but I'd offer even money that's what it'll show." He shifted, like getting set for the long haul. "How exactly did you find out about Zack?"

"It's all in the—"

"Let's try again. How did you find out about Zack?"

I'd taken the same chair as before, facing his desk. "He sold uppers to one of our kids. She told her mom and her mom told me." I tried leaning back. The chair wanted to tilt.

"So you decided you had to make sure the local police took a look at what Zack was doing?"

"Wouldn't anybody?"

"What happened to the kid?"

"Her mom got pissed that I got her involved and they went to another barn."

He ran a hand through his bristly hair. "Always the way, huh?"

I'd tried hard not to name the girl. The police back then hadn't given me many options. Wardle moved on where he probably always meant to be going. "But then there was that other issue with Cassidy. That . . . uh, torch we talked about."

"That *really* doesn't have anything—"

"Let's give it a try."

150

I wanted my sigh to signal exasperation, not surrender. "He was beating her up. Getting him out of her life had a chance to stop it."

"And you threatened to kill him, didn't you?"

"Yeah, I thought you'd probably read the report."

He made a face. "Not beach reading. So that was why they made you produce the girl as a witness. So the defense couldn't claim it was all about you going after Zack."

"You'd have to ask them."

He folded his hands across his broad chest, lacing his fingers. His thick wedding ring matched his gold badge. "Whoever Cassidy was running errands for didn't get caught up in your net and he hasn't named them, as I suspect you know."

He must have worked the phones hard about Zack since he'd come back from dealing with Brian. "I didn't know that. I didn't ask."

The laced fingers rose, flattened. "What I'm asking you—again— is whether, in the time you put into that situation, you heard or saw something that would help us. You must have seen things. She must have told you things."

"One more time, just for the hell of it—I told the police everything I know."

He moved a coffee cup from the corner of his desk closer to the center. "Word is you were in her pocket and angling to get closer. Word is you'd still like to be. I asked you last time if you had any conversations with her. Had any since then?"

Could he possibly be shadowing her? Then he'd know about her visit to my camper. If he did, let him call me on it. "I saw her Tuesday when that horse got loose. She didn't have a lot of time for conversation."

"Yeah, I heard about that horse. More strange stuff you're involved in. And one more time, from what I hear, when you didn't see anything that would help."

I didn't answer. So he didn't know everything Jenny was doing— but seemed to want to. The coffee cup got moved another couple of inches. "We've had a death now," he went on. "You don't want to expose Ms. Silver to any suspicion—" he put a hand up as my mouth came open, "—that's obvious, but you don't care about any physical danger she might be in."

I fought to bury an angry reaction. Maybe she was in danger, but not from anything he was asking about. I had no call to hand her over to him when for all I knew she had done nothing wrong. But I was tired of the way he kept using her to bait me. "If you think that kind of threat will make me invent things that didn't happen, sorry. My mind doesn't work that way."

He shook his head, a move so slight maybe he didn't mean for me to notice. He laced his fingers again. "I'm sure you know this—dangers to others aside, there are penalties for withholding relevant information."

"Apparently we disagree about what's relevant."

"I just want you to be aware of the chances you're taking. You might not like the way they turn out."

Yep, more bullying. In fact, threatening. I quashed another dumb retort and stood. " Maybe once you ask the right people, you'll find out what you what you want to know."

His brows went up, stayed up. "The right people?"

I said over my shoulder, "Definitely not me."

But from behind me his voice came. "Mr. Slaughter."

Not Robb now. I looked back.

"I saw you have a history," he said. He rubbed his knuckles against his teeth, blocking what looked like a chuckle. "Let's call it a history of maybe taking other people's problems a little too personally. Maybe in ways that go pretty close to the edge."

Yep, he was fishing. Two cases now and from the look of it no clues in either. "Sometimes over the edge can be the right side of . . ." Again I got my mouth tamed. I shrugged.

"Yeah, I know," he said as he reached for his glasses. "Justice." He sighed like he was remembering something so far gone it wasn't worth explaining. "You can get in a lot of trouble thinking justice is your job."

CHAPTER 24

At DINNER NATURALLY the kids wanted to chatter about Brian. Brett said if we heard anything we'd tell them. "Let's not get caught up in rumors."

"They all do that stuff over there at Skyhaven," said Scott.

"Over where?" said Sherrin.

"The barn with the fountain," said Cadence.

"Let's just wait on this," said Brett. "Like I said, right now it's all rumors."

"Should someone tell the police about this Skyhaven?" said Taylor's dad. "I mean, if—"

"I've got a feeling someone will," Brett said.

I'd been distracted trying to process Wardle's tactics. He seemed more interested in implicating Jenny than protecting her. Maybe I had finally sent the message I wasn't going to help him make her life any worse than I already had. Fortunately, before anyone noticed I wasn't paying attention, the food came and Taylor started on a tale about Cadence once trying to eat a whole tomato and ending up looking like blood was coming out of her mouth. That made for a more appetizing subject. Jorge started teaching Scott the Spanish names of all the dishes on the table, and we got out of there without Brian coming up again.

During the meal, my phone vibrated. I looked down. Valerie. Brett saw me looking. I dismissed it. We both dismissed calls during dinners; it was a policy we'd made long ago. A moment later came the ding of a voice mail.

He came to the camper to get Dozer before heading to the La Quinta. "What did Wardle want?"

"He thought I might have seen or heard something when I was around Zack."

He went on playing tug-of-war with Dozer over a frayed lead rope.

"I didn't."

Still silence. I poured a finger of bourbon, sat on the bunk.

Finally he said, "A cop asked me about you and Jenny."

I sighed. Who else around me was getting those kinds of questions? "Seriously? What did you say?"

"What do you think I said? I said she hates your guts."

"Thank you."

"Jenny could have been mixed up with Zack in the drug shit."

"Maybe. I've never asked."

Dozer slung his head with his usual bear grunts and growls. Brett held steady, didn't pull back. "So that was it with Brian? Drugs."

"Wardle didn't have the coroner's report."

"Let's hope this shit stops with Brian. This gets out of hand, they could shut the whole series down."

Not impossible. In my head I did a quick take on how much our barn would lose in coaching revenue if that happened. And what I'd lose that had nothing to do with our bank account. "Maybe whoever's supplying the stuff will be a lot more careful."

He surrendered the rope to Dozer, who collapsed at his feet, gnawing. "They found out anything yet about Romp?"

"Not from the looks of it."

"They'll never get the creep who did that."

For him, creep was a mild word. Like he couldn't think of one ugly enough. He got up, dusting his jeans. "For fuck's sake, try to keep us out of it."

"It's not like I'm trying to get us in it."

He maneuvered Dozer out the door and down the steps toward his truck where it waited. He looked back up at me. "Quit mixing it up with that reporter. She's trouble."

"She's harmless."

He shook his head before he closed the truck door between us. "Fuck she is."

Once the truck disappeared, I pulled up Valerie's voice mail. "Got your woman," said the message. "And more. Call me."

It was past eleven. She didn't answer. Sure as shit, she'd turn up tomorrow in the middle of classes, her every appearance not only making people wonder what I was messing in but also riling Brett. I left my own voice mail. "Tomorrow's crazy. Sunday, too. I can't talk to you in person." I'd have to find ten minutes when no one around me was paying any attention. "I'll call you before dinner tomorrow night."

Saturday was as crazy as I expected. We had multiple conflicts, with Raul and Jorge and Martha running from in-gate to in-gate shuffling our horses around in the order so Brett and I could get off Snap and Zenith and Growly in time to coach our riders. You get used to that hoopla. Teaches you focus. We didn't win any classes, but picked up high ribbons in all our divisions. Every jumper earned a check.

There was no official mention of Brian. No police driving visibly in and out. No one in management showed any interest in shutting down the series; like with the attack on Romp, the hundreds of thousands in entries already banked had a lot to say about that. Jorge had heard from one of Dever's grooms about half Dever's barn being roped off with police tape and some sort of drugs found in Brian's tack trunk. Apparently some of the other trunks had been searched. A Mexican groom had disappeared; the police were looking for him, Jorge said somberly, busy brushing out Jane's tail. It seemed to me that he and Raul stayed closer to our aisle than usual, but that could have been just me.

I supposed I could have told Wardle about the Skyhaven bunch. But that was where Brian had ridden, where he'd been found. So that situation would get enough attention without my contribution. Sure, any kind of drug stuff could lead to all sorts of crimes, including, I supposed, attacks on horses, but what I was piecing together about the Paxtons and their million-dollar jumper seemed a lot more relevant to the attack on Romp than Zack's petty drug dodge. A kid's misadventures had turned out tragic, but what went on around the diamond fountain was the kind of problem Wardle should be well-equipped to handle. It wasn't like I was withholding what little I had learned about Zack from Jenny. That was one thing Wardle was right about. I didn't have to let myself be dragged into every heartache that came along.

The million-dollar chestnut didn't show. Greg Drakow turned up to hack their Dutch horse, presumably to loosen him up for tomorrow's Grand Prix. Ricoeur's bald-faced stud didn't show, either, but he picked up checks with two of his other horses, Jenny holding them at ringside for him to make the switch.

Seeing Drakow called up his winning ride on Romp at the first series Grand Prix. I'd heard they could finally handwalk Romp in the mornings, drugged up. Pitiful, dropped two hundred pounds. I thought about stealing ten minutes to drift over there, glance in. Then Bernie rode up on Gildy, five trips to her round, and it was time to focus again.

Once more, I got lucky. When we'd bathed and fed the horses, Brett took everybody, parents and all, on a tour of the mobile tack shops clustered in a field beyond the rings. New coats, new breeches, new helmets for the kids; try on boots, talk endlessly about how a coat fell, ooh and aah over rhinestone studded browbands, as if the horses cared. During those excursions I always looked for some urgent task only I could complete. I had one that day.

Around seven I took a chair out by the wash racks. Valerie answered, said, "So what's this about some kid and an OD?"

Shit. Not where I wanted her investing her energy. "Ask Wardle. He'll give you the *New York Times* angle."

She scoffed. "A bunch of rich kids coking up is not New York Times material. Not like Russian oligarchs."

"So are we any closer to nailing any Russians?"

"Well, I did talk to Marci Hagen for about twenty minutes. She even sent me some pictures. Says ol' Solomon's not a superstar but he's perfect for her."

"Terrific."

She warmed to what she had to tell me. "So where did she get him, what did she pay? She did wonder why I was asking. I told her I was thinking about getting back into riding and I'd found this horse that I thought might come from the same place she got him, Sommergate, and I wanted to know how it went with her. She asked me how I knew about her buying him, and I said USEF records. Hope that was all right."

"Okay."

"Anyway, she said she didn't think Solomon had come from Sommergate. I said it was on his records and she said she hadn't looked back that far. Then she said—by this time we were pretty chatty—she got him from a woman who'd had a really bad experience with the dealer *she* got him from."

What path would that horse's life have taken? From Sommergate straight to a dealer? Dealers often bought and sold horses like cheap stocks: buy a lot, buy low, mark up, sell fast. They could trade in nice horses, but not likely Grand Prix horses. If a dealer was the buyer from Sommergate, that horse fell hard.

"Anyway," Valerie was going on, "seems this other woman— Marci's friend, who she got him from—was told Solomon was going to be a champion, sold for a million dollars or something, but this dealer was giving her a break. Said the dealer showed the woman a bill of sale for a million plus, presumably from when the previous owners bought him, so she believed him. She was going to pay some astronomical price thinking he had a great future, but the person she took lessons from said Solomon wasn't worth a tenth of what she'd agreed to pay. Marci said there was some kind of lawsuit, the dealer saying the woman had committed to buy and she'd cost him another sale. Best I could get from Marci, this woman got Solomon at some kind of reduced price in a settlement, and then she didn't like him, never showed him. Marci got him for ten K."

"Did you get this other woman's name?"

"Can't you get that through the USEF?"

"Not if she never showed him." Horses had gone through our barn where we acted as brokers; others we bought and sold but never showed. We weren't required to report our ownership to the USEF if we never showed the horses in our names. If we put up our own money, we had bills of sale both ways for our protection, but no one looking up the horses through the USEF would know we'd been involved.

In my ear Valerie was silent. Finally she said, "I think Marci might tell me the name. Or maybe there're court records."

"Whether the dealer the other woman did business with actually bought the horse or just tried to broker a sale, we're back to the main question: who was *he* dealing with, where did the bill of sale he showed Marci's friend come from? Who claimed to have paid Sommergate that big price?"

"Hmmm." Concentration tightened her voice. "So we're sticking with the idea that somebody—Sommergate, probably—sold him for a lot of money. Then he ended up on the skids. Or he wasn't worth that much to start with. But don't people pay more than they should for these critters all the time?"

"Sure. Selling a horse for more than it's worth is the name of the game for some people. But if it happens enough, people will figure it out."

Her voice went skeptical. "So you're saying that if somebody kept selling horses for inflated prices, people would notice. Why haven't they?"

"That's one thing it would be good to find out."

Her voice went gritty with even more challenge. "And this dealer—do people like that really get taken that easily? Wouldn't somebody like that have a pretty good idea what a horse is worth?"

"People are funny about horses. Everybody wants to be the expert. Especially pros, they buy a bad horse, they don't like it broadcast. Sounds like this one got suckered by a chance to make a big score, then wanted to hide he'd been scammed."

"But if he told this woman Solomon really was that good . . ."

She was reaching deeper than I wanted. Once she got her teeth in, she'd be like Dozer, latched on. But if I was going to keep using her, I needed to keep her gnawing. "Maybe the people who paid too much for the horse knew exactly what they were doing."

She went silent again. Then: "I'll see if I can find the dealer."

I checked the time. Raul would have set up the ponies and the hunters, but I still had to do Snap and Zenith. "Keep sticking with phone calls. Don't let anyone know how to find you."

"Excuse me, I'm not stupid."

Hell no, she wasn't. "Text me when you know something."

She laughed, not sweetly. "I'll either text you or the *New York Times*."

Everything Valerie had told me fed my growing theory of what the Paxtons might have been up to. I still had to figure out exactly how their schemes put Romp in that trailer. At least Valerie seemed willing to wait for more facts before texting the *New York Times*.

I was the one who had to tamp down my hope things were starting to happen. I fought the urge to look down the line to see how close the wall was. I needed my head level. But I couldn't help being a little pumped. What I'd said about this dealer being suckered gave us a chance. If you were trying to screw somebody, the last thing you wanted to give them was facts to check. From the sound of it, this one had wanted that sale bad enough to flash around the kind of documentation I needed, probably with names.

I wanted those names. Anyone who paid all that money for Solomon didn't give a shit about reputation, not like legitimate dealers and trainers did. For serious professionals, buying and selling bad horses was nuts. People didn't pay big money for horses because they wanted to build equity like in real estate or to earn back a purchase price. They wanted to campaign them. They wanted to win. So top farms and trainers wanted to be known for handling winning horses. And when you sold one, you wanted it out there still winning so customers would flock to you for the next winner. You didn't want horses you sold to disappear into someone's back yard.

Whoever had bought Solomon XI from Sommergate wasn't worrying about whether he ended up in someone's back yard.

I tried out the chance the Paxtons were just bad judges of horses. Maybe they'd been really high on Solomon, on this chestnut they were showing, on the others Drakow had ridden for them. When they found out the horses were duds, the high sales prices would have been lucky windfalls.

But the show records hinted at more windfalls than luck could explain.

CHAPTER 25

SUNDAY MORNING WAS EVEN CRAZIER than Saturday. Management wanted classes ending in time for the big Grand Prix, which this week would start at three. A lot of the morning classes were flats, different divisions going simultaneously, a recipe for chaos made even more hectic with Rianne and Baby Jane entered in the Hunter Derby. On top of jogging from ring to ring, Brett and I had trips on Growly and Snap. Focus times ten. I'd scratched Zenith. Brett caught me in the aisle. "Why'd you do that? You okay?"

"I can't do him justice. I don't want him to have a bad trip."

"You okay to ride Snap?"

"If you had to strap me in the saddle I could still ride Snap."

He smiled at that, but it was a tight smile. "Don't guess it'll come to that."

Truth was, I'd grown super self-conscious about my riding. What might happen—no, had to happen—crouched on my shoulder at every stride. Sooner or later it was bound to snatch the reins when I needed to soften, belly-kick when I needed to squeeze. Riding well meant saying "I'm still here" to our clients, to Martha, the guys, and Brett. To me? *I'm still in control.* With Snap it wasn't so tough. I really could ride him with half my body and mind, though I did my best not to let that happen. But Zenith made it so much easier to look like I couldn't manage even the basics like not catching his mouth over a fence.

What helped that day was our riders' successes. Scott was second in his Medal division; if he could do a couple more summer shows, he might make Regionals. Rianne collected a nice check for third in the Derby. The girls were fourth and sixth in their Medals, but then Clown of all things won his Pony-Hunter flat class and surprised the shit out of me by ending up Reserve. Taylor didn't place Whisper in front of the judges like she knew how to; he was fifth, which was low for him. But she seemed really glad Cadence won.

My faith that I wouldn't fuck Snap up turned out worth trusting: one turn shorter and riskier and he would have won it all. Pat was gushing. I thought she was about to kiss me, but she veered off and kissed the horse.

I wished I could enlist Pat to chat up Dierdre Paxton, find out who they were selling that chestnut to. The horse hadn't showed again. Was it even still on the grounds? But I wanted to leave our little world of horses and friends whole behind me, and getting Pat involved would open a crack. It was bad enough with Brett watching every move I made like he'd have to rush in and pick up stuff I dropped.

This time at the Grand Prix I sat down low with everyone, part of our little cheering section in the stands. The kids all had favorites, horses they dreamed of riding and riders they were in love with. The only horse I wanted to see was the Paxtons' Dutchbred, trying to repeat his win from last week. He went early, went double clean, with a really fast time. The next three horses didn't even come close.

But I couldn't concentrate on the class. I kept hoping my phone would buzz with Valerie's call. Halfway through the class I saw Malloy across the ring, coaching his riders over the schooling jumps. Since my last talk with him, I hadn't just stayed away from his barn, I'd stayed away from asking anyone about Romp. Other people might echo Malloy's hint—and Wardle's, for that matter—that I was investing too much of myself in what had happened. And maybe I didn't really want to see too far into Romp's future. But now with Malloy busy coaching and all our folks concentrating on the arena before them, I found myself wanting to sneak a quick look. See if the horse had anything new to tell me. I said to Pat, who was sitting beside me, "Be back in a bit." When I swung by our barn, Jorge and Raul stood with their backs to the wall, facing a uniformed cop.

I hadn't realized they weren't in the stands with the rest of us. All three men looked around when I walked up.

"Mr. Crider?" the cop said.

"No, Slaughter. His partner. What's this?"

"Couple questions," said the cop.

He was a young white guy, starchy in blue. He wore a Ranger-style hat, his shaved scalp showing at the back. I looked at Raul and Jorge. "What's he asking you about?"

Jorge jutted his chin, sort of at a whole lot of places. "If we know Juaquim Navarro."

"Who?"

"Kid we want to talk to," said the cop.

Rumor said the kid ran because he was illegal, not because he was into the drug stuff. "Anything he wanted to know Wardle could have asked me."

"Seems he did," the cop said.

I handled that in my head for a moment. Not part of this conversation. "These guys have things they have to do here."

"It's okay," said Jorge. "We're caught up."

He held my gaze, dark eyes steady. Raul looked off to the side, fingers digging in his pockets.

"Okay with you, Raul?" I asked.

"Yeah, sure." His gaze shot to me, then past.

I edged around until I got the tiniest bit between the guys and the cop. "We'll be going to dinner soon," I told the cop. "I owe them both a beer and I want them there to get it."

"Won't take half an hour."

"Fine then." Raul was tucking in his T-shirt. I waited but he didn't look at me. "As long as you're okay with it."

"Yes," Raul said.

Raul insisted on driving himself back from dinner while Jorge rode with me. I couldn't legitimately ask Jorge where Raul took off to. I did ask about the talk with the police. "We told them pretty much what everyone knows." He flipped a hand in dismissal. "Some of the kids were getting stuff. They need to talk to the kids."

"Did they hassle you?"

"They were very polite."

At least Wardle's troops hadn't watched too many tough-cop movies. Or maybe they'd gotten the memo that some of these men had friends. I tried to decide if Raul had looked keyed up at dinner, couldn't tell.

Brett deposited Dozer in the camper because he and Cindi were going to a movie. It was a gift that Dozer usually ended up tagging along with them. There was not only his volcanic snoring; too often

Brett left the bedroom door open, and the damn dog slurped water in the night like some kind of wallowing hippo, got in and out of my bed, stomping on my stomach half the time. No surprise, he was busy with his body parts on the bunk beside me when Valerie texted. "Call me tonight."

I punched her icon. "I think we hit a zinger," she said. "You need to talk to this guy."

"What did he say?"

"He seemed to think I had some connection to the outfit he got Solomon from. I said I was interested in knowing what happened to Solomon, his history, the people who'd owned him, and the guy seemed on a hair trigger about any clue I might be working for them."

"What's his name?"

She was eating something. I let her finish chewing so she could spell it. "Tock, T-O-C-K Mercer. I looked him up." She took on a flat tone, maybe reading. "Buys and sells quality horses, any sport."

"So thinking you had some connection to the outfit he got Solomon from pissed him off?"

"He said, 'Tell 'em to peddle their goddamn horses somewhere else.' Said he thought he made that clear long ago."

"He tell you why?"

"Seems to have to do with that woman Marci told me about. The one he sold Solomon to. He apparently thinks he got burned." At my end, Dozer had gone to sleep on my feet. At hers, dishes clattered. "That's why you need to go see him. You can talk the talk."

"Where is he?"

"Ellijay, Georgia. It's not that far."

"Actually, it is." No easy Interstate routes from where we were; more like weaving mountain driving. "I can't take off in the middle of a show."

"Don't you have tomorrow off? No showing? Besides, it's supposed to rain."

All I could see was the shitload I'd trigger if I took off out of the blue for some place in Georgia. "We have things to do."

Her voice took on a funny lilt. "Hey, kid, this is your rodeo, not mine."

"It's your *New York Times* byline."

"Hell, I'll share."

"Didn't you even get the name of the outfit he got Solomon from." That was what I'd banked on.

"He thought I had it."

"But if he got sued over trying to unload Solomon, there's records. Can't you find them?"

She was prompt. "Actually, there aren't any. From the look of it he cut his losses over Solomon before they got to court."

I gave Dozer a shove that might free my feet. "This is bullshit."

A loud clank. Like an exclamation mark after a curse. "I found him. And I found out there's something screwy about how he got that Solomon. That's two things. Remind me what you've done."

I sighed. She probably took my sigh to mean I was pissed, not tired and up against a wall. "Call him back."

"I'm about to hang up on you, Robb."

"Tell him you're—"

"When you've figured out what you're going to do next, text me." She hung up.

I eased my feet the rest of the way out from under Dozer. God help me if he woke up and clambered onto my gut. He started snoring. I plugged in my headphones, but I didn't turn on any music. I stared at the sleeping dog.

Yes, Mondays were dark. But Snap, Zenith, and Flight had early Tuesday classes. Claryce had decided to stay over, and that would commit us to dinner Monday night. Zenith would need to be hacked since I'd scratched him on Sunday. Brett had never left me holding the bag the way Valerie thought I could leave him. If I wanted to trigger the earthquake I'd been avoiding, I couldn't think of a surer way.

What it came down to, I couldn't have everything I wanted. Sooner or later I'd have to make choices. Sooner had caught up with me. I looked up Mercer online.

An LLC, go figure. Like Valerie said, he handled all kinds of stock. Probably as a broker, keeping an eye out for people looking for certain kinds of horses and people selling horses like that. Photos of his place—a big warehouse-type barn and arena—confirmed my judgment: he didn't deal in high-priced jumpers. He didn't boast about recent spectacular sales.

I called up a maps app. Three hours driving time from where I was to his place.

Surely you could talk the talk over the phone. I'd make time tomorrow for that talk. About when I decided that was how to work it, Dozer flopped over and plastered his smelly blubber on top of me exactly like I'd expected. Maybe it was his warm heartbeat against my shoulder that coaxed me into a restless sleep.

I didn't order up the wild weather for Monday, and I didn't call on some powers-that-be to answer my prayers. Once the rain started, it was clear my life had arranged itself so the only excuse I had for not tackling Mercer was that I'd piss Brett off. The day was fast coming when pissing Brett off would be the least I had to worry about.

No point in calling Mercer before daybreak. I hacked Zenith as the sky turned from black to smudgy, and even before full sunrise I could feel the dirty day coming, a lot worse than our weather apps had prophesied. The air piled around us, "like snot," according to Brett.

By eleven we were all dripping with sweat just standing around. The mares had lather between their butt cheeks and they hadn't been out of their stalls. We hung the fans, first time we'd needed them all summer. Martha and the guys were taking turns leading the horses to the wash racks to rinse them when Brett held up his phone for me: a big line of storms sweeping out of the northwest.

"Great." Three years before, the grounds had been hit by a deluge and the creek that circled the back paddocks had burst its banks. All the rings had flooded. They'd canceled three divisions because there wasn't time to reschedule the classes. "My app showed rain this morning," Martha said, "but that looks like more than rain." She handed me the bucket she was using to sponge Growly with liniment. "I should get Whisper out now." He'd turn destructive in his stall if he didn't have some fresh-air time.

She rigged the pony in a lunging harness and headed out. But she was back fast, a snapping wind behind her. "Lightning. The other side of the ridge. Thunder came up quick." Whisper trooped obediently back into his stall, where he immediately started molesting his water bucket. Dozer slunk into the tack stall, curling behind our medicine trunk where he didn't really fit.

"I'm taking him to the camper," Brett said.

"Put him in the bedroom." So he'd pee in Brett's bed, not mine.

"He'll be happier here," said Martha.

"Yeah, and he'll thank us by devouring the nearest bridle." Brett hauled him out into the aisle. "I'll throw him one of Robb's tennis shoes. He'll love that."

He was gone only minutes before the announcement came over the speakers. "In the barn area. We're getting severe weather warnings. We're closing the rings. You might want to tie things down. Stay inside and stay safe."

By two o'clock the rising creek had turned the jumper rings to a dirty sheet, poles and panels floating as if a big boat had gone down. Once the first squalls passed, Jorge and Martha and I joined a crowd in ponchos and muck boots going out to see. "Beating the hell out of those jump standards," said Martha. "It's still rising," Jorge said.

Back in our barn, the five of us spent an hour talking to the horses. They were used to heavy rain on the metal roofs of our barns at home, but the crash and flare of the lightning had set them circling in their stalls. I wondered if Romp in his darkness heard the rattle as crackling. At least when the wind died, our bunch settled. But we wouldn't be lunging or riding any of them soon.

Quarter to three came another announcement. "Folks, we're postponing tomorrow morning's classes. We'll aim for a two-o'clock start time on the published Tuesday p.m. schedule. We'll let you know about the morning classes once we get the times sorted. Weather service says we should expect rain until early tomorrow morning, but no more flooding, so that's good news."

Martha and Jorge went down to the rings again and reported that the ebb hadn't started but the flood had stalled. Brett and I did some tack repair we'd been putting off; then he wiped his hands on his jeans and said, "I'm gonna run over to Cindi's for a while."

"Take Dozer with you."

"He'll be calmer in the camper."

My mouth had already decided what it was going to tell him. "I might take off somewhere myself. I might not be there later to take him out."

He stopped in midstride on the way down the aisle. Normally I wouldn't have made a big deal out of a quick run somewhere on a Monday. And he wouldn't have asked or cared. I zipped up my helmet bag. "I might go look at a horse I heard about."

He knew if I was telling the truth I'd say what kind of horse, where it was. He wanted to question me, I saw that, but not about some horse.

He ended up saying, "See you later, then."

In my poncho I splashed to one of the pavilions between the rings. The raised deck was deserted, chair and tables stacked, some blown over by the storm. Unfolding a chair, I took out my phone, keyed in the number for this Tock Mercer guy.

CHAPTER 26

THE PHONE PROVED USELESS. Some woman wanted to know my business with Mr. Mercer and when I wouldn't play, told me Mr. Mercer wasn't available, what could she do for me? What I could do for me, it became clear, was not piss her off. I had to agree to look at live horses before she finally penciled me in for the morning if I could be there by eight. By the time she gave in, I could have been a fifth of the way there.

The storm tracked me every inch of the way. My app said mountains were faster than the roundabout interstate option, but most of the drive I couldn't see the road in front of me for the spray off all the trucks and cars taking the same route. I spent a grim, Benadryl-sodden night in a Motel 6. I was choking down motel waffles and bilge coffee when Martha called.

"You didn't tell me what you want me to do with Snap."

I'd meant to text her but in my exhaustion I'd forgotten. "Is it still raining?"

"You mean here?"

"Yeah, there. Rent a paddock and turn him out."

"Can't. Everybody's beat us to them."

"Then maybe lunge him. If you can't don't worry, he'll be all right."

"Robb, where the hell are you?"

She'd never before had to ask such a question. "His class won't go till three at the earliest. I'll be there."

"Pat's on her—"

"Martha, I will be there."

"Sorry, sorry. Everything's all fucked up with the weather."

"I know."

169

Driving from the motel, I argued to myself that my only lie to Brett had been one of omission. Maybe I could square this betrayal. From the look of his website, Mercer bought and sold a lot of good-looking Appendix-registered—half-Thoroughbred—Quarter Horses. Some of our nicest junior and amateur horses in our early years had been Appendix. They tended to combine Thoroughbred spark with good Quarter Horse brains. Maybe I could fool a whole raft of people by "looking at a horse."

The online pictures had prepared me for Mercer's warehouse operation: an indoor arena with banks of stalls around the outside. A light dust filtered over the huge ring, smelling of close-packed horseflesh and a sweet note of good hay. The website said Mercer sometimes ran Western or roping or barrel-racing events in the well-lit space. His office took up a corner at the end of one of the long rows of stalls.

He grunted "Come" when I knocked. He got up from his desk to reach across for my hand. He was shorter than me, thick-built, with chunky arms and thighs. His square face was creased with a grin that looked permanently chiseled. I got the impression he wanted me to see the Rolex on his wrist.

Dust coated some of the things in the office, like the framed pictures of Saddlebreds and Western ribbon ceremonies and a couple of big, round-butted Paints. On his desk sat two bronzes of cutting horses. The sculptures looked pricey enough to make your eyes pop if you stumbled across them in some fancy store.

"So you buyin' or sellin'?" he asked with the grin.

"Right now, maybe buying." From the first second, this was dicey. He wouldn't like being strung along; plunging right in felt less risky. "But actually, I made a trip down here from a show we're at up in Timberburg to ask for your help."

The grin dimmed. He settled into his high-backed black leather chair, waved at a similar one in front of the desk. I sat, not leaning back. He put an ankle across a knee. "That so?"

"A woman who works for me—" Valerie would love that, "—called you the other day."

Nope, the grin wasn't permanent. He gripped his chair arms, chin going up. "Son of a bitch."

"She didn't work for the people connected to that horse, Solomon XI. Neither do I." At least he gave me time to talk. "I had a problem with some of the people who once owned him. I heard

170

from a woman named Marci Hagen, a friend of the woman you sold Solomon, that you did, too."

Only part of a lie. I wondered if he could tell which part. "So what the fuck do you want from me?"

I wanted him to let me keep going. "It's not actually the Solomon horse I'm interested in," I lied. "But based on what Ms. Hagen's friend told her about you and Solomon, I just think he's an example of this problem with my customer and a horse *she* bought." I'd pieced together what might have happened if I'd been in his shoes. "A dealer—" his brows went up, lips jutting, "—not like you. It wasn't anybody registered with any of the professional organizations." Especially since this dealer was my invention. "Anyway, the dealer sold her a horse, told her that the people he'd bought the horse from had paid a lot of money to some LLC for him. Like a million dollars. Had her talked into a big price because he was some kind of potential Grand Prix star."

I wanted him to consider what he had in common with me. For example, the desire to do right by clients. He waved some fingers, brows still up. I continued, "Horse wasn't worth a hundredth of a million. She got a lawyer. The dealer she'd bought the horse from claimed he'd been scammed."

The stories should intersect. Mine was close to what Marci had told Valerie, with Mercer the "scammed" dealer who'd tried to sell a horse he'd been told was worth a lot. I detected a motion of his chin, I hoped a subconscious nod. The trickiest part was coming up.

"Anyway, the dealer is using this line about how much *he* paid for the horse to get her to settle for a lot less of a refund than she's owed. But he won't cough up a bill of sale or proof anybody ever paid the first LLC a million dollars, so we can get an idea of whether he got burned."

He put steepled fingers to his mouth, a forefinger stroking his pursed lips. "You're saying he actually bought this horse himself before he went to sell it?"

"We don't know."

The finger rubbed hard. He rocked back. "Nobody with smarts buying and selling horses would sink his own cash in a deal like that."

"You didn't, then?"

For a moment he glowered. But he crossed his hands on his gut. "I think you know how this business works."

171

I did know. He'd almost certainly reached an agreement with whoever owned Solomon—presumably the outfit that claimed it paid Sommergate a big price for him. This outfit and Mercer set a price Mercer would give them if he found a buyer for the horse. Then he'd piled a big killing on top of that price, suckering his own customer with a claim she was getting a bargain. I didn't spell that out; jacking up prices was perfectly legal. And maybe even mildly ethical, if the bill of sale he'd waved around was real.

So I nodded, veering away from what we both knew Mercer had done. "We don't know whether the dealer my customer bought from staked his own money, but like I said, he justified his price based on what he said the previous owners paid for the horse. But he doesn't have any proof of that. No bill of sale."

Mercer's eyes narrowed thoughtfully. "You think maybe he got scammed by the same outfit that scammed me. Like they're some kind of common denominator in a pattern."

Another nod. I had to hope the glint in those eyes meant he was wondering if the "outfit that scammed me" might be in for a little comeuppance. People like Mercer (and my fictional dealer) wouldn't be experts in Grand Prix horses and would make easy marks for someone wanting to get rid of a jumper cheap but not too cheap.

"So," he said after a long pause, "you heard of an outfit called Sommergate?"

I hadn't wanted to be the one to name Sommergate, since the transaction with the Paxtons I was about to claim was pure lies. "USEF records show Solomon started out at Sommergate. The horse my customer bought did, too. So yeah, maybe a pattern. Who knows what this middleman who buys these horses actually pays Sommergate, but he tells dealers it was a lot so his price looks like a steal. Maybe he comes up with a sob story, divorce or taxes or something, to explain why he's taking a loss."

He blinked. Hardly an admission that I'd hit close to the truth. He rolled his hands off his belly, thumbs up. "So again, what do you want from me?"

Keeping it simple would probably work best. "The name of the outfit that came to you peddling Solomon, saying they'd paid big money for him."

"No reason to assume it's the same outfit. A lot of people could be buying horses from this Sommergate and selling them for jacked-up prices."

I shrugged. "But like you said, the pattern fits. The way both horses started out at Sommergate and ended up with a dealer scammed."

He came up with a different version of the grin, thinner, ticking at the corners. "You don't just want the name, you want some sign how much this outfit actually paid Sommergate for Solomon. You think that'll tell you whether your dealer is bluffing about what they told him. What makes you think I know that?"

I could hold back the one card I held with Mercer, but I'd come a long way to clench this. "Ms. Hagen's friend says *you* got a bill of sale."

"And your dealer didn't do that."

"He won't cough up the price or the name."

"Well, Mr. Slaughter." He shifted forward, then twisted in his chair. "I'm real sorry for your customer, like I was sorry for mine. I don't want to get mixed up in any more of this kind of shady business. I got no idea if the people that pushed that horse on me are the same outfit you're after, and I don't want to make no accusations. The last thing I need is to get dragged into court over a horse I've never seen."

Shit. I understood him. I could guess why he'd settled with Marci's friend out of court, even if the bill of sale gave him a good defense. She could make a big stink in the local horse world about how he'd tried to bilk her, and showcase how he'd been taken in himself. If he admitted he had the names and sums I wanted, who knew, I might go get myself a subpoena. He might even have to admit the big killing he'd made on Solomon even after cutting his price. Why open himself up to someone else's woes when he'd dodged his own?

But as he spoke, he opened a file cabinet behind him. He gave a short laugh. "Now if you want to look at some horses . . ." He laid a sheet of paper from the cabinet where I could see it. "What exactly you looking for?"

I reached to pull the sheet toward me. He stopped it with his finger, shook his head. I took out my phone to take a picture. He shook his head again.

"Like hunter stock?" he asked. "I've got a couple of nice young horses. Make your trip worthwhile."

I read the sheet before me. Spelled it out in my head so I'd have a hope of remembering it. A bill of sale for Solomon XI. An LLC,

Kristoff Fields, Terrell Bowles, agent, had paid Sommergate a million two for Solomon XI.

I said, "I love to look at horses. I've got time."

He slid the sheet back, returned it to its slot. He picked up the phone. "Hey, Reg, I got a guy here wants to look at horses. Hunter types. Show him that Gold Tempest horse and that mare from Fenton. Slaughter's this guy's name. Yeah."

He stood. I pushed up. "Hope your client gets a good deal," he said. "Sorry I couldn't help you more."

CHAPTER 27

I GOT A COUPLE OF VIDEOS that might make the trip look marginally kosher and texted Martha I was on the way, ETA before one. She answered promising to have everything ready. "Everything" covered a lot of ground.

The rain had stopped. Once on clear roads, I texted Valerie what I'd entered into my phone after the talk with Mercer: Kristoff Fields, the address, the agent's name. I gave her time to get the message then called her on the truck speaker. "The guy's dying to stick it to this outfit but he didn't want to be on the record. He made sure I couldn't prove he told me anything."

"So we know what now?"

"That Sommergate does sell cheap horses for astronomical prices. To this Kristoff Fields, at least."

"That tells us what about what happened to Romp?"

"Nothing yet. We need more information. Like who this Kristoff Fields is, what's their deal."

She snorted. Annoyingly. "Mercer sounds like a pushover."

"He got greedy."

"I mean for you."

"You weren't all that eager to do the pushing."

This time a scoff, from back in her throat. "I know how to delegate. If you get him in trouble, he'll sue you, not me."

"I'll remember that the next time you tell me I'm not pulling my weight."

"Whatever. I'll see what I can find out about this Kristoff Fields."

"If you can't call before two, wait till after eleven." I'd be pulling my weight somewhere else till then.

Heading home I chewed over what I'd learned. Whatever was going on with Sommergate sounded less and less like insurance fraud. According to the bill of sale I'd seen, they *had* sold Solomon to this Kristoff Fields for north of a million. Maybe if Valerie tracked down the current owners of a couple of the other Sommergate castoffs, we'd find more connections to Kristoff Fields.

Meanwhile I had to keep Valerie hobbled. She'd figured out that the idea I was toying with didn't involve insurance, but I didn't want her running with her own version. I didn't like her between me and my distance. I had a lot to figure out still; a couple of questions to the wrong people could mess me up good.

One thing I'd concluded: if the scam had nothing to do with insurance, it had nothing to do with Jenny's story. I hadn't told Valerie about the drugs in the feed, so at least she couldn't hassle me about that.

I tinkered with pieces of the theory. In the case of Solomon, either Kristoff Fields had been ripped off by Sommergate or they knew exactly what they were paying for. Or maybe they hadn't paid anything. Anyone could write a number in a blank space in a document like that.

So then I wondered, why would you put down a number like that if it wasn't accurate? Apparently the number had worked on Mercer, inspiring him to take on selling Solomon thinking he could get top dollar for him. For all I really knew, he could have written that number himself.

At a fast food stop I looked up "Kristoff Fields" on my phone. Miracle of modern technology, I found it in LLC records, registered in Connecticut, not Delaware. But it had gone "inactive" two years after Sommergate sold Armistice and one year after they dumped Solomon. I slid that tidbit into my mental files.

The bottom line was that a big number showed big money changing hands. Turning cash into tangibles, my cousin Phil had said. As a rule, horse people did the opposite, turned tangibles into cash. Maybe you could do both at once, with the right number on that line.

As I put the miles home behind me, I crept closer to believing Dyan's story. That they do this "all the time."

I made it to the showgrounds by 12:30. Martha met me at the tack stall wiping leather balm off her hands. "You got time, take a breather."

"I'm okay. Rianne and Bernie here?"

"Down at the tack shops. Brett's at the camper." She didn't ask if she should let him know I was back.

The weather had gone flat, cloudy and damp but no rain. I went in to see Snap. He ignored me, dozing over a pile of half-eaten hay. Zenith was asleep, too. The way I liked him. When I came out from Zenith, Brett stood outside Growly's stall unzipping shin boots to put on him. He made the fastener pop as it came apart. "So did you buy us a horse?"

I double-checked Zenith's latch, finding stuff to look at. "Got videos of some."

"Ride any?"

"No."

Martha loitered nearby watching. But it was Brett I was going to have to settle with. "I'll show you the videos later."

"Yeah, I'll make popcorn." He went into Growly's stall. It was too early to be putting boots on, but he did it anyway.

Sooner or later all the shit I'd been ducking had to come crashing down.

I couldn't keep on not sleeping and thinking about what I was going to do or not do and what it would be like on the other side of the wall and still be able to do justice to a horse.

Two horses.

The worst was how little Brett said.

We'd moved Snap up to meter-thirty, the same class as Growly and Flight. We got Zenith in his meter-twenty early so he'd be done and the other two would have time to school. The jump crews had dragged the rings to make the footing safe, and the course designer had modified the courses to prevent slips on tight, sloppy corners, especially in the jump-offs. It should have been okay.

In the schooling ring Zenith couldn't seem to find where to put his feet. Brett watched him manage barely decent distances over the simple schooling verticals. All he said was, "He'll pay more attention in the ring." By the grace of some god I knew better than to call on, he went clean. He had a rail in the jump-off because I didn't set up well out of the corner. Brett said, "Okay."

With Snap, I thought, all I had to do was get the stride I needed and maintain. But somewhere between coming around the corner to the schooling oxer and getting to the base I figured out what had happened with Sommergate and the million dollar horses and Romp. And suddenly I was locked into that distance to the future as plainly as I should have been to the distance Snap had settled on to the fence. All my determination collapsed into tremors. Every muscle in my body did not want to go to that spot.

The next thing I heard was the clatter of falling poles and the deep thud of a horse's body hitting the ground. The crash reeled past me in flashes as I rolled. I had time to think, "rotational," the kind that breaks a horse's neck and crushes the rider he lands on, but then I was up in the wet sand and Snap was trotting away. Figures I identified as people ran after him. The only one who came to me was Brett. "You okay?"

"Yeah." My shoulder felt jammed but not dislocated. That wasn't where the pain was. "I didn't see it. I didn't think he'd be crazy enough to leave."

Brett looked at me, his mouth open like his words were sticking somewhere. He took off, like everybody else, after the horse.

Around me trainers and grooms were lifting the fallen standards. I picked up a pole. A groom took it from me, silently nodding, grinning too, maybe because he didn't know the English for *here, I'll fix what you broke.*

Brett came leading Snap. Beyond him, among the almost unidentifiable figures watching from the fence, was Pat.

"I don't think you should ride the class," Brett said.

"What?"

"You're off, like the other day. Something. I don't know what it is, but it's fucking with the horse."

"That's crazy. I'm fine."

"Yeah."

You can put a lot of history in one word. A lot of punishment. A word that said, *we've never ever lied to each other before but now you have.* I made myself say "Yeah" back. He handed me the reins. "Okay."

Someone had run my irons up. I led Snap to the mounting block, pulled the stirrups down, positioned him to get on. A hand touched my back, on the arch of my shoulder where the weight hurt. Pat said, "Is he all right?"

I hadn't looked at him. Hadn't even asked that question. I guessed I thought Brett had. "He looks okay." So useless. Pat's face, her buried loss always there, seemed more fragile than ever. "I'll see how he is."

"Are *you* okay?"

I couldn't get "yes" out. She touched my arm. "Robb, I think you should let Brett ride him today."

Someone at my shoulder said, "Do you mind if we get there, please?" I was in the way of the mounting block. I said, "Sorry," and led Snap behind Pat.

Pat didn't play the standard record we all used: *It's only this one class. We all have falls.* She just said, "I don't want my horse hurt."

I had trouble handing her the reins. She fumbled them, dropping them between us. After a moment I picked them up.

She said, "I'm sorry."

I said, "I'll take him over there."

Brett took the reins. His eyes had never looked darker. I said, "You better fucking win."

His scoff wasn't a laugh. I thought he really didn't want to win. But he couldn't help it. The day was laid out that way. Pat stood at my shoulder and gave a hard little sigh as his blazing time went up.

I took Snap back and led him over to Raul as if the horse and I were still one. Snap didn't know the difference. They don't unless you hurt them. I didn't hurt him on purpose, and he knew I would not, ever. I didn't have to remind Raul to check him out thoroughly. He knew what to do after a fall.

Brett said, "I need you to watch Growly." Maybe he did. He could get into his own battles with horses, and both of us knew he was in a fighting mood. Probably he didn't know any other way to make things better. I said, "He's going through his left shoulder a little." Brett said, "Thanks, I didn't feel that." On the next schooling pass, he fixed the drift. Growly ended up third, behind Snap, time getting him the way it often did even when you were on a good horse.

At the barn the hunters were waiting, braided and glistening. Rianne and Bernie didn't mention Snap. I don't know what I would have done if either of them had had a bad school. As it was, my only job was to hand out familiar instructions, stuff they already knew, and tell them how good they were doing. Bernie had a good day; Gildy seemed to like the sloppy footing. Both hunters pinned.

Then we had to go to dinner and Rianne wanted to know if I'd seen any nice horses in Georgia. I said I had a couple of good videos.

Appendix horses. Brett and Martha started talking about all the nice Appendix horses we'd had. So that took care of dinner.

Except for the way Pat smiled at me way too much. What sat worst with me was the moment at ringside, when I realized she'd seen the torment take hold of me, a hunger I couldn't satisfy. It was bad enough when the ache inside me went snarling after the people around me. Now it wanted my horses, too.

CHAPTER 28

I LET EVERYONE BEAT ME AWAY FROM THE TABLE to duck the commiserating chats. But Brett didn't leave. The dining room had emptied so it was pretty much the two of us. He stood wadding used napkins and tossing them onto dirty plates as if cleaning up was his new job.

I folded my napkin, then rose and pushed my chair back. He kicked the chair beside him hard enough to rock it. "What the fuck, Robb?"

"I had a bad day. Shit happens."

"We've had maybe six bad days between us like that in eight years. There's always been a reason."

I was too tired to hide the edge I was a heartbeat from sliding over. "The very definition of 'shit happens' is that there's no reason," I heard myself snap. "It just happened."

He shoved the chair again. "It happened because you hadn't had any fucking sleep because you were trawling the damn countryside for some bizarre reason. I want to know where you went."

I took a breath. Could I hold off the meltdown a little longer? "I told you, to look at a horse."

"It must have been a hell of a horse."

"Horses." I rubbed my eyes, not clearing the haze of exhaustion. "I told you, I'll text you the videos."

He drew back blinking. "This is us."

That was one answer he'd set himself up for. "You spent the afternoon with Cindi. I spent the afternoon and a morning looking at horses. So yeah, this is us."

He scraped his hands on his trousers. He shook his head, not really at me.

181

After one of those seconds you're not sure you can live through, I asked him, "Aren't you worried Dozer's chewing up your seat covers?"

"Dozer doesn't eat anything he has to chew." He straightened. He couldn't quite fit the chair he'd kicked back under the table. "That fall could have been a lot worse."

Maybe he wanted me to say it wouldn't happen again. I couldn't. So much to get through. Wishing so hard I could keep him out of it.

"You staying in the camper tonight?"

He shrugged. "Don't know yet. Cindi's got more drama with her kid."

Cindi's son had a lot of problems. I'd heard about them over many a beer. "Sorry."

"Her worries." He sighed. "I'll go by the barn, make a last round." He circled the table, opened and closed the fist at his side, then shook himself. "Send me those videos."

He looked worn down walking out. I waited until I leveled my own breathing, then headed for the men's room. Once inside, I stood at the urinal willing my mental rattle to shut off. When I came out, he'd gone. With Cindi otherwise occupied, he'd almost certainly end up in the camper. I went into the adjoining bar and let the waiter bring me a Coke. Once she'd set the drink in front of me, I called Valerie. No answer. My watch showed ten-forty-five. I said, "If you can't call back in the next five minutes, don't call."

The phone rang about two minutes later. "Something going on there?" she asked.

"Yeah, my partner."

"He there now?"

"No."

"How much of this you keeping from him?"

There was only so much I owed her and that wasn't part of it. "So what did you find out?"

A silence like she might push. But she said, "That Kristoff Fields, get this. That LLC was dissolved four years ago. The year after Sommergate sold Solomon."

"Yeah, I did a quick search and saw that."

"They were only registered for three years. In Connecticut." Her voice dropped, like she was the one worried about someone hearing. "That's not the best part. The Kristoff Fields address on the Connecticut registration. It's the same address as on the court documents when Dierdre Paxton got into it with the insurance companies after the Arabian died."

I'd picked up the Coke. I set it down carefully.

"Did you hear me?" she said.

"Yeah."

"They owned both LLCs. The Paxtons. The one that sold those two horses and the one that bought them."

"Yeah."

"You can't tell me you figured this out."

"I sort of had."

"What else have you figured out you're not telling me?" She sounded like she'd come to a ditch she'd have to cross and she wasn't sure which side looked dicier. "Like about the Paxtons? Why they'd buy their own horse?"

I shouldn't have to explain to her. Probably didn't have to. "They're laundering money," I said.

A silence. Then, "So they have some money they can't spend because they can't report it to the IRS and they have to find some way to make it look like legitimate income."

"Their other, secret LLC pretends to 'buy' a horse from them. The only thing really that gets transferred is the money. Then they get rid of the horse itself, probably for enough to cover some of the capital gains tax they owe on the haul from the big sale."

More silence. Behind it, I could almost hear her brain clicking. "Why would they try to kill Romp? How could he be part of some money-laundering scheme?"

"I don't know yet."

Now the kind of silence before a pot boils over, and a pop in her voice after. "The word 'partners' occurs to me."

"I'm not keeping anything from you, I'm trying to work it out. I don't want to go around making accusations until I'm sure."

"Until *we're* sure."

I tried to put a shrug in my answer. "Then you see what you can come up with. When you've figured it out, tell me. Then we'll see where we are."

"We could go to the cops about the money-laundering. The Paxtons would have to talk then."

I stiffened, my neck muscles clenching. I'd seen, three strides out from the wreck of that schooling oxer, how Romp fitted in. If I shared that flash with Valerie, the next thing I knew, I'd find Wardle and his courtroom getting between me and the wall. I couldn't back off, but I had to make sure she did. "We're accusing people of fraud. We need proof. I don't want to get fucking sued."

"I bet we can get proof." A pause. "I can get it."

"Partners," I said, too quickly. "That means we tell each other before we do anything."

"I have this bad feeling you're going to do something crazy."

She couldn't see me shaking my head but I did anyway. "Not without telling you. I promise."

"Oh, so you *are* planning something crazy?"

"I'm just saying, wait till we see what else we dig up."

A sharp chortle. "And if I do dig up something, you want to tell me the five minutes out of your totally nuts life when we can talk?"

"Text me. I'll find a way to call you."

"Robb . . ."

"What?"

A new note. From somewhere deeper. "Here's another bad feeling. There's something you don't want this to be about, but sooner or later it will be."

"That's stupid. This is about a horse somebody tortured."

"Yeah." As if she thought I needed telling. "It is."

I took a big swig of the Coke, wanting the sugar. I needed it to spike the ball Valerie had tossed me. What she'd told me about Kristoff Fields slid into my plan for the Paxtons like a key into a lock. I didn't think I really had to worry she'd land on the same conclusion I had about what had happened to Romp, at least not before I could act. But I wasn't convinced I'd stopped her from nosing around the Paxtons. Warning them.

A shout down the bar made me jump. Two guys cheering a ball game on the overhead TV. A shadow fell over me. I thought it was the waiter, making last call or something. It was Jeff Carr.

With all the shit that had happened that day, I'd almost forgotten he existed. "Hiya, Robb." He slid into the chair opposite before I fully registered him as a flesh-and-blood body. "Let me buy you that beer."

An impulsive "No" almost escaped me, but the waiter descended. "What'll it be?" Carr asked.

I nudged my Coke glass. "I'm fine."

"Ice all melted," said Carr. To the waiter, "Bring me a lager draft. And freshen up Robb here."

White flash of teeth. Did he have them fucking painted? Maybe he meant all that glare as a promise. Something I wanted he had to sell? Valerie's news meant I might not need his little bargain. But here he was with his smile on and I couldn't judge what he was hawking until I saw what it was. Snake in the feed room. Rat snake or copperhead, could be either. I took another hit of Coke to wake up better, slouched like I could dredge up a blink of attention. "So we're both out late again."

A big sigh swelled his chest. "I saw you and realized, seems like every time I run into you I act like a shit."

"Yeah, you do."

He ran a hand through his curls. He'd spiffed up, the red tangles slicked, his thick shoulders packaged in a conservative sports coat and open-necked blue shirt. Like he'd been out with the big boys. Some of them horse killers. "It's like, I just get pissed. Then I feel bad after. I start thinking you and I might not be all that different. Two guys nobody appreciates."

The waiter brought the drinks. I picked up the fresh Coke for a reason not to answer. If I was like this guy, I wanted to know how. The waiter gone, Carr pushed his beer aside, its creamy head fizzing softly. "Ah, hell. You know how it is with horses. Everybody wants to be the guy who can throw a leg over anything, ride anything, right? Then one of 'em plants you." He clicked his tongue, a frown flitting past, maybe a memory registering. "Like you today. Bet it chapped your ass when Crider won that class on your horse."

"He's not my horse."

"Just letting you know I know what it feels like."

"What what feels like?"

He raised the glass to his mouth, drained foam off it. "You know."

I thought about it. What I knew. All of it. "So you take it out on the horses."

"Now why would you think that?"

I let the question lie there. Too bad he wasn't drunk.

"Anyway. Whatever." He laid his elbow on the table and leaned close. "I wanted you to know I get it. How if you had some really good horses—"

"We have some."

185

"No, like *really* good horses. The kind that take money you don't have."

That sounded like a door unlocking. I'd come this far, so I pushed. "Are you trying to make some kind of deal?"

But any opening I'd sensed slammed shut. "Now what would either of us have to deal with? We're just staff." A hesitation, then what looked like a plunge. "I would have been a great rider. Even better than you. If I'd had a chance at the horses." He rapped the table hard enough to shiver the ice in my glass. "That's what it comes down to in this business for all of us, isn't it? Getting our hands on the horses." He sat back. He showed me the blades of his teeth. "Unless we get our hands on the good horses, don't kid yourself, we're staff."

"So whose staff are you?"

He drank a third of the beer down, watching me over the glass. "Like you, the rich people's. Big shots. You're a smart guy. You know the game is all about money. Theirs."

The dim bar light brought a yellow glint to his eyes. Fake anger? Or real? "So we're talking about money? How much?"

He picked up the glass and upended it, then set the glass down hard.

"I'm telling you," he said like he was shoving some sort of religion on me, "I'm not gonna be staff forever. Doing dirty work for some big shot." He made that gesture with thumb and forefinger, a gun aiming at me. Fired it with a pop of his lips. "I bet it got to you, all right, Crider winning on your horse."

The first time he'd said that about Brett winning I'd shaken clear of it. But what I didn't like was how much I hadn't liked seeing Brett win. It was all Carr's fault, the shit you set in motion when you led a horse you were planning to kill up a road in the dark. Anything I could do to him, he'd deserve. I shrugged like I had a lifetime for his bullshit. "Whatever you want me to know."

"One thing you might want to know." He lowered his voice, like maybe delivering some kind of sex hack. "Keep a lid on that reporter woman. She's got a reputation for a big nose and people are starting to notice her sniffing around."

"What people?"

"Everybody's got something they don't want in the paper." He leaned close, the beer on his breath more than a single glass could account for. "I mean she's a nice enough gal, huh? Not fuck-ready, but who'd want her to get hurt?"

He'd caught me between wanting to throw my drink in his face and wanting to know what he was leading up to. He pulled back from my silence, spreading his hands. "See what a nice guy I am?" He pointed a thumb at my glass. "Let me buy you that beer. I mean, the show's almost over. Who knows if we'll get another chance?"

Maybe I should take what he'd said about Valerie as a warning, try to coax more out of him. "I'm not much of a beer drinker."

"It's not like beer's all there is." He sucked down the last of his own drink. "Name it. What you want."

So. He wanted *me* talking, laying out what I had to bargain with, showing if I could make it stick. It wasn't like there was no deal I would have considered, but any deal with him would be messy. I'd have to think what I'd risk for it. After what Valerie had told me, not much. I said, "I'll think about my options." I shrugged.

He let me study him for a long moment. Then he scraped his chair back. "So tell me when you've picked your poison." He straightened his jacket, standing. When I didn't answer, he pulled out a crisp twenty and snapped it. "Anyway, like I said, I wanted you to know it's not you personally when I get pissed and say something stupid. It's all the pretty horses." He snapped the twenty again. "You know about those."

He crossed and dropped the bill on the bar. I half expected him to pop off another finger-gun at me but he didn't. He waved off change from the bartender. It was a thumbs-up he sent me over his shoulder as he sauntered out.

I wondered how late the bar served. Brett would be in the camper, probably not sleeping well for a lot of reasons; he'd know when I got there. I turned down another Coke, watched the TV batters. No hits.

I thought about calling Valerie to tell her about Carr's warning, assuming he meant it as more than idle bull. But even if he did, it covered pretty much what we'd already locked horns about: her impatience, her way of racing off on her own hook. And she'd want to know who the warning came from and why Carr was the one to deliver it. Questions I wasn't ready to answer. I took several minutes to compose a message that wouldn't trigger her. "Just FYI, I'm getting rumors you're asking a lot of questions. Maybe chill a little until we know more about what's going on?"

As I could have predicted, her answer was a quick, "Got it, boss." And a grimacing emoji. Well, she didn't need telling a sixteenth time what I had told her fifteen times before. Besides, the threat to horses would still be on hold, waiting for the last of the excitement to settle. Jenny was probably in more danger than Valerie, if not from the same sources. Neither of them wanted my protection. At least having passed Valerie the warning freed me to think about Carr.

Some big shot at these shows had apparently used Carr hard, and it looked like staff work hadn't paid as well as he'd hoped. Left him worrying he'd be doing the clean up if I told what I knew. I couldn't help flashing to Dever. No bigger shot at this show. But the only dirty work I could lay at his door would be the drug stuff, and now I knew for sure the drugs had nothing to do with the attack on Romp.

Still, Carr must be wondering what I was up to. Sucking me into a deal would insure him against any accusation I could make. But it looked like I didn't need his kind of risky deal. Not when I knew where else to go for the one thing he could have provided: the names of the big shots who'd paid him. I didn't have to rely on staff.

Once I had those names, the call I had to answer would get real fast. The wall right in front of me, no stopping. The days beyond it— my life—a blank. The pricks of a sweat started. I got out of the bar and into my truck. I didn't dare drive until I was sure I had beaten the seizure. Would it be like this in the fatal moment? A crippling sweat when I most needed control? I made myself picture Carr walking up that dark hillside, Romp kindly following. A twist, pain, not in my stomach but where my heart was. I made my own little gun gesture. Pointed it at my reflection in the mirror. Made myself hear the blast of a gunshot, not his feeble pop.

But that pretend blast didn't knock Carr out of my mind. On the winding roads back to the show I kept seeing him rap that table. Anger. You could do a lot with good hot righteous anger like that. For several foggy miles I slid into visions of Carr using that anger on the big shots who had enraged him. But at some point, with a jerk, I woke up. Carr's anger crowded against me, solid and living, coiling into what I'd been waiting for, a brand new plan.

I parked on the gravel road, far from the sleeping show, far from anyone who would see the sweat wanting to build. This really was the snake in the feed room. The one you had to drag out and take a good long look at with the light on before you panicked and killed it. The kind of snake that could take care of a really big rodent problem you had.

My heart thudding, I made myself eyeball the snake's promise like I was a stranger on the sidelines. Slowly my tremors stilled. Yes, the plan would be tricky, maybe even crazy. There would be suspicion. Even charges. Wardle wouldn't be fooled. But as the cool night closing round me clouded my windshield, the sweat dried to a crust on me and bits of this new plan lined up smooth and clean like the scales on that snake's skin. I hadn't realized the weight of the commitment I'd made until this new plan lifted that weight off me. All this time I'd plowed forward thinking that "throw my heart over" meant letting my own anger claim me the way Carr's anger looked capable of claiming him. Giving it my life as if I had no other option. But my life wasn't what my anger wanted. It wanted justice. The snake said, all you have to do is fill it up with justice and it will let you be.

And if my idea really was crazy . . . well, it wasn't like I was pulling up and quitting. I still had the gun.

A dog barking. Tires growling on the nearby highway. The quiet engine stutter. The snake in the feed room kept hissing: if Carr was Part A of my new plan to deliver perfect justice, Part B was in my possession, always had been, ready to hand. I climbed out, opened the storage box in the bed under the cab window. With my phone flashlight, I dredged among the jumbled tools, old tack, cables, repair stuff for the camper. I put my hand right on what I was after, right where I thought I'd stashed it. Karma. A perfect set up, almost as if I'd ordered it from Amazon.

CHAPTER 29

A<small>T THE BARN WEDNESDAY MORNING</small> everybody was obnoxiously cheerful. Even Raul seemed to smile a lot. Martha moved fast after every sweet little comment, like she knew I wanted to punch her. I wished she would say, "Get over it," the way she usually did.

A lot to get over. A new hope, a fresh determination that flared in nervous shivers. I had to put the excitement behind me. Normal came hard.

Brett showed up late, messing with the neck of his polo shirt as if it didn't fit right. He and I didn't always speak—if we had business to deal with, we handled it and didn't chatter. Especially not at six in the morning. Today he just said, "Sleep okay?"

Martha accosted me when I went down for a wrap and coffee. I couldn't think fast enough to avoid her; all the little tables were taken so we leaned against the schooling ring fence, balancing our cups on the rails.

"So something's fucked up here," she said.

I should have known after all her pussy-footing she'd pull the trigger. "Like what?"

"Like that wasn't you riding yesterday."

"That was my evil twin Cosmo."

She snorted. "Fuck off."

"I can't have a bad day anymore?"

"Here's what's worrying. That you just handed Brett the reins."

I had to look at her. No real way to know how much she understood.

"I thought it was for the best," I said.

"You *knew* it was for the best. That was my point."

Her sharp brown eyes promised some unwelcome common sense coming. I dodged. "What can I say? I'm a peacekeeper."

"You're a damn liar." Her voice held no malice, just truth. "You're up to something, you and that damn reporter. She's going to get you in trouble."

"You've been watching too much Netflix. Nothing's going to happen."

"Something's already happened. When that horse got loose, you could have been killed." A drag to her words, of speculation. "If somebody thinks you know something—"

"Look, I appreciate you're concerned, but that horse getting loose was an accident." My coffee had cooled but I drank it. "Nobody's paying me the least attention."

She grunted. "Well, I hope to God she'll be the one they go after."

"I've told her to be careful."

"She listen?"

"Not much."

We leaned against the fence through a long quiet moment. She stuck her untouched wrap in her vest pocket. I fiddled with the foil on mine. "An angel passed," she said. "I hope it touched you. I hope you felt it." She took a step, then turned back. "I hope to God you don't *need* it."

She smiled, quick, her mouth in and out, but not the way she usually did.

There were a lot of important moments that Wednesday, the last Wednesday of the series, even if I wasn't there mentally to recognize them all. Claryce won a big meter-thirty class with the kind of ride that would make the Olympic Team come calling. Bernie won her eq class. There were twenty-seven people in it. "I quit worrying about winning," she said.

As for me, I'd ridden bad enough times I had a plan to fall back on, so I could dodge the pitying glances everybody kept trying to disguise. It was the same plan as Bernie's. Quit obsessing. Ride like a technician. Every corner, every stride, every feel of the reins. Get the basics right. And look where I was going. Keep my eyes on my line.

It got me through the day. The angels touched Zenith but they didn't kiss him. He had a rail in the combination even though he met it right and jumped high and clear the rest of the trip. Snap went double-clean and lost by a wide hoof mark and Pat hugged me when she took over the reins. Growly won his class, first win at that height, first win of the series. A trainer from a Virginia barn, next to me at the rail, said, "Good footwork on that one." I produced a causal nod, like if we never sold Growly it wouldn't matter. At least we didn't have to sell Growly for any million bucks to get what we needed. If my plan worked, he'd go on being one capable, profitable horse in a line of many. I went back to the barn with angels' breath on my neck.

I accidentally-on-purpose tipped a bucket of water on my breeches that afternoon so I had to go to the camper to change. I dragged on jeans at Mach speed. From under my bunk mattress, I retrieved the gadget I'd dug out of my truck storage box last night.

The question I could answer now was whether the device still worked. I'd improved the odds by dusting off the terminals at the business end, changing the batteries in the remote. The question I couldn't answer was whether the remote would still work at the quarter-mile range the box advertised. Last July Fourth it had lived up to its promise; our barn family oooohed and aaaahed as the spitting pinwheels it set in motion threw reflections across our placid little lake.

This time of day, people were hanging out at the rings; the campers facing the unused barns were closed and still. Slipping into one of the empty barns at the end of the row, I snagged a handful of old hay that the grounds crews hadn't swept out of the empty stalls. Not a horse or person anywhere near; I was totally alone. I dropped my little pile in the unraked dust in the middle of the aisle, far from any wood structures, snapped the cables from the surprisingly tiny contraption onto a fan of hay tendrils, and drifted nonchalantly the length of the aisle. Surveying the showgrounds, the living rings and schooling paddocks, the clustered horses and riders and trainers and families and friends, the whole miniature city paying me no attention, I pushed a button. The handful of hay sixty feet from me flamed happily with a soft crackle until I went over and kicked dust over it. I rubbed out the trace of ashes and made sure to smear my own boot marks as I sidled away.

I knew what I was going to do now. Next stop, find out who I was going to do it to.

The afternoon passed without word one from Valerie. At least she hadn't jammed herself between me and the next move on *my* agenda: getting the names.

I'd seen from the list at the in-gate that the Paxtons' Dutch horse wasn't in Growly's class, probably wasn't showing at all until Sunday. So they wouldn't be down by the rings. Once I'd finished up with the hunters and eq trips and got everything put to rights at the barn, I told people I was going down to the tack shops. What I really did was detour to Malloy's barn.

Good timing. The Paxtons were relaxing outside Malloy's tack stall in deluxe patio chairs with people I'd seen around but didn't know. He had beer and she had one of those canned cocktails. Her off-white skinny jeans and pink silk blouse weren't what I'd have advised around horses; he wore jeans and a gaudy cowboy shirt.

I'd actually been thinking about a bay gelding Malloy had showing in the Baby Greens as a move-up horse for Scott. Malloy came around the corner from the wash racks leading one of his jumpers and I asked if it was okay if I looked at the young horse in the stall.

He slipped the jumper into the grooming crossties. "Glad to get him out for you."

"No, that's okay. Right now I'm just thinking."

"Any time you want to try him," Malloy said.

So I talked to the bay gelding for a few minutes. Then it was only a few steps to the closed door of the stall that was still Romp's.

The wails only I could hear were there, as always. Always would be until I stopped them. I didn't know how long I'd have to stand there ignoring the disapproving vibes Malloy might be sending or wondering which of them I'd get. Not long, it turned out, and I got her.

"So sad," she said at my shoulder. "We wanted to take him home but we aren't going to be around until the end of the month and we wanted to be there to make sure he gets the best care."

She must think she owed me some kind of reassurance; I gave her a nod as she reached for the upper latch. "It's so awful," she said. "He mostly stands in the corner with his head down."

I made myself look. Like she said, the horse sagged there, head hanging. Washboard ribs, hips jutting, coat graying, muscle turned to drooping slabs. I wondered if he was getting regular grooming. I said in a low voice for her, "I can find out who did this."

Her eyes widened, like I'd meant them to.

"Oh, my God," she said, louder than I liked. I worked to hold her gaze. She lowered her voice. "How?"

194

I took out one of the cards I'd stuck in my breeches pocket for exactly this moment. "I have to go to dinner soon. We can talk afterwards. I'd appreciate it if you didn't say anything to anyone about this."

She took the card. "I have to tell Rich."

"Sure. But I don't want to jump the gun. I want to make sure I'm doing it right."

"But don't the police—"

"I'm not even sure how much the police are still on it."

Her face clouded as she flipped the card back and forth. "Well, that's true. Especially since that poor boy . . ." She looked across at her husband, but when I followed her gaze he was bent in conversation with another of Malloy's owners. "I'll talk to Rich and call you." She shoved the card in a tight jeans pocket. "No one's in any danger, are they?"

I shrugged. "Not yet."

At dinner I probably overplayed the cheer I thought I ought to be showing; a couple of times Martha gave a small shake of her head like she wanted to reach over and turn the OFF knob. Jorge was the one who actually said something. "You not having another beer, Robb?"

"Maybe later."

He gestured. "Starving kids in Cancun and you not eating those fries."

"Here, you want them? Not that *you're* starving."

He gave me a wry grin. "Don't want what you've got, boss."

Rianne, at my right, saved me from having to pump out a snarky answer by asking whether Jane really needed a martingale.

At least Dierdre didn't call during the dinner when I might have been tempted to answer. I maneuvered Rianne and Bernie and Claryce into my truck coming back so I wouldn't have to put on an act for Martha and Brett and the guys. I dropped the women off at their car, then I drove up the road and stopped at the bottom of the trailer lot.

I hadn't invited the danger yet. But I was about to. It wouldn't come that night. They'd need time to think about what I told them. The danger lay out there, beyond them. Where I would take them. Not only danger to me. To them.

195

I'd about decided she wasn't going to call soon and had reached for the ignition when the phone rang.

It wasn't her, it was Rich. "What's this all about, Robb?"

"We have to meet somewhere."

"Now? Can't you just tell me?"

"No."

"We should take this to the police tomorrow."

First step into danger. "You don't want that."

"Excuse me?"

"I don't know exactly who did it," I said, "but I know why."

"Why doesn't have anything to do with me and Dierdre."

The exact wrong thing he should say. "I didn't say it did."

"Then you can tell me. We can deal with this together."

"That's why I want us to meet."

The sound on the phone wasn't the exasperated intake of a tired guy wanting his pillow. It was a flat silence, then a grab of air.

"Sure this can't wait till morning?"

I wasn't about to spend the night tossing and turning, obsessing over every possible lie and line I'd have to come up with. "Tomorrow's a crazy day. Our kids are coming."

He went away a minute, one of those changes in the connection that says you're on mute. He came back before I could get impatient. "Come to our hotel. We're at the Holiday Inn Express."

I knew the motel. Scotty and Sherrin usually stayed there.

"Come up to our room, 326," he said.

"No, the lobby." There were a couple of private corners there.

"Why not the—"

"The lobby. In about ten minutes." I hung up.

CHAPTER 30

THE FURNITURE IN THAT LOBBY was fat, dark, and glossy, but it wasn't leather. It squeaked. When they came in, I let them stand over me, awkward, where I lounged in the big armchair I'd chosen. When they realized I wasn't moving, they looked around and picked nearby chairs.

She wore a robe-like thing, not a bathrobe but floor-length with big sleeves and big pockets. He still wore his jeans and flashy shirt. He peered around for a moment as if he could find someone to bring him a drink, but the Holiday Inn wasn't that ritzy. She looked at me with her face creased. Her white-blond hair, tied back, was slick.

"So," said Richard, giving up on whatever he was looking for, "you got us down here." He folded his arms, the picture of a guy who wanted you to know how hard he was working not to be pissed. "Not how we wanted to spend our evening. So what's up?"

I tried to play somebody who didn't care what he thought. "I'm curious about a couple of horses you once had. One named Armistice and one named Solomon XI. You sold them to an LLC called Kristoff Fields six or seven years ago."

"Yeah, sure." Rich fanned his hands. "I remember them. What do they have to do with Romp?"

"You sold them for a lot of money. More than a million, in both cases." I hadn't seen a price on Armistice, but if my theory was right, it would have been up there.

He shrugged. "A horse is worth what someone will pay for it. So?"

I couldn't read his mind, but his face had gone from what looked like open perplexity to a knowing grimace with a smirk underneath it. Like he was out ahead of me and happy to be there.

"Kristoff Fields dumped them both right away," I said. "For about one hundredth of what they'd paid you."

Dierdre sat forward. "What in the world is all this, Robb? We had nothing to do with what happened to those horses after we sold them. You're not . . . accusing us of something, are you? Because if you are, that's plain nuts."

From the way Rich cut his gaze at her, he'd also recognized an accusation. I spread my arms across the chair back, propping an ankle on a knee. "Kristoff Fields was your company. It dissolved shortly after the deals with Armistice and Solomon. You'd set that LLC up before you realized you needed a shell company registered in Delaware."

I'd imagined all the ways people in their position might react. Like the option Richard picked. He mirrored my pose, ankle on knee, ultra-comfortable. Like we were getting ready to bargain. "Unless I've misjudged you over the few years I've known you," he said, "you're in over your head. I'm not sure exactly what you're implying, but to bring some kind of charge involving the ownership of our corporations would take a court order. Unless you've got one up your sleeve, you're wasting my time."

"Whatever you think you're implying," she put in, "we had nothing to do with what happened to Romp."

Odd, I thought, she should go there. Beat me there.

"There are people in the world who are a lot smarter than me," I said. "Who would be interested in this kind of investigation."

He tapped a manicured finger against his temple. "Yeah, but it takes money to hire them. You have enough?"

"Some people don't need to get paid to track down money laundering."

His voice got away from him at least a notch. "And you know how many of these folks?"

Dierdre leaned between us, tugging the robe across her knees. "I can see why you think what you do."

Rich twisted to face her. "He doesn't—"

"Yes, he does. He thinks we have some money hidden away somewhere—in this other LLC or somewhere—that we can't spend because we can't tell where it came from. Isn't that right, Robb?"

"What the fuck are you doing?" Rich asked her. "He's probably recording this."

I took my phone out, set it on the table beside me. Clicked it off.

He perched forward, hands fisted, like he was going to jump up and rip open my shirt. "You could be wearing a wire!"

She whipped around at him. "So what if he is? You're the one acting like he's right. I don't want to sit here all night playing games." She came back to me. "To be absolutely clear, you think—you hypothesize—we've been buying cheap horses from ourselves for big prices so we can show the sales as income. Very clever of you to hypothesize that." She leaned forward, her voice finding an edge. "But you know what? You don't care if we're stealing from starving children, do you? You don't care what so-called crimes we're committing with our money. This is all about Romp."

I said nothing. Rich drummed the fingers of both hands on the chair arms. She flounced the sleeves of the robe. "What do you really want?"

"I want to know who's blackmailing you."

Her mouth fell open. He did a set of crazy whirls, me, her, me, her. Finally me. "What the hell are you talking about?"

"You're doing something illegal." I'd warned myself to expect an eruption at this point. Where I showed them the real threat I meant to them, the flash I'd had heading for that fall. "You sound like you're small time. But you don't want somebody to come along asking questions, maybe getting that court order to find out the beneficiaries of all your LLCs. So somebody demanded a cut and you didn't give it. So they went after a horse you really care about."

"That's nuts!" Richard said.

"Really?"

"Nobody knows—" But he shut off what he'd been about to say.

"Like you said," I told him, "I'm an amateur. But that means if I can figure out what you've been up to, lots of people can."

"But like *you* said," she protested, "even if we are doing what you say, we're small potatoes. A cut of what we're getting is . . . is peanuts."

"The prices on horses with Grand Prix potential are skyrocketing."

She sighed, chin in a hand. Rich twitched in his chair.

"Nobody's blackmailing us," he said. "We don't have the faintest idea who did that to Romp."

Again, she was the one who wasn't into game-playing. "You're not going to believe us. I see that. But what do you really think you can do?"

The first thing I unwrapped wasn't a lie, though I kept it in the same package with lies. "You know you're compromised on Solomon and Armistice. Kristoff Fields was registered at the same address as on the court documents when you got sued over your Arabian's death." Bringing in the dead Arabian delivered a visible jolt. I went quick to where I had to go next. "I have a signed affidavit from someone who tried to do business with Kristoff Fields and got burned. This person tracked down the truth about that LLC. Decided not to sue. But I suspect there's a trail of people who got tangled up trying to make money off your scam horses. Armistice and Solomon are a pattern. And once somebody gets that court order . . ." I shrugged.

They looked at each other. I hadn't done enough blackmailing to know what people's expressions looked like when blackmailing worked. But with four days left, I was closing in on do-or-die. The skin on my spine prickled. For now at least, what I'd find on the backside of the wall was in their hands.

She reached across the space between their chairs and put her hand on his. "So you're threatening to expose us? Our little . . . way of passing on decent horses to genuine buyers who treasure what we have to sell?"

She was talking about people like Marci Hagen's friend, who had to threaten court to claw back the big bucks they'd paid for those decent horses. Rich growled in his throat.

She went on. "And we can't stop you unless you tell us about somebody blackmailing us by doing that horrible thing to Romp?"

I said, "I want to know who did it. I don't care what I have to do to find out."

She nodded. "Yes, I see that."

We all sat there a moment. Rich bounded up and paced to the front of the lobby. The room was empty, not pleasant enough that people would clump there for pleasant things. He stopped at the well-lit registration desk. As far as I could see, the counter was also deserted. No help for him there.

She draped the robe over crossed ankles as she leaned toward me again. She tried an intimate whisper. "Robb, will you give us a couple of days to think about this?"

"I want this settled before the end of the series. Which is Sunday. A couple of days is too long."

"I don't know if . . ." She looked toward Rich. He had his back to us. "I'll call you tomorrow."

200

"No. I won't be able to drop everything to talk. We'll have to set up a meeting. Text me."

Her hand clutched the folds of the robe maybe a little tighter than she meant to. "All right. But please. Be thinking how we can solve this together. How to find out who did this. Whatever we did, we don't hurt horses." I thought she was going to touch my knee. But she drew back. "I think you know that."

"If you let one get hurt to protect yourself, what's the difference?"

Her jaw clenched. "We wouldn't. Please." For the first time she pleaded. "Believe us."

I pushed to my feet. I hadn't realized how much adrenaline had kept me going until I saw how dizzy I was, how far below me she seemed in her pretty robe, her deep chair.

And I still had to make it past Rich, who'd parked himself between us and the doorway. But I'd made it past a lot and I was still standing. "Text me." I turned and passed Rich. He didn't speak, just watched me walk out the door.

Halfway through that Thursday, I wished I'd let her call me. The wait wouldn't have loomed like that huge fence I was racing toward, not sure how much horse I had. Once she called, I'd know how much engine I could count on. Nothing to do now but wait.

Still nothing from Valerie. She'd promised not to move without telling me, but she hadn't promised to stop digging; maybe she'd tunneled close enough to Carr to prompt his threat. No news didn't feel like good news, but I could hope it meant she hadn't dug up much.

The kids' classes started on Thursday this week, so I had plenty to occupy my mind. Getting Clown to pretend he really liked being chased like a damn mustang down his lines. Getting Taylor not to stall Whisper out of his spot when he was a little too forward but to let him sit up on his own. Getting Scott not to override in his first attempt at Beginner Jumpers. The hunters helped, too, for example figuring out how to make Gildy sharper so Bernie could pin higher in her hunter classes. Understanding how each horse and rider and course fit together. For myself, persuading them all I still fit somewhere.

When Raul led Snap to the ring, he didn't quite turn his gaze full on me and for the briefest moment, he didn't seem to want to hand me the reins. Like he was going to ride him? If I landed in one piece I'd have to follow up on the hint of hostility I was reading into his expression and deal with whatever was bothering him. No time for that now. Then he walked away, lithe and quick, and I thought, maybe he *could* ride. Maybe on the other side of the wall somebody would put the magic under him like someone had put it under me. He'd watched enough, good and bad fences, so when he finally rode, he'd already have the rhythm in him. I had a quick flash of coaching him in his first classes. So many hopes waiting if I could survive the other side of the wall . . .

After the class, Pat took the bridle, a little too bubbly to suit me for our fourth-place finish. "Such a great ride," she said.

As for Zenith, he had a rail, but he made me happy. He practically hunted around a really tricky course. It was like he was finding a track through another world. It must have had something to do with the way I was riding, down lines that led somewhere he'd never been before.

During dinner that Thursday night I played tired. That wasn't hard. Brett and Dozer went off to Cindi's. In the camper I sat in my going-out clothes, holding my phone, checking every function on it, waiting for the call that refused to come. I couldn't convince myself anything was broken. Eleven, eleven-thirty, eleven-forty-five. Twelve.

The Paxtons stayed out for a late dinner, I said to whatever part of my body was listening. Rich people didn't have to get up early. Rich people didn't have to do anything but figure how to spend what they'd stolen. They didn't have to do business with an amateur like me. With staff.

I stretched out on the bunk. The sweat lurked under my skin. If the Paxtons called my bluff, I'd have to turn back to Carr. Would he know all the names I needed? What would bait him, threats or money? But no, the Paxtons were hooked and if I could stay smart I could play them. How should I act if I saw them on the grounds tomorrow? Assuming they hadn't summoned their private jet and fled to the Cayman Islands or wherever else they'd stashed their loot. More likely they thought they could outlast me, thought this was all about money. If only something as simple as money could solve it. You couldn't buy your way over the wall.

I bounced so high when the phone rang that I bumped my head on the camper siding behind me. The phone had fallen into the covers. I dug it out. Valerie. A text. "I'm in a trailer like the horse. Come fast."

CHAPTER 31

FIRST THING I DID WAS CALL BULLSHIT. Of all the things I'd imagined the Paxtons doing, this wasn't it. Second was to text back as I grubbed for my boots: "Where?" No answer. Still no answer by the time I staggered to my feet, thinking fucking *New York Times* reporter, too fucking smart ass. She had dug too damn deep with the wrong people and the threats got real. Fucking Paxtons. She had managed to alert them and this was their answer. Using her to get at me.

I threw on a vest, got out the door. The gun? I went back, snapped in the magazine, and hooked the holster in my belt. If I had to fire that gun tonight, self-defense might make pulling the trigger easier. Self-defense or saving a person instead of a horse.

"Trailer" had to mean in the hillside lot. And "like the horse" had to mean fire.

I gunned my truck up the center track of the lot, thinking if they'd done something to her, she couldn't have texted me, they'd have taken her phone.

She wouldn't have sent that message as a joke, either, not a *New York Times* reporter. The message had to be a trap. Somebody wanted me to drive into the middle of whatever they'd done.

I revved faster. The rows of parked trailers stretched away on either side of the center lane. The moon had slid behind broken clouds. If the message meant another fire, I'd see it. Unless the burning trailer was way down on either end of one of the rows. I'd saved Romp because I'd been on Carr's heels. I couldn't save someone I couldn't find.

I stopped when I reached the top of the hill behind the last row. I had to turn left or right. I idled for a moment, opened windows, listened for cries of terror. No sound but wind in the trees at the top of the hill, some bird. A car on the distant highway. My panting. I held my breath. Reached under my vest for the comfort of the gun.

I turned right on a fifty-fifty guess, looking down each track between trailers as I passed. When I reached the corner I had to either go down and look along the horizontal gaps, or go back and try the other side.

By now, a fire would have bloomed into the night the way Romp's had. I eased down the lane along the side of the lot, the main highway off to my left in the distance. The track here was rutted, jarring. I braked. A smell. Unmistakable. Smoke. But not rubber or gas or hot metal. Like Romp's smoke. Hay smoke. But sour, as if the hay was damp.

I lurched forward alongside a big trailer. Ahead of me a car sat on the grass on the side of the lane. My headlights suddenly clouded with belching murk. Coming from the trailer row to the right.

I pulled up to the car, stopped. Enough moonlight I could see that no one was in it. I turned off my engine and jumped out in the thickening smoke. I held my breath, fought off sudden coughs, listened. A muted clanking, banging. And a strangled rasp. *Help*.

I thumbed the safety off the gun in my belt and edged down the row of trailers. The shadows snarled with smoke, and the smell grew. And the sounds. Louder banging. The cries grating, choking. *Helphelphelp.*

The smoke boiled from a side window of a two-horse trailer, a logo on the side I didn't recognize. It rocked on its tires from the frantic bangs inside.

I looked around, behind me. Anyone might jump from the shadows. I had my phone but no time for that; first, get to her. "Valerie!"

The sobbing cries stopped. Then began again. "Help! Help me!"

I raced the last yards, leaped for the door to the space in front of the stalls. *Don't be locked.* It wasn't. Smoke gushed out, blinding me. Inside in the murk hung hay nets, tie ropes. A shape at my feet. "Oh, God," she said from inside black billows. "Oh, God."

For a moment I was back with Romp, adrenaline-crazed, frantic. I coughed, tears starting. It took me a second to realize: no flames. Stacked bales in the two stalls, the smoke pouring off them, a suffocating fog. Smoldering. I waved smoke from my face, blinded, blinked, felt her against my boot, knelt.

She lay on her side, face pressed to the floor mats. She thrashed, gulping. "Stop," I told her, probing. A length of chain around her waist bound her to the metal post separating the stalls.

She'd known to get down low where air pooled; her knees were drawn up for another kick at the trailer siding. No side ramp on this trailer I could let down. She struggled again, jerking uselessly at the chain. "I can't . . . I can't . . . "

"Stop it. Be still." She was sucking in more smoke in her thrashing. I didn't waste time looking to see how the chain was fastened; her hands were free, so there'd be some kind of lock. "The pole comes up." They were made that way, so you could open up the whole compartment if your horse needed the space.

Working blind by feel and memory, I reached overhead. Sometimes the levers that loosed the poles from the floor slots stuck; this one fought me. I gave the lever a wrench, another, and the mechanism creaked free. I yanked the pole out of the floor.

She writhed, panicking. "Stop," I said through buckling coughs, "I'm getting it." I held my breath, braced my foot against her struggles, wrestled the tall awkward pole between the chains and her back. When it came clear she kicked and scrabbled. I flung the pole aside and caught her shoulders, dragging her convulsing body into the front compartment away from the bales. She clutched at my legs, grappling. I pivoted to swing her toward the door I'd come through.

I'd left it open. It had swung closed. She yowled like an animal, lunging. I thrust her aside, reached for the door handle. It turned but the door did not open. Someone had come up while I was struggling to free her and shut us in.

CHAPTER 32

I PUSHED PAST HER AND WRENCHED the handle on the escape door on the far side. Firmly locked.

I snared the back of her shirt. "Lie down." She gave me her eyes long enough for me to find sanity in them. "Oh God," she said, her breaths lost to coughs.

I reached for my phone. But in this smoke by the time someone came to help us we'd be dead. No time to wait for a pick-up. "I'll get us out."

Like I knew that. Like I prayed she did.

I turned to the stacked bales. The smoke was solid now, dense gusts. I batted uselessly. Above the smoldering hay were the sliding side windows. I pressed closer to the hay, gritting my teeth at the heat coming off it. Through running tears I located the window on my left, the one I'd seen smoke pouring out of. Cracked for oxygen so the fire would catch? I stretched over the stacked bales but my reach wasn't long enough.

"Robb!" Valerie screamed from where I'd left her.

I squinted at the window. Wide enough. Wide enough.

"I got it!" I shouted back.

I thought about pulling the top bale off, climbing onto the bottom one. But that would expose the smoldering hay inside to air. Set off an inferno. I knew from long practice you could climb a wall of stacked bales if you dug your toes into the spaces between them. If they were heavy enough they wouldn't topple on you while you bellied up.

I stretched for the top bale. A sear in my palms. But I had a vest to shield my chest. I also had a gun against my belly and a phone in my pocket. How much heat would it take to set off bullets? Melt my phone? I had no idea.

I heard myself growl. I wound my hands in the twine holding the top bale together, shoved my toe beneath it, launched myself, and sprawled on top. I frog-kicked like I was swimming, toward the open window. My vest didn't stop the heat but I squirmed, twisted, didn't give it time to reach me, got my hands on the edge of the open window, and pulled.

Wide enough. Barely. My body making its own space, like Romp shoving through that side door.

I went out head first, a twelve-foot drop maybe, my fall slowed by my jeans and boots snagging on the window frame. When I hit the ground, I tucked and rolled. A single pin secured the metal door latch. I yanked it out, flung the door open. The chain still looped around her, Valerie plunged into my arms.

We fell together onto the grass, both gasping, sobbing, smoke pouring out above us. She clambered up, fell, clambered up again. I got to my knees, then to my feet after her, grabbing the chain. It slid down her hips, clanking around her knees as she scrambled. Between coughs she gasped, "God, oh God." She half-ran, half-crawled, toward the lane and her car. I didn't try to stop her. When she reached her car, she flung herself against the door, yanking the handle. The car was locked.

"Damn damn damn damn."

I was shaking almost as hard as she was. I took her shoulder, turning her, pushing her against the car. "Stop."

"They . . . they . . ."

"Stop."

She drew a sleeve across her wet face, bent double in a savage coughing bout. When she straightened, her gasps didn't flatten but they slowed. I looked around. Smoke still curled toward us. Still nothing moving among the close-packed trailers. No sound but our strained breaths.

But somebody out there? It came to me that whoever had set that fire hadn't been as expert or as careful as Carr. Or maybe had had even less time. My mind tried to work. Someone had sent me a message that brought me up here in time to save her. Maybe the plan hadn't been to kill Valerie but to get me here. Get me into that trailer so that door could be slammed on me. Whoever it was thinking the smoke would get us before I figured out how to escape.

She wiped her face again, pushing off the car. "Where are my keys? And my phone?"

"I got a message from your phone."

"I didn't send it."

"You need a doctor—"

"Fuck you, Robb. I need my keys and my phone."

She was upright, even if the amount of smoke clogging her brain muddied her thinking. I clenched my fists to stop their shake. "I have a flashlight in my truck. We'll look."

She let me steady her with a hand on her arm while we walked the short steps to my truck. "So what happened?" I asked.

"I don't . . . do you have any water?"

"No." I hadn't thought of that.

She shook loose. I got the flashlight, more powerful than my phone app. I thought she might not want to go back to the trailer with its stinking cloud, but she wove beside me as the light swept the ground. I thought about the police. All that would happen if I called them. The problem made a hard knot at the back of my brain. She said suddenly, "There!"

No phone, but a key fob. I swept the light around. She picked up the fob, then dove for something that shone in the light beam. I thought she would hand the thing to me, but she closed her hand around it.

"What's that?" I said.

She shook her head, turned back toward her car.

We locked ourselves in her car, me in the passenger seat, the dome light off. The moon had come and gone a couple of times. The pall of smoke had cleared or drifted away, the fire in the hay bales finally dying out, but not the stench. We had brought it into the car with us, on our skin, our hair, our clothes. We had not called the police.

She claimed she didn't know what had happened. "They must have hit me. I can't tell the police anything."

I dug my hands deep in my pockets. "The fucking Paxtons." I tried to read her expression in the shadows. "I told them what I knew. Just yesterday."

She'd put the thing she'd found in her own vest pocket. It crackled, like a plastic bag. "So you think Dierdre or Rich followed us up here and shut that door?"

"Hell, no. They paid—" I choked back Carr's name. "Someone." *Their dirty work.* "They're using you to get at me."

211

She slumped back, eyes out the window, didn't speak.

I'd straightened my mind out. No police. We were both alive, and I was deep in my own business with the Paxtons that Wardle could only interrupt. I surrendered one of my few cards to give her the kind of info I'd give a partner. "Someone's blackmailing them. By attacking the horse they care about." Again she was silent. "I confronted them about it. They're trying to make me back off."

She coughed, reached across me to her glove box and got out a package of wipes. I took the one she offered. She scrubbed her face, the wipe turning black. "Did it occur to you someone might be after *me?*"

The wipe felt gritty in the soot on my cheekbones. I wadded it, dropped it, laid my fingers flat on my thighs. They cut into my muscle. Carr's warning echoed. "You did something today. Triggered somebody. What the fuck did you do?"

"I didn't talk to the Paxtons."

"You did for your article."

She ran another wipe across her mouth, spitting into it. I said, "What's in that bag?"

"I'll tell you later. Some shit I have to look into."

"Something to do with the Paxtons—?"

"I said I'd tell you later."

"What the fuck are *you* hiding?"

Her lip hardened. "I need to think about me for a change."

"If you're thinking of calling Wardle," I said quickly, "he's clueless."

But she had gone off on her own wavelength, staring straight ahead. "I'll call Wardle, all right, but when I do, I want to go with the right package. Not a bunch of bullshit accusations that get him nowhere and make me look like a fool." She tossed the dirty wipe to the dashboard. "I'm gonna go look for my phone."

I opened and closed my fists. As if I had anything useful to do with them. She pushed her door open. I said, "I'll come with you. You shouldn't—"

She looked out at the silent trailers. A dry snort. "I can find it," she said.

She set off in the darkness. After a moment I caught up with her. I offered her the flashlight. "Here."

She hesitated, then took it.

"I'm not leaving you here."

She ignored me.

"I'll wait in my truck."

"If you think you have to."

"I'll be right here," I said. "I'll wait."

I ended up leaning on my truck, shivering, probably from a kind of shock. She didn't find the phone. She didn't tell me what she had in her pocket, either, and I made what may have been a naïve decision not to beat her senseless to find out. There would be a chance to get the truth out of her later if the object turned out to matter, maybe once we got our heart rates in order. She handed me my flashlight and got back in her car. From the base of the hill on the gravel road I watched her drive away.

I'll call Wardle, all right . . .

So sooner or later she would block me. But I still had time. To figure out what she was hiding, who she had triggered, what she had done.

I drove to our camper and parked in front. I stripped on the step with the door open, dropping the clothes in a pile. I had the gun in my hand, a bullet chambered, when I walked through the camper to the bathroom and the bedroom. No one there.

I showered faster than I wanted, dressed in sweats, and hid the ruined clothes in the truck. Tomorrow they'd go in a Dumpster. Back inside, locked in, I crawled into my bunk.

Fire. What a convenient weapon. Especially around horses. All that wood, all that hay, all those dry shavings or straw. To blackmail the Paxtons. To terrorize Valerie and threaten me. But anyone could play with matches. I lay back and for once it wasn't the sight of the wall that consumed me. It was crackling fires. Some of them set to trap me. Some of them I had set myself.

213

CHAPTER 33

As USUAL, A FULL DAY OF SHOWING AHEAD that Friday. And all day both Valerie and Dierdre squatting in my mind. Time was running out. Surely one of them would call before the day's madness got started. Had to. They didn't. So much for my luck.

My worries about Valerie grew with the rising daylight. Her silence. The way she had left me alone in the dark. Had she made some guess about what I was up to and wanted out? What was in that packet? I hadn't seen it well enough to make more than a guess. Some sort of drugs?

I made nuclear-grade coffee, my brain on a nitwit circuit. Could someone really be trying to frame her? Or was she mixed up in the drug stuff herself? Either possibility would explain why she'd shied off calling the police. I'd more or less concluded that someone at Dever's barn was behind the drug operation, maybe Dever himself. I'd seen no sign Valerie was interested in Dever. Did she even know who he was? But what if somebody had tried to drag her in by planting drugs where she would find them—then had lured me to the trailer lot so I'd be there when she did?

Maybe there'd even been someone hidden among those rows of trailers videoing us, her picking up the packet, the two of us ducking into her car. Both of us framed.

I worked on linking that idea to the locked door. Valerie didn't have to be alive for a drug-crime set-up. Me being there, dying with her—two for the price of one. A corner of my mind coughed up the hints from Carr and Wardle that I was unstable, capable of all sorts of craziness. Like arson? Not such a nitwit circuit: somebody making it look like I'd dragged Valerie into that trailer to silence her, only to make some amateur mistake and get stewed in my own pot. Our dead bodies could be spun all sorts of ways.

I wanted to wrestle Carr in. He had to be antsy: hinting at a deal, then regretting he'd been so reckless, now afraid I'd tell. He couldn't know about the role I'd penciled in for him in my plan. The piece that didn't fit any of my theories was the text from Valerie's phone. She said she hadn't sent it, hadn't had the phone. Someone who didn't want us to die might have sent it. Or someone who wanted me in the trailer with her. Carr again?

Could the Paxtons be the big shots he resented? A trap to set me up would explain their silence. They wouldn't have to deal with me if I was fighting some drug charge or arson. Or piled up with Valerie in a smoking ruin.

Theories were still boiling in my head when I ran out of time. I showered again, shaved, got into my breeches and paddock boots and polo. All clean. But I felt raw under my fresh clothing, as if I really had set a fire that was searing off hide. I stumbled out in the first gray light and went to our barn. The horses knew I was there and started clamoring for breakfast. Jorge came out of the gray and saw me. He stopped for half a stride, then went into the feed room without speaking. How much did it all show this time?

I texted Valerie. No answer. No way to know why. Because her phone was still up there among the trailers? Or because she didn't want to tell me what was in that plastic bag?

Friday morning I knew who I fooled and who I didn't. Our riders were easy: the kids, their parents, the husbands and boyfriends, all backslapping and laughing, almost too cheerful for me to take. I found ways to tell them all how well they were doing. I lived off the light in their faces for a while.

I listened for rumors about another trailer fire. Nothing. Whoever owned that trailer didn't have to be involved in the attack on Valerie; they might not discover the ruined hay for days. Smolder like that could be put down to moldy hay working, like compost. You didn't have to want to kill somebody to burn down a barn that way.

Hardest of all that day was steering my mind off Raul and Jorge. They turned away as they worked, talking low. Then they'd shut up. I worked to read Raul's gaze but couldn't. At one point he disappeared for half an hour, not at the time for his usual lunch break. Asking Jorge where he'd gone was unthinkable. When he came back, he dug in as always, helping Jorge with ear trims, but he didn't look at me until I asked a direct question, then only answered with a nod and a brief, cool smile.

Maybe even worse was the time I'd wasted, the two hours of rising dawn after Valerie left that I could have used to take the next steps in my plan. I couldn't let Valerie's stubbornness or the Paxtons' silence bump me off course. I didn't know what maneuver the Paxtons would come up with so I couldn't plan how to counter it, but at least I could get part of my own scheme in place.

Since I'd given up the cover of darkness I had to steal daylight time. Around eleven, with the Special Hunters taking forever to come up to the gate, I told Jorge I'd be back in a bit like I was heading out for grub. If he heard a false note in my voice he didn't show it. He nodded, his gaze on the shavings he was brushing out of Jane's tail.

From one of the empty grooming stalls we'd commandeered at the end of our aisle, I retrieved our golf cart. I'd have preferred the invisibility of walking, but the cart would be faster. Martha caught me pulling out. "Bring back one of those gallon bottles of fly spray."

"Sure thing."

All I meant to do now was preliminary set up. True, if I got caught before I flipped the switch, I'd face some fancy explaining. I tinkered with cover-my-ass lies as I stopped at our camper for a quick foray under my mattress for the igniter. No story I came up with would float with Brett and Martha. At least, what I did today I could undo in half an hour if my odds turned to shit.

As usual during classes people were down at the rings and not up among the trailers so I had the lot to myself. I parked the cart between our six-horse gooseneck and the big slant in front of it so that no one driving by casually would notice me there.

I unlocked the door to the tack compartment behind the gooseneck. The compartment was a good-sized space almost big enough to use as a small camper. Plenty big enough for the little party I planned.

My first step was to disable the webcam that opening the door activated. Ordinarily, during daylight hours, Brett wouldn't bother tapping the icon if his trailer-alarm app went off; he'd assume the guys had opened the trailer to retrieve more feed. But what if one time in a hundred he opened the app out of idle curiosity and saw my setup? If he tapped and noticed the camera wasn't working, I'd promise to check it. As always, counting on my luck.

As in most goosenecks, the tack compartment extended over the hitch that fitted into the bed of the truck, giving us a space the width of the trailer and about five feet high where we could haul gear for setting up our tack stall at the show. Now the space contained only some old tack-room drapes and extra buckets. I climbed up and crawled to the latched windows on either side of the extension. I opened the one on my left an inch.

Sliding back down, I circled to the ramp that opened onto a storage space in front of the first row of stalls. On the road we tied ponies side by side in this area so we could haul up to eight horses. Now the space held bags of shavings we'd bought from the on-site vendors for fetching as needed. Hay we'd purchased was stacked in a stall in the main trailer space. I'd counted the hay and shavings already unloaded to our feed room. Friday, Saturday, Sunday nights. The guys would need most of the bales and bags stored here before we packed on Monday. I dumped four bales out on the ground, all the golf cart could carry. I'd have to be the one driving up each night for the rest of them, as well as the one locking up Brett's and my saddles. I'd done that chore often enough no one would wonder if I volunteered.

Partially full hay nets hung on the stall partitions in the trailer, waiting to be refilled for the trip home. I cut open one of the remaining bales and packed the nets, then dragged them around to the tack compartment, where I stashed them in the extension over the gooseneck. The hay smelled sweet, clean and dry. The sacrifice of that lovely hay that could feed so many horses . . . a small piece of what justice would cost.

Finally, watching the time, I dragged four bags of the shavings from the storage area into the tack compartment and piled them against the side wall. That done, I circled around to the golf cart, hoisting a single bale into the back. I knew from experience that from a bale in the back of the cart I could reach the windows over the extension. This was the riskiest moment. Anyone looking my way from the car lot might notice. At least the trailer between me and the showgrounds sat at a bit of angle, blocking what I was doing from anyone glancing up the hill.

So I drove the cart around the side of the trailer and parked it where I could reach up to the window. I retrieved the fireworks igniter from the golf-cart. Climbing onto the bale, I pushed the igniter with its cables and clamps through the open window. Come time to issue invitations, if that ever happened, I wouldn't count on the hay alone to catch, but for now I wanted the pieces in position. I'd need a line of sight to the igniter, but I'd already found I could aim for the trailer roof from a corner of the empty barns. As a last step, I tied a length of hay string from the bale I'd cut open to the igniter, tucked that inside, too.

I loaded the other bales I'd tossed out; with all four wobbling on the cart, I drove down to our barn. "Thought I might as well bring these," I said to Raul's raised brows. He shifted feed bags while I slung the bales off the cart.

I parked the cart, realizing I'd forgotten Martha's fly spray. "I'll get it later when I take up the saddles," I promised.

Her squint ran up and down me. "Whatever. We'll need it tomorrow."

I'd have to be more careful. The lie that trapped me would probably be one of the small ones. At least if anyone went up to the trailer the alarm app on my phone would beep. I'd have time to think of an answer for "what the fuck is all this?"

Jorge came back from the rings to say they were waiting for the last ten trips in the Specials. Time to get the girls on for their flats and Scott for his over-fences. Following them down to the schooling area, I couldn't resist looking up toward the trailers. Toward our trailer sitting innocently in its slot.

CHAPTER 34

MALLOY CAME UP BESIDE ME while I waited on the rail for the last Special Hunter to finish. He propped his chest on the top board and hung his elbows over. A small smile, sociable. "Your kids look great, Robb."

For once, an ordinary ringside conversation, a taste of normal I needed. "Yeah, they're doing great."

He clasped his hands over the fence rail. "About Rich Paxton," he said.

No, not normal. But I'd expected something like this. If Paxton had been the one to shut that door on us, he'd be pretty desperate to know how I'd escaped. He'd need a go-between like Malloy to pump me. "What about him?"

"He wanted to know a lot about you. Like what kind of reputation you had."

I locked in on those hints being spread about me. Grist for Paxton; discrediting me might be his best option. "Why would he want to know that?"

"Not sure. I got the feeling something had happened between you and him."

It worried me that Malloy was doing this. His best bet was to stay out of squabbles unless they cost him money. I knew what my plans for the Paxtons would cost him, but I couldn't exactly lecture him on his stakes. "You got me. I don't know him that well but he's always seemed like a nice guy."

He grimaced like he was trying to translate subtitles. "This have something to do with Romp?"

I shook my head. My kids were lining up to go into the ring. No time to push him the way I wanted. "If you find out what he's bugged about, tell me."

"Yeah." He said it heavily. He backed away from the fence, planting a shoulder so I'd have to step around him. "Robb, that horse is not going to get better."

I spread my hands, like he was telling me the obvious. "I told you, I get that. Gotta go."

When I reached the girls, I stood between them in the in-gate, hands on the ponies' necks, enough of a clench in my fingers I had to stop myself from crushing their tight little crests. "Go hack your hearts out," I said. "Have fun." I stroked the ponies' butts as they passed to loosen the cold knot on the back of my neck.

That they both pinned high didn't stop me from watching for the Paxtons. What message had Malloy meant to deliver? A warning of some sort? *Mind your own business.* That had been his mantra. But I was way past worrying about what was and wasn't my business. My whole plan depended on getting the names the Paxtons could give me, and a part of my brain was running scenarios I could try in the next two and half days to shake those names loose.

At least Malloy's questions confirmed that my little talk with the Paxtons had set things in motion. So, for a little longer, my best bet was sitting tight.

If only I could get Malloy's words out of my ear. *That horse isn't going to get better.* I thought, he has to live forever with what I can't fix for him. I should have let him burn.

I turned to find Scott at the rail beside me, holding SP. We had slotted him in about halfway down in the third rotation, his rides four trips apart. These classes were bigger than last week. The trips were terrific, one blowout after another. Scott said, "I'm gonna do so bad."

"Is that so?" I said as light as I could, running down his right stirrup.

"Everybody's better than me."

I said what my old coach told me. "There'll always be somebody better than you. There's always somebody better than all of them, and sometimes that's you." That didn't make a lot of sense to me, but the way he plain meant it always made me smile. Scott didn't smile. He climbed on, biting his lip.

We had a decent school. Not brilliant, but at that point I wasn't holding out for brilliant. But the first thing Scott did when he rode into the ring was blow his lead. I wiped any judgment off my face before he looked over at me. Post-mortems later, not with the course still ahead. He fixed the lead, then ran SP right under the first fence, got one of the scramble distances that made the rest of the line at best a hope.

It got better. He did what I told them all to do once you know you've blown it: make it a school. I watched him checking his mental notebook, all the little steps that somehow created a picture. He didn't have the flow his best rides managed, but his last line was lovely. He was in tears when he rode out.

For moments like this—they happened a lot—a trainer needed a bag of things to say. My stuff was old, frayed, but comforting, even to me. I patted SP. "That was terrific, how you put it together for that last line. I hope your mom got video."

"God, I hope she didn't."

"Hey, you know . . ." I wanted to say something about taking bad odds and pulling a good end out of them. Then my gaze slipped past and it was Valerie I saw.

She was stalking through the horses and riders beyond the schooling area, heading for the barns. Long strides, shoulder-strap bag clutched across her body, focus straight ahead.

"The next trip'll be better," I said. "Look, I need to take care of something. Keep him walking."

"I can't believe I blew that lead," he said. "Next time I'll—"

"Be back in a minute. If I'm not, get the gate lady to move you down in the order." I was already jogging. I lost sight of her in the scrum of horses and grooms and trainers but when I reached the lane in front of the barns, there she was, way ahead. I didn't want to shout. Too many people. She turned down Ricoeur's aisle.

I ran faster, didn't care who saw. When I skidded into Ricoeur's barn, the aisle was empty, one of the jumpers in crossties but all the others quiet in their stalls. I raced through, came out on the backside. Valerie and Jenny stood beyond the row of wash racks. Only one horse tied there, a groom hosing it. The splatter drowned out what the women were saying. Jenny's head was thrown back. She rose on her toes as if to wheel and leave, but Valerie snapped something and she spun back with a vehement headshake. Valerie raised a hand but whatever she'd been about to do, she ditched it when she glanced past Jenny and spotted me.

She froze for an instant. She shouldered clear of Jenny and headed up the road. I sprinted to catch her. Ran hard into Jenny, who'd flung herself in front of me. She grabbed my arm, spinning me, clawing. "It's all lies, Robb, what she's going to say about me."

What Valerie was going to say was disappearing around a corner. I stood a better chance at truth if I followed. "I can't talk now. Let go."

"No. Listen to me."

I raised my arm to free it. She hung on with both hands. "Whatever you want, Robb. I'll do anything. Don't believe what she says."

Whatever I wanted? What did she think I'd ask for? "So what is it I'm not supposed to—"

"*What's going on here?*"

At the boom of his voice I looked past her at Ricoeur.

He strode toward us in his automaton walk, his big ugly face reddening. "Let go of her!"

She turned loose, jumping back. Ricoeur jammed between us, glaring down at her. "Did he hurt you?"

She looked at me, not him. For all the world like she actually considered saying yes.

He pointed, ordered, "Go back to the barn."

"He's not—"

"Go."

She shot me a glance between scathing and a collapse I could only call pleading, then turned, a forced stride back into the aisle. If for even second I thought of going after her, Ricoeur blocked that madness. "You will leave her alone," he said in his clipped accent. "You will stay away from my barn, my horses, her camper, her." He reared up, as big as his goddamn million-dollar jumpers. "You will stay away."

"I didn't—"

"I will have you charged with assault, and I will make it stick."

I locked my mouth shut. Like she'd have any use for me when she had this baboon for a protector. He raised a hand like he was going to shove me. I stepped back. The groom hosing the horse had stopped to watch. People I vaguely knew had come out of the barns farther down. I turned and walked away.

Scotty sat on SP by the rail, tears running, his mom beside him. "They wouldn't move me down. I had to go."

Without me there, he wouldn't have known he could ignore the gate person's insistent urging. "He did really well," said his mom with a dry smile.

"It was awful," Scott said.

"I'm sorry. I had an emergency."

She opened her mouth, I'm sure to ask what the hell kind of emergency would make me race off and leave her son in the middle of a class. Thank God she only snapped her lips together. I put an arm around SP's neck. I needed to feel something alive against me. After a long shitty moment Sherrin said, "I hope you were able to take care of it."

"Yeah, it's okay."

"I got video."

So I watched the small phone screen. He actually had done well. He wouldn't pin but who cared? "Ride like that in the Medal," I said. So little I could say. "Why don't you jump off, give him a break."

"I want to stay on."

"Do what Robb says," said Sherrin.

Rianne came up leading Jane. I gave SP a last pat. "Not sure we'll need to school again. We'll see a little closer." I followed Rianne out of reach.

CHAPTER 35

GETTING EVERYBODY COACHED and in and out of their classes and debriefed and the videos watched so we could talk about what to do next time all meant that taking off after Valerie wasn't an option. God knew where she'd gone. Finding out what had triggered Jenny would have to wait until Ricoeur was out of the picture. I hadn't set eyes on the Paxtons, or on Carr. Behind the routine was a growing panic. I brooded over Valerie's stiff back, her chin jutting in Jenny's face. *Whatever you don't want this to be about.* It had started to look like Jenny was what she meant.

Back at the barn Brett stood talking to Claryce outside Flight's stall. At the sight of me, he pinched his mouth tight, then grunted, "I need to talk to you." To Claryce he said, "I'll only be a minute." He led me around the barn corner, outside and out of her view.

He had to be riled about Scott. Anything less, he'd have waited until we were alone. He swung to me, black eyes snapping. Percussion. "Now more shit? What the hell is the matter with you?"

"Lame" wasn't a strong enough word for the answer I came up with. "There's things I'm dealing with that don't have anything to do with you or the barn or—"

He pushed me with a balled fist. I reached for the wall behind me to stop my stagger. He pushed again. "The hell it doesn't have anything to do with the barn. Not just that craziness with Scott, yeah, I heard. But that goddamn reporter coming here and scaring the shit out of Raul and Jorge. Who the hell does she think she is?"

"Valerie?"

"Yeah, that's her. Your friend."

"She's not my friend."

"Then what the hell is she? Asking them shit about that drug stuff. About that kid Brian. Like those guys know anything about any of that stuff."

I tried to fit what he was saying into what little I seemed to know about what Valerie was up to. "I've never talked to her about any of the drug stuff. I don't know what she thinks she's doing." What she was doing was what I'd left Scott to ask her. That and what she'd hidden in her pocket last night.

But he wasn't in any mood for excuses. "What have you talked to her about?"

"We've talked about what happened to Romp. She said she was trying to find out more about that."

I waited for him to keep going on the drug stuff. But he uncurled the fist he'd pushed me with, jabbed a finger. "Our people depend on you," he said. "You've got to fix this."

So much that needed fixing. "I'm trying to—"

"You having some kind of breakdown? Do you need a fucking doctor?"

"No, I'm—"

One last jab. "Then fucking straighten out."

He turned, shaking what looked like an ache from his clenching hands. He headed back to all the cheerfulness with a last stab of those angry eyes.

I stood there a few minutes. I had known from the start I would never have the answers he wanted. I couldn't see having them tomorrow or the next day either. I forced my mind to my immediate problem, what he'd told me about Valerie. So now it was the drug stuff and not Romp she was into. Our guys couldn't have been involved in any of that. But they might have told Valerie something that sent her to someone who was. Maybe after all horse killings wouldn't get you a *New York Times* byline. Maybe a big fancy plot like drugs was the ticket for that.

She'd better think twice about involving Jorge or Raul in her big ambitions. It was one thing to trip up Scott and his mom in my clumsy stumble. But they would manage. Jorge and Raul, maybe not so easily. I hoped they wouldn't be stuck picking up the wreckage if I blew my landing from the wall.

By the time I went back into the barn Brett and Claryce had left to learn courses. I sent the kids and their little family circles down to watch trips before their Medal classes. I took a few seconds longer to put Brett's anger in the box I needed to keep it in. Funny: we all had things we wanted to fix but couldn't, not and leave everybody safe and happy, even Brett. Obviously he thought I was what needed fixing. I wished he had the right tools.

From the front of the aisle I caught sight of Raul. He was talking to a groom I didn't know well, a guy from an Illinois outfit. Nothing odd there; of course he had made a lot of friends in his years working the shows. I had to stop imagining that he'd started ducking my gaze. Even if he was mixed up in some garbage, he wouldn't be into harming horses. Eventually I would have to tease out whether he was in trouble and see if I could help him—assuming I survived the next couple of days.

Behind me a noise. I jumped more than I should have. I turned, found Wardle looming at the back of the barn.

He was uniformed again, the stiff blue jacket broadening his shoulders. "Got a minute?" he asked.

If he had some new way to harass me, he'd have to wait until I had time for it. "Nothing more to tell you. My kids are waiting. Gotta go."

He raised his voice. "You set any fires last night?"

That turned me. So much for trying to stall him. I didn't know where Jorge was, or Martha. I hoped not in hearing distance. "What do you mean?"

"We got a report of another trailer fire, moldy hay that didn't catch. You came to mind."

So the trailer owner had discovered the damage. But no way they could know Valerie and I had been there. "I don't know what you're talking about."

"It seems the metal fixtures inside were pulled out of the floor. Somebody did that. Freeing somebody trapped? You?" He scratched his neck before getting the words out. "Or by you?"

I stole a few seconds to figure out where I stood in this confrontation. No point feeding him more lies like the others I'd never talked him into swallowing. But I'd run out of time for this shit. It was even more pointless now to worry about how level my voice sounded. "From the start you've had bad shit going on and all you've done is hassle me. You keep hinting you're going to charge me with something. If that's what you're planning, do it now."

He came to me, face to face. Looked up and down the silent aisle. Scraped the back of his hand across his mouth. "I think it was one of you riders in that trailer. Riders wouldn't think twice about a tumble like that. Who do you think it could have been?"

I registered his mean-movie-cop growl more than his words. Time to find out what kind of hard-ass he thought he was playing. "I haven't heard you charge me. Let's get it done."

He tucked his thumbs into his belt. His gun made the one in the camper look like a cap pistol. "So you weren't anywhere near this burning trailer last night?"

"Asked and answered."

His gaze ran up and down me, couldn't find a landing. So his threats were empty. "Just so you know," he said with a new crispness, "maybe we could find out who hurt that horse with more cooperation." He hitched the gun belt under his belly. "Your story never has made sense, how you didn't see anyone at that trailer that night."

"Sorry you're stuck on that," I said. "Waste of good manpower." I couldn't leave until he did. Jorge came around the corner with the manure cart, grabbed a pitchfork; he gave me a raised brow and disappeared into Clown's stall. Wardle took a couple of laden steps away with a grim headshake.

"You're not the only place I can get answers," he said brusquely. "You might not like some of the places I look."

If he meant Jenny, that was old news. I shrugged. He reached the end of the barn, his grimace over his shoulder an odd one, almost, I thought, of pity. "Don't leave my jurisdiction."

"I'll be here till Monday."

He jerked his head in dismissal and stomped off.

"Text me if he comes back," I told Jorge.

"Gotcha."

"Don't let him make you think you have to talk to him."

"No chance of that."

So Wardle had moved on from bullying to threats. Desperation? If he had a trap ready to spring, he'd have used it. His time was running out just as fast as mine.

Was Valerie one of the places he thought he might get his answers? I had to get ahead of him with her, just in case. Besides, I'd had it with her, too, the way she was running me in circles. Before I set off for the rings, I stopped and thought.

I needed some trick to lure her out of hiding. I didn't know where she lived so I couldn't go find her. I had to rely on texting— and lying, since the days when we told each other everything had apparently passed. I needed a lie big enough to yank her chain. After a moment I wrote, "I talked to Jenny. She told me everything." If Valerie got the message, it meant she'd either found her phone or had a new one and she might check with Jenny. So I added, "She said not to tell you but I thought you should know."

If only I could quit flashing on that grim scene between her and Jenny. Jenny feeding drugs not to horses, but to kids?

I had to survive a big, noisy dinner, more parents and boyfriends than ever, my heart tight with fear that Valerie would pick the moment I should be listening to one of the kids' excited recaps to call. Afterwards, Brett took off with Cindi, thank God, and everyone else finally headed for their hotels to rest before the big Saturday ahead.

I couldn't stand the thought of barricading myself yet again in the camper. But walking around the grounds alone at night didn't appeal to me anymore. Maybe I should carry the gun. I circled around to our barn, jumping at innocent shadows, checking all the latches. Wishing we really could lock the horses in.

At last I settled on the metal steps of the camper, listening to the gentle rustles of horses and people bedding down. I should have been worrying about the silence from Valerie and the hassle from Wardle, but those strange, desperate moments with Jenny took over my mind. She had asked something of me but I had no idea what it was. Thinking about her laid an exhaustion over me that had nothing to do with lack of sleep. It had to do with a sense of loss when I didn't even know what I should have wanted, when I should have been thinking about my own plans. It wore on me thinking about what she might have done. And who with. A nagging thought took shape: she was making stupid choices, and what I'd done to her might have been the cause. One thing was clear, she was what I needed to let go of. She had nothing to do with the challenges I faced.

Fuck with it. So stupid to think what I'd felt for her was ever any kind of love. She was just this broken thing I kept cutting myself on, like I was one of those people who wanted the cutting. Fuck with it all.

I dragged myself into the camper to pour bourbon. No Ativan tonight. I had to clear my head of fairy tales and think what came next. Looked like the Paxtons thought they could run out the clock. Either that or try some new way to silence me. It was easier to believe Rich had slipped up and closed that trailer door than, say, Dever. I hadn't threatened anybody about the drug stuff. So it was the Paxtons. They had lured Valerie with promises she'd get a scoop on the drugs, and then used her to trap me.

I should have taken uppers. Maybe a little of Dever's coke would have stopped my eyes closing on a hazy raft of useless possibilities. I was reeling through some scene where someone had hidden Romp and I couldn't find him when my text app dinged.

I didn't want Rich Paxton in our camper and I didn't want him near our horses. But I wasn't about to trot along like a good boy to the damned Holiday Inn.

I wrote, "There's a bar at the Four Seasons on the Asheville highway. Twenty minutes." I shut off the phone.

At the hotel I parked across the lot and watched him arrive. He stopped on the sidewalk at the bar entrance, peering around before he disappeared inside.

I drove over, sat for five minutes by my dash clock before I followed. I hoped the wait would make him fret.

The bar was roomier than the one where Carr had caught me: long, with booths along the wall and tables at the far end. I'd expected a Friday late crowd, but the place was almost deserted. A guy at the bar watching some sports channel on the big TV, a woman in jeans and a sequined top bent over her phone in a booth. Paxton waited at one of the shadowy tables, nursing a full rocks glass. He wore the same leather jacket I remembered from the day of the fire. Then I'd thought fake country. Now I thought motorcycle bad. He watched me sit with a cocksure smile, like you'd use on somebody you knew a lot better than he knew me.

"Let's don't drag this out," he said.

The bartender came over. I shook my head.

He leaned over his glass toward me. "There's not a word of truth to it, whatever fantasy you've dreamed up."

If he'd failed at attempted murder last night, no surprise he'd follow up by offering a bargain. I wondered what he thought would move me. "Then why am I here?"

He sipped from his glass. Smell of Scotch. "Because I hate to see somebody like you—young, with a good business going and a lot of talent—get into trouble. Turn into a troublemaker."

He rattled the glass so the ice pinged. A TV Mafioso couldn't have put the threat better. I shrugged. But he surprised me. "You care about the horse," he said. "Right? You want the horse to go to a safe place where he'll be taken care of. Right?"

I leaned away from him. So this was what he thought I'd take.

"We all do," said Paxton. "But it's your call."

"Let's not drag this out," I said. "You want me to keep my mouth shut about your dirty tricks. You think you can use Romp as some kind of bribe."

He tilted his head, mouth hardening. "So you don't care about the horse after all."

I set my hands on the table. The motion made him blink.

I said, "I don't care how many scams you run or how many shell companies you own or how many people you cheat. Or how many times you threaten me or attack me. I want the names. All of them. Who did that to Romp."

The smug look clicked off. He tried to bring it back but the effort didn't convince me. "What the hell are you up to? I don't have your goddamn names."

I rocked back in my chair.

He plonked the glass down on the table, so loud the man at the bar looked our way. He leaned forward again, covering the space between us. "If I had any fucking idea who did that, I'd be up to something on my own. But I don't. So I've only got one thing for a bribe, if that's what you want to call it." He took an angry swallow. "That horse can live a quiet happy life for a long time. If that's what you want."

I shoved my chair back. Braced my fists on the table and got in his light. "We all want long happy lives, don't we? If that's what *you* want."

He lifted his glass with a jerk as I left him. The ice had melted and it didn't make any more of those little pings.

I let myself into the camper. Took the gun from the drawer.

I unloaded it, put both hands around it, found the line of sight like I'd been taught. Dry-fired twice, hard snaps in my hands.

Didn't have my goddamn names? Bullshit. He wouldn't cough them up to blackmail? He'd puke them out just fine at the point of a gun.

What a stinking little fantasy I'd made for myself, thinking I didn't have to throw my heart over. Getting all cozy thinking I could clear the wall and never land. I might have lived forever telling myself the screams I didn't have the guts to stop were meaningless whimpers.

But now there were those few moments in that bar.

He had the names and I had to get them, no matter what it took. Finish this. Or leave Romp in the hands of a man so obscene I couldn't find a word filthy enough to describe him. A man who'd already let that horse be tortured if he hadn't personally done it, and who would torture him again for a few dirty bucks.

I almost jumped up and went out in the night to find him. I'd track the others down once the names poured out with his piss and shit and vomit. The trigger would pull itself. Each shot I fired, I'd say, this is for what you did to Romp . . .

What stopped me with a round chambered and my hand on the door latch was something the gun guy had told us. *If you ever have to kill someone, the worst thing you can do is fire wild. A bad shot won't drop somebody, two bad shots won't either. When all hell's breaking lose, you have to maintain control.*

Wild didn't begin to describe what I wanted to do in that moment. Until I saw my shots spinning nowhere and Paxton climbing to his feet. The cops who came for me wouldn't fire wild. Wardle might even smile as he plugged me. He'd drop me and leave Paxton to take out what he wanted to do to me on the horse.

First time in what seemed like a long time, the sweat spewed out of me, full-blown. Because I'd let the rage take me, lost sight of my goal. I sank to the bunk, locked my mind on the gun. Ice in my hands, clenched between my thighs. Dim awareness of my finger alongside the barrel like the gun guy had taught me. Sweat giving way to shivers and then to slow breathing. Space came back into focus. All hell hadn't broken loose. I'd beaten the sweat and the madness, taken control.

Paxton had been my best option. He might think he was my only option. Might think he'd won. But control meant being smart about what you had to work with and what you wanted to happen.

I put the gun back in the drawer. Under control.

CHAPTER 36

LAST SATURDAY OF THE SERIES, crazier than ever: setting fences, checking jump orders, wiping boots, adjusting spurs, making them tell me their courses, learning my own courses, making sure their reins were straight and their coats pulled down to make their backs flat and painting hooves and all the rest of the chaos. I smelled last night's sweat on me. I kept moving so no one else would.

Through everything, I watched and thought, my mind baiting traps to see what they caught. Valerie was out there somewhere, hugging her schemes. Ricoeur never looked my way. I saw Jenny once or twice from a distance that had to be deliberate. Thank God for that distance. Even short glimpses of her reminded me of how little I could do to get her out of her crazy mess.

The kids' folks hung around closer than usual, though maybe it just seemed that way. The guys did their stuff and Martha did hers, and if any of them looked at me cock-eyed, I didn't turn around fast enough to catch them at it, though I was sure I felt their gazes on the back of my neck. Still things to prove, even to myself. Still work to do so that all this would still be here if I could salvage my plan. I went over Scott's course with him inch by inch even though I suspected I was piling on too much information: ride forward and sit up and wait and outside aids off the turn and don't knee pinch (but he knew that) and reins even and . . . sheesh. I calmed down with the girls, lecturing Clown about how his ears should perk and showing Whisper how to win the flat by waving my arms back and froth to demonstrate a swinging stride. The girls didn't seem worried I might be conning them. Their sweet, blind trust fed confidence in me. I didn't dwell on how nuts my plan was. I didn't add up the thin odds of the best option Paxton had left me, sealing a deal with Carr.

So I watched for Carr, over the ponies' necks, behind the girls' backs, and under their folks' radar. By mid-morning he hadn't popped up anywhere, though between the ponies' first and second trips Dever emerged across the jumper rings in his spiffy golf cart, feet up, elbows spread, grinning down at Dyan. Dyan laughed so loud at something Dever said that I missed who won the Junior Hunters. If I was Wardle, I would have been all over Dever. Wardle must be off baiting fresh hooks for his ongoing fishing expedition. If yesterday was any sign, they'd be useless. Not least because I wouldn't leave any fish in the pond.

I glanced back after Dyan's chortles quieted and in her place with Dever—at last—was Carr. Neither of them paid me any attention across the mish-mash of people and horses and rings. I had to pretend to listen to Taylor reciting her course while I kept them in view. Carr's mouth moved fast, close to Dever's ear. Dever frowned as he bent to listen, as if Carr was handing off something rank.

"And soften for the six coming home," Taylor said, pointing with her crop, and I dutifully nodded, thinking the way Dever sneered down at Carr shouted "staff." The flip of his hand as he fired the cart up looked like dismissal. Carr didn't glance my way as he trudged off, not all that cocky, and I couldn't break free to lope over and find out what frame of mind Dever had left him in.

Would I have the goods to turn him? So far in all our run-ins, he hadn't shown any fear. Money seemed the best bet. I had some, not all that much, but he couldn't check my credit score. I was calculating how much somebody like that would hold out for when he resurfaced at the jumper ring in Tannenbaum's cart with a saddle for a tack swap. As he got down to take the horse's bridle, his gaze slid over mine, came back. His look was thoughtful. I held it until he broke the link with a shift of a shoulder. But he glanced at me when he climbed back into the golf cart and I thought I saw him nod.

A big risk, getting down to pay dirt with him. But no one else to turn to. I should have practiced firing that gun more often. If I couldn't rope Carr in, I'd need it. Either way, my mind filled with lines of fences, combinations, with impossible distances between them, challenges no normal horse or rider could hope to adjust for. Then here came Pat, handing Snap's reins to me, and I had to stop thinking about killing people and ride.

The last class in Snap's division. I told myself with this grand young horse beneath me, I didn't have to throw my heart over any fences, I just had to let him jump. Whatever I carried, I had to leave

238

on the ground. Pat ran a hand down his glowing neck in the in-gate. "I've been really happy with this summer. You've done a great job."

I wanted to win that class more than I'd ever wanted to win anything. Too much. He went double-clean but I picked safe over bold and choked in the jump-off. We were third.

Pat had no idea what had ridden that last course with me. "Good decision," she said lightheartedly. "He's still learning. And this is a step-up. Good job."

A note of forced cheer in her voice? Relief that she'd gotten Robb through this summer before he crashed any more fences? Her relief was nothing to mine when I handed her that horse unharmed.

Time to get on Zenith. Brett came to the schooling area with a tight-lipped neutrality that made a poor show of his version of normal. Somewhere between his sparse suggestions and adjusting my feet in the irons, the realization swamped me: whether I ever rode another class depended on what I could sucker out of Jeff Carr. I had to rope him into the plan I had going, gamble that I could buy him. A gamble no sane person would have taken on. Sitting on Zenith waiting for my trip, it came to me like a blow what a fool I was to count on that desperate gamble. If my fate depended on turning Carr to my purposes, the odds were better than even that this would be the last class I'd ever ride.

And how fitting, I thought, that if this was my last ride, it should be on crazy little Zenith, the horse who was a gamble by definition. The horse who demanded you get your heart over long before he left the ground. He needed so much more from me than Snap did, you had to take what he was and ride what you had and give him more of yourself than you could sometimes spare. Of all horses to have to carry me over a course of big fences when all my concentration was fixed on a leap far beyond the show ring that had nothing to do with him.

Except that it did. What happened in the next twenty-four hours had everything to do with him. If I failed with Carr, what I'd imagined ahead for Zenith would be his true future: Brett's guilty caretaking, then a life in cheap-horse hell. Any saving spark he had in him undiscovered. Too late now, when this trip, my last chance to let the spark out, was just a pit stop in a blind gallop toward a place where he would never consent to go.

My mind took me back where I'd been that first day after I'd climbed into the burning trailer. All at once, once more, I was scared.

239

In the in-gate my hands shook. The reins wanted to slide out of my fingers. My feet couldn't find the edge of the irons. I couldn't get him around this course even if that was what it would take to save him, couldn't do what had to be done. Like before, I got into the ring by some dim magic, helpless. In front of me loomed shadows that had to be fences. Like before, somebody knew how to get over them. Not me. I was so amazed when I looked back and found them all still standing that I almost forgot there was more to it, the real crazy gamble: the jump-off.

Under me Zenith sidestepped. The jump-off buzzer sounded. I owed him a last chance to show what he had; I had to at least try. I fought to remember the shortened jump-off course, picked up my canter blind. If I could have seen the wall ahead it would have saved me. All I saw was our futures if I didn't pull off a feat no sane person would have attempted. A fucking miracle. More than one.

The first fence fled behind us. One of us knew the answers to all the standard questions: a hard turn to six, then a rollback to four-a-and-b, the combination. Next the bending line from five to eight, then somebody found a perfect spot to the next-to-the-last fence, the oxer before the final turn. That turn, a right around a couple of fences, put you on a long straight run to a final vertical near the gate. Rider after rider turned that vertical to firewood charging to make up time. Others wasted precious hundredths of a second checking to set up for that big stark fence.

No one had cut inside the center obstacles to the final vertical instead of taking the sweeping track around them because it couldn't be done.

But Zenith was small and quick and if this was his last class who cared what shambles he left behind him? Time to see what miracles he could produce. So I asked for what moments before anyone normal would have called hopeless—hauled him hard right inside the fences I was supposed to go around.

Flying down the ring at that crazy angle meant that when we turned to the vertical Zenith had only three full strides to get his eye on his job.

For a moment I knew I'd blown it. We were too flat, not enough impulsion, the spot wasn't there. You couldn't fix it at that point. You were done. We either had to slide through that big hard fence pulling up before it or take it with our chests.

He left from so far back you could have landed an airplane under him. Hit the ground hard, zoomed through the timers on his belly. I listened for the thud of a pole falling and when I didn't hear it looked back over my shoulder. Clean.

We'd gained a full second over the next fastest horse.

Martha turned up grinning beside me, smacking my boot as I rode out. An odd damp luster on her sallow cheekbones. "Death wish," she said.

I let Jorge take Zenith. Claryce's course in her ammy class was the same as mine, same jump-off. Brett said, "Watch Flight school. See if he's sharp enough to try that inside turn."

A job to do. I needed it. I was still sailing, clearing big fences. Thinking of other things that minutes ago I'd sucked back from because they couldn't be done. "He's too big, too much power," I said, even if Claryce didn't want to hear it. "He'll jump past the turn." I caught Brett in a nod. He said, "A bunch of them are gonna try it and blow it. That should clear the field pretty good." Watching Flight go clean with the leading time, I had to ground myself, like I'd landed off my own ride in a place I'd never been.

Valerie answered my text as I pulled my boots off and settled in a chair between Cadence's mom and Rianne. Rianne offered me a beer from the ice chest beside her. I took it, drank long, then clicked the icon.

They're doing it again. Ask Jenny which one this time.

Rianne shifted in her chair beside me, making me start. "You should take us all to dinner to make up for scaring the shit out of us, Mr. Inside Turn."

They were cheering Zenith's win, his second that series. Scott, sitting across from us, laughed, a laugh with depth, a boy's growing-up laugh. A step-up horse for him next summer . . . "I can't go to dinner. I have something I have to do."

"Oh, no!" Rianne stomped a boot. "We're all done tomorrow! Except for the Grand Prix, this is your only chance." She hollered. "Brett! Robb says he's not going to dinner!"

Brett looked out from the tack stall, fiddling with Growly's bridle. He shrugged. Rianne gave me a pout. Martha came into the aisle. She bent to fish in the ice for the bilge she drank, some lager. "What's all this?"

"Robb won't go to dinner! It's almost our last night!"

Martha got interested in wrestling with her pop tab. "I don't think we're his first love anymore."

I made a teasing show. "I have a secret girlfriend."

"You can't," said Cadence, coming up behind me. "We're your girlfriends!" She smacked me with the hairnet she'd just taken off.

I tilted my head back to look at her upside down and wiggled my eyebrows. As always when I did that, she burst out laughing. I caught Martha in my upside-down sights, too. Didn't turn her frown over. I trapped Cadence's hairnet as she flipped it at me. "You can all be my girlfriends tomorrow."

"We'd better be." She snatched the hairnet.

"For God's sake, don't rip that," said her mother. It was one of the special horse-show hairnets, to keep long hair under helmets. "I don't want to have to buy another one."

I pushed from my chair and headed out, for the first time pumped for one more inside turn.

CHAPTER 37

CARR WAS UNLOADING TWELVE-PACKS of beer and soda from a pickup and hauling them to a fridge in Tannenbaum's tack stall. Gofer work. When I came up, he eyed me from under his rusty brows as he grabbed two more cartons and disappeared inside. I propped an elbow on the side of the truck bed. He came out wiping his mouth with a sleeve. "Ain't you got things to do somewhere else?"

Not a tooth in sight. But I hadn't expected a pushover. A lot safer for him if I did the offering. I gave him room to work around to where we were going. "Things any better for you than the other night?"

He gave a crisp nod. "Yeah, I've been thinking about the other night."

"Me, too."

"I bet." He picked up another twelve-pack. Craft beer. Our customers sometimes brought their own in case I didn't buy the one out of a hundred they liked. A crease between his brows now as he got a firmer grip on the carton. "I'm working real hard to forget whatever I said in that bar and you should too."

A clang in his tone like a rock under the surface. "What do you want me to forget?"

A groom down the aisle shouted something to him in Spanish that I didn't catch. Carr whistled in response, then called, "*Momentito*." The groom gave a thumbs up and went into a stall. Turning, Carr swung the twelve-pack wide enough that it almost hit me. "We're busy here. What do you want?"

The rock wasn't below the surface. It was the grit in the sweaty planes of his face. I told myself, he's a survivor, he won't sell cheap. Sort of like buying and selling horses except that more than a commission rode on the deal. "The other night I thought you wanted something. Maybe something I've got."

He set the carton on the tailgate, looked down the aisle. A lot of activity there, grooms, riders, horses, a girl dressed for her class lining up her blaze-faced bay beside a mounting block. Tannenbaum himself glanced my way, raised a hand as he followed his rider out toward the rings. Carr produced a grin. Maybe to the people down the aisle it was one of his stock versions. It looked staged close up.

"I know what you're up to, Slaughter," he said, fists tightening. "The more I thought about it the more I figured it out. You got some kind of dirty work you want doing. Just like the others. Like I said, looking to hire staff." He jabbed a boot heel in the raked shavings between us. "Let me clear up one thing for you. I have a list of ten people who'll say where I was that morning. In case you got any ideas."

He studied my face. Maybe he thought he saw me hurting. He laughed.

And then maybe my rage showed. The look he'd get when I lined him up next to Paxton. My trigger finger aching. With all that meant. Because his laugh died to a strained grin that stretched his face almost to breaking. "The police will want that list," I said.

His teeth turned to a wall the words had to squeeze through. "Fine. Let me get you some postage."

"No." My own words had to break past teeth clenched against them. "I'll deliver it."

"Yeah, see where that gets you. Not where you think." He glanced around, as if making sure no one was looking when he aimed his finger gun at my shoulder. It didn't stab, just tapped, as if he wanted to see how hard I'd be to knock over. "So get out of my face, Slaughter, you're not such a big fucking hero."

I pushed off the truck. I wouldn't mind if he read that I could have killed him as he stood there. "I don't know," I said. "Maybe to the horse."

I stopped outside in the lane to let the heat rise off me. I could feel the fury coming, through the insides of my bones.

I was lucky no one spoke to me, at least not that I was aware of. I didn't know how long it would take, not to quiet the rage inside me, that wouldn't happen, but to wrap my muscles around it so it couldn't explode through the walls of my gut.

I wasn't going to persuade the names out of anybody. Or buy them. That had all been Disney. Taking them was my only option.

With all that meant.

The truth of it, as I waited for air to push through to my brain, was what I'd known from the start. No justice until I committed the part of me I'd held onto. Nobody else to do this. No other path to justice except over the wall.

My phone dinged. Martha. "We're at Brewster's if you change your mind."

Above it on my message list, Valerie's text. *They're doing it again.*

I walked, passed our camper, going nowhere. Saying over and over, Carr and Paxton. A fucking chant. Starting to ache to get it over with. Tired. Exhausted. Wanting to run headlong into traffic. Fire wild.

That wasn't good. I dug my nails into my palms to stop the pulse from pounding in my wrists. This was the dangerous moment. Do it wrong and all I'd have were the gofers. Staff. The big shots would walk, wouldn't even end up in that courtroom. They'd be free to do it all again and again.

And their victims would go on screaming. I'd hear.

Control was the answer. Being smart. How? Act normal? Show up for dinner with our barn? I thumbed Martha's text up. Saw Valerie's again.

Valerie. What the text said registered suddenly, clawing up from where I must have buried it when I kidded myself I could seduce Carr. "They're doing it again" said she knew something. Or thought she did.

Valerie and her little notebook. And that mysterious bag. Once I'd thought of her as one of the tools I had to work with. Maybe secrets there that would make me smarter. I texted to the number she'd written from.

CHAPTER 38

I PICKED WOODY'S ON TIMBERBURG SQUARE because it was the kind of family soup-and-sandwich restaurant where our barn group wouldn't wander in. Like with Paxton, I let her get inside, then drove over and pulled up next to her car.

She'd taken a booth in the bright, open room on the side away from the windows, a glass of soda in front of her. An aproned woman came over as I slid in but I shook my head. Valerie wrapped both hands around her glass and leaned toward me. "For starters, I don't think Jenny told you a fucking thing."

So she thought she was going to handle this conversation. "Excuse me, I did save your life."

"Yeah." She twisted the glass in the condensation puddle it was forming next to her paper placemat. "Thank you."

"Brett told me about you messing with Jorge and Raul."

"'Messing with them' is a loaded way of putting it."

"It's an accurate way of putting it. They're here on visas they could lose any minute. You know that. You were poking around to stir up trouble and you got some. Our guys don't have anything to do with that shit."

She studied the little bit of condensation she hadn't already rubbed off the glass. "This shit they don't have anything to do with—did Jenny tell you anything about that?"

I scoffed. "She didn't have to. Everybody on the showgrounds knows where the drugs are. The kids all hang out at the Skyhaven tack stall. It has nothing to do with our barn or our horses or what you and I were supposed to be working on."

An older couple, both in shorts and sandals, took a booth across from us. Valerie lowered her voice. "That Dever guy."

I folded my placemat, folded it again. Yeah, it was the drug stuff, not saving horses, that would take her where she wanted. "Look, the

247

police are on the drug stuff. Maybe they won't care if you come up with a big story." I saw a distance I hadn't fully expected and took a Zenith leap, long spot, wide spread, maybe enough horse under me. "You've been going around asking questions about the drug stuff, I guess for your *New York Times* thing, and along with riling everybody up you said something to Jenny." She blinked. Another leap. "She didn't tell me exactly what you said to her, but whatever it was, she ran straight to the Paxtons. Whatever they're up to, they'd kill over it. Now it sounds like they're going to kill another horse, isn't that what you texted me? Like they tried to kill you?"

Her mouth worked in a sideways S shape like two things were trying to come out of it at once. She reached in her vest pocket, pulled out the plastic bag. "What is that?"

I picked it up. A vial inside, empty. I read the label. Succinylcholine. Not something I would ever be likely to use. It paralyzed horses undergoing surgery. Killed in the wrong dose. And easy to miss because it broke down fast into natural substances in a horse's system. I dropped the bag on the table. "Yeah, it can kill horses. You should ask the Paxtons if they used it on her Arabian stud."

She pulled the bag to her and toyed with it, eyes on me. "You're right, it was sweet little Jenny I asked things. And yeah, about that guy she lived with and the drugs. Got the cold shoulder. But then out of the blue she called." A twist of the crinkly plastic. "Said she'd been asked to give something to horses. To kill them for insurance. Said she didn't know what it was she was supposed to give but she'd told whoever it was no." She eyed the bag where it lay between us. "But somehow she would get something to show me. There it is."

"She couldn't just 'give' this to horses. It has to be injected." I shoved as far back as the booth would let me. "Jenny may be a lot of things, but she's not a killer. Get that straight."

"Oh, you mean killing reporters isn't part of this 'everything' she told you, then?"

"That's bullshit." I kept my voice level. "You're not gonna tell me Jenny attacked you."

"Depends on your definition. She sure set me up."

I picked up the ketchup bottle at the end of the table to keep my hands busy. No way to derail this until I saw where it was headed. She twirled the bag on the table. "She gets me up to that trailer lot in the middle of the night. Big secret. Going to give me this shit." She rattled the bag. "So she gets out of her car, leaves her headlights on so I'm blinded. Hands me this. Then she's looking past me and she gives this little yelp. The next thing I know I'm on the ground with a knee in my back."

"Paxton?"

"I don't know who it was. And the next-next thing I know I'm in that trailer, scared as shit."

I popped the ketchup bottle open. "You said they hit you."

She pulled her hair back from her face. The bruise had bloomed on her neck behind her jaw.

"Yeah," she said. "It hurts."

"Jenny didn't do that."

She let her hair fall back into place. "No, you're right. Not that." Her gaze drifted, the way it did when she was thinking. "I don't think she ran to the Paxtons, but I do think you're partly right about them. I think they're mixed up in this drug stuff. People threatening their horses to make them play. After all, they've got a sweet money-laundering conduit already there for the taking. So I don't think it's insurance at all."

"So nothing to do with the succinylcholine—"

"That was meant to throw me off track. Note that they left it there for whoever found me. I guess they thought sooner or later someone would."

I leaned back. The booth was padded, but something about it cut.

"If you got hit," I said, "maybe you don't remember everything that happened."

Her voice got its edge back. "I went up there yesterday. To the trailer where they put me. I found my phone, smashed in the road. I tracked down her truck. Found shards of glass in one of her tires."

"That's nuts. Glass wouldn't have stuck there."

"So don't believe me. I got in her face and you saw her reaction. Of course she didn't know what the hell I was talking about."

"She made that call. To get me there in time." That was a guess, but Valerie didn't contest it. I shifted. "There's still no connection between her and Romp."

"Okay, so who tried to kill Romp?" She waited out my silence. "Maybe that guy Carr?"

No way to know what my face told her. All my work keeping that name on the shelf and now she'd flung it at me too fast for me to catch. I said with a broken calm that maybe came from losing the one piece of leverage I'd held onto, "What does any of this have to do with Carr?"

"I had a conversation with a guy who knows him."

"Who?"

"Apparently a guy who's been sitting on a grudge against Carr for a long time. When he found out there was another horse on Carr's agenda, he decided to come looking for me."

Easy to believe that scenario. I'd rather trust Carr's enemies than his buddies. But the story led downhill faster than I could keep my footing. I said, "Which horse?"

"Another one of the Paxtons'. He said their best one."

"When?"

"There's only a couple of nights left, right? Tonight or Sunday, after the Grand Prix." Another thinking journey. "Sunday night people will be partying. The coast'll be clear."

I drew a tight breath. Carr's name had put me in new territory. "Are you saying Carr was the one who mugged you Thursday night?"

"I told you I don't know."

"Jenny wasn't there that morning with Romp."

"You just didn't see her."

I stopped the violent headshake I almost gave her. "She wasn't there."

"Let's think about it. She's up at all hours in the dark, right? Braiding horses. In and out of the barns. Carr, or somebody like him, they'd stand out. Not her." She tapped the table. "She's mixed up with Carr, that's obvious, in case you weren't watching. She delivered him Romp. I bet she'll deliver the next one. God knows what's in it for her, what hold they've got over her."

I focused past her on the plain, white-painted ceiling. Couldn't find any answers. A long silence. When I looked back at her, her mouth was doing things. Finally she said quietly, "Sooner or later I'll have to tell Wardle about Jenny and what I know about this guy Carr."

"Wardle can't fix this."

"If you think you can, you're running out of time."

As if I wasn't sitting there counting the minutes. "If you tell Wardle about Jenny, he'll arrest her. That won't stop what's going to happen. If you're right, she's part of it, but not all. Giving her to Wardle will just mean you and I can't do anything about it."

"What can we do about it now?"

"Give me tomorrow."

She shook her head. "Next time she might not call you to come save me. Or herself, for that matter. She might not be able to."

I smoothed what sounded too much like desperation. I had to stop her from going to Wardle. "Until morning. Keep your doors locked. You'll make it till then."

She studied me. For the first time, she drank from the soda. Set the glass down.

"Come to the barn before classes," I told her.

The S of her mouth turned to a V. It could have been a smile if it hadn't looked so pointed. "What are you going to do, warn her?"

The anger locked my jaw and I saw her flinch. But truth was what she would respond to and I found some. "You went off on your own asking questions. I had to risk my life to save you because you did that. Now you owe me one night to ask questions of my own."

Another sigh, deeper. I clasped my hands between us, bent close. "Look at it this way. We still don't know who's behind this. You say it's not the Paxtons. You turn Jenny in, if she's involved, Wardle won't get it out of her. We'll never know. They'll keep doing it, just using somebody else to do their dirty work."

In the pool her glass made, she drew a tic-tac-toe grid, a slow X in an upper corner. "And you think you can find out in one night?"

"You said yourself they'll probably wait until Sunday after the Grand Prix. And it's not like she has anywhere to run."

Now an O in the center. A draw almost certain.

I threw in my last chip. "Don't you want to know who it is? Or are you dragging Jenny in regardless because you know I care for her? Is that it?"

Her eyes were always alive; now they flared. She demolished the grid with a swipe. "That was fucking low."

I was ready to go a lot lower. I didn't want her to make me. "Nothing will happen tonight. You said so."

She shifted her purse onto the table. "Your barn. Daybreak." She slid the bag into the purse and rose to stand over me. "Whatever you're going to do, stay out of fucking horse trailers. You can't solve anything for anyone if you're dead."

CHAPTER 39

THE ONE THING I KNEW when I got back to the show was that Valerie would not make all this up. I might not know where she lived or how many pets she had or for that matter how old she was, but I knew that.

I also knew I was lucky to get this much reprieve. Valerie had a normal conscience, one with limits. She wouldn't keep risking lives to beat Wardle to what Jenny might tell him, not even for the *New York Times*. Still, she'd said she would wait till morning. I trusted that. She had flinched at the idea of turning her unsolved case over to Wardle like it had jabbed a pain center in her brain.

And now I understood what Jenny had been afraid I would listen to.

In the camper I poured a double bourbon in a plastic glass, no ice, and slipped outside. It should be a while before our group made it back, buzzed and bubbling, but I didn't want to take the chance. I needed to get my head around what had come down on me. What I had to do next.

Dusk was falling; headlights glowed as people drove in after dinner for a last check on their barns. A dusty sheen over the showgrounds, natural for a rider to wander down to see if the jump crews had finished setting up for the next day. The pavilion overlooking the rings where I'd talked with Phil was deserted. I climbed up, sipping the bourbon. In the ring below the crew was unloading the last poles from a flatbed and measuring lines.

A few fences over, someone was hacking a big chestnut in one of the schooling rings. A lot like the Paxtons' Dutch horse, but with more white. The low sun behind me spilled over the horse, something in him flaring. The way you sometimes see them on a summer night at home, drifting in the sunset, in the green grass.

253

I'd unfolded a chair and settled when a car crept down the road behind me toward the pavilion and the rings. God, not our people coming back early. The car pulled up beside me. A black police car, unmarked but with the telltale spotlight in front of the mirror. Wardle leaned across the seat toward me. "Thought that was you. Maybe now you've got a minute or two?"

The time had probably come when normal people would have held out for a lawyer. The only task for my lawyer would be keeping Wardle at bay until I finished my job. This time I did keep my voice level. "What do you want?"

He climbed out, stretched wearily. "Just a couple of minutes. Some stuff I thought you might want to know."

The chestnut horse was walking now, cooling, gold in the dust off the sand in the rings. Below us the jump crew cleared out, their quiet calls echoing in the growing dark. Wardle stepped up onto the pavilion platform and unfolded a chair for himself, filling the metal frame to overflowing. "To cut to the chase," he said, his tone as matter-of-fact as if we were discussing the sunset, "this guy Zack Cassidy, seems like he got knifed up there where you sent him. Serious enough to put him in the hospital. Some kind of warning, I was told."

Zack again, like a freak wind blowing over a jump standard as you cantered around the turn. Like then, pulling up and waiting for someone to put things right so you could keep going. Except in that case they stopped the clock for you. "I guess that kind of thing happens. Anyway, it does on TV."

"Wasn't TV."

I sipped bourbon. The horse walked up the lane toward us, a woman on him, reins floating.

"It's funny they didn't kill him," Wardle said.

"Funny?"

"They certainly could have. Stopped short."

"They?"

"Haven't pinned it on anyone. He won't say."

I took a long swallow. "I'm supposed to care about this why?"

He looked at his shoes, shrugging. The horse walked past us, the woman waving. "Hi, Robb." I drooped my cup of bourbon between my knees, waved back.

"Pretty horse," Wardle said.

"When I turned Zack in," I told him, "I didn't give a fuck what happened to him. I still don't."

He shifted suddenly, getting up. The lights coming on around the barns made the poles on the jumps below us shimmer. He said, "Seems to me you think keeping your mouth shut makes people safer. But sooner or later you'll have to tell me what you know. Who you've talked to." He seemed to take a moment to work on his last line. He bent close to me to deliver it. "It's easier than it looks to get at people you think are safe."

That edge he had once told me I tended to slip over was several steps behind me. "Nobody's safe until you do the job you're fucking paid for."

If I touched a nerve he didn't show it. He gave one of his big sighs, then rose and folded his chair and returned it to the stack. "Told you it wouldn't take long." Damn if he didn't smile. "Have a nice evening," he said.

He stepped down to his car, climbed in. With a wave through the windshield he drove away.

The dust from the ring settled, a graying haze rising from the nearby creek. One really hot summer here we'd flatted our horses in this kind of near dusk. You could see well enough if you didn't drift out of the track into the rail.

I decided Wardle thought Zack's name would do to me what his threats couldn't. Shatter me so he could sift through the wreck he'd made of me for the shards of his pitiful case. I couldn't think of any other reason for him to tell me what had happened to Zack. He thought he could bleed me for leverage on Jenny, since she was the only lead he could come up with. A dirty trick that might have worked if Valerie's ugly claims hadn't tunneled into my imagination, where they sat eating at the ruin of my pointless love.

Lights shone from the camper. Brett. His truck sat out front. With me not there, he was playing music off his phone through his speakers, loud enough I could catch the notes. Usually when he was alone he played hard and tooth-rattling—old stuff, the Stones or the Who. Now for some reason he'd turned up the volume on Patsy Cline.

Parking his truck close to the camper like that probably meant he'd soon head off somewhere. Even if he didn't, he usually went to bed before midnight. That would be the next piece of luck I'd need. I walked back to my own truck where I'd left it in the car lot, sat with the windows closed.

I had no idea how they would have done it. Surely not in writing. Passed her in somebody's barn aisle and whispered? So far as I knew they'd only done it once, so maybe there was no pattern. I took the owner's manual out of my glove box, tore out a blank page. I tried to imagine what the person Valerie had described was expecting. I wrote, "The Dutch horse tonight."

I got out and slipped past our camper down the lane toward hers. The windows were dark and her truck not there. I slid the note into the camper door frame, then sank into the shadows between the barns fronting her space. She might not come back till very late. It was okay. I wasn't going anywhere.

She came at eleven, drove past without seeing me, headlights cutting a wedge. She parked across the nose of her camper, got out, took a shopping bag from the back seat, then disappeared between campers toward her door.

She'd get maybe five hours of sleep. Or not. All I could see was the front of the camper, a light breaking beneath the lowered shade. Then, dim, a glow from farther back. The bedroom where she'd fled that last time Zack beat her silly. It would do things to you, being pummeled like that. For her the pummeling had been double, the physical blows on top of grief.

At least I thought she grieved.

When she came out, she came fast, jerking the door shut. She passed me in the white shadows of the sentry lights.

It wasn't hard to follow. I didn't try for silence. If she had only looked back.

She passed our barn. At Malloy's she stopped.

Malloy would have grooms posted. But she'd know which stall, which horse. If she'd made it out with Romp, she'd make it out with this one. She disappeared into the aisle.

I slipped fast back up the row to our camper. It was silent and dark, Brett's truck still there. But no Patsy Cline now, just tinny voices, and through chinks in his bedroom curtain, flashes from changing TV scenes. I eased the door open. The main space was empty, his bedroom door down the hall shut, the TV music swelling. Dozer would be sprawled on the bed with him, but no growls came as I worked the drawer open. With the gun holstered under my jacket, I headed back toward Malloy's behind the camper row, out of sight.

From a gap between campers I watched Malloy's aisle. No sign of her. Or a horse. I'd been away five minutes by my watch. Maybe she'd gone out the front and I could catch up to her. With my luck.

But my breath jumped at motion: the Night Watch lady, emerging from one of the aisles and headed Malloy's way. So much for this excursion. Unless Jenny had somehow figured out the woman's schedule and was working around it. That turned out not to matter; the woman merely glanced down the dark aisle, then sauntered on.

She was well away before the sentry lights struck the white gold of Jenny and the gold of the horse's head and the pale flash of his stable sheet. He followed at the end of a plain lead, no stud chain, head down, feet slow. She'd been the one who was lucky. A quiet latch, grooms drowning each other out snoring, too slight a figure in the dark to stir up the other horses. She'd shot him with ace, waited till it worked through his system, not enough to make him wobble, but enough to calm him, so he wouldn't ask where or why.

Our luck.

I slipped back, unseen, as they passed. He ambled, kind, drowsy, unknowing. They always follow, don't they? You say, let's go over here to ugly death, and they say, sure.

I fell in behind her, well back. On my phone I had Wardle's number. And hers. But I had that glow to follow. I didn't feel like a fool, didn't feel tricked, didn't even feel angry. I felt locked in, pulled down to that arcing glitter with a kind of craving. I didn't call Wardle. I followed her.

She led the horse up the path behind the campers, a muffled clipclopping ghost. If anyone saw, no one raised an alarm. Up the hill into the trailer lot. So they weren't afraid to pull the same shit again.

Some gofer was bound to pop out to take the horse, like Carr must have before I spotted him. I hung back, I hoped out of sight of anyone watching, but it did no good to plan. There might be several of them. After all, Carr hadn't done a very good job singlehanded. They'd be armed. Who doing this kind of thing wouldn't be?

My mind, making plans anyway, plotted how I could get them to talk. To tell me who was in charge. They'd be like the Paxtons, they'd never expect me to kill anyone. They'd think they could lie, bluff.

What would they do when they realized? Blab? Panic? Rush me? It wasn't the confrontation I'd imagined. It felt haphazard, unfinished. But if this was all I'd get, I'd take it. They would soon find that out.

Then I thought, I should take her first.

I thought, I have to. I can't stand and look at her, watch her waiting. I have to take her before she knows.

I made the moment take shape. Forced it. Her face on one of the blank forms. The image wavered. I fixed it there.

For now, though, her physical body moved through the night before me, unalarmed. She climbed the hill, farther than I'd expected. Close to the top she turned left down a row, the horse still plodding behind her. Once she reached over and patted his neck. Three trailers in, she stopped.

I stopped, too, put my hand on the gun in my belt. No one materialized to meet her. She started forward again, then turned right alongside a four-horse head-to-head, much bigger than the trailer where they'd trapped Romp. She led the horse to the back of the trailer. I edged forward, ducking under the trailer gooseneck so I wouldn't stand out against the white siding if she looked back.

From that shadow all I could see was the horse's rump. He swished his tail lazily, his halter rattling when he shook his head. Silence from her. I chanced a look. She'd tied him to one of the ring bolts on the trailer. No sign of her, but clear creaks of the ramp on the far side coming down. She'd leave the horse, then. Collect her murderous pay in her own good time.

The anger came, the rage I should have felt from the start. Betrayal. All the heartache I'd spent, trying to make sense of her bloody love. And now all the lies about insurance and dosing horses and not hurting anything. I shook with the simplicity of where I'd arrived, how easy it was to fix this, this small part. The idea of playing it smart drained out of me in an instant. I could have killed ten of her, each one exploding, bam, before they could open their mouths.

She came back. She untied the horse. She talked to him as she led him around the trailer, loud enough for me to hear. Her sweet words sent the sweat worming down my ribcage. "Come on, baby, it's okay, I promise. Nice hay. I'll bring you water. Just a little adventure. Come on."

His hooves thumped up the ramp on the other side, the trailer shaking slightly with his weight. I stepped out and eased forward, feeling for the gun. The same hook scored my gut that had lodged there when Romp screamed, a call I couldn't jerk loose from, nowhere to hide. Once I raised the gun, I would be used up, the future gone. No matter. For days now the horse I'd been riding for that wall had been floundering. Let the thing find its own distance. My hand gripped the gun and moved it even though it dragged me, like a chain tied to some wheel deep in the ground, turning. I met her rounding the back of the trailer. She saw me and screamed.

CHAPTER 40

T OO LATE TO CATCH HER UNKNOWING. Her stricken gaze on me. I was not in a place to make sentences. I said, "Why?"

Her eyes fixed on my hand, the gun. So wide they sucked up the thin light from the stars. She put her hand to her mouth, wiped. Words came out. "Someone . . . a note . . ."

"Not someone. Who?"

A headshake, her white hair whipping. "I don't know. Oh my God, Robb. Oh my God."

"Who?"

A snap now. "I told you, I don't know."

"Yes, you do."

She peered around wildly. "They followed you. Did they follow you?"

"Who?"

Her voice quickened. "I'll bring him back in a couple of hours. This was . . ." Hands on her face, in her hair. White strands pouring through her fingers, melted stars. I took the gun in both my hands and raised it to waist-level. She covered her mouth. "Oh my God. You can't think—"

"Yes, I do."

She stumbled around to the other side of the trailer. I followed, cut my gaze around. No sound or movement in the ranks of trailers. She sank to the wheel well beside the lowered ramp.

"I wouldn't . . . I didn't . . . I was trying to hide him . . ."

She spoke to the ground, mumbled. I moved to face her, still aiming. "What did you say?"

She looked up, straight at me. "They'll kill him."

"Yes."

"All it will take will be one person."

"Is that how many it took with Romp? Or two? Carr and you?"

She shook her head. It was too dark to see what her frown meant. "Not the horse. Zack."

Again. Always. Zack. I jerked the gun toward the downed ramp, the horse in a stall at the top of it. "So that's why you're doing this." An echo of Wardle's words, distant: *It's funny they didn't kill him.* "To keep these people from killing Zack."

She laid her pale hands in her lap in the oddest manner. Clasped and still, like women in paintings I'd seen in an art book in one of my foster homes. "They did that to Romp because I wanted out, I said stupid things, like I thought I could bargain, do the soft stuff, nobody getting killed." Her eyes glistened. "A kid died at Southern Pines, in April. An OD. And now Brian. Stuff I did, bad stuff no one should be selling." She hunched toward me. "I begged."

The horse fluttered his nostrils. A contented sound, above us in the dark. "This note, was it how you got directions?"

"No!" Her hands fluttered. "Somebody was warning me. Somebody who knows."

Maybe she could have taken the four words of my note—the Dutch horse tonight—that way. She breathed on her fingers, her voice now toneless. Maybe the way you'd read the sentence for your coming execution. "I've tried and tried to think of a way out. Once they kill Zack, they don't have anything to hold over me. So now they've changed to using the horses, hurting them. But I can't do this every night. If I get caught taking him back how will I explain it?" Her strained breath broke up what she was saying. "The only . . . way out is to . . . to make them kill me. Without me they'd leave Zack alone."

"That's crazy. No one is worth that."

She looked almost startled to find me still listening. She shook her head.

"Tell the police."

Bleak scorn in the flick of her hand. "Maybe if *you* killed me. Isn't that what you followed me here to do?"

I took a hand off the gun, lowered it to my side. She watched it. The light couldn't find her eyes now. After a moment, I said, "Why not let fucking Zack save himself. Let him tell the police what he knows."

She stood with a snort, scraping her palms on her jeans. "He doesn't know anything. He just did errands. I only know because—"

One hand rose and fell. "Some people traded me information for something they just had to have."

"Sex."

She didn't even shrug. She swayed on her feet for a moment, then grabbed air and staggered up the ramp. Beyond her the big horse's shadow as he tore at the full hay bag. She touched his nose. "I was going to get him water. But he won't be here that long."

The gun had started to feel cold. I looked up at her. "So you delivered the stuff."

Her nod was a tremor in the trailer shadows. "And collected the money. Sometimes people came while I was braiding. Or I hid things where I'd been told."

"That night with the candle—"

Her breath stuttered. "Yeah, a little message. You were pretty smart."

"And Empathetic?"

"There's a lot of ways for a horse to get killed."

I wanted to ask who came around in the dark while she braided our horses. "All that stuff you told Valerie. The succinylcholine you gave her."

"I didn't plan that. But I had to go along to steer her off. I thought she knew."

"So you tried to kill her."

A snapped headshake. "I texted you. You came."

No way to test the truth of that. "Someone locked us in there. You?"

She looked down from the ramp at me like I was a sign in a foreign language. "I warned her. I told her people might get killed. You—she—were making trouble. Worrying people over what you knew and wouldn't tell."

"Maybe if you'd told me who was doing the killing."

"And get Zack killed?" A shudder tensing into anger. "For God's sake, Robb."

"Now?"

She studied my face as if rewriting what she saw there. "Now you want to do the killing? To fix things? Like you wanted to kill Zack to fix me?" She made a sound I couldn't name. "I wish like hell I was the kind of thing somebody like you could fix."

If her partners were coming to finish this, they'd better hurry. But nothing stirred, no sound from the big dead boxes. I didn't know much about the stars, but I could see they'd moved.

I tucked the gun in my armpit. "You know who's behind this," I said.

"Yes."

"But you won't tell me."

"You'll get yourself killed if you know."

It wasn't like I had any threat left to jerk the names out of her. "The Paxtons."

I thought her sound this time was a laugh.

"Why Romp?"

"They knew I liked him."

"Dever."

This time the barest shrug.

"Romp screamed in that trailer," I told her. "Maybe I'm the only one who heard him."

"No," she said. "I did."

The cold gun sucked heat from my body. I lowered it. Her gaze didn't even track it. "People can buy all the fucking drugs they want," I said into her silence. "I will stop the screams."

Now she did laugh. At least I thought so. "Getting yourself killed won't stop jackshit."

"That's my business. Leave it."

"You used to think you loved me—"

"I didn't."

"Yes, you did." She came down the ramp at me, a wild blur out of the shadows. Spitting. "You were crazy. You wanted to kill Zack, didn't you? You thought all I needed was one good fuck to take care of him forever and fix me. Didn't you?" I barely got a sick sound out, got the gun overhead aimed skyward, before she was on me, wrenching at the waist of my jeans. "It's just us here. Nobody will see us." She ripped my jeans open. "If it'll knock this crazy killing shit out of you, God, give it a try."

She grabbed my dick. Hurting. The moment came when I could have done it. Fucked it out of her forever. But I found it in me to jab the gun in my jacket pocket with one hand and circle her wrists with the other. She fought, but I won.

I hitched up my jeans. Pulled my shirt down.

"It wouldn't have worked, would it?" she said, panting.

That would have to go unanswered, but I said anyway, "No."

She clasped her hands, that prayer move again. "There is a way you can fix me. If you ever loved me. If you will."

Over the sound of the horse now I heard my own breathing, with a funny whine to it. "What?"

"Tell Wardle. All of it. About me and Zack and Carr."

I stared at her. "That's stupid. You're not the ones behind it."

"He'll see you don't know that."

"That's crazy. He'll arrest you."

"Yes."

I understood then. "They'll kill you to stop you from talking." In that place where people weren't as safe as you imagined. "You want them to."

She looked around as if she'd opened her eyes on a bleak desert. She backed away and sank onto the ramp. Above us the horse chewed, peaceful. The moon must have risen somewhere because there was a glow.

"Not going to happen," I said. "I'm not going to live for fucking ever with *your* fucking screams."

She made a white rope of her hair, pushing it off her shoulder. Ignored me.

"It's not going to happen," I said again.

"Two fucking lives wasted."

"I will stop the screaming."

Her gaze passed over me blankly. "I'll take the horse back in a few minutes. But if you think I'll hurt him, you can take him now."

I closed my hand on the gun. Almost as if there was something I thought it should say but wouldn't. I took my hand off it and left her there.

CHAPTER 41

BACK IN MY TRUCK I laid the gun on my thigh, stroking it like it was breathing. *Tell Wardle. Tell it all. What she'd done for Zack.* Put her in Wardle's jail cell, where the people she wouldn't name wouldn't wait to see if she stonewalled. Wardle's small-town jail wouldn't protect her any more than federal prison was protecting Zack.

She'd asked me to make them kill her. Take away their reason to threaten Zack.

Nothing I did would save her. If she lived, she'd live with a hell she couldn't will away. Like Romp did. Like me. I couldn't change that for her; Zack here or Zack in prison, as long as she lived, he'd have her. Even if I had killed him when I should have, that wouldn't have changed anything.

All I could really change was the dying she'd been part of. Children I couldn't name, and horses whose screams I'd hear even if only in the nightmares. Children and horses—and her—all of them dying for the sake of one ugly bastard. I had the power to stop all that dying, right under my hand.

The last Grand Prix day. Today or never. I went to the camper to shower and shave and dress. In my mind the day ahead had a strange shimmer to it, as if I'd be floating out into a cloud. In that coming haze, the word "might" would have no meaning. No more thinking this "might" be the last time I told Cadence to shorten her reins or Rianne not to carry her hands so high or Scott to think about riding his own course and not everyone else's or Taylor to for God's sake check her diagonal or Bernie to let go a little, let go and ride. The word "will" replaced it. This *will* be the last time.

Brett sat at the table as I entered, cradling a coffee cup, staring. His gaze barely changed when he saw me. He didn't speak. I grabbed

267

my clothes and went into the bathroom. He was gone when I came out.

I picked a windbreaker light enough that no one would question if I needed it even as the day got warmer, pulled it over the gun where I nestled it against my side. I still didn't know how I was going to make it all happen, just that I'd reached the point where it *would* happen. Where I'd corner Carr and break him open, read in what he spilled where my feet should take me. I hoped sunlight would burn off the shimmer so I could see through to the end.

Then there was Valerie, leaning against the plank siding, our barn already buzzing behind her, come to claim the payoff she'd contracted for. I stopped to face her before anyone in the aisle saw me. She tilted her chin sideways, still keeping her gaze dead on me. "Morning's here."

Her sharp, frank face stripped off the shimmer. Turned everything hard. With one word to Wardle, this woman could make all I'd been through pointless. "Yeah, I see that," I said.

The chin went up higher. "And?"

I wouldn't have to stall much longer. "I'll tell Wardle everything I know." My last lie if luck didn't desert me. "After the Grand Prix."

"That'll be too late for him to do anything."

"He'll have tomorrow. It'll take them time to pack."

She gave me her cutting V-for-Valerie smile. "Didn't we say the horse will die tonight?"

"They won't do it now." I had to make her hear that. "They'll wait for another show."

But her eyes narrowed. "Let's see here. Assuming you're right and they wait, Wardle will take Jenny in, and maybe this guy Carr. Nobody else unless one of them named names, and you think they'll do that in the short time he can hold them before they get lawyers to clam them up?" She spread her hands like showing me a book of the future. "So the whole damn mess will just move on?"

Move out of her reach, I could hear her thinking. Take her big story with it. How to keep stalling her? "Maybe something will happen today. Maybe we'll know more later."

Her brows went up. "Oh, will we?" She looked past me, at the show coming to life, people leading horses out to be lunged, grooms trundling wheelbarrows, the rings with the newly set courses catching the young daylight, a scene she'd clicked into focus for me. "You know what? I've never spent a whole day at a horse show. Never thought I'd want to. But I might learn a lot."

"You can't hang around here. Or around me. It's going to be crazy."

"No argument from me on that assessment."

Here came Brett, still distant, but he had good eyesight. "I have to go. Please do me a favor. You know these people are dangerous. For once, be careful."

She actually laughed. "Coming from you, that's rich."

I shouldn't have been astonished to see our horses braided and waiting, but I was. Something blind, driven, in how she could do this, silently, alone in the dark with her thoughts and her crimes. The same as with me, maybe—heading out to the rings as the light rose, studying the lines and turns and combinations as if those piles of painted wood and stacked brush were landmarks in another country I could will myself into, where I could drift unmolested until the fucking end of time.

But knowing what this last day held kept me moving. Watching for Carr kept my mind racing so I didn't have to stare into the moments when I found him, what I'd have to do then. Planning. How to get him away from all these innocent people. How to surprise him so it all happened fast. How to get what I needed from him before I had time to think about anything more than *this is for all the screaming. All the dying. All the children and her and Romp* . . .

In the end I didn't have to find him. He put himself in my hands.

It started with a screaming shitstorm. I was following my kids toward the crowded gate for a huge twelve-and-under equitation class when a barrage of shouts erupted from Dever's barn. I pivoted toward the commotion alongside the dozen or so people nearby. Carr's voice rose, a whine of hysteria underneath it: "You fucking dirty bastard. Fucking dirty dickwad bastard!" His stocky figure reeled backward out of the dim aisle.

Dever emerged after him, face flushing. "Get out of my sight, you fucking asshole, get your ass gone!"

Carr tried to keep moving and still snap at air. "Treat people like shit, yeah, you'll see what that gets you."

"Take your cheap shit where somebody gives a fuck!" Dever yelled.

269

Carr flung him a finger and scuttled. Dever tossed a disgusted wave after him, spat, and disappeared into the barn.

Around me people gave themselves a shake like they'd been spattered with piss. Beth Hawley, a couple of feet from me, saying, "Jesus. Whatever that was, hope it isn't catching." Adam Blanchard, an Ohio trainer, answering, "The steward'll be on that. It's not like that guy Carr's much use for anything."

Blanchard was right, management could kick Carr off the grounds for that kind of exhibition. Gofers weren't like owners and trainers with entry money to anchor them. To me the outburst sounded like a staff-versus-big-shot relationship gone pretty sour. Maybe Dever hadn't paid what Carr thought he was worth for a little bit of dirty work.

Down the row of barns I could still see Carr in his blue windbreaker, shoulders hunched, moving fast. Behind me the ring opened and the girls and Scott made their way through the crowd to find space for themselves on the rail. Brett and Martha were over by the jumper ring for the last class in Claryce's ammy division. The judges in the kids' class would split the riders into two groups when they cantered, a standard practice at the faster pace to keep the more excitable mounts from exploding. That meant the class would take half an hour. Maybe I couldn't settle my business with Carr in half an hour, but I could find out what hole he'd ducked into. I turned my back on my kids on their ponies and took off on Carr's heels.

To my surprise, he veered into Malloy's barn. When I jogged up, Nia was adjusting a martingale on one of the barn's jumpers. "Jeff Carr come by here?" I asked.

"Think he went back to talk to Mel," she said, turning as the rider came up to mount.

In an open stall I found Malloy girthing up another jumper. "Carr?" His broad face hardened. "That douchebag? What makes you think he'd come here?"

I couldn't exactly challenge a flat denial. "Sorry, I thought I saw him."

"What do you want him for?"

"Just had a question for him."

"What question? Something I can answer?"

"No, just a deal he mentioned."

"Jesus." His brow creased. "He's trouble, Robb. I wouldn't believe a word of what he says."

"Yeah, well, thanks."

Okay, so where would the bastard go? I scouted from the camper row to the tack shops. No sign. The announcer in the flat class began calling the winners. I heard our kids' names; they had placed high and if I wasn't there for the debriefing they'd come looking. It wasn't like Carr had a helicopter waiting. I headed back to keep faking normal for a few more minutes at the ring.

But as I drew close, I felt a touch on my shoulder. I started, turned. A young groom I didn't know shoved a slip of paper at me. After a second I took it. *Your camper at eleven.*

Not Jenny's handwriting. Valerie's? I'd never seen it. An impulse surer than logic told me it was Carr's.

Sure enough, it was Carr.

He was propped between our camper and the bigger one beside it, one boot propped on a tire. His jeans were dust-smeared, as if he'd been unloading hay or cleaning stalls. A raw nerve in his jaw was ticking. He jerked his chin at the closed camper door.

Reluctantly I opened the door for him. Another person I didn't want in our camper. But I also didn't want this meeting taking place in public where a video might end up on somebody's phone. The gun under the windbreaker weighed against me but my gut said this wasn't the moment I'd need it. Based on our last talk, this meeting shouldn't be happening. Something had changed.

He crossed and fiddled with the spigot at the sink, twisting it on and off. He didn't look at me, tossed over his shoulder, "What do you want and what are you going to pay?"

I flattened my voice, stifling a twitch of reckless anticipation. "Last I heard you weren't selling."

"You don't have enough time left to act all innocent." He flipped the spigot again, almost hard enough to break it. "Fucking dirtbag bastards. Call in markers and all you get is spit."

Maybe it was the relief behind my breastbone that fed me the words I needed. "Jenny's going to tell Wardle about you. See how your list of ten people stacks up against what she's going to say."

He looked over his shoulder, his gaze sly and bitter. "So it's like that with you and her now."

"Yeah, it is."

He scoffed. "Then you're a jerk. Is that all you've got?"

"It's enough. Just so you know, she's out of it. I know everything she knows so it won't do any good to go after her. I'm the one you have to worry about now."

He faced me, hands on the counter behind him. "You want whoever's behind what happened to that horse to get whatever they've got coming. Turning them over to Wardle won't get you jackshit. You got to do better than that."

"I will when you tell me who they are."

"Huh? She didn't tell you?"

"Let's see if you tell me the same thing."

He chewed on my bluff. He couldn't know what I was thinking. That here it was, the moment I'd find out my future. If it had to end right here, in this camper, where even now memories of the last eight years were playing, I was ready. Not even breathing hard. A flash of Brett, walking into the blood. I dismissed it. Carr sucked the inside of his cheek, wiped his mouth. I put both hands under my windbreaker against my belly. This was the man who had tied a horse in a trailer and set a fire behind him. His gaze didn't leave my face.

"I'm not playing that game," he said. "Not till I know what I'm getting, hell, not till I get paid. Look, let's say half of my price is knowing they get shafted like they shaft the rest of us, like they did that horse. We got to talk about the other half."

The fury I'd felt with Rich Paxton flared in my chest. He would damn well play the game the gun wanted if I drew it from my belt. But that was the short game. Playing it now would cost me the big score. Playing it smart was that gamble that had scared me, but worth it. "Money," I said.

He squinted. "How much?"

"Name it."

He didn't blink. "A hundred K. In cash."

"For that much, it gets a little more complicated. How bad do you want to get back at them?"

He didn't consider more than a couple of seconds. He ran a thumb along the edge of the counter behind him. "Complicated how?"

Claryce won her final class. Everybody had to hug Flight, pissing him off. They didn't pin the Hunter Classic until after twelve; Rianne was second, and Bernie picked up her first big score and her first check, finishing fourth. Twice I caught Valerie in the distance, perched in the hunter-ring bleachers or sipping a soda with her elbows on the schooling-ring fence. From there she couldn't hear the bubbling, the laughing, cheers for all our championships and reserves and what a great summer! Down the hill they were building the Grand Prix fences for the Paxtons' horses to jump and Ricoeur's and I thought one of Dever's, and the kids walking back to our barn chattered about their favorites, how beautiful they were.

At the barn the voices rattled around me, loud debates about where to go to lunch and whether to go back to the hotels to change for the Grand Prix. I agreed with everything everybody said and dodged every invitation, handing Raul all the untacking and bathing, leaving Jorge talking with Brett about packing up. I told Raul, "I'll take our saddles up to the trailer. Be back in a bit."

"You coming with us?" Bernie called gaily as I loaded the golf cart. "I'll catch up," I said. I'd managed to keep everyone out of the trailer. One more trip now, the one that mattered. Carr had been right. I didn't have time to act all innocent anymore.

I didn't let myself calculate whether my plan would play like I'd spun it out. The odds I would survive the landing weren't that dismal, except that if you had to have a weak link, you couldn't pick one weaker than Carr.

I'd had to explain what I wanted three times, talking fast. I think he got it the first time, he just liked making me brazen it all out. "I don't hear me getting paid in that," he said.

"It's Sunday," I said. "I can't get it today. I'll have to get it wired here."

"Oh, sure. Like I risk my neck with these guys for that."

Guys. All men, then. I didn't like the stall I came up with but it might keep him on the line till I saw if I had the hook set. "I'll write a check. You'll get there first, it'll be under my saddle cover, at the cantle. You'll have that to hold over me until the money comes." Forever blackmail, sure, but I owned his forever. It wouldn't last long.

At the trailer I hoisted the saddles onto the racks in the tack compartment beside the bags of shavings I'd stacked. Beautiful saddles, but one more small loss of what justice cost. I considered resetting the webcam. I'd have liked seeing the real-time luau Carr would put together. But the cops would seize my phone for certain and I couldn't risk it showing what Carr did. I thought of disabling

Brett's alarm app but he had worn his phone on his belt all morning; with luck, if he saw the door had been opened, he'd assume the guys had started packing. Even if he did wonder, the fun would be over before he caught on.

On my last couple of trips to the trailer I'd created a little stash underneath it that I dragged out now. A half-full gallon gas can. A plastic sack, its neck knotted, packed with lead ropes and rags I'd soaked in gas. A handful of plastic shopping bags. I carefully filled the shopping bags with a couple of inches of gas and tied them off. I climbed into the compartment, humped into the storage area over the gooseneck, and set the bags in the center. I drew over the cable from the igniter that I'd left inside the cracked window and fastened the clamps under the knots. I slid back down and repositioned the packed hay bags on top of the gas-filled bags.

I fed the gas-saturated lead ropes out the window over the gooseneck and back inside through the barred window above the stacked shavings bags and saddles. I cut open the bags, tucked the ends of the lead ropes inside, and crammed the rags into the dry, clean, pine curls. The shavings themselves gave off a scent of resin, though not enough to mask the gas smell. The open window would help some. Sure, the guys would catch on, and they'd have their cell phones. But if my set-up did its trick, Carr would get them inside, get the check, get out, and get the door slammed just as the trailer went up in a conflagration that would melt the phones in their hands.

The plan wasn't all that complicated, except for the part about counting on Carr. "It has to happen before the Grand Prix is over," I'd told Carr. "So I'll still be in the bleachers. When do their horses go? Early?"

He'd chewed his jaw. "I don't know."

"Find out. People need to still be in the stands, not wandering around."

He'd looked at me sideways. But he scratched the back of his neck. "I'll see."

So, sitting in the bleachers, I'd get Carr's message that some people wanted to meet me in our trailer to talk about what happened to Romp. I'd climb down, head for the trailer, still be on my way when the fire started. I had to be sure to be seen near the barns, far from the trailer lot, when the blaze went up. From there, I had to make sure I was the first one to reach the trailer so I could retrieve the igniter before help arrived. By the time anyone thought to look for the device or something like it, I'd have reduced it to a pile of metal on a highway or in a lake somewhere.

Of course, even without the igniter, the cops would come at me. They'd have a case. But there'd be a lot of confusion and "reasonable doubt." Who was to say I wasn't the intended victim? After all, these guys had every reason to want to silence me. They'd already set two fires; Jenny could testify to that. A little bad blood, one guy betraying his buddies; with the webcam off, no way to prove who closed the door.

Who would Carr deliver? So far I could list only Dever and Paxton. Somewhere among all the show people I thought I knew could be others. I'd told Valerie that first day that I'd recognize a horse killer when I saw one. Maybe by this time tomorrow I'd know who I had missed.

Carr as the loose end set my teeth to grinding. But he couldn't implicate me without incriminating himself. His line would be that he'd agreed to set up the meeting, that was all. That he wasn't even there, let alone responsible for closing the door. I wasn't sure he'd figured out quite how far our brotherhood in vengeance was going to take us or how short and ugly I planned to make it. The time to deal with him would find me. For example, when he finally decided he'd have to threaten me to get paid . . .

Again, only one risky step in the prep, the moment when I pulled the golf cart around to the side of the trailer, climbed up on that last hay bale, fished the igniter out, and set it on the trailer roof in my line of sight from the corner of the last empty barn. If anyone saw me position the igniter and trail the length of hay rope down where I could give it a jerk after the fire started, I guessed I'd find out in the courtroom I'd be the one headed for.

A lot of worries riding back to the show with me. I squelched them. No better way to crash a big fence than to mess with your horse's head three strides out.

CHAPTER 42

THE BARN WAS QUIET, no giggling and bubbling, no kids. Down the aisle Raul was throwing hay and Jorge topping off water. No sign of Brett. My phone pinged as I made room for the bale I'd brought. Valerie. "We'll see you at the Grand Prix," the message said.

Shit. "We" had to mean Wardle would be watching the class with her. If she'd already talked . . . Wardle had made clear that I'd be on his list with Carr and Jenny—for lying, withholding evidence, obstructing justice. Could he arrest any of us without a warrant? Could he get one on a Sunday afternoon?

I stifled that tic of panic. I'd have to stall Wardle if he made a move. So far I'd kept him off me. I only needed a few hours. I'd find some way to buy those.

At least, I thought, now when Wardle picked up Jenny, she wouldn't be a target because there'd be no one to pull the trigger. I didn't know or care what happened to her precious Zack.

Zack. His name brought on what I guess I could call sadness. A letdown? Maybe an almost normal feeling, now that I had nothing to do but wait. Into a gap in my mind slipped a sense of so much left undone. I couldn't get Romp away from the Paxtons, I'd burned that bridge. Hopefully Malloy would be the one to put him down; he'd make it quick and painless. As for Paxton himself, if he wasn't part of Carr's haul, I'd lose him in all the mayhem. But sooner or later I'd find him. I'd track him through time and space and ride his shoulder forever, raking at his heart.

The Grand Prix would start at three. A little more than an hour away. In the camper I tucked the igniter remote in a pocket but locked up the gun. Valerie's "we" clued me not to have it on me. If by some chance Wardle made a move before my little party, he might miss the remote but if he found me carrying, permit or no permit,

277

he'd take the gun. If all went okay I could leave it in the drawer forever. But I wanted it there, waiting, just the same.

Brett stepped out of the tack stall as I passed on my way to check on Zenith. He looked at Jorge, who looked back at him, not at me.

"Where is everybody?" I asked.

"Walking the Grand Prix course." He jerked his chin. Outside.

"You owe it to me to tell me what's going to happen," he said.

Dumb to think I could dodge this moment. "Why do you think something's going to happen?"

"Because whatever you were going to do about Romp hasn't happened. It's going to. Every time you walk past me I see it. And that woman hanging around here." He snorted, a sound sour as a piece of wet shit he'd flung at me. "I'm done with all this worrying. If we live through this day, we're over. Get your lawyers lined up."

"I don't need lawyers." I didn't know I was going to say what I said until I said it. "All I need is for you to take care of Zenith."

"Zenith? For God's sakes." His face changed. Like he'd opened a door on me and found a pile of bones there. "What's the name of that fucking policeman? Ward? Woody?"

"Wardle."

"I'll get him to fucking arrest you. Stop this."

"If he had a reason to arrest me, he would have."

He shook his head like he needed to clear a burning sound from it. "Jesus." He turned and stomped away.

Left there behind him, all I could think was that he was the one who looked broken, like I had taken something from him, and it wasn't something he could spare. I stood there wishing I could call him to come back and get it. But he'd want to know what it was, and even though I thought I knew what it was, I couldn't have explained it. So I said nothing, and then he was gone.

Down at the arena our barn crew was one knot among many, exploring the crazy garden of a big jumper course. Bernie and Rianne and the moms trailed the kids. The kids piled on me when I crossed to where they'd stopped under an oxer built to look like the engine of a train. I pointed down the line to the vertical that led to the oxer. "Okay, how many?" All the voices clamored. Five. Five and a half. No, six, you didn't step long enough. Let Robb do it! He'll get it right.

"No," I said. "Let me see you all walk it. Whoever gets it right, I'll pick your horse's feet for a week."

The moms went, too, giggling as much as the kids. They had horses at home, took lessons. They knew how to count strides.

So we played, for me next week a blank, chopped off the calendar, these lives around me unseeing, their next week as unknown as mine. The girls doing near splits trying to match what they thought would be my stride, Scott off by himself trying the set of the poles in their cups, to see how hard you'd have to hit them to make them fall. Bernie taking selfies with Rianne and the moms under the top rail of the final fence. I was surprised at how it all took me. I wanted to laugh like they did, laugh and laugh, really hard.

The girls wanted to sit with me; they followed me up the bleachers. Below Brett sat with all the families and couples, but the girls clung to me.

"Guys, I gotta watch a couple of horses for some people, I promised." I put my hands in the air so they couldn't grab them. "As soon as I'm done I'll come down."

"We'll be really quiet." Taylor made moon-eyes at me. "I'll be, anyway. Don't know about *her*."

"I can be the quietest," said Cadence. "I promise."

"Save me a seat. Not next to Brett. Let's make him jealous."

"It's your secret girlfriend," said Taylor. "We'll finally get to see her."

"Not today. I really have to concentrate. Go back down."

They did finally, with enormous sighs. I climbed to my regular perch at the top, the shadowy row that hadn't filled yet. The place where I could see the good spots when the horse did, the clean, sure choices of the really good riders. Valerie showed up as promised, a thin figure far below. At her shoulder, a dark shadow in a plain denim jacket and jeans: Wardle, the black gun at his hip. They edged into the third row, off to my right. Valerie twisted and searched above her. She found me. She touched Wardle's shoulder. He looked up at me, too.

I had to still my clenching muscles. If he thought he could arrest me, I had only minutes. To do what, lie some more? Run? My body hadn't picked a plan when Wardle turned back to the ring, and after a moment, slowly, Valerie turned away too.

279

I sat quietly while the bleachers filled, waiting. I wondered what choices Jenny had made. I had done the best I could to protect her, telling Carr I knew everything she did; I had to hope he had passed that bluff on where it did some good. I couldn't shut down the worry. Or the sadness. At least after today no one would be gunning for her. No sign of her. Or of Carr.

The Paxtons' Dutch horse went fifth.

Last night he was a shadow at the top of a trailer ramp. Now he showed me yet again how grand he was. The glow of him, fiery chestnut, the white knees flashing above the poles, not even stirring them with a breeze. He was the kind of horse who came out of every turn and put his mind on every fence before him and in every breath of his body there was that magical answer: *yes*.

Back in the barn was another horse who'd glowed like this. Dark, but the kind of dark that brings out stars and moonlight you never saw before. Romp had hit his wall that cold morning and nothing I'd done had made a difference. Even if he jumped in my mind with me I'd be leaving his body on the ground. I was the only one who could know what it was like for him, living forever with those endless tormenting moments. Again I wished for his sake he was already dead.

After the Dutch horse's round, Malloy's show manager Nia took him back to the barn. I quashed a dumb urge to leap up and follow, make sure she put him somewhere safe. But surely he'd be fine for the moment. I wasn't as convinced as Valerie they'd try again this show. Besides, night was when they did their killing. He'd get his bath and his grooming for his victory lap later. He didn't need me yet.

Turned out Dever did have a horse in this. One of his clients, a small, energetic woman, rode him, a bright bay with one white leg. Dever followed her to the in-gate, pulling out his own stopwatch as she cantered onto the course.

Wardle took no visible notice of Dever. He had to know by now that the drug-dealing hot spot was Dever's barn. If he picked up Jenny or Carr, whichever one talked would name Dever. Valerie might even have heard the shouting this morning, passed that on. I convinced myself again that Wardle wouldn't make a move until the class was over. Dever's horse went double-clean; so did three more, but too slow to win. No word from Carr. Another twenty horses to jump. I stopped kneading my hands. All kinds of time. The seconds pounded past in a beat I could feel between my shoulder blades.

Ricoeur's horse would go late, the bald-faced horse we'd chased that night. He'd step over the fences but he was ponderous. I was past caring how well Ricoeur did.

I filled some of the waiting rehearsing my theories. Dever. Running a slimy game with the kids who came and went through his ritzy barn. Maybe some of those kids even helped run the drugs for him. Like Brian trying to rope in Scott.

Meanwhile, like Valerie said, the Paxtons had a ready-made set-up for sheltering dirty money. Dever could have threatened to expose their laundering scheme so they'd play banker for him. They balked and he went after their horses. Dever had used Carr to keep an eye on Jenny. Romp had played double duty as a weapon against both Jenny and the Paxtons. Converting tangibles into fear.

It held together. It would have held together for Valerie, too. I waited for Valerie to climb up to harass me. But she kept her back to me, Wardle like a salt brick beside her. If they talked, I couldn't detect it. They were watching something, but not the class.

Maybe after all he'd scored a warrant and they were waiting for it to arrive.

That was the danger that really spooked me, the moment that would let Wardle handcuff me and take me away. By the time I got bail, what mattered to me—who got hurt, who got saved, who got what they had coming—would all be filed under "left unfinished." Too much already damning me from there.

Too much time, then, the waiting. Time for the sweat to break out. *Goddamn it. Not now.* I put my hands to my mouth and bit down so hard on my knuckles I broke into flesh. If there was pain I didn't feel it. A pressure rose in my belly, like my insides were surging into my brain. I bit down harder. The stab of my teeth close to bone called up all my planning, the karma that patience now would bring me. The flood slowed in my chest. I picked up my copy of the class program, smoothed it until the letters stopped jerking. A tight distance. You could do those. You had to let the fence come to you.

Sixteen trips left now. Below me, Wardle rose, his phone to his ear. He barely glanced at Valerie, moving toward the end of the bleachers and out of sight. Could he get his warrant over the phone? Valerie twisted to keep her gaze on him. Then she looked up at me, frowning. I did not want her to come near me, to see me bleeding, the sweat pooling. She looked away again.

I wished I could get down from my high row, be a little closer when I got Carr's signal. Moving, doing something, would make the heartbeat seconds easier to take. Where was Wardle? Around the corner, under the end of the bleachers? I hadn't planned on having to slip past him. He'd want to know where I was going, might even follow. Cadence peered up, waving. I gave her a stab of my hand, *in a few minutes*. She gestured wider. *Come down.* Her mother turned with a questioning squint. I waved again, made a show of focusing on the horse on course.

I'd been a fool to trust Carr. What if he'd gone to the trailer early? But my phone would have told me if the trailer door had been opened. Before the end of the Grand Prix, I'd insisted. "I'll see," he said.

Below me Wardle hadn't come back; Valerie still sat alone. Learning way too much about horse shows? I caught motion in the bleacher row to her left, someone working past the seated spectators, forcing them to lean back and crane. My breath caught. Jenny. Arriving to stand over Valerie at Wardle's empty spot.

At least she was still alive. A tiny piece of good fortune maybe I'd had something to do with. Valerie stared up at her, shoulders squaring. Jenny talking. Another shoutfest? Now? I stood; would the strangers on either side get between them? But Valerie shifted a millimeter and after a second Jenny sat. Two bent backs now, Jenny talking, a phone on her thigh. They pressed close together, giving me one hunched back for a confab that lasted barely a minute. Jenny rose and wriggled back through the spectators as Wardle resurfaced at the end of the stands.

So had Jenny told Valerie—and by extension Wardle—what I had kept from them? Had she betrayed the plans she wanted to stop me from carrying out?

I spent a fateful minute sitting, standing, sitting again, not deciding. So I was still there to hear the voice from below and behind me calling my name.

I jumped six feet. Mentally at least. I leaned over the bleacher seat behind me. Not Carr. Raul, head tilted back.

I hooked an elbow over the seat back. Something wrong at the barn? Christ, an attack on our horses? Raul wouldn't let anything come between him and their safety—of that I was sure. I got up on a knee. "What?"

I was high enough he had to raise his voice to reach me. "They're moving him. They're going to kill him. You have to come!"

The Dutch horse? In broad daylight? A sickening answer: why not? Pure fucking logic. Not after the class when the barns would be full of people partying. *Now*, when everyone was staring down at the arena, the aisles deserted. They were taking the horse with them to the trailer. Any threat to them and the horse would be hostage. Another fire set, another animal tortured—possibly by that sick arsonist Robb Slaughter who got caught right there at the scene?

"Hurry!" Raul shouted, bouncing on his feet.

I wished to God I still had the webcam. Raul could be wrong. Or he could have been lied to. Someone could be taking the horse out for a little grass. To take pictures. To comb his tail out. But if Raul was right . . . "Did you see him?"

A nod. A quick hook of his arm. "Come now."

I peered over the back of the bleachers. A criss-cross of girders, a long way down. The only path that wouldn't alert Wardle. Nobody visible in the aisles of the nearby barns. Raul fretted as I slipped over the seat back, held on until I found a foothold. The girders were cold, my grip treacherous, my boot soles slick. But I wedged my feet in each bolted cross and with one long reach after another, squirreled my way down.

Raul danced ahead of me, waving. I caught my breath from the jolt of landing. "Where?"

"Empty barn. Hurry. Now."

No reason to doubt him. It made sick sense. They'd parked the horse—long enough for calming drugs to take hold? We moved fast. For all that emptiness, watchers might be tucked into those shaded aisles. People witnessing my crazy climb and Raul's urging. They'd know we weren't out for a stroll. We passed Dever's barn, with its stupid splat, splat, splat. I hadn't seen him at the class since his horse jumped. Malloy's barn, ours, Causey's, Beth Hawley's, all silent. A breathless jog past the last occupied barns. Raul stopped, panting, just short of the next to the last aisle. I pushed past him, peered into the shade.

A figure outside a stall halfway down. Raul at my shoulder, I raced forward. The figure turned toward me. "Oh, thank God, Robb. Help me here!"

Malloy. Panic in his voice, he was too late, we all were. The top door of the stall was open.

Not the Dutch horse. Romp.

He stood plastered to the back wall, awash with sweat, hooves stabbing up and down in a demented rhythm. Hazy dust boiled from behind the closed bottom door. Dust with a stench to it. My sweat froze. Smoke.

"What the hell!" I pressed past Malloy, fumbled at the latch. Malloy elbowed me aside, jerking at the jammed metal. "The loudspeakers were driving him nuts. We thought if we moved him, he'd settle. But somebody's set another goddamn fire."

If there was a world outside that stall and beyond that horse I forgot it. Even if we opened the door, the horse might freeze, shrink back into the stall instead of braving the flames. "We need a blindfold." I tugged at my shirt.

"You!" Malloy shouted at Raul. "Find Nia. She'll be in my barn."

I'd seen Nia return to the bleachers. But Raul was gone before I could speak. Even unlatched, the door stuck. Malloy wrenched it open. He undid his belt, pushed it at me, "If you get his head, I'll try to get behind him. If he sees the light maybe he'll head for it." I took the belt, held a hand out to Romp as I edged through the rising smoke toward him. He scrambled, climbing the planks. Cries, *those cries*, from so far down in us I couldn't tell who was screaming. I reached for the halter to thread the belt through it. I never knew what Malloy hit me with.

CHAPTER 43

IT WAS THE SCREAMS that kept me from dying there in hellfire. Romp's screams.

No other sound could have plowed through my addled consciousness, reached me in time.

He was a black whirr through stifling darkness above me. Crashing over me where I lay at the back of the stall. Straw inches from my feet giving off a spitting glow of flames.

I scrambled up, my ribs throbbing, my shoulder shot with pain where he'd already stomped me, too blind and choking from smoke to dodge when he spiraled into me and slammed me against the wall.

I gulped back the breath he'd punched out and hunched into the corner when he ricocheted past. The lick of the flames showed me why I wasn't already dead. Romp's hooves clattered on bare concrete, the straw kicked against the walls in his frenzy. But the smoke was packing my lungs with soot.

My vision blurred, dizziness and throbbing pain. Past Romp's spins, the streak of light between the top and bottom doors. Oxygen to keep me breathing. If I could get close enough—

Something clanged as Romp kicked it. A metal can. Lighter fluid? A sickening spit of heartache: Raul? Leading me here? For them? So it would look like the horse had stomped me as I went to kill him? The flames shot up the end wall.

Between me and the door Romp was a black cyclone, rasping on the concrete, his cries gone to wheezes. Not seeing me, seeing those flames.

If the fumes left me upright, I could edge along the wall toward the door, bracing against his frantic wallops. Had to. Malloy no doubt hoped the horse would do his killing for him, but he wouldn't take any chances; he'd be back. First to tackle the fire, or so it would look like, but really to check. How long did I have? The wall supported me, my legs holding. But Romp bore into me, hard hip in my chest, spinning me back into the corner. I clawed up again. The light was brighter, sparks arcing from the straw to the dry wood of the front wall. I could still beat the fire to the door if I just—

A burst of licking tongues, crackling wood. Romp hurled himself on top of me in my corner, the only place he could run. He reared, raking the wall above me, coming down on me, hooves slashing. I rolled sideways, sank under him, hands over my head.

The front planks spat fire now. Through his skittering legs, only a light where the door was. Only a white light where—

I blinked. Nothing through my weeping eyes but glows and shadows. But yes, white light.

I beat him to drive him off, his legs a living wall of pistons. Everything shutting off but the pain in my lungs.

If only Romp would leap for that light. Take out whoever had brought it. Malloy, coming to finish me off? Instead the horse quivered against me, hooves pounding. I had to plunge through those punching spokes toward whatever waited if I wanted to survive this. Leave him behind me to burn.

Then beyond him, below his belly, movement. Human legs. In my blurred vision the legs turned thin and jeaned. Sneakers. Vaguely, a voice. Not Malloy. I couldn't make out what it said. It grew in my mind, louder than the screams.

Every nerve in me shrieked don't wait, dive for the light, fuck it, run. Again, the murmuring. Romp froze, trembling so hard the air shook.

The jeaned legs rose up on tiptoes. A frail lifetime while my lungs closed against me and my mind cooked. I waited in Romp's shadow for his body to gather under him, the way it had to if he was going to clear the wall.

He moved. A step. Another, the thin human legs easing backward. Then the explosion, a high wail, and air rushing at me. He was gone.

He'd knocked Raul sideways. I tackled him chest-high and tumbled us both onto the blessed dirt of the aisle.

He pushed to his knees but I couldn't. I lay and twisted and coughed. He knelt beside me for a moment, then stood. Through the tears pouring down my face I watched him pick up a dark cloth, turn on a spigot, run water. Only when he wrung the cloth over my head did I realize it was the shirt he was not wearing. He'd used it around Romp's head to coax him toward the flames.

He tugged on my arm. "They'll come. We have to get safe. Hurry. Now."

He propped me on his shoulder, dragged me toward the back of the barn. I spat. Black spit. Stopped to cough. He tugged.

But still in the shadow of the aisle I held him, taking the wet shirt from him, wiping my mouth and face. "Malloy . . . ?"

"He'll come here. Jenny said—"

"Jenny?"

"She said where were you and I said in the barn with the horse, Malloy was there with you. She said no, hurry back and get you away."

"You didn't see him?"

"No, but she said he'll be coming—"

"Where was Wardle? The cop?"

"I don't know."

From far off toward the rings the clamor of confusion and panic, Romp hurtling in terror into the middle of a show. Behind us the roar grew, smoke boiling. I handed Raul his shirt, coughed words out. "Go to our barn. Is Jorge there?"

"I'm not sure."

"Text him. Text Martha. The three of you don't leave our horses. Text Brett. And these numbers . . ." I reached for my phone. It wasn't there. I couldn't remember Wardle's or Valerie's number. Something else missing but my mind wouldn't register it. "Text Brett."

He hung there a long second, face creased with worry. I said. "Go."

He ran, sprinting between the barns and the campers. I followed. No sign of Malloy coming back but he would. To do whatever the horse hadn't. At our camper, I staggered inside. Part of me wanted to collapse there in that familiar hideout, weeping, pulling up hard even as my horse gathered under me. Instead, I took out the gun.

I was in a space between dream and will. I wasn't okay, but I didn't care how okay I was. I didn't even feel where Romp's hooves and muscles had caught me. My shirt was torn, littered with straw, caked with dirt. I tugged out the tail and let it fall over my belt and the gun.

I walked into the sunlight. Up the row behind me, a barn was on fire. I didn't care. People shouted, off underwater. People ran toward me. But they parted for me. My face black, my clothes scorched and tattered, straw in my hair.

Still no Malloy. At his barn two grooms leaped to their feet, wide-eyed. "Where is he?" They looked at each other. One of them put a hand out. I shrugged past it. "Where?"

They shook their heads. The Dutch horse was in his stall.

I went back out into the lane between the barns and campers. A sense, a claw in my consciousness: something I should be doing, something I had planned to do. I felt in my jeans pocket and knew what was missing. No matter now.

I started for Dever's. The shouting down by the rings muted, maybe Romp cornered. The shouting behind me louder, the smoke stench building. By now Malloy might be back at the fire he'd set, dragging hoses, spewing water, not seeing the corpse he hoped for. I turned back that way.

Beth Hawley raced past me, stopped, turned. "God, Robb. What happened? You okay?"

"Yeah, yeah." Normal came back to me, that lifetime of practice. "Did somebody call the fire department?"

"Yeah, I think so. Seriously, you okay?"

"You seen Malloy?"

"No. Why?"

"Nothing." Nothing but I was going to kill him. "I have to check on our horses."

"Well, be careful." She brushed straw off my shoulder. "This is really nuts."

She joined the panicked stream running toward the smoke plume. I let her get ahead. Was I okay, they'd all be asking. They didn't know the right questions. No one knew the right questions but me and Romp and some of them, Raul.

And Jenny.

Jenny, who'd sent Raul to save me from a trap because she knew who was doing the setting. Who I had vowed to save from the grief of killing if nothing else. But I'd bought her time, hadn't I, giving Carr the message there was no point in harming her as long as I was around?

Except now for all they knew I wasn't around anymore.

She filled my head, the one all my failures would come down on. The broken stars in her hair. In the fog where she called from I saw Malloy as clear as that spot you know will get you over: where he was, what he was doing, who he was making scream now.

CHAPTER 44

So I FLEW. Her camper door was closed. I leaped up the shallow steps, wrenched it open. Malloy's back to me, camper drawers open, littered paper, scattered clothes. Beyond him in the narrow hall passage Jenny with her feet spread and hands braced on the walls. He was speaking as I filled the doorway. "Like fuck you ditched it. Where is the fucking phone?"

Her gaze moved. He turned. The sight of me did numbers on his eyes. He corralled the shock, brows coming down, a mask of astonishment. "God, Robb, you look like hell."

I took out the gun.

He stared at it, hands choke-holding the jacket he'd been plundering. He laughed, a broken-metal crack in it. He shifted toward me. "Oh, come on. You're not going to shoot anyone."

Know what's behind your target, they'd taught me. *Bullets can go right through. To her.* In the second I wavered, it was Malloy's gaze that moved. I glanced behind me from reflex, the gun still brandished, and Malloy plowed into my side.

The gun cracked, bullet piercing the ceiling of the camper. I tumbled down the steps into Wardle's waiting arms. He slammed his own gun into my wrist as I fell, spinning my gun to the ground. Adrenaline good for something. I shoved a shoulder into his belly, knocking him off balance, then scrambled clear, landing with my back to the camper steps, squatting on my heels.

"For God's sake!" shouted Malloy from the camper doorway above me. "Fucking shoot him!" He plunged down the steps, snaring my shirt collar, his weight bearing down. My movements were now all reflex, no hope in them, just grabbing for what I could. I doubled over, backed into him, flung him over my head into a somersault that caught Wardle in the gut, knocked his gun loose, slammed him off his feet. I bent for my own gun, straightening and aiming. Clean shot.

291

No half-measures. But Wardle clambered up between me and Malloy, scrambling for his gun. Malloy clutched Wardle's shoulder to pull the cop in front of him, making Wardle stagger and miss his first grab at the gun. "He's got nothing you need," Malloy shouted, dragging Wardle backward. "Hurry, just shoot!"

Then without sound or any flicker of motion, she was there. She put her palm on the end of my gun, fingers spread. The bullet would go through her hand, her throat. She wound her hands around mine. "Romp's yours," she whispered. "I bought him. He needs you." My mouth opened. If I spoke neither of us heard me. "Your friend has my phone and she'll get them. Give me the gun."

The metal slid free of me, into her shining space.

Beyond her Wardle caught up his gun and shook Malloy off. Malloy yelped and bolted. Wardle straightened toward us and raised his gun.

She wheeled and shot him. He grunted, doubled, his gun firing but the bullet plowing dirt. She fired again. He sank on his haunches, his gun falling, hands finding the holes she had made.

In all this I did nothing. I watched her like I had that dog dying on the highway, my arms and legs unmoving. She turned to me at last.

"There, it's fixed now," she said.

Then, close enough for me to share her breathing, she raised the gun. Not toward me but upward, and only when it drew to the level of her open mouth did I understand its aim. I reached like she had, my hands around hers. I wrestled our arms above us, and pressed our cupped fingers into the trigger until the gun gave up its last bullet. She sank clinging to me, and I caught what was left of our lives.

EPILOGUE

Two Months Later

I WOKE UP SOME MORNINGS wondering where I was.

Oh, yeah, in a shabby little apartment over a shabby little barn.

I had signed the lease but the stalls below were empty. I hadn't been able to make myself bring the horses here.

You have your freedom, I said to myself, morning after morning. Be happy. Every day I went down to saw more boards and hammer more nails and toss out moldy hay and mow weeds on my rented tractor. And tell myself again that one day I had to go and get Romp and Zenith and bring them here.

But I couldn't. Not because the barn couldn't be cobbled together, but because I couldn't imagine myself keeping horses safe. I'd dream of fires in the dim little stalls. I should have dreamed of Malloy or Wardle setting them but instead the ones I dreamed of were already raging. The screams drowned out by the whoosh of flames taking the horses right in my own barn after I had trusted myself to bring them there.

I hadn't talked to Brett, but Martha had texted. "They're perfectly fine right where they are. Nobody's counting. Whenever you're ready is fine."

Or maybe it was just the hassle of renting a trailer, or the look on Brett's face as he led them out to load them, both of us hating what *us* had become . . .

I was free because they couldn't find anything to charge me with.

That was Ricoeur's lawyer's doing. Ricoeur had shown up at Jenny's camper minutes after the show security and the show EMTs, stalking through the hastily thrown up police line. He stood over Jenny and me where we huddled on the camper steps in a shared oblivion, shuddering heart to heart. To her he'd said, "You say

293

nothing." He turned to me. "You, too." He put a hand on her arm and without a word she unfolded herself from me. "I will send you a lawyer and you will listen to him," he told me.

The steely old man with the fat gray mustache hated me. "I don't care about you. I care about keeping clients happy. I don't think of you as my client but the guy who is wants you taken care of, so that's what I'm going to do." He treated me like a cheap computer he had to program. "You know only five words," he told me. "'Yes,' 'no,' and 'I don't know.'" He allowed me one more word for the state-police and FBI interrogation: "Fifth." "They know you set up that trailer to burn but if you don't admit to it, they have to prove it in court, and with no witnesses, how will they do that?"

The plain script worked fine for the next questions. Did I start the fire that burned the trailer—and Jeff Carr in it? "No." So who did? "I don't know."

They didn't know either. The remote for the igniter and my phone never turned up. I had them both in my pockets when Malloy opened that stall door on Romp. When Raul hauled me out they were gone. "So you ditched them," said the pumped-up young Timberburg deputy who sat in on the interrogations. "No," worked fine for that, as well.

It rankled the Timberburg guy when Raul claimed he was wringing his wet shirt over my head in the aisle dirt when the fire started. The deputy went after Raul like he thought he could break him. The lawyer sat in on that interrogation, still on Ricoeur's nickel. "Good guy," he told me later. "He did fine."

For the lawyer my freedom was never in question. "If it comes to the point," he said, "you went to that camper with a gun because you knew Ms. Silver was in danger. You surrendered the gun to her and events after that were literally out of your hands. In fact, there's not a turd's worth of evidence you ever pointed that gun at anyone."

The script for Jenny's preliminary hearing had more words in it. I said Wardle had been aiming at her when she shot him. That was one true thing I said.

"Easy self-defense," said the lawyer, gloating. It was pretty clear he liked her. I would have thought he might appreciate that I was the only reason she was still living. But all he said to me the last time he saw me was, "If we'd gone to court you'd have ended up in an institution. On probation till you finish a rehab program." I started to say I wasn't some kind of addict, but sometimes you take even gifts people don't want to give you. Like the look Jenny gave me as she sat with Ricoeur hovering as close at they let him in that courtroom. Her flat gaze didn't say thank you but it didn't say the shit it used to say, either. The lawyer didn't understand that he didn't have the power to set either of us free.

The lawyer said he wasn't getting paid to tell me news I could read in the papers. I didn't need the papers, I had Valerie. She was in my lap because I had gone back to being human interest for her story about the drug ring. She had nibbles from the *New York Times Magazine*, she said.

She actually interviewed Wardle after he got out of the ICU, which almost certainly wasn't where Jenny meant to send him. "Dripping cooperation," Valerie said. "Going for that plea bargain. The way he tells it, all he did was look the other way. The whole sweet little set up every summer during the horse shows, shoveling money to him—all Malloy. Going after that horse to terrorize Jenny when she started balking? All Malloy."

"Bullshit," I'd answered and she nodded. But since Malloy didn't talk to reporters, we'd have to wait for a jury to decide if Wardle was telling the truth.

She had read the transcript of Jenny's hearings. "So you saved her ass three times. Once from Malloy, once from Wardle, and now probably from an attempted-murder conviction. She knew about Wardle and Malloy, more than enough to make them want to kill her. It was all there, on the burner phone where she kept all their texts, the one she gave me at the Grand Prix."

That was the handoff I had witnessed. A couple of women's backs in the bleachers, bent over a phone. The phone Malloy had been demanding when I showed up with the gun.

"Wardle would have shot us both," I said.

"Her, yes. You, I'm not so sure. I think he wanted to know what Jenny had spilled to you and who else you had blabbed to. Me, say, or Brett. He thought he could get you in a cell and sweet talk all that out of you."

It made sense. Malloy shouting for Wardle to shoot me and Wardle not pulling the trigger when he came up behind me at the camper door. Should I have caught on about Wardle? I understood how I'd missed Malloy; I'd seen him too long as a father figure, dismissed his constant needling for information and warnings about getting too close to Jenny as perfectly normal, friendly concern. Reliving those short weeks far too often, I'd thought of a single moment with Wardle I should have picked up on, the moment he told me how a rider could take a tumble out of the trailer Valerie and I had been trapped in. He wouldn't have known I'd needed to take any tumble unless he knew the door was locked on us. No one could have known that who didn't have the story from someone who was there.

And then there was Jenny, wanting me to tell Wardle what she was doing for Zack, so he would see that was all I knew.

"So Ms. Silver owes you big time," said Valerie, giving the dingy little over-the-barn apartment her usual acid inspection. "Of course, she did buy you that horse."

No one had dug up how much Ricoeur had given her to buy Romp or what she had had to do to get the money. "Sex, obviously," Valerie said.

I didn't answer. I had made myself see the sex she surely gave him as one more sad chore between bathing his dog and managing his bad-mannered studs. Why wouldn't she fuck him? Piling up her pennies. In case one day she wanted to buy a horse . . .

"The Paxtons aren't telling how much they got for the horse, either," said Valerie. "Word is they called Brett to send someone to come and get him. Apparently that woman Martha went."

Martha would have taken one look at that horse and started fantasizing a vengeance so grisly even I would cringe. "The Paxtons."

Valerie snorted at the bite in my tone. "Give it up, Robb. Nothing ties them to the drug ring." Nobody had tied Mack Dever to it, either, but I had my own opinion about who knew what when. "For what it's worth," Valerie said, "the Paxtons are actually in more trouble than you are. People with clout are asking where the money they were laundering came from. My sources say there's enough involved to warrant prison. We did good work there, Robb." She didn't seem to like the look on my face. "They didn't hurt any horses. Don't you have better things to do than schlep around after them?"

She hadn't been in that bar that night with Rich Paxton. Hadn't heard those little pings.

The other thing she told me was that someone had finally showed up to claim the remains of Jeff Carr. "He had a brother, it seems. Nobody admits to luring him to that trailer or knowing what he was doing there." I thought she was probing for guilt in my expression. "A little loose end there, given he almost certainly helped with Romp, wouldn't you say?"

She waited a stretched-out minute, I guessed for the one detail I'd never surrendered. I said, "Since Malloy's not talking, you'll have to ask your buddy Wardle."

"Shame of it is, since there's no way to know who set off the igniter, neither of them is looking at a charge for Carr's murder."

"They'll be liable for what happened to Brian." I didn't know the legal ins-and-outs of deaths due to drug dealing, but maybe Jenny's cooperation with the police would let her slip out from under that charge.

She frowned, brows rising. "There were probably other kids, weren't there?"

"Maybe kids even they don't know about. Deaths no one will ever answer for."

All tied up, then. I should have been okay. I was letting go, wasn't I? I couldn't fix Jenny's life, I'd saved her so her hell could have her, but wasn't that all I could do, wasn't that okay? I hadn't been smart enough to spot what lay before me and deliver the justice Wardle and Malloy deserved, but they faced long sentences, didn't they? I'd signed my share of the farm over to Brett; he hadn't done the paperwork yet, but that was his problem. I knew I'd fucked up his life, but he would manage; he hadn't lost a single customer, had even gained some. So I'd given him something for his trouble. That should be enough.

But with Brett especially I just kept thinking I'd made choices he hadn't signed on for and I'd taken something I should repay. But beyond the farm, what did I have? Well, I had the horses. They weren't worth much, but I didn't have anything else that mattered, at least not to me. He might not "get" Zenith, but he wouldn't abuse him, he didn't do that, and he'd give some thought to whoever he finally passed him on to. And if Romp had to be put down, Brett should be the one to do it. It occurred to me that I was just handing him my responsibilities, but the more I thought about it, the more I decided it was the horses' safety that mattered, and the thought that he would be the one taking care of them cooled a burn in my chest. Like there really was some chance the barn would collapse around them. Or that its flimsy dry walls would burst into flames . . .

Of course, his scoff when he saw the bills of sale I pushed across the table at the pub where I had persuaded him to meet me said my plan was doomed. He sat down with his chair pushed back and looked around at the little room as if the walls had said something pissy. I said, "I'm not sorry for what I did, but I took something from you and I should give something back."

"What you took?" He leaned forward, elbows on the table, fists crushing air like he wanted to strangle me in them. "Eight years, Robb! Eight years of being damn good at what we did, having what it took between us, showing everybody it was us and not some pile of money, it was us who were so damn good. Now all that's gone. Now we're the barn where the crazy guy is." He slapped the papers hard enough to make the bartender stop drawing a beer and frown at us. "*Was*, thank God."

He picked up the sheets and tore them. He stood up. "Not enough," he said.

The question then was what would be. But what could he possibly answer? Shit had happened. I said, "It'll take me a few days to be ready to get them."

"Whenever," he said, and walked out.

Well, I had tried. So I should have been okay. Maybe I would have been, if both Martha and Phil hadn't come down on my back. Martha caught me dragging rotten hay bales out of one of the stalls and stood there partly her usual self—drooping T-shirt, hair pointing in all directions, and a curl or two of fresh shavings stuck in the cuff of her jeans—but the rest of her a scowling combination of worry and disgust. "Thought I'd stop by to see where my horses are going to be living. Or from the looks of it, maybe not."

She swung open the top panel of a stall door where I had replaced the old corroded hinges with shiny new ones. Gave the brittle wood a jerk. The hinges tore loose; she caught the door panel as it tumbled. "Well, shit," she said.

I grabbed the splintered panel. "Just let it go. I'll put it back."

She aimed a damning finger. "You need whole new boards there." She peered all around, up and down the row of dilapidated stalls and musty storage rooms, into the age-stained rafters. "A lot of them."

So had she come just to harass me? "I'll get them."

She made her mouth into a thin hyphen, then blurted, "This is not okay, Robb. You need to fix this."

My throat wanted to close on a bitter heat. Not just to harass. To torment. "I can't fix the past."

"Not the past I'm talking about."

If confession would end this, I was all for it. "I appreciate what you're trying to do," I told her. "I know I fucked up. I'm handling it. I've accepted it. A lot of stuff got broken for nothing. I've accepted that."

She scoffed. "He told me about you trying to give him the horses. He doesn't want the damn horses. He doesn't want your share of the farm, either. He doesn't know what the fuck he wants. He wanders around like a zombie trying to figure out what's gone."

"I don't know what I can do unless he tells me."

She chopped her words into chunks. "He doesn't *know*."

I didn't see that it would help to keep saying I didn't know either. "So we're fucked."

"You know what?" she said, suddenly urgent. "If you'd gone to jail, they'd have made you get help figuring how to fix what you started." Her gaze got even fiercer. "Much as I hate to say it, I wish you had."

I poked at the scattered hay so she couldn't pin my gaze down. "Thank you, Dr. Martha."

She spun, and I breathed a hope that this grim scene was over. But when she was far enough out of range I would have had to shout my answer, she called over her shoulder, "I don't know what you have to do, Robb. Except that somehow you have to find a way to fix this. You're the only one who can."

Phil had called Valerie right away to offer me a lawyer. Valerie said she was pissed I already had one. Her visit was even worse than Martha's because she piled her abuse on top of news.

"I thought you knew," she said.

So the sex wasn't just a job like any other. She was going to marry him.

I watched from the ratty sofa while Phil poked around the apartment. "What if she gets convicted?" I said, hearing myself sound like the kid who didn't get the last candy apple. "Can he marry her then?"

She frowned like she wanted to slap my wrist for grabbing at the apple. "You can't seriously think there might still be something there with that woman for you?"

I was thinking about Jenny, all right, asking myself why. For money? Protection? For something she obviously hadn't wanted from me or hadn't imagined I could give her? But Ricoeur?

"I never thought there would be," I said.

Phil's silent inspection of the apartment didn't mean she'd come to help me decorate. She opened the refrigerator door, checked out the beer and pizza, then got down to business. "About that promise, Robb."

So that was it. One more thing wanting to be fixed, how I'd betrayed her. She'd know I wasn't sorry, so I didn't say it. I remembered her talking about absolution, her own guilt. "You have no responsibility for any of this, Phil. What you did or didn't do twenty years ago didn't make a flying owl shit's worth of difference."

"Or what I did or didn't do a few weeks ago."

"We already decided you couldn't have stopped me."

From the fridge she picked up a beer, inspected it. Yuengling, good enough for the time being. "You were a danger to yourself and others," she said.

"You had no proof."

She arched her eyebrows. "And now?"

"You won't have to wait for any call."

She found the bottle opener screwed to the kitchen door jamb and popped the top off the beer. Looked at the bottle some more instead of drinking. Twenty years ago I drank more kinds of beer than Yuengling on the fake IDs she got me. "Here's something hysterical," she said. "Your partner—Brett?—called me. Valerie gave him my name. He wanted to know if I wanted your horses. Isn't that a sad hoot?"

It was enough of a surprise to jerk a sputter from me. "I'll get the goddamn horses. I just want things safe here."

"Safe?" She smacked the beer bottle down hard enough on the counter to send foam spewing. "And the next time you decide to right some injustice and get yourself killed or sent to prison, what if there's nobody like Brett to hand your horses to? I told you to keep yourself safe so you'd be there for the next horse that needed you, but now I see it's the horses I should be protecting." She eyed the beer as if she couldn't figure out where it had come from. "I don't like the guy who runs this place. I need that guy to be somebody different. Not somebody fucked up like you."

I got up and walked out. She followed a few moments later, down the narrow stairs. I didn't look around. I was counting up all the hard work that needed doing. She said, "I'm working on my peace with all this and I think Ms. Silver has made her peace. I wish you could make yours."

She turned to leave, her footsteps scraping on the aisle concrete. But even before she came, I had thought about her and that night when she took that gun from me, what it must have been like for *her*, doing that, and what she had lived with ever since. She wouldn't buy new promises any more than she would a lame "sorry," but at least with her there was one more option, thanks. "If you hadn't stopped me that night," I said to her back, "or if you had turned me in, I never would have met Brett, I never would have put a leg over a horse. I would have missed out on the only real joy I've ever known in my life since that summer, maybe the only joy I ever would have known. So you shouldn't feel guilty for giving me all that."

She looked over her shoulder. "I just want you to go on having that joy," she said.

No kiss this time. Not even a touch on my wrist, the only thing she'd risked giving me in front of our parents as she took off to grad school that summer long ago. But she turned away slowly, as if she was still waiting for me to offer her more than I had.

I stood there for a long time after she left. Missing, the more I thought about it, that last touch, that connection. The way she left was a pretty clear message that she was the one letting go.

She really thought someone was going to have to take another gun off me, and this time she didn't plan on that person being her.

The one thing I should hang onto was some chance I could become the guy she would trust with her horses. But between me and that guy was the one thing so far I hadn't come close to letting go of, the only thing I did it all to accomplish. I still hadn't stopped the screams.

And now it seemed as if a big loud chorus was screaming. The horses I had abandoned. The people I had let down. The justice I hadn't delivered. Unfinished and wailing, failures on top of failures to do what I should have done. I was exactly who Phil thought I was, the guy who'd burn it all down to stop the goddamn screams.

301

No wonder I didn't want the horses anywhere near me. All I could think to do was make the little barn a palace. A fortress too strong for even me to destroy. I looked around at all the sagging lumber, littered storerooms, hanging roof shingles, gaping holes. How far away was that miracle? How many tens of thousands of the dollars I didn't have would it take? For some reason, my head still echoing with Phil's retreating footsteps, I plunged into a frenzy of cleaning, clearing, undoing: ripping out rotten siding, whacking down cobwebs, even digging up and repacking the dirt in the stall floors. At some point in the night I stopped to feel the sweat dripping off me and realized what was happening, realized I was on the back side of the wall. How I got here I didn't know but as I sank to the cool concrete of the barn aisle, I thought, this is how I really failed. I didn't kill the right person. He was still here, doing damage, he still lived. As the teeth-chattering shivers came over me I knew I had to make Brett take the horses and there was only one way to do that for certain and I took out my phone to tell him what I was about to do to make him take them and it was only when I heard her voice that I knew the person I had called was Phil.

EIGHT MONTHS LATER

I DIDN'T TELL BRETT about my decision. I guessed Martha did. She drove over the Center a couple of times, bringing, of all things, cookies, which the staff liked more than me. I didn't ask about Brett. If he still couldn't tell me what he wanted she sure as hell couldn't. I did ask about the horses. "They're fine," she said. "Settle all that up later. Just do what you have to do here."

But most of the time in my sessions, I ended up talking about Brett. How to answer the questions I hadn't heard when he asked them: "What the fuck, Robb?" and "What's going to happen? You owe it to me to tell me," and "This is us." I had no better answers after weeks of working to construct them. Brett was the one person I could never answer, not with apologies or explanations or any of the debris that boiled up in the nights now that I only sometimes woke up from the screams and the dreams about fires.

So the day he came—no call, no warning—I had no fucking idea what to say or do. He surprised me in one of the public break rooms looking at barn plans on my laptop. I had been trying to get used to having funds from my share of the partnership he had never let me sign over, hoping I wouldn't have to deal with leaking roofs.

And like an asshole I caught myself being pissed because he hadn't given me any warning. Like I'd done a really good job of warning him. I fished through the thousand and one remarks I had planned to make the day I finally saw him, but none of them sounded like excuses. So all I did was close the computer screen, turn to face him, and say stupidly, "Hello."

He didn't sit, stood there stiff in pressed jeans and a sports short crisper than he'd ever worn to visit his various Cindis. He looked thin to me, and too sunburned. Beat up from all the chores the partner he still hadn't recruited would have shared. I'd lost my tan; gym hours and jogs around the grounds didn't make up for days spent teaching and riding. Why had he come? He couldn't possibly think I had anything new to give him. It came to me with a jolt: something had happened to one of the horses. I jumped up to face him. "What's wrong?"

He raised his brows; under the dark tan spread a darker shade that could be a blush. "Nothing . . . not . . . I have something I have to show you." He reached in his pocket for his phone.

Nothing wrong? Romp still alive, no crippling injury to Zenith? Then what? I accepted the phone gingerly. He had opened a video.

In our far outside field, a flood of green, slopes and valleys of new spring grass, where we did our galloping work, building bone and wind. In the frame, on a level stretch, cantered a gray horse. He *was* different, Zenith, moving past me with a lightness of stride, a soft arch to his neck, perfect self-carriage, a singing rhythm across the ground. On his back was a slim, dark figure, in gentle balance, given up to the motion. Raul.

I sank into my chair, hypnotized. As I tapped the replay button, my horse swept past me again and again. Against the green in a long flowing canter I'd have died to coax out of him, reveling in his stride with a joy I didn't remember ever feeling beneath me on that horse.

"If you're not going to take him," Brett said hoarsely to my bent head and my silence, "I'm hoping you'll let me give Zenith to him."

Not a single remark among the thousand and one came close to what I wanted to say. He gave me a long moment, then sighed. "Just worth asking," he said.

I finally looked up at him. I don't know what I expected to see. What I did see was worry that almost ran to fear. Did he think I would be angry? Jealous? That I'd start raging? He held out his hand and I let him take the phone. To my surprise, he scrolled again, offered the phone back. "Well, whatever. Just so you know nothing's wrong."

Another video. Zenith and Romp together in one of our big paddocks, first nuzzling and nipping, heads over necks, play-rearing. Then a bolt, together, a million legs and snorts, bucks like the air was there to be jumped. Romp black as a chess piece to the near-white of Zenith, glowing with fat-dapples, his mane too long and whipping, his tail high. Again I watched and watched, then watched again.

Finally I gave the phone back. I propped my elbows on my knees, put my face in my clasped hands. Waited till I dared to look up.

"Have you ridden him?" I asked.

"Not yet."

Another question I had to decide I was okay to ask. Okay with any answer. "Why not?"

He looked around the room as if measuring some invisible danger. "How much longer is this stuff here going to take?"

I ran my thumbs down my cheeks. "I don't know yet."

"They give you some kind of certificate or something?"

"I don't think it ever actually ends." I said what I had learned was true, canned as it sounded. "It's a process."

He stood, put the phone in his pocket. "A little longer won't hurt him. Let me know when you're ready."

This wasn't the way I thought it was supposed to work. I should be the one doing the giving. I said, "Does Raul really want Zenith?"

"I'll have to ask him. I don't think he knows that's an option."

"Will you send me those videos?"

"Sure."

"If he wants him . . ."

The worry fell away as if he'd just come out of a class where a bad school had turned into a victory gallop. Relief, and the kind of joy only a good ride can give you. No surprise: he fled the work it would take to tell me all he was feeling. "I'll find out," he said from the door.

I sat until my eyes quit burning. So he'd finally asked for what he wanted. He wanted me back as the guy he could trust, not just to ride and teach and schmooze but the guy who wouldn't, ever again, try to burn it all down. Showing me that video was his way of asking if that guy was in me somewhere, and I knew now, from the looks of it, he was.

Because I was relieved, too. Relieved to find no anger, no jealousy, no sense of betrayal, in the sight of my horse giving himself to someone who could ride him better than me. Instead I felt what you feel when a rider you're coaching suddenly finds the magic you know you made possible but didn't teach. I sat there thinking if I could let go of this, there were other things I'd thought I could never shake off I could let go of. It would just take practice, the process. I relived my horse galloping past me, strides lofting in a joy I could let someone else give him, and all I could think was how glad I was.

THE END

ACKNOWLEDGMENTS

Like many writers, I've had a lot of help along the way. For me, asking for a read is a huge favor, and I'm often reluctant to request it, especially among captive friends. But over and over, my insightful and patient friends have come forward. Wild Bill Sweigart, one of my most valued long-term teaching colleagues, has read multiple drafts of multiple novels, always with great care and attention to what I wanted to achieve. Other uncomplaining victims of my literary excesses include two who taught me about being a better human while putting up with my writing, Terry Lynn Danner and Susan Romano, both of whom know me and my writing at our best and worst. Then there are two who read and read and read: Deanna Hopper—who is a genius at catching inconsistencies and mistakes, and Mary (Ernie) O'Dell, founder and president of Louisville, Kentucky's Green River Writers, whose support and friendship have carried me through more years than I can count. Finally, I want to thank the anonymous beta readers of The Spun Yarn reading service (highly recommended), and editors Carolyn Haley and Alyssa Matesic, without whose valuable advice this book would not be half as good as I hope it is.

ABOUT ME

I've always been a horse nut, and as a young person, I was a rabid horse-racing fan. So it's no surprise that my novels so far are about horses: the Kentucky Derby and the glamour of a Thoroughbred breeding farm—but with a little of my favorite ingredients—mystery and mayhem—thrown in! For *King of the Roses* and *Blood Lies*, I drew on my years of moonlighting on the racetrack, and for a while, owning and galloping my own racehorse. For *Three Strides Out*, I've incorporated knowledge from a lifetime of riding and showing hunters. Since then I've used my doctorate in English to teach writing at a regional campus of a Midwestern university—right across the river from Louisville and the Derby, in fact! Today I live in southern Indiana with my evil cat Peep, write, watch a yardful of birds, and ride Paddy, my sweet, sweet horse.

Made in the USA
Columbia, SC
19 May 2024

35850269R00176